Ring of Hope

Anna-Leigh Brooks

Published by New Generation Publishing in 2021

Copyright © Anna-Leigh Brooks 2021

First Edition

The author asserts the moral right under the Copyright, Designs and Patents Act 1988 to be identified as the author of this work.

All Rights reserved. No part of this publication may be reproduced, stored in a retrieval system or transmitted, in any form or by any means without the prior consent of the author, nor be otherwise circulated in any form of binding or cover other than that which it is published and without a similar condition being imposed on the subsequent purchaser.

ISBN
  Paperback   978-1-80031-084-1
  Hardback   978-1-80031-083-4

www.newgeneration-publishing.com

Prologue

Corporal Jamie O'Halloran left his first base on Sunday 27 June 2020 at the tender age of twenty, though of course he believed himself to be mature for his age, having been in a serious relationship with a thirty-six year old divorcee, Jess Willets.

Jamie was deeply in love with Jess and planned on proposing to her the night before posting out, until a couple of weeks before his planned proposal, a reckless one night stand changed everything.

He left that base a broken man and moved onto a new base, working hard and pushing himself to ignore the pain. Enduring long hours of physical training, he pushed himself harder still as the physical pain was nothing in comparison to the emotional pain he felt.

The ring he had bought Jess remained in his possession. It was his only hope that one day he would give it to her, as he never stopped loving her and told her he'd wait for her, no matter how long it took.

Now, five years on he is engaged to be married to someone else, but feels he needs closure so decides to return to that base on a twelve week secondment. He has no idea if Jess is with someone else, or even still living in the village but what he learns on his first day back after a visit to The Bowl will change his life forever.

He discovers that not only is Jess still living in the village but she's been harbouring a secret from him since he left. Will he get the closure he's looking for and go on to marry his new fiancé?

Chapter 1

Something To Think About

Jamie has that inexplicable feeling again, in the pit of his stomach, like he's missing something or someone.

He's awake early, it's just gone 0350hrs, and he can't remember the last time he slept more than four hours in any one period, and even achieving that has been a struggle. When his relationship with Jess ended, he slept even less, the odd hour if he was lucky and it was a good eighteen months before he started sleeping for as long as four.

He'd lie awake thinking about Jess, their sex life, their relationship and most of all how he had managed to destroy everything they had for a one night stand on a drunken night out, fueled by rage after an argument with Jess over her parents.

He never understood why she couldn't tell them, she would always say to him "my mum's difficult, she's complicated" she didn't like people like Jamie, he figured that much, he wasn't someone she wanted her daughter with, she wanted her to be with someone who was posh like them.

He has recently come across an opportunity for a secondment, for 12 weeks initially and it will be a great opportunity to showcase his skills as a newly promoted Corporal, but it does mean going back to that same base and the village where he lived with Jess.

He books a meeting, with his Sergeant, to talk to him about the secondment. He wants to apply but he needs his Sergeant's recommendation, which will secure the placement for him for 12 weeks, with a possible extension to 12 months.

In the meeting, his Sergeant tells him that going back isn't always a good thing and asks him if he is sure about doing this. He saw him after the break up and watched him punish himself hard as a result of his actions.

'I need closure Sarge,' Jamie answers.

'Are you sure it's closure you're after Corporal O'Halloran?'

'Yeah Sarge,' he says, very convincingly he thought.

The Sergeant tells him to go home for the weekend and think it through, before he puts him forward for the placement, if he's 100% certain when he arrives back to base on Monday morning, then he'll put him forward with his recommendation. At this stage Jamie hasn't even told his mum or Tara, he doesn't want to give them any cause for concern, not yet, not when it hasn't even been confirmed.

Chapter 2

Holiday Romance

Leaving work at 1630hrs, he needs to call Tara and update her on his change of plans. He was going home to stay with his mum for the weekend, but he needs to put Tara off from coming tonight, he needs to talk to his mum, tell her what his plans are and his reasons behind it.

Tara picks up and it's nice but a little awkward that she sounds happy to hear his voice.

'Tar, I'm not coming back till tomorrow,' he says, and listens to her sighing in response and asking why not. He tells her he's got "loads of shit to catch up on" and needs to have the training logs ready for Monday. She sounds disappointed, but tells him she understands, and he arranges to go round to her tomorrow, stay the night and then head back on Sunday.

He doesn't like lying to her, but he just needs a bit of space, some time to think, he needs to be alone and figure out what he wants - his future's in the balance.

He and Tara are due to get married on 18 July, 2026 - next year, it's all booked and paid for, but he's not sure if he can go through with it. He's been questioning himself lately - does he want to spend the rest of his life with Tara?

He loves her in his own way, but he's realised that he is not 'in' love - he knows that for definite. He thought he could love her, he did when he was in Cyprus, he missed her when she went home and looked forward to her visits, in fact for Jamie it was like a long holiday romance, now he wonders if that's why he proposed, maybe he got caught up in the moment.

He's been back in the UK for a year now and is receiving his second promotion to Corporal, but he's become unsettled again, he hates this feeling, he's not been able to settle or find any peace in himself since he split with Jess back in June 2020.

He left her house on the night of 5 June 2020 after confessing to her that he'd had a drunken one night stand, and he hasn't seen or spoken to her since. He wanted to go and see her on many occasions but his heart was broken, he couldn't risk seeing her, as he knows he would not have been able to handle it. All he wanted was to be back there with the woman he did - and still does - love.

Jess cut all contact immediately with him and his family and their mutual friends, and he thinks she also must have changed her number as whenever he called it, it went through to voicemail. He hasn't left her a voicemail for more than five years now, but he still feels the temptation to. He wants to tell her how much he missed her – and still misses her. He wants her to know how he's just had his second promotion, how he knows she'd be so proud of him, but more than anything he needs to tell her how much he's changed and matured. He's twenty-five years old now, not that stupid twenty year old boy that fucked it all up.

He unlocks the file on his phone, where he has stored all the messages from Jess or photos of them together or the selfies she had sent him. He couldn't delete them, so he has them in a locked file and every now and again he'll look through them and re-read their messages. He realises he's been looking at them a lot more often of late.

Chapter 3

Mother's Advice

He pulls onto the drive at his mum's lovely three bedroom semi-detached house. It was built in 2020 and he purchased it that same year for his mum to move into after Sean joined up in July 2020 - he wanted to get her away from the old estate.

There's no other way to describe it, the area he grew up in was rough. It was tough staying on the straight and narrow, avoiding getting caught up in the gangs and the drugs. When Sean joined up, Jamie was seriously worried about his mum living in the house alone as the estate had changed a lot even in the two years he'd been in the Army, definitely for the worse.

He walks in to the house and sees his mum looking surprised to see him as she'd heard from Tara, telling her he wasn't coming back tonight. Anne looks concerned, she knows her son and she knows when he's troubled - and she can see on his face, he looks troubled.

'Don't tell anyone I'm here Mum, will yer?' he asks.

'I won't Son, but what's wrong?'

'I need to talk to yer, but first I need a shower and some food,' he replies and heads off upstairs for a shower.

When he bought this house he made sure he'd have one of the double bedrooms and a double bed, unlike the last house where he had the box room with a single bed, which was fine when he was on his own, but when he was with Jess and they'd stay, it was difficult sleeping in a single bed - even worse when they were trying to have sex, discreetly on the floor – the memory of this is making him smile now.

His mum shouts up asking him if he wants a take away or if she should rustle something up.

'It's ok, I've ordered a Chinese, it should be here soon,' he shouts back to her.

Jamie comes down in his Regiment branded T-shirt and training shorts. He keeps clothes here now for when he stays, training and running gear, that way he doesn't have to bring anything with him, his mum will wash his clothes and put them in his room ready for when he comes next time, be it a weekend or on a week's leave.

They sit at the kitchen table talking as they eat, Jamie needs a beer, he's sure he left some in the fridge last weekend. Getting up to get one, he sighs – his heart feeling heavy. He knows he has some big decisions to make, life changing ones, he just wants to feel happy with life again after all.

Anne is worried, she saw him at his worst when he was completely broken after his split from Jess. Even though there was a big age gap, she liked Jess, they got on really well. She tried to contact her a couple of weeks after it all happened but it just went to voicemail. She sent her a text message also but it came back un-delivered. She even thought about getting one of the girls to drive her down as she needed to speak to her, to ask her if she could possibly forgive him and give him another chance.

In those early days after the split, there were times she thought that her son wasn't going to pull through, she worried he'd do something silly. She dreaded her door bell ringing or an unknown number calling her phone. She had nightmares of someone telling her Jamie was gone. She doesn't have a favourite child and she loves all her kids equally but Jamie, well, he has a special place in her heart, he's sensitive and caring, in a different way to the other four of her kids - he's the one she worries about the most, always has and probably always will.

She's noticed a big change in him since posting back from Cyprus, just over twelve months ago. Something is bothering him and she knows he's not happy

'What's up Son, you're very quiet.'

'I don't know how best to tell yer, so I'll just come out with it. I'm going back, I've put in for a twelve week secondment,' Jamie says and takes a drink of his beer and stares straight ahead.

'Do I need to ask why?' Anne questions, concerned that she already knows the answer.

'I need closure Mum, I can't marry Tara with this cloud of doubt hanging over me.'

'Jamie, what if she moved away, back to her parents or worse still she's married now and still lives there? What then? How are yer gonna feel?'

'That's just it Mum, I don't know. If she's moved then that's it. If she's married, I don't know but I need to see for myself.'

'Have yer spoken to Tara about any of this?'

He shakes his head, he doesn't know how to tell Tara as he doesn't want to hurt her, none of this is Tara's fault.

'Listen Jamie, if yer feel like this yer need to tell Tara, it's not fair on her. I know yer don't love her, not the way yer loved Jess, but Son, don't put yerself through this, or Tara.'

He looks down at the table, shaking his head as he says, 'I've tried mum, I've really tried, she's a sweet girl, she deserves better.'

'Go Son, if it gives yer the closure you're looking for then things might be different with Tara. When yer gonna tell her?'

'Tomorrow, I have to, it's an immediate start - a week Monday, on the twenty-seventh.'

Chapter 4

A Special Friendship

Jamie heads out for a run. It's early, 0500hrs, the mornings are dark and the clocks go back next week. He doesn't like running when it's dark, but he can't wait for sunrise, not this time of year when it comes so late. He'll be on his way back by 0700hrs.

He puts his pods in, turns his music on and heads out into the still of the dark morning, no house lights, no traffic, just the moon and the odd street lamp.

He needs to figure out how he's going to tell Tara and what he's going to tell her - he doesn't want to hurt her. After all is said and done he cares deeply for her, he's known her since she was a teenager and watched her grow into the beautiful woman she is today.

He can't deny it, Tara is stunning. She's only 5ft 3 inches tall with a petite size 8 figure, long blond hair and deep green eyes. She's beautiful and he's sure if he'd never met Jess he would have snapped her up long before now.

He thinks about how very different she is to Jess. When they started dating she was only nineteen and he'd just celebrated his twenty-second birthday, nine days before his sister Rosie married Tara's brother Jed on 28 May 2022.

She looked beautiful in her bridesmaid dress - a pinky colour, full length, flowing dress with very thin straps. He couldn't help himself, he did fancy her that's for sure, she told him that night she'd fancied him since she was fourteen - a spotty, brace wearing teenager.

She always cringes when he laughs anytime they talk about her teenage days.

Looking back he can see that she was quite a rebellious teenager, but in a subtlc way with her piercings and tattoos. He wasn't really a big fan of Tats - that was until he got his own done, now he understands how addictive they can be.

She got her belly button done for her thirteenth birthday, then after that her tongue, along with a tiny nose stud, and a couple of holes in her ears. Her tattoos are a different story, they all have a meaning, when she used to lie on the beach in her bikini he'd find himself looking at them, thinking how sexy they looked.

The time in Cyprus was special to Jamie. Tara would come out every six weeks or so, spending her days on the beach while he worked, but he kept her away from friends who knew Jess. He knows that wasn't fair on her, but it seemed to him that it was for the best, even though she was more their age, especially Clementine, Tommo's girlfriend.

Clementine didn't speak to him for more than two years after what he'd done, only when they posted to Cyprus did she start to talk to him again as she loved Jess and missed her. In an emotional drunken conversation one night she told him that her friendship with Jess had been special and what a stupid prick he was -he couldn't deny it, he knew he was.

Chapter 5

A Bit Of Privacy

Driving to Tara's he picks up some flowers. Like any woman, she loves her flowers. Whether it's a simple bunch from the local supermarket or a big bouquet from the florist, her face beams when she sees him with flowers. He'd like to think she's pleased to see him rather than the flowers, but who is he kidding?

A couple of years after her dad died, Jean, her mum, decided to move. They'd lived in that house for twenty-odd years and she said it was too big, which it kind of was I guess - four bedrooms and a huge extension on the back and only her mum and Tara living in it. They now live in a modest three bed, on a new estate that's still being built. It's like a town in itself on an old industrial estate, you'd never know that about it now mind.

Parking his car a little down the street as there's no room on the driveway with Tara and Jean's cars, he picks up the flowers and his rucksack with his clothes in. He's only brought enough for tonight and tomorrow as he'll head back to base tomorrow evening - he has a meeting booked for 0830hrs to go through the paperwork for his secondment.

He hears her before he sees her. Tara let's out a little shriek as she opens the front door, throwing her arms around him and standing on her tip toes to kiss him as he wraps his free arm around her and kisses her back.

'Hello darling, sorry about yesterday, I just had shit loads to sort.'

'It's fine, you're here now, and with flowers - you spoil me Corporal O'Halloran,' she replies with forgiveness.

He laughs - he hasn't quite got used to that title yet – and walking into the house he says 'hi' to Jean and takes his stuff straight upstairs with Tara following behind him. He walks into her bedroom with the en-suite that he likes, it's a little bit of extra privacy even if it is just instead of walking to the bathroom and back. It means he doesn't need to worry about what he wears, not that he stays too often, he prefers Tara to stay at his mum's with him when he's home for the weekend.

Tara lies down on the bed and pats it with her hand, a gesture that she wants him to lie next to her. He tells her to be patient as he needs to hang his stuff up and that she wouldn't want him going out tonight in a creased top - what sort of respectable soldier would he be then?

He lies down next to her, pulling her closer to him. He feels guilty, as he doesn't want to hurt her and never thought he'd find himself in this situation, but here he is and he knows exactly how she'll react.

Tara never liked Jess. He knew it was a jealous thing as she was in love with him, she's told him on many an occasion. Whenever she talks about the times he brought Jess home - the New Year's Eve party in particular - Tara will always refer to Jess as 'her' or 'she', not that Jamie likes Tara to talk about Jess at all, in fact he makes a point of changing the subject.

'So, where are you taking me tonight?' she asks.

He lifts her hand up to his mouth and kisses her engagement ring. He struggled choosing this one as he didn't know what would suit her tiny fingers, but in the end he settled on a trilogy of emerald cut diamonds on a platinum band.

'A nice Turkish restaurant that's recently opened in town.'

'Oh that reminds me, we still have the wedding rings to buy,' she says watching him kiss her hand, 'I fancy a diamond band to go with this one.'

'Yeah, okay, but we still have loads of time Tar, wait until after Christmas.'

To distract her, he turns towards her and kisses her lips, he can't talk about the wedding, he's not even sure that it's going to happen. In fact he's not sure of anything anymore.

She tells him how much she's missed him, that she can't wait until she's living on base together in married quarters and that she just wants to be with him, but she's looking forward to the wedding, to which she's invited one hundred and twenty guests, although he's never met at least half of them.

Jamie wants a nice simple wedding, something quiet, just the people who are closest to them - their family and a couple of close friends. But Tara's having none of it as she has told him more than once "I'm only getting married once J, so I want it to be the best day of my life".

Chapter 6

Tattoos

Jamie's lying on the bed ready to go out and watching Tara as she gets ready, doing her makeup - she doesn't wear a lot but it seems to take her ages - then her hair and *finally she just needs to get dressed* he thinks to himself.

He tells her the table is booked for 1930hrs, and if she takes any longer they'll be needing to book for breakfast, laughing as he says it.

She stands up and looks in the mirror, then asks him what does he think she'll look like when she's pregnant.

'What?' he says, taken aback by this comment. He's not thought about that, he's not sure if he wants any children, he knows he did with Jess and they were trying for a baby, but he hasn't thought about kids since, in fact they're the last thing on his mind.

He tells her he has no idea and that she needs to hurry up and get ready. He doesn't mean to be short with her but he's nervous about how tonight will go and it's an effort not to let the stress show.

As she starts to get dressed, he watches her put on her deep red, lace underwear - he loves this colour. He moves to the end of the bed and tells her to "come here". He puts his hands on her hips as he starts to kiss her belly, working his way up to her breast, he tries to take her bra off but she tells him a firm 'no' that they're going out and she hasn't got time to take another shower. He tuts, rolls his eyes and calls her a spoil sport, but she's right, they haven't got time, it takes her too long to get ready.

He watches her pull her jeans on, her thigh tattoo is a piece of art - an elephants head with its trunk wrapped around one of the two 3D effect roses and petals that are either side of the trunk.

He looks to her tattoo on her rib cage, it's just below her right breast - 'Faith, Hope & Love' - with the symbols that represent each word above it. She's told him that this was the most painful - that he can believe, she has no meat on those ribs at all.

He doesn't however, understand the feather on her wrist with the infinity sign wrapped around it, but it's pretty with the purple shading. He guesses it's something to do with her teenage days as it was the first tat she got.

He understands why she got her ankle tattoo, as this was a tribute to her late father, Brian. They're rosary beads which wrap around her ankle with the cross on the front of her foot, and she actually has some of his ashes in the ink and his initials engraved in the cross.

He loves watching her get ready, but he's not sure about her choice of clothing - she literally is top to toe in designer clothes. He's told her that she'll get a shock when she has to start shopping on a squaddie's salary, it definitely doesn't stretch to all those labels, to which she has replied "that's ok, me Mam will look after me, she knows how much I love me clothes".

Chapter 7

Turkish Meze

Jamie decides to drive, he needs a cool head, a sober one - he needs to be able to think about what he's saying and how he says it. Tara may be petite, but she's feisty, if she gets one on her, there's no point telling her to calm down as that just riles her more. It's best to leave her, let her calm down and then talk about whatever it is that got her all riled up in the first place.

Town's busy, he thinks as they drive through. He'd love to go out 'on the lash' right now, it's been ages since he had a good blow out so he thinks perhaps he should organise a lads night out, he'll drop a message in the Whatsapp group later in the week, try and sort something out for some time before the Christmas break.

He holds her hand as they walk from the car park to the restaurant. She's struggling to walk in her four inch heels along the cobbled stones and he listens as she's cursing and frightened she's going to damage her shoes. He's more worried about her ankles than her shoes.

'Fuck it,' he says aloud and picks her up. She screams at him to put her down and he laughs at her, telling her that he will once they're off the cobbles. People walking by are pointing and smirking at them, prompting her to tell him he's "embarrassing them".

When they reach the restaurant he puts her down, she calls him a 'dickhead' and he laughs and tells her it turns him on when she talks dirty. She can't help laughing with him at this and he takes her hand and leads her into the restaurant.

They opt for a Turkish Meze for starters as they used to have this kind of food a lot in Cyprus when they'd go out in the evenings and they decide to wait a bit before ordering any main, as the meze sometimes fills you up too much to eat anything else. He holds her hands across the table, plays with her engagement ring, and tells her he has something to tell her, it's to do with his job and his recent promotion.

She looks at him a little confused and wonders if he's thinking of leaving the Army. It wouldn't matter as he could come and work for her brothers in the family business. Jed would find him a position for sure - he and Jed are like brothers rather than just in-laws.

'Tar, yer need to keep her cool and listen to what I have to say.'

'Okay, but if you're thinking of leaving the Army, it's fine, you can come and work…'

Jamie interrupts her mid-sentence, shakes his head and tells her, 'It's not that, I have no intention of ever leaving the Army, not if can help it anyway.'

'Well then, what is it?' she says with a worried tone.

'I'm going away on a secondment, it's for twelve weeks initially with a possible extension to twelve months.'

'Away, as in abroad again?' she asks, her head naturally tilting to the side as she tries to understand.

He shakes his head again and tells her 'No, it's in the UK, I'll be on a base here in the UK.'

Her heart stops. She doesn't need to ask him which base - she knows. The one base she wants him to stay away from, to never return to. It's that one, the one where *she* was and still could be. Tara pulls her hands away.

'You fucking what?' she shouts at Jamie, channeling all her fear out as anger.

'Tara, shush! People are listening!' he says, trying to calm the situation.

'I don't give a fuck, they can listen all they like.'

He's beginning to wonder whether he should have told her at all, perhaps he should have just gone - she would have been none the wiser.

'Look, it's been five years,' he says, still trying to give all the reasons that he himself would like to believe in, but all the time knowing that this was a losing battle.

'So fucking what? What difference does that make?'

'A lot Tara, we're engaged to be married, or has that escaped your mind?'

'Take me home. Just take me fucking home now!' Tara demands, with one of the most severe looks on her face that he thinks he's ever seen.

'Tar, stop, just hear me out will yer, it's not as bad yer think.'

'Carry on, I'm listening.'

'I'll be in the blocks on base, I'll be working long hours Monday to Friday, coming back every other weekend, if I'm not away on exercise, there's no reason for me to go out in the village, I'm not with any of the lads from my Reg. Think about it will yer, think about what I'm saying before yer start jumping to conclusions.'

They sit and eat in silence for the rest of the evening before driving back home to Tara's in silence. If there's one thing Jamie hates, it is the silent treatment.

He needs to snap her out of it, he can't go to sleep like this so he turns over and pulls her close, telling her he loves her and that for once in their relationship she needs to trust him. The irony is, he doesn't know if he can trust himself.

Chapter 8

Leaving The Regiment

The paperwork is sorted, it's been fast tracked and he leaves this base on Wednesday 22 October 2025. He's leaving his Regiment behind and his gut feeling tells him that the next time he sees the lads will be on the next posting at the beginning of November 2026.

He will go home to his mum's until Sunday, when he'll need to go back to the base and pack up his room, hand in his pass and head south. He's anxious about what awaits him, he's not seen or spoken to anyone since leaving more than five years ago.

He deactivated his Facebook account when he split with Jess as he couldn't face changing his relationship status back to single and removing their profile photo of them together at Nobby and Shelley's wedding. One day he will reactivate it, when the time is right, he's sure of that.

It's been a tense few days as Tara has blanked him for most of it. When she has replied to his texts, they've been one word answers with no emojis or kisses. He knows the next couple of days with her are going to be difficult to say the least.

Driving back to his mum's he thinks of all the times they've argued and it seems that they bicker a lot, something he hadn't realised until this week. It can be over silly, trivial things too, which is then followed by hours of the 'silent treatment' which drives him insane, as she well knows.

He arrives at his mum's and he can see Tara's car is on the drive so he'll park behind it on the drop curb, he's not parking down the street as it's pointless - if they go out they'll go out in his car anyway.

Tara looks tired as she comes to the door to greet him, he can see she's not slept much. He actually feels guilty for putting her through this, he knows he's the one being selfish now, but he can't move forward to a future with Tara without closure, this is something he's adamant about.

He can see her eyes are red and puffy as she walks towards him, she's obviously been crying. He holds his arms out as he says, 'Hey, come here,' and wraps his arms around her petite body, kissing her on her head as she lets it all out. They stand at the bottom of the driveway, embraced in an emotional hug. His heart is breaking for her, he knows what it feels like to be in love with someone and feel that fear of losing them. Why couldn't he just love her like she loves him and be happy to be getting married next year? Perhaps he should have just married her in Cyprus. Would they be in this position now or would it be worse?

Chapter 9

Signing In

He's packed up his car and is handing his pass in at the front gate before heading south on a three hour journey that he's not at all looking forward to. He's got used to the nice short distance between his mum's house and this base.

He calls Tara once he's on the road as she was crying her eyes out as he left. The last few days at home were very emotional and he was glad to leave today if he's honest. She was planning to go home, so he calls her mum's house and her mum answers the phone. Tara was too upset to come to the phone, she tells him. Her mum then tells Jamie that she's disgusted with him, and, 'How could he put her daughter through this?' He tried to explain that he had no say in it, that he was put forward for it by his Sergeant, but she cut him dead, telling him that "Tara might be gullible enough to believe the bullshit" he tells her but she doesn't, she sees right through him, seeing exactly what's going on.

He continues his journey in a sombre mood, Jean was right, Tara doesn't deserve this. Perhaps he should finish it now, after all, what irreparable damage has he caused them?

Finally, after what felt like an endlessly long drive, as if he was driving from one end of the country to the other, he signed in and picked his pass up from the gate house, asking the soldier if The Bowl was still open. He's heard that some of the pubs have closed down on other bases, so it was good to hear this one was still open and decides he will pop by later once he's unpacked and prepared his kit for tomorrow.

One things for sure, it doesn't matter what military base you stay on, the blocks are all the same - even in Cyprus it was no different. They're not meant for comfort, they're just blocks, he decides. Designed for young lads to live in until they either move on or get married and then it changes to married quarters, something he'll find out if he and Tara make it to July.

Jamie gives Tara another call, texting her first to tell her he'll call her in five mins because he really doesn't want to speak to Jean again, he figures if Tara doesn't want to speak to him she'll text back telling him 'not to bother' or something similar, but to his surprise she doesn't.

When she answers, her voice is hoarse from crying. They chat for a few minutes and he tells her he's going to nip to the mess and get some Sunday lunch and that he'll either call or text her and that he loves her. He's not lying when he says this as he does love her - in his own way.

Chapter 10

Catching Up

'Jamie'

The mess was closed so I decided to take a wander down to The Bowl - the beauty of these places is they're cheap, they do good food and like me if you've been on the base before, you either bump into an old friendly face or at least the bar staff remember you.

'Well if it isn't Jamie O'Halloran,' says a familiar voice and I look around to see my old friend Fred sitting in one of the booths. He beckons me over and I'm happy to join him - at least I'll have a bit of company for the next hour or so.

I order a pint and take a seat opposite him. He asks me how I am and what I've been up to and what in God's name brings me back. I tell him I need to order food and then I'll fill him in afterwards, I also ask him if he has eaten.

'No not yet, Hazel is away for the week so I've been left to fend for myself,' he says.

I laugh and tell him, 'Yer doing a good job so far as I can see!'

With the food ordered - and another pint - I start to tell Fred what I've been up to these past five years and the reason I'm back here for the next twelve weeks. He listens intently as our food arrives and it's at that point I ask Fred where Hazel has gone and who with.

'She's gone abroad for the school half term with Jess.'

My heart misses a beat as my stomach practically hits the deck, she's still here, still in the village. Shit!

She stayed. I was sure she'd have moved back to her mum and dad's by now. Perhaps coming back here was wrong, perhaps my mum and my Sergeant were right - you shouldn't go backwards only forwards. Shit! What have I done?

'Did she ever re-marry?' I ask casually, secretly dreading the answer.

'No she never re-married,' Fred says between mouthfuls, 'in fact she's been on her own since.'

I'm relieved to hear this for my own selfish ego, but I'm sad to think she's still alone, that's not fair, she deserves to be loved and cared for.

'You know Jamie Lad, I always thought you were good together, it's a shame you did what you did. I'm sure in time she would have told her parents.'

'I was immature Fred, thought I knew best, thought I was getting me own back, yer know, I was feeling hurt so I wanted to hurt her, but the truth is Fred, it destroyed us, me included.'

I feel a rush of emotions and that pain again, five years later I still feel it as raw today as it was back then.

I can hear Fred is still talking, so I pull myself back to the present to listen again as he tells me, 'Little Mikey started school in September so now she has to go away during the school holidays. So that's what they've done, they're on holiday. Hazel has gone with her to help look after him, the little ball of energy that he is.'

I actually can't think or speak at this moment but I have to, I open my mouth but nothing is coming out. I take a sip of my lager.

'So, she has a child, a little boy is it?' That's all I can muster up.

'Yeah, little Mikey - and to think she was told she couldn't have kids, that she'd need IVF!' he exclaims in mockery. 'Hang on, you don't know?'

All I can do at this point is shake my head.

'Look I'm not saying he's yours, but I told Hazel that if he is, then you have a right to know.'

My mind is running at a million miles an hour. Little Mikey, is that short for Michael, my middle name? I need to listen more, I need to concentrate on what he's saying, though I actually feel like I'm going to be sick.

'She was adamant it was a direct result of a fling with a work colleague, to get over you apparently, only she falls pregnant and he didn't want to know. Anyway, Hazel and I have been on hand to help out because even though her mum and dad moved closer when he retired, they're still half hour or so away. But it's great for us, not having any children of our own we've been there to help her and him 'cause he's the cutest little guy, the biggest blue eyes you ever saw and the blondest hair.'

I think by this point the colour has drained from my face.

'You ok Jamie? You look like you're in shock.'

I nod, what else can I do? 'What date was he born?' I manage to respond, barely able to string two words together

'12 January 2021. She called him Michael, but I call him 'Mikey' or 'Little Mikey.'

He carries on talking about how amazing Jess is with him, that she now only works three days a week and that it can't be easy, being a single mum.

I can hear him talking about this and that but all I can think is *I need to get out of here, I need to get back to my room.*

I barely finish my dinner and then make an excuse that I have to be up early tomorrow for my first day. I say goodbye and he tells me he'll be back here tomorrow if I fancy some company.

When I get back to my room and think about everything Fred told me I put the 12 January 2021, in my calendar and rewind 40 weeks…to 21 April 2020. Fuck!

Chapter 11

Catching Some Rays

Sitting on the edge of the pool with her feet dangling into the water, Jess was enjoying the half term break. She always struggles at this time of year, as it is coming up to Halloween and that means it will be six years this Friday that Jamie came into her life.

Michael is playing with his water gun, he's wearing his UVA sun suit as well as his life jacket. He's quite fair skinned and Jess worries that he'll burn so she always applies extra sun cream, much to his annoyance. He always protests but it falls on deaf ears "no point in protesting, if you're not wearing sun cream Michael, you don't go in the pool" she tells him every time.

She watches Michael playing, and thinks what a happy child he is - she's so lucky - and he's beautiful, just like his father. Even if she wanted to forget about Jamie, she couldn't as Michael reminds her every day with his blonde hair and big blue eyes, he is the spitting image of Jamie, there's no denying.

She sits quietly, realising that she's thought about him a lot lately, she's not sure why, but whatever it is, she feels it in the pit of her stomach. For some reason she's been getting butterflies, like the ones she used to get when he was around. She misses him, always has and always will.

She can hear Hazel on the phone to Fred, she's so grateful to Hazel for coming away with her. She's been coming to Majorca for the past three years as it's a short flight for Michael and it is lovely and hot. Once he's old enough to handle a longer flight she'll take him to Greece as she has lots of happy memories of holidaying there as a child with her parents.

Michael is playing pretend ,make-believe shooting his gun and calls 'Mummy, watch me, I'm a soldier, look.'

Aww Michael, you'll make a great soldier one day, that's for sure, she thinks to herself, *it's in your blood.*

They're staying on an all-inclusive complex, as it works out cheaper, with all the free pop, ice cream and snacks, it's one less thing for her to worry about. Plus, staying together means she can have an alcoholic drink without worrying about getting drunk and not being able to take care of Michael. Hazel is another pair of eyes and ears, and rarely has more than one or two herself.

When Hazel comes off the phone, she looks like she's in shock and Jess asks her if she's ok. She

shakes her head, and Jess is immediately worried that something is wrong with Fred. She calls Michael over as she needs him to get out for few minutes, explaining that Nanna Hazel isn't feeling happy. He grumbles a little but he loves his nanna Hazel and as she lifts him out, he runs to her shouting, 'What's up Nanna, why you upset?'

She holds a towel out and wraps him in it like any protective Nanna would, and as Jess approaches the beds she can see something is bothering her. Hazel looks at her and laughs, 'You'd never believe you're a forty-two year old woman with a child Jess, you have the most amazing figure. You really do put some people to shame.'

Jess laughs too, 'You're just being kind Hazel,' but she is slim, after having Michael she was back into a size ten jeans by the time he was a week old, but then again when she looks at photos of herself when she was pregnant, she had the tiniest bump, it's no wonder he was only 5lb 9oz.

'Is everything ok with Fred?' she asks, as Hazel doesn't seem to be forthcoming with any news from her call with her husband.

'Yes love, he's fine.'

'You look worried, I thought something was wrong,' she says, prompting a little more for information.

Hazel looks at her, there's something wrong but she isn't saying which makes Jess is even more worried. What if it's her mum or dad?

'Tell me Hazel, what's wrong? I can see it on your face.'

Hazel looks at her and says, 'Jamie's back.'

Chapter 12

Fainting

Jess can hear mutterings around her and someone saying, 'She's coming to,' and as she opens her eyes she can hear Michael crying. Michael! She sits up, still dazed, and the man next to her tells her not to sit up so quick, or she'll pass out again.

'What?' Jess says, in disbelief.

Luckily for Jess, the man - another holiday guest - is a Paramedic back home in England. He smiles at her, a nice kind smile and hands her a drink of water. 'Here you go Jess, you fainted, I think you might be dehydrated,' he says.

She takes the glass of water from him, realising she really is thirsty and taking a drink she looks around - Hazel is holding Michael, she can see he's been crying and she puts her arm out, gesturing for Hazel to pass him to her.

After a few minutes everyone has dispersed and the holidaymaker who came to help her gives Hazel his mobile number in case she passes out again 'No matter what time of day, just call,' he tells her. Hazel thanks him and goes and sits with Jess.

'What happened to me Hazel?'

'You fainted Jess.'

'Why? I've never fainted before, not that I recall.'

She tries to remember the last thing they were talking about. She tells Hazel, 'I remember walking over to the bed, you had a really worried look on your face, and then I'm coming around on here with a stranger helping me. I thought for one moment I heard you say "Jamie's back",' and she laughs as she says it, not a jovial one, a nervous one.

'I did Jess.'

Jess's heart skips a beat, she can't believe what she's hearing. 'Why? How? When? When did he post back?'

Hazel tells her, 'It's not a posting, he's on secondment, for twelve weeks, he walked into The Bowl last night, sat with Fred, had a couple pints and some food and left. Fred told me "He's just been promoted to Corporal, that's why he's here".'

'Did he tell him about Michael?'

Hazel nods, 'But he told him it was from a fling after he left, but he's not convinced he bought it. Jess you're going to have to face up to it, he's back, he deserves to know and Michael needs to know who his father is. You know I've always kept my opinions to myself, but sometimes you don't have a choice in life and this is one of those times.'

'Is he married, did he say?'

Hazel shrugs her shoulders, but tells her that Fred said he looks really well - mature and bulked out and he's also got tattoos.

Jess looks at her, confused, 'Tattoos? He hated them. Wow! I guess he must have changed.'

Chapter 13

Memories

Jess and Hazel decided to head back to their room, Michael was tired so it was a good opportunity to give him a nap. The afternoon sun is very hot, even though it is October. Jess is very quiet all the way back and Hazel doesn't disturb her thoughts with idle chit chat.

She takes Michael into the bedroom and lies on the bed with him while he chats away about his friends in school, his teachers and how big and strong he is. Jess laughs at him and says, 'Yes you are, you're Mummy's big little soldier,' then she kisses him on the cheek and tells him, 'Stop talking now and go to sleep.'

As she lies on the bed her mind wanders back to the time when she was pregnant. The first few weeks were hell, she wonders how Michael even made it - she never ate, she didn't sleep, she cried non-stop but most of all her heart was broken, and still is. She's never looked at another man, she can't. She knows she'll never love again - how can she when she's still in love with Jamie?

That's been the hardest thing for Jess. Even after what he did she never fell out of love with him, she wishes she did as she's sure life would have been easier if she'd have hated him.

She can see it now, the day she decided she had to have a clear out and the box that's locked away in her cupboard, filled with everything he bought her. If it didn't fit in the box it went in to the bin. His photo from beside the bed, the photos of the two of them from Nobby's wedding downstairs - the frames went in the bin and she rolled the photos up and put them in the box .

She remembers how she frantically went into the bathroom and gathered the ovulation sticks and the pregnancy test kit, then back to her room for her butt plug - she was never using that again -perfume, her beautiful bracelet with its 'Lady and the tramp' charm in the box and finally his calendar and she rolled that up too and put everything in the box. She couldn't throw it away, she wasn't ready, but one day she thought, *I'll have the courage to do it.*

She had then decided to start on her wardrobe, getting the black bags from downstairs, she opened her wardrobe and took her dress from his birthday party, the dresses from his work's Christmas party and the wedding, her New Year's eve outfit, all the shoes she'd bought recently and finally her beautiful coat he bought her for Christmas. She normally gave her clothes to the local charity shop but she couldn't bear to think of someone else wearing her stuff, not this time, so she took the bags outside and opened up the bin, put them in, closed the lid and walked back inside.

Next, she'd started on the spare room, taking the curtains down and the curtain pole, stripped the bed, filled the black bags up, took them out and left them by the bin too. Even the bed she put out on the front garden with a note attached saying 'Free'.

The room was clear, there was nothing left of Jamie in the house only her memories, which she knew she would never erase, because for all the pain she was in, she still loved him. 'One day,' she said aloud looking down at her belly, 'One day, I'll tell you about him, your daddy. I'll tell you what a beautiful man he was, the best soldier in the world and most of all how much we loved each other,' but until that day she decided she'd tell her baby that daddy had to go away to work, because one day he'd be back. She didn't know when but she knew.

She lies there now, looking at Michael sleeping and whispers to him, 'Your daddy's back from work.'

Chapter 14

Words

Tara booked the day off - "it's an emergency" she told Finlay, her brother "I have to go down south, I need to sort this out once and for all".

She hasn't slept since Jamie told her about him going back to that base. Her worst fear. She can't believe it, she looks at her engagement ring. 'Why didn't I just marry him in Cyprus?' she says aloud, knowing it was because she had wanted the big wedding, she hadn't been bothered if she had to wait.

She's waited for him since she was fourteen, and she's not going to let *her*, *that woman*, Jess, take him from her, not this time. She had her chance and she let him go. She knows he's not in love with her the same way he was with Jess, but she doesn't care.

Tara thinks about the time she asked him why he doesn't call her 'baby' or 'babe'. She heard him say it to Jess numerous times throughout the night on New Year's eve, he even introduced her to Tara by saying "Oh, baby this is Tara, Jed's little sister".

"Why don't you ever call me baby or babe?" she had said to him.

"What?"

"You never call me baby or babe, you used to call her it though. Why not me?" she had continued.

"Tar, what the fuck yer talking about, what does it matter anyway? I call yer darling and other nice words" Jamie had tried to reason with her. He just couldn't bring himself to call her baby or babe, he said these words to Jess, and couldn't use the same words with Tara, as it would remind him of Jess, and that pain was too much.

"Yes I know but never them, why not?" Tara had not given up easily.

"Tara, enough, it's a fucking word. Are yer seriously trying to start an argument over a poxy word?" Jamie had become angry, he didn't want to have to explain himself, and he wasn't going to, he had turned over and gone to sleep.

Tara's eyes fill with tears as she recalls the conversation.

She gets in her car, opens Google and looks up Jamie's base, opening her satnav she puts the postcode in. She knows if she heads for the base it'll be easier to find the village.

'Estimated Time of Arrival 11.05am,' says the digital voice of the satnav.

Chapter 15

Confusion

Tara turned into the village feeling very nervous. Frightened that Jamie might see her car, as he'd definitely recognize her registration plate, TAR4S – a twenty-first birthday present from her mum.

She had no idea where she was going, so pulling over on the main street, she opened google maps to look up the village. She could see the social club ahead and now looking on Google she can see there's a shop somewhere in the centre.

Starting the engine again she heads to the centre. It's half term, and there are lots of kids playing out and people are decorating their homes ready for Halloween. She has a drive around, all the houses look exactly the same - she remembers when she used to go to Cyprus and how all the houses were identical. Jamie told her it's for security reasons, in case anyone is followed - whoever is following them won't be able to identify the house again as it's no different to any other.

She has no idea if Jess still lives in the village, if she's married or what house she lives in. The only thing she does know is she can't have children, that she'll need IVF as Jamie told her one night when he was drunk - one of the few occasions he spoke about her or them. Tara always wondered why they split up – that conversation he used to avoid, he'd shrug his shoulders and say "we just did". She knew not ask any further questions by that response.

Tara's desperate, she's clutching at straws, her heart is breaking. She's feels she is losing the man she loves and has loved for the last eight years, albeit secretly for the first six of them.

She finds the village shop and sees that it is very busy as it's nearly lunch time. She can see military personnel walking in and out and she's nervous and scared. She sits and waits in the car for a while watching who is coming in and out, trying to think of what to ask, so as not to raise suspicion over why she's looking for Jess.

She runs a few scenarios through her head, one being that she is looking for her old baby sitter, they lost contact just after she moved here. She doesn't know her surname, but she'll improvise, tell them she can't remember as she was a child.

As she gets out of the car and walks towards the shop, a couple of young squaddies walk out. Her heart skips a beat as for a split second she thought it was Jamie and her fear takes over. She tells herself to get a grip, that he's not going to come off base during the day to use the shop, that's the reality.

She walks in, sees it is deserted and taking a deep breath she approaches the counter. A middle aged woman greets her warmly and Tara smiles, takes a deep breath and begins.

'Hi, I don't know if you can help me, but I'm looking for my old baby sitter, her name is Jess and she has long blond hair and she's taller than me,' then she laughs and says, 'but that's not hard really.'

The shop assistant laughs with her and tells her to hang on a sec. She calls her colleague asking if she knew where Jess was. To Tara's amazement the shop assistant seems to have bought her story and she listens in as her colleague replies, 'She's away this week with Michael.' Tara is slightly relieved by these words, this means she has someone, she's not single anymore.

The lady behind the counter asks if she wants to leave a message and she'll pass it on when she sees her next. Tara, being a little curious who Michael was, she couldn't help asking her, and the shop assistant replies, 'He's her son.'

Tara walked out the shop, even more confused now and thinks to herself that she must have had IVF with her new partner or husband. Jamie would never take on someone else's child and feeling somewhat relieved, she starts her car and sets the satnav for home. Driving out of the village, she feels a sense of happiness - for the first time in ten days she's looking forward to her wedding again. She's going to marry the man she loves.

Chapter 16

A Trip Down Memory Lane

Jamie's had a really good week, he forgot how much he enjoyed this base, The Bowl and the locals, they're always so welcoming. He nipped to the sports and social club a couple of times this week too, they were showing the midweek football games, it was lovely to see so many familiar faces. He's glad he came back even if it's just for twelve weeks - he's going to enjoy himself and make the most of his time here.

He leaves work early on Friday, he's going back home and has arranged for Tara to come and stay over at his, he's not in the mood to speak to Jean - he doesn't want to cause an argument - so it's safer for Tara to come to his until Sunday, then he'll head back to base. Before he leaves he wants a quick look around the village, see if anything has changed.

To his surprise, quite a lot has changed, there are definitely more parks for the kids. It's Halloween, a date etched forever in his memory, the houses are all decorated and he can see some of the kids out already, dressed in their costumes. It's just gone 1500hrs and he has one more stop to make then he'll get on the road - with the teatime traffic he should be home by 1730hrs.

He parks the car on the opposite side of the road, he knows she's not back yet, they're still on holiday until tomorrow. Fred dropped them off at Luton and he's picking them up, they have an afternoon flight, so they'll be back home by 1800hrs latest.

He wants to get out of the car and go and look through the window but he doesn't, he resists. He sits and stares for a while at her car, a new one, a nice white SUV, she does love her German cars. The sign on the back window makes him smile - Disney's the lion king cub with the writing 'Little Prince on board'. From this Jamie knows he's the most loved child you could meet.

He thinks back six years ago tonight, he and Jess started seeing each other. The chemistry was instant, they had amazing sex and the energy between them was on fire. He can see it now, even though he was pissed he can remember stripping her off for the first time, her thong, her smooth lips and the taste of her juices.

He remembers how it felt pushing his hard cock into her wet pussy, he looks down, he has a hard on already just thinking about it. Even after all this time he still gets an erection from her sexy photos or his thoughts of what they did.

He'd pulled her thong to one side and he was so turned on, it was the first time he'd ever had sex without a condom and it felt amazing, that shudder as he climaxed. It was pure pleasure, something he's only ever felt with Jess.

Fred hasn't said much to Jamie about Jess, in fact he avoided any conversation since Sunday, which was fine with Jamie, he'll find out in time all that he needs to know. But for now, he's going home to his mum's and intends to enjoy this weekend. He's not sure when he'll get to go back before the Christmas break in six weeks as the training schedule has him away for a few weekends .

One things for sure, Tara won't like it, not one bit - these are testing times for them.

Chapter 17

Home Time

Jess and Hazel have had a lovely week away, Michael enjoyed the pool and the beach, building sandcastles and swimming in the sea, so all in all, it's been really relaxing.

Jess has no idea what to expect when she gets home. Will Jamie contact her or will he stay away? Either way she's decided she's not going to let it worry her anymore, what will be will be.

They get to the airport for 1.00pm as their flight is at 3.00pm. They are due to land in Luton around 3.30pm with the time difference, so by the time they get through to arrivals and home it'll be nearly 6.00pm. That's ok, Jess has booked an online food delivery for 7.30pm.

The flight back was a breeze, Michael managed to fall asleep for the last forty minutes. He is totally worn out, and so is Jess, she just wants to get home to the comfort of her own bed now.

They pull into the village and she can't help but look at the base, she wonders if he's here or has he gone home to his mum's, wherever that is these days. When Jess went up to see his mum in the November, she was seven months pregnant. She had thought it through very carefully, and decided that she'd go, that he did have a right to know.

She had driven all the way there with her stomach in knots for the whole journey. Two hours she was feeling like that, plus her sickness which didn't stop until he was born - something she didn't enjoy about his pregnancy.

She'd turned into the street and seen the usual lads on the corner, the ones she'd seen on her previous visits, only this time she'd heard Ash calling her, so she'd stopped outside his mum's. She was a nervous wreck, what did Ash want? He'd come running up to her car and she'd panicked, she hadn't known what to do - Jamie had always told her to stay put while he dealt with him.

Ash had knocked on the passenger window, so she'd lowered it a bit and he'd asked her was she looking for Jamie, to which she'd said "No, I've come to see Anne". It was then he'd told her she'd moved two weeks previously, that Jamie had bought a house on some new estate near the motorway and Anne was living there.

Jess remembers Jamie telling her about it – he'd showed her the estate on the weekend of his birthday. She thanked Ash and left, she wasn't going to drive around some new estate looking for Anne, it just wasn't meant to be, so she drove back home crying. She had so wanted to see Anne, she wanted Jamie back in her life as she'd forgiven him for what he did and just wanted him back.

Chapter 18

Time To Think

Jamie has had a lot of time this week to think about his future. He knows he's here until Friday 6 February, and he has the Christmas shutdown in between (19/12/2025 – 05/01/2026). If they offer him the extension and he wants to stay he will, which means if he and Tara get married in July, he'll still be based here, there's no way he will move her into married quarters down here. No, she can stay with her mum and go to his mum's when he's home until he joins back up with his Regiment - only then will she join him, only then will they live in married quarters.

When he gets home he needs to update his calendar. It takes pride of place in the kitchen, that way his mum knows when he's home. She has a secret lover, well not so much secret - they're both middle aged, Jamie thinks he's around fifty-five, and for his mum's fiftieth this year, he took her away for two weeks to Portugal - but no one's met him yet, though all they know is his name is Pete and they've been dating for two years.

Jamie is pleased, his mum deserves someone who will look after her - he's not going to be around all the time. Sean never comes back these days, he's settled in Dorset, met his husband down there as that's the area he's based.

That was a shock for Jamie and Joe, Sean coming out as gay. His mum says she always knew. It all made sense, once he found out - he remembers on a few occasions trying to set him up with a nice girl but he shrugged it off, he just thought he was focused on his training for the army, which he was as well.

Sean's just turned twenty-two and he got married six months ago. Jamie didn't go. He knows it's wrong of him, but he couldn't stand there and watch his kid brother kiss another man, it didn't sit right with him – and still doesn't if he's honest.

But, he's happy and that's all that matters. After what Jamie went through, he realised that everyone deserves a right to happiness, no matter what your choice of partner is. You simply can't choose who you fall in love with, it just happens.

Anne told him Sean's doing really well, he's on his way to his second promotion to Corporal and at this rate he's going to overtake Jamie on the promotions. He laughs to himself as he remembers that conversation.

The two hour drive home is going well, it's giving him time to unwind on the journey, time to work out how he's going to approach the situation with Tara. How he will tell her this is his last weekend home until 19 December. If he can squeeze it in, he'll try and get back 21 November, three weeks from today, it doesn't sound so bad after all.

The Regiment he's with are all young lads, some on their first post straight from training. The eldest is only nineteen and the youngest seventeen. He listens to their conversations about girls and shagging, cringing but laughing at the same time, they remind him of himself at that age, what he was like. His attitude was to "fuck 'em and leave 'em".

Looking back now, that was awful - he never realised or thought about how that would make a girl feel. No wonder he had a bad reputation, as he later found out from the lads. The local girls he'd slept with or the girls at the lap dancing club had said he was a proper player, made them feel cheap.

That hurt him, he never thought himself a player and he never wanted anyone to feel cheap, he just saw it as a way of not getting involved. After all it was just sex, a one night stand, he didn't see it as anything else. Perhaps the girls he fucked wanted something else - something more? Who knows, it's in the past now and he's more than happy to leave it there.

Chapter 19

Feeling Horny

One things for sure, he was certainly feeling horny on the way home, he even text Tara to tell her. She sent back a laughing face emoji - not the kind of response he was looking for but then that was the Tara he knew and loved.

I really hope she's in the mood for sex, it seems like ages since we had any he thinks, and realises this is something he needs to sort out with her. She's not shy - well she says she isn't - but she's not bothered by it either, she can go for weeks with no sex, whereas he struggles with it. He's ok without it for a few days when he's away at work but once he's home at the weekend he needs it.

He parks up and gets his kit out, having brought it home for his mum to wash as she still gets a sense of pride washing his kit - he'll iron it on Sunday morning before he leaves at lunch time. He's got a really early start Monday, they're on parade for 0800hrs which means he needs to be in the office by 0700hrs.

A full week ahead of training, plus they're away next Wednesday through to Sunday, although the lads don't know it yet. He remembers these training exercises, he used to send Jess flowers whenever he went away unexpectedly - it was his way of saying "sorry, but I'll be back".

He tells the lads in his group how important it is to make your woman feel safe and secure, to let her know you're thinking about her whilst you're away. You don't, in reality, you simply don't get the time - but they're not to know that. "A bunch of flowers cost nothing in comparison to what they mean to the women" he tells them. Some agree but there's always one who's a cock, another Gavin.

He has to laugh, his good mate Gav, his brother from another mother as Gav says, was his saviour after Jess. He looked after him and made sure he didn't do anything stupid, they all looked after him really but the others were either married or in relationships. Gavin was single and he stayed with him, trained with him and was simply his rock during those few months, actually more than a few, probably eighteen months to be fair.

Tara comes running out to him, wraps her arms around his neck, stands on her tip toes and kisses him. She tells him she is horny too and that she loves him and has missed him. He wraps his arms around her, practically engulfing her with his body as she's so petite. He's relieved to hear it, it means they are going to have a good weekend so he decides to leave the calendar until Sunday, he doesn't want to spoil a good thing, not now anyway.

Chapter 20

Home Wrecker

She hears the alarm going and thinks to herself *it can't be 7.00am already*. She hits the snooze button, hoping for another ten minutes, planning to then get up and get Michael ready for his first day back after the half term break. She smiles at the thought of his chunky little legs in his long trousers now that it's becoming too cold to wear shorts.

She's going round to see Jodie after she's done the school run, to fill her in on the holiday and also to tell her that Jamie's back.

Jodie and Jess are best friends. Martin, Jodie's husband, was posted here six years ago and the kids are in secondary school so when it was time to move after the three years was up, Martin put in for an extension. This was not something taken lightly, as it meant he had to join a different Regiment on a temporary basis. Now he's re-joined his Regiment as their base is only forty-five minutes away so he commutes every day.

Jess is feeling horny so she looks at the clock and wonders if she has time for a quick play with her vibrator, but then decides to put it off. Instead she'll come home after Jodie's, put some porn on and have a good play -that's all she can do these days. She resigned herself to a life of celibacy after Jamie so she bought some new vibrators, they are her saving grace, she gets so horny, something that never changed, even after Jamie left. He definitely awoke something in her, that's for sure.

She gets up, has a quick wash, throws her sweat pants on, vest top and sweat jacket, and finds a pair of trainers to wear. She really has swapped jeans and boots for comfy sweaters and trainers, *oh the joys of motherhood and school runs,* she thinks with a big grin on her face.

Jess walks in to Michael's room and stands there for a few moments watching him sleep. She remembers the rare occasions watching Jamie sleep – as she was always the sleepy head - 'two peas in a pod,' she says out loud to herself, and sits on his bed, bends down, gives him a kiss on his forehead and brushes his hair back, 'Michael, time to get up darling, you're back to school today.'

He stirs, and mumbles, 'I don't want to go back today, can I have five more hours mummy please?' She laughs, *if only,* she thinks - the irony of it! Come Saturday and Sunday when they can sleep in for 'five more hours' he'll be up by 7.00am, if not earlier, something she can never understand.

8.30am and they're ready to leave. It's definitely chillier than before the break, but then again it is 3 November, she thinks, and realises she needs to start Christmas shopping - Michael's list gets longer and longer as he's getting older. She also wants to organise a birthday party for him as he'll be five in January, and he wants to invite his school friends to it – better start planning it now so it doesn't get hampered by the Christmas break from school.

They walk to school with a few of the other mums. No one knows Jamie as these are all either recently new to the base or arrived after he left. Fortunately they never got to meet Angela either, she left a couple months later, which was a blessing. She slept with the wrong husband and his wife went after her in The Bowl not long after it came out she'd slept with him. She threatened to kill her and apparently it took four MP's to pull her off. Angela left soon after. She was definitely a home wrecker, there's no beating around the bush on that one!

Chapter 21

Catching Up On The Gossip

Jodie opens the door and hugs her bestie, she's missed her while she's been away. 'You look amazing, so tanned, I'm so jealous right now!' she says, and they both laugh as Jess walks in.

'Kettles already on.'

'Good. I'm parched, you had breakfast yet?' Jess asks.

'No, I was going to wait till you arrived. Do you fancy a slice of toast now and then we can nip out for lunch?'

'Sounds like a plan to me, I'll pop home before hand and get changed,' Jess says. She doesn't mind doing the school run or going for a coffee in someone's house in what she's wearing but she's surely not going out for lunch in it.

They sit at the table and Jess notices that Jodie has a concerned look on her face - Jess knows her best friend and she knows when she's worried.

She asks her, 'What's up? You have that look on your face.'

'Jess, I have something to tell you, it's not good and I don't know how to say it, so I'm just going to come straight out with it.'

Jess is scared, what if they're moving? How will she cope without her best friend? She hates this part of the military, you make so many lovely friends and then after a couple or three years they move on, well in Jodie's case six years, but that's not the point. She loves Jodie and Martin, and how is Michael going to cope without them?

'Jamie's back.'

'I know.'

'What? How? You've been away, have you seen him?'

She tells her about Hazel on the phone to Fred and that she was sat on the pools edge, and she looked at Hazel and she had the same worried look as Jodie did just now. Fred had told her, he'd walked into The Bowl the night before and the reason he's here. She also told her about the fainting and they both laughed. Jess asked her how she knew, because Jamie is living in the blocks and Martin isn't on the Base.

Jodie explains that Martin saw him in the social club on the Tuesday night. Mart was home early as he wanted to go and watch the football and have a couple pints. He walked in, saw Jamie sat at a table with a couple of guys from the base that Martin knows, and left - didn't even bother going in.

'How does he look?'

'Good apparently. He looks different, but the same Jamie, just broader and with tattoos.'

'I know! What's that about? He hated them.'

'The thing is mate, this secondment, it's not something you get asked to do, you have to apply.'

Jess looks stunned, she's not sure what Jodie is saying. 'What do you mean?'

'He put in for it Jess. Martin made a couple of phone calls, it turns out he asked his Sergeant to recommend him - told his Sergeant he needs "closure".'

Jess is stunned, she's in shock, 'What does he mean by "closure",' she says quietly.

'Fucked if I know, but one things for sure, this isn't a coincidence, this is something he's planned.'

The two of them sit there in silence for a while, a million thoughts going through Jess' head.

'What you going to do?' Jodie asks her.

'Nothing. There's nothing I can do, he knows where I live. When he's ready, he'll come knocking.'

Only then will Jess know what to do.

Chapter 22

Training Day

Jamie's packed and ready for the off but first he needs to give the lads their four hours notice. He walks into the training room where a couple of them are talking about the weekend, he hears one of them say he's got a hot date, and he laughs as he thinks to himself *you 'aint anymore mate* as the only thing hot about the weekend will be his shower when he gets back early hours of Monday morning.

He texts Tara to tell her he's going out on exercise until Monday, so he won't have any mobile phone coverage but not to worry and he's arranged with the local florist to drop some flowers to her work place around lunch time.

They had a lovely weekend, including sex Friday and Saturday night. He was quite surprised when she made the first move in bed Saturday night as she's never done that. He's not sure what's happened but since the middle of last week she's been different. He can't explain it, but something's happened, whatever it is he wasn't going to question it at the time, he was just happy she's happy.

He started to update the calendar on Sunday morning as she sat with him at the table and he was prepared for whatever the reaction was going to be, but there wasn't one. She sat there calmly and even added all the events to her diary. He jokingly put his hand on her forehead like he was checking her temperature, making sure she was not sickening for something - but nope, she didn't have a temperature.

He watches the lads for their reactions as he tells them, as you can generally tell who's going to last in the army by who'll bail at first opportunity, but to his surprise none of them reacted badly, they were all stoked about it, after all this is what they joined for, the excitement, the adventure, the fact they get to play with real guns instead of plastic nerf ones - this is what being a soldier is all about.

As they leave the room to go and get packed he hears them say to Jack, 'You gonna send your girl some flowers?' He nods as he walks out. His hot date will wait once she gets her flowers, she'll know he's serious but work comes first and when you date a soldier you have to live with the unpredictability of everyday life.

Chapter 23

No Alarm Needed

'Mummy, Mummy, Mummy wake up its morning.'

'It's too early Michael, come here and get into bed,' Jess looks at the clock 06.48am, 'You're kidding.' Every day this week she's struggled getting him up, but like clockwork, it's the weekend and he's awake. She considers telling him he has school tomorrow - perhaps he might just lie in.

She lifts the quilt up and he climbs in next to her. Wrapping her arms around him she kisses the back of his head and tells him she loves him and what a good boy he is.

He's non-stop chatter, so there's no point going back to sleep. How can you, with a chatty four year old in bed? She asks him does he want breakfast and then does he want to go to soft play today - probably wasn't a good idea mentioning soft play, he's now even more excited.

They get up, go and have breakfast and then get showered and dressed for soft play. One of her new friends are going as her fella is away on exercise - from what she's heard, it's very similar to what Jamie went on when they first got together.

Becky is knocking on her door by 10.00am, even though they aren't leaving until 11.00am. This is her first base, she lived with her mum until she got married three months ago. She's very young, only twenty years old but has been with Ben since she was seventeen. Ben's a Lance Corporal, his first promotion, he joined straight from school and is slightly older by about two to three years, and they have a gorgeous little girl, Isabella - she's coming up for her first birthday at Christmas, and Jess can't deny it, it's made her very broody for a little girl.

Jess can't help but wonder what Jamie is up to, she's been back a week now and hasn't seen him. In fact no one's seen him this week, he hasn't been to The Bowl and he's not been to the sports and social club either. She's beginning to wonder if he's gone back to his base and given the idea of 'closure' up as bad idea.

She invites Becky in, makes a cup of tea and tidies up the breakfast dishes. Becky talks about how grateful she is for her friendship and that she was scared to move here, but Ben would always tell her that the locals and wives would welcome her with open arms – and he wasn't wrong.

She's talking to Michael, telling him what a handsome boy he is and she says to Jess, 'He's going to be a heartbreaker when he's older.' Jess laughs, and can't help thinking *like father like son* while she stands by the sink clutching her cup of tea, she wonders if Jamie ever will come back into their lives, if only for Michael's sake.

Chapter 24

Soft Play Date

Jess and Becky are non-stop chatting on their way to the soft play area - it's only a twenty minute drive to get there but first they have to drive on to the base as Ben forgot to leave the car seat for Isabella. They drive into the car park by The Bowl and Jess looks around at the cars, they're all pretty decent - *these aren't the cars of young lads or new recruits* she thinks to herself. She's just looking but not really paying much attention when a registration stops her in her tracks, her heart thuds and then misses a beat.

J13 JMO. She takes a photo and sends it to Jodie with a caption. [His private registration plate].

Jodie texts back. [How do you know?]

She tells her it's her initial and birthdate, he found it when they bought his car before they separated.

Jodie answers [Shit mate he's still here, where's he been all week?]

She replies with a couple of emoji's but Jess has a fair idea of the answer.

Becky comes walking back with the car seat - she's struggling but Jess can't do much to help as she's holding Isabella. Jess tells her if it's an Isofix seat, she can slot it straight in and fortunately for Becky it is so she relieves Jess of the baby.

Becky gets back in the car, all smiles, excited to be going out as normally when Ben is away or he's on nights she's stuck in the house. She tells Jess she really needs to learn to drive, that way when he is away, whether it's a few days or a short tour like the one he has coming up next year, she'll be able to go and stay with her mum so she's not house bound, stuck hundreds of miles away on her own.

Jess agrees with her, it's a very good idea, but tells Becky never to think she has to feel isolated, that she knows what it's like to be lonely with a baby and if she's feeling like that she should tell her and they can come and stay with her - besides there are times when Jess would love some company.

Jess needs to question Becky, to see if she knows anything about Jamie, if Ben has told her about a new Corporal on secondment - but she doesn't want to make it obvious, she doesn't know her well enough to let the cat out the bag.

They arrive at the soft play area and it's pretty busy, which means it's going to be noisy so she'll not be able to talk to her in here. Perhaps that's a good idea, there are some things best left unsaid and she decides that maybe Jamie is one of those things.

Chapter 25

A Choice Of Stars

Jamie was glad to be back. He's truly knackered - as much as he loves these kind of exercises they take it out of you, but they're as close to real life combat as you're going to get so they're essential training. However, travelling in those wagons is pants, they don't seem to get any more comfortable and like all the other lads he always sleeps on the way back.

They arrived back on base on Monday morning at 0410hrs and unpacked the trucks, now the lads have got forty-eight hours break, they're not back until 0900hrs on Wednesday morning when they'll have a day in the training room recapping what they've learnt, what they did well and what they did badly.

Jamie remembers the time Nobby dropped his rifle on one of these exercises, in fact he told everyone about it on Nobby's wedding day - it was part of his best man speech. That was an amazing day, Jamie thinks of that day often, happier times. He always feels guilty for Tara when he thinks of Tommo and Clem's wedding as he didn't take her. Even though he had a 'plus one' on his invite, Jamie thought it best not to.

Jamie walks into his room sure that he's going to sleep for England after his shower. He's lived on a couple of hours of sleep each day for the past five days. At one point he told Ben he's "getting too fucking old to be sleeping rough" and Ben laughed saying "mate you're not alone there, I didn't mind when I was sixteen, in fact I loved it but a comfy bed is way more appealing these days". Jamie laughed and told him he should have joined the RAF, he'd have a choice of 4* or 5*. They both burst out laughing, but in all fairness a comfy bed really is so much more appealing.

Jamie wakes at 1423hrs after just over eight hours sleep, the most he's had in a long time - he's thankful, he genuinely needed it. He decides to turn on his phone as he needs to let everyone know he's back and he listens as a chorus of tunes start to play out on his phone from text messages, WhatsApp, emails and Instagram notifications.

He throws on a pair of jeans, a sweater and trainers as he's going to the mess. There should be some food for him, - hopefully a good cooked breakfast as they always keep something back for them when they know they've returned back in the early hours of the morning.

He opens a message from Tara [Thank you for the flowers, you're the best, love & miss you xx]

He replies with a simple [Hey, I'm back, miss you too xxx]

His mum has text him also [Missing you my son, let me know as soon as you're back. Love you Xx]

So he sends her a simple update same as Tara [Missing you & love you too mum, I'm back now xx]

He'll sort the rest later as he's hungry and wants food. It's busy when he walks into the mess, the lads have all got up with the same idea, after a few days of ration packs, a reheated English breakfast tastes like something you'd get at the Ritz, not that Jamie's ever eaten at the Ritz, but that's the best way he can explain it.

Chapter 26

Stalking

Jamie parks up and turns his lights off, it's a good job he has a black car as no one will really see it if they look outside. Plus it's the middle of November and everyone's curtains are closed. He thinks *if anyone has seen me this week, they'll think I'm a stalker*, and laughs to himself.

He watches as the landing light goes on, then her slim silhouette standing at the window as she closes the curtains in Michael's room, then a moment later he watches her close her curtains, then he sees what he thinks is the bathroom light go on. He's watched her every night this week and it's the same routine - 1800hrs she starts and by 1900hrs she turns a little lamp on in Michael's room, 19.15hrs she turns it off and a few seconds later she turns the hall light off, the bathroom one is left on, then he sees her shadow walk past the living room window after she's put Michael to bed.

He has to get the timing right, he's decided tonight's the night. He tries to imagine what she does and what her routine is. His best guess is that she's bathing Michael, then reading him a bed time story. Having thought it over as the week has progressed and the timings stayed the same, this version in his head makes the most sense.

He likes her routine, children need a routine, he also likes the fact that Michael sleeps in his own room. He thinks back to what it was when he left - it was a newly decorated spare room and he wonders what colour scheme she's chosen for him. He also has questions in is mind such as what his likes and dislikes are, what he likes to eat, or is he a picky child?

He wonders what he was like as a baby. Not that he knows much about babies only what his sister Rosie told him about Archie, his nephew. He's two years old now and she's pregnant with her second – she's hoping this one isn't a sickie one like Archie was.

He's upset he missed out. He should be angry with Jess but he's not, he can only think about how hurt she was after what he did, he has had to live with that regret every day since. He can't even think about it, it literally turns his stomach, the thought that he could even go there with her, Angela, of all people, but he did what he did, there was no one else to blame but himself and he's learnt to live with it.

He just hope's that Jess has finally forgiven him. He has hoped and prayed for her to forgive him, for a very long time.

He looks at the time on his phone and it's 1844hrs. Turning it off he puts it away in the glove compartment and gets out of the car, shutting the door quietly. He locks it and the alarm activates and the indicators flash *well, if she didn't know I was here already, she does now, bloody indicators* he thinks and he tuts and rolls his eyes.

His stomach is in knots as he crosses the road, he actually feels physically sick, his heart is pounding, but he has to do this. Walking up the path, he's surprised there's no outside light on, but then thinks *why would there be it's not like she's expecting anyone*. He knocks on the door and waits, then the outside light comes on as he's standing there waiting and then she opens the front door.

'Hello Jess.'

Chapter 27

A Busy Week

Jess has had a busy week sorting out her Christmas list, she's text her mum and dad asking if they'd come to hers this year. Now that Michael is older, she wants to stay at home so he can play with his toys rather than having to lug everything to and fro. Besides, it's not going to be easy to pack the car with his presents anyway as he'll see them. She's also booked some time off on the run up to Christmas, 23 and 24 December and if she can she's also requested the two days leading up to New Year's eve, if she can't then she's sure Hazel or Jodie will help out.

She dropped Michael off at school this morning and headed straight in to town to do some Christmas shopping as there's only five and a half weeks to go. She's been back from her holiday a fortnight tomorrow and curious as to why Jamie hasn't been round or tried to make contact. She's resigned herself now to the thought that he isn't interested, as if he was he'd have come around by now she's sure of it, the Jamie she once knew was very impatient.

She gets home and hides his presents in her wardrobe, she's bought him the pilot outfit he wants, along with a toy garage and some cars. She's also bought some educational books for his age today *so that's three items crossed off from his list of about a thousand* she thinks and laughs to herself, in any case he will have plenty to open. She's also going to start getting some towards his birthday, and tomorrow she's got to go to the soft play centre and book his party.

She goes upstairs and closes his curtains and next goes and closes hers and then runs Michael's bath. She calls Michael to come up as his bath is ready and when he comes up the stairs, she tells him he's a cheeky monkey for not coming up with her like he used to. Michael tells her he was busy watching television and she laughs at him, knowing that's an indication of things to come as he grows up, then she kisses his head and puts him in the bath.

She gets his PJ's, dressing gown and slippers ready and after she's washed his hair she tells him it's time to get out and that he can have longer play tomorrow. Jess is tired tonight and wants to get him to bed so she can relax, she's even thinking of having a nice bath and an early night herself.

Once he's dressed in his PJ's she takes him downstairs, 'It's coming up to six-thirty, time for your milk Michael,' she tells him and he sits at the table to drink his warm milk. Jess is in the kitchen tidying up their tea things, when Michael calls her.

'Mummy, someone's knocking the front door,' and he gets down off his chair and goes to the front door, asking Jess, 'Who is it?'

'I don't know Michael, not until I open the door. It's probably Auntie Jodie come round for a cup of tea.' She puts the outside light on and opens the door.

She sees him standing there before she hears his voice. He's still in his uniform and her first thought is how hench he is. He was always muscular but now he's even more so, his sleeves are rolled up so she can see his tattoos - a full sleeve - she has to focus but the shock of seeing him is too much. She wasn't expecting this at all, her hand covers her mouth and she can't speak as he says, 'Hello,' and smiles that beautiful smile. Her heart is pounding, she thinks she's going to faint again, but then she feels Michael tugging on her trouser leg.

'Mummy, who is it?' his little voice shows nothing but curiosity.

She can't answer, she wants to but the words aren't coming out, she sees Jamie bend down to Michael's level and he holds out his hand and introduces himself.

'Hello, my name's Jamie, what's yours?' he says to the small boy in his pyjamas and offers his hand for him to shake.

Michael giggles as he says, 'My name is Michael.'

'Well hello Michael, I'm pleased to meet yer.'

Jess watches as Michael shakes his hand, it's so tiny in Jamie's.

'Are you a real soldier?' Michael asks.

'Yes Michael, I am,' Jamie replies, and laughs as he stands back up.

Then Jamie looks towards Jess and says 'Are you going to invite me in or are we going to stand here all night?' He laughs his cheeky laugh and winks.

Jess just smiles and invites him in with an almost invisible nod of the head as she still can't talk, her head is still fuzzy. She swears if Michael hadn't been there she'd have fainted for a second time.

Chapter 28

Emotions Take Over

Jess walks in behind Jamie, watching his peachy bum as he walks. Michael is chatting away to him, she can't help smiling at how open and friendly he is, she loves that about him.

Looking from one to the other, they have the same shaped heads and the same walk already, she finally finds her voice and asks him, 'Would you like a drink, tea or coffee?' then she tells Michael to drink up his milk as it's near his bed time.

Michael sits back on his chair and Jamie sits opposite him, still chatting. Jess can't deny that it's wonderful to hear them talking. She never thought she'd ever see this, she had only hoped and prayed that one day she would.

She makes Jamie a cup of tea and hands it to him and he looks at her and thanks her. Her stomach is mass of butterflies and she still feels shaky but she takes a seat next to Michael and listens in as they carry on chatting. She tells Michael that it's bed time now and asks if he is finished with his milk, to which Michael nods and shows her his empty cup. They both laugh at him with his milk moustache and Jess uses her thumb to wipe it off. She gets up as Michael gets down off his seat to go to bed, he looks at Jamie and asks him if he wants to see his bedroom. Jamie looks at Jess and she nods for him to agree.

Michael holds out his hand to Jamie and gets up from his chair. Jamie tells him he'd be delighted to see his bedroom and takes Michael's hand as they walk upstairs with Jess following behind them.

Michael takes Jamie into his bedroom and shows him his toy box - it's full of cars, toy guns, colouring books and crayons. Next he shows him his dinosaurs on top of the chest of draws, then his dinosaur duvet cover and tells Jamie they make a really loud 'Roaar' noise. Jamie can't help laughing at his cute impression.

Jess tells him to get into bed and pulls the quilt back as Jamie backs away. He walks out onto the landing and waits for Jess to join him. Jess bends down and gives Michael a kiss goodnight and tells him she loves him very much.

'I love you too mummy. Is Jamie my daddy?'

Jess is shocked, she wasn't expecting this. Michael sees soldiers walking around the village and on the base every day but not once has he ever asked if any of them are his dad.

'Yes darling, he is,' she answers as she can't lie to him.

'I'm happy he's come back from work to see me, will he be going back to work soon?'

Jess' heart is bursting and she wants to cry but she mustn't, she needs to be strong. She can't answer him so she shakes her head, gives him a hug and a kiss and gets up to walk out the door, saying good night again as she turns the light off.

'Night Mummy, night Jamie,' Michael says as he pulls the quilt up to his chin.

'Night Michael,' Jamie manages to say, though he can barely talk with the lump in his throat from listening to Michael talking with his mummy.

'I'm glad you came back from work to see me Jamie.'

'Me too Michael, me too.' Jamie wipes his eyes with his thumb and fore finger, his emotions now taking over.

Chapter 29

The Right To Know

Jamie walks down the stairs and Jess follows him. He's visibly shaken and could never have expected this. Michael is amazing and he feels so proud of Jess for the way she's raised him. He can see already that he's her world, but he feels sad that he didn't know about him before and can't help thinking how much he's missed out on.

He knows he needs to talk to Jess, to ask her why she didn't tell him and what right she had to deny him his son and Michael his father, but for now he can only think how Jess is as beautiful today as she was when he left - he can't deny it, he's still as much in love with her today as he was six years ago.

He walks into the living room and stands by the table, his legs crossed and his arms folded. He's comfortable but nervous - nervous of what's going to happen next and also scared that maybe nothing will happen.

'Yer look really good Jess, motherhood suits yer.'

'Thanks.'

'How are yer?' he asks her, genuinely wanting to know after all this time.

'Good.'

'Is that it, one word answers?' he says, and laughs nervously.

'I don't know what to say Jamie,' she says honestly, she really doesn't have any words to get her through this awkward feeling.

'I'm sorry, I shouldn't have just turned up like this, but I didn't know what else to do or how else to get in touch, yer must have heard I was here.'

She nods in acknowledgement as she's walking towards him, she bends to pick Michael's cup up from behind him and he takes the opportunity and cups her face in his hands and kisses her, lovingly and passionately, his tongue looking for hers. He feels her arms around his waist as she kisses him back, he doesn't know why he kissed her, he just couldn't help himself, his feelings and emotions took over.

He uncrosses his legs and pulls her closer, wrapping his arms around her, he wants to strip her off and make love to her - he's missed her. He wants to tell her that there hasn't been a day he hasn't thought about her, that he's never stopped loving her and is still as in love with her now as he was the day he left, but most of all he wants to tell he's sorry - sorry for destroying everything they had.

He stops kissing her, let's out a little laugh, and apologises. She laughs at him and tells him it's ok.

'Wc need to talk, seriously. I need to know why yer never told me, I had a right to know,' he says, trying to think clearly and get a grip on his emotions.

'I know, I tried honestly. I went to your mum's but she'd moved, even went to your base and left a letter for you.'

'What? When?' he asks, puzzled.

Jess tells him it was the end of November, when she was nearly seven months pregnant. He shakes his head, fuming that whoever she gave the letter to didn't pass it on to him. He works it over in his mind, trying to make sense of it all. He concludes that there's not a lot he can do now, what happened has happened but he sure as hell intends to make sure he's there for Michael from now on.

Chapter 30

Planned Ahead

Jess goes to make another cup of tea with her heart still pounding. She wasn't expecting him to kiss her but she has to admit that she loved it. She's missed his kisses and his tender touch, and she couldn't get over his muscles, the strength of his arms - she can see he's matured, physically and emotionally. He left here five years ago as a boy and returned as a man.

She hears Jamie going upstairs to the toilet so she quickly sends Jodie a message

Jess: [He's here, Can't talk. Will call you tomorrow when coast is clear xx]

Jamie nips up to the toilet, he can't help himself, he has to take a sneak peek of Michael sleeping. He looks so tiny - Jamie smiles. He uses the bathroom but then on the way down he takes a look in Jess's room. He sees that she has decorated it since he was living here, the bedroom looks lovely and he imagines her lying in bed playing with her vibrator and watching porn as he knows she's not been with another man since he left.

By the time he gets downstairs Jess is sitting on the sofa clutching a cup of tea, Jamie picks his up from the other end of the sofa and sits next to her. She smiles, she knows what he's up to.

Jess asks him what he's been up to and he tells her that after leaving here, he did two years at the new base, then went out to Cyprus for two years, coming back to the UK just over a year ago.

He doesn't tell her about Tara or their engagement as there's no point, even if he and Jess don't have a future he has made his mind up this week he won't be marrying Tara. He doesn't love her enough to marry her, he wants to get to know his son and Tara would never accept Michael.

'Did you ever marry or live with anyone after me?' she asks him, having no idea of the answer that may come.

Jamie shakes his head, but he does tell her that he's been seeing someone, but now it's over, well, on his part anyway.

'Look Jess, for what it's worth I'm sorry. I'm sorry for what I did - to this day I don't know why I did it.'

'You aren't the only one to blame, I was as much at fault as you were. The situation with my parents, I should have just stood up to my mum, I was a grown woman.'

He nods his head, moving forward to the edge of the sofa. He leans forward with his elbows resting on his knees, as he continues to talk.

'The thing is, I've missed yer every day since the night I left. I'm not gonna lie babe, erm, Jess, I need yer in my life. I don't know how yer feel, I don't know if yer've forgiven me, but I can tell yer this, I'm not that twat that left here all those years ago.'

'I can see that, where've all the tattoos come from?' she asks, not able to contain her curiosity as it's such a big change for him.

'Yeah, I've loads. Some on my chest, my back and a couple on my legs.'

He stands up and takes off his top to show her. His body is like an oil painting, his ripped muscles, his six-pack and the tattoos look so sexy on him. Jess gets up from the sofa to take a closer look and he turns around so she can see it, his angel wings that span his shoulder blades with a cross down the middle of it, she touches lightly, his skin is so soft and smooth.

Now he turns around so she can see his chest tattoos. There's one on his left side, a quote which reads "Life is not measured by the breaths we take, but by the moments that take our breath away" and underneath it are the Roman numerals 'X-XXXI-MMXIX'

Jess knows what that date is, she looks at him and asks him why that date. He tells her, 'That was the date my life changed, Halloween, only I ruined it, with my stupidity or whatever you want to call it. I destroyed everything, including myself.'

She touches his chest with her fingers, running them over the quote as she looks at him, she feels his hand on the back of her neck as he pulls her in closer to kiss her, she feels his tongue in her mouth, touching hers. She lifts up her arms for him to take off her top and her heart is pounding, she hasn't had sex for five and a half years, how will she remember what to do?

He unhooks her bra and removes it, her breasts are exactly how he remembers them, not a mark on them, even though she's had his baby. His hands cup them as his thumbs play with her nipples, she lets out a moan, this still turns her on and he knows it.

Jamie turns her around so her back is leaning against him, she can feel he's hard, she wants to feel him inside her, she's wet already, she's dreamed about this moment so many times, how he takes her and makes love to her like he used to. She remembers his shudder as he climaxed, she wonders if he still does that, something she will find out soon enough, she hopes.

He kisses her neck as his hands caress her boobs, he tells her how much he's missed her, her soft skin, her perfect shaped boobs. He tells her he wants to make love to her, he wants to feel her juices on his hard cock and that he's missed the taste of her cum, then he asks her if she's missed him.

She nods, she can't talk, she's enjoying his kisses and his hands caressing her boobs, his hand moves down to her jeans, he unfastens the button and then the zip, slides his hand inside and feels her smooth stomach. He starts to push her jeans down but then stops abruptly. She opens her eyes, she doesn't what him to stop, *why has he stopped?*

'What's wrong?' she has to ask as she stands there half naked, feeling a little embarrassed.

'I don't want to do this here, it's not right,' Jamie answers. He pulls her jeans back up, lifts her head and kisses her. He explains that he wants to make love to her upstairs in bed, he can't do it down here, he can't have their juices all over the carpet, not when his son will be playing on the carpet tomorrow.

He bends down and picks up their discarded clothes and tells her to go up to bed but leave her thong on. He'll lock up and then he needs a quick shower and he'll be in. He puts his top back on as he hands her top and bra and she looks at him, totally confused.

'I have an overnight bag in my car with toiletries in and clean clothes for tomorrow. I need to go and get it,' he smiles his cheeky smile. She knows he had this all planned, she laughs at him as she walks out of the living room and upstairs to bed. She'll wait for him there, after all she's waited five and a half years, what difference does another twenty minutes make?

Chapter 31

Just Like Old Times

She hears him coming up the stairs, after dropping his boots on the floor in the hallway. He walks in with his ruck sack, sits on the bed and takes out his clean jeans, T-shirt, boxers and socks, hangs his T-Shirt up and lays the rest out on the chair in the corner of the room.

Standing up he starts to undress again, taking off his top, undoing his belt, button and zip and then he looks at her and smirks, 'I'll be back soon,' he says and she blushes as he catches her looking at his cock. Bending down he gives her a long lingering kiss.

While he is showering, she puts her fingers in her pussy and feels how wet she is. Taking her fingers out she wipes them on her nipples, *he can lick it off once he's finished in the shower*, she thinks to herself, a smirk crossing her lips at the same time.

He walks back in to the bedroom with a towel wrapped around his waist. She can see the tattoos on his legs now, his left one is his Regimental badge and slogan 'Ubique (Everywhere); Quo Fas Et Gloria Ducunt (Whither Right and Glory Lead) and on his right leg he has some sort of tribal tattoo just below his knee, it's about three inches in depth and she can see that it stretches around his whole leg.

Standing there in just his towel, his sleeve really stands out. She can see it's a story on the battlefield, with a poppy on the top of his arm, the black silhouette of a soldier, the dark skies with a plane and lots of shading. It's a very good piece of artwork, but sad, as she can see the story behind it - it's definitely a military tattoo that's for sure.

He looks tanned, like he's been away, she thinks it could be a result of Cyprus, but won't ask him in case he tells her it was with another woman. That is something she doesn't want to hear, the thought of him with another woman or touching another woman fills her with dread, she's just not going to go there.

She lies down and smiles as he takes off his towel and gets under the covers. Leaning over to Jess he pulls her towards him, he begins to kiss her tenderly, telling her how amazing she looks. He brushes her hair away from her face as he climbs on top of her, he's aching for her, his cock is pressing hard against her pelvic bone as he kisses her.

His hand caresses her breast and he moves to suck on her nipple. He stops and looks up at her and smiles, he knows that taste, and he starts to suck again, moving from right to left. She arches her back and moans softly, she's turned on, she wants to feel his hard cock deep inside her wet pussy now.

He moves down the bed to see that she left her thong on just as he asked. He kisses her belly, it's so flat and smooth, he looks up at her and asks, 'Are you sure you've had a baby?'

'Why?' she asks, and he says there are no stretch marks. Jess tells him she wasn't very big and she kept herself moisturized throughout.

He smiles, and goes back to kissing her belly along the top of her thong, kissing and licking the front of it he pushes her legs apart and pulls it to one side as he starts to kiss and lick her smooth lips. He pushes his tongue between them and tastes her juices. He feels sure he's going to explode before he's even penetrated her with his hard cock.

His tongue feels so good licking and sucking on her clitoris and she moans with pleasure as his two fingers go inside. They slide in deep with her juices all over them and her moans get louder, she remembers how he used to love to hear her, the louder she was the more excited he became.

He sucks her juices from all over her pussy lips and clitoris, his fingers getting steadily faster, she's going to cum on them soon, he can hear it in her moans, he sucks her clitoris a little harder as his fingers go deeper and starts to feel the tension - she's cumming, she tells him.

He takes his fingers out, dripping with her cum and moves up the bed and watches as she licks them one by one, he puts a finger in her mouth and leans forwards and kisses her tasting her juices on her tongue and letting Jess taste her juices on his lips and tongue.

He kneels up and removes her thong, then climbing back on top of her he places his hard cock just inside her wet pussy and pushes it in, it feels amazing, he can feel her warmth all around his cock, her pussy is tight, as he slides his hardness in and out he begins to thrust his cock deeper, gyrating his hips from side to side, her moans getting louder, the deeper and faster he goes, the louder Jess' groans become. He kisses her neck as he makes love to her.

He whispers, 'Louder baby, let me hear you,' and his hips move faster, her groans are gut wrenching as she cums. He's close to cumming too and as he thrusts harder and deeper, faster and faster, he tells her he's about to cum. One more thrust deep and hard and his cock explodes deep inside her wet pussy, mixing his spunk with her juices.

She feels his body go rigid, then comes the familiar shudder- she knows he's just climaxed. She opens her eyes to see him smiling at her and sees the look of pure pleasure written all over his face. Smiling back at him she lifts her head to kiss him, telling him how much she's missed him. He smiles and says, 'Me too baby, me too.'

Chapter 32

Early Alarm

He rolls over as they both catch their breath and she gets up as she needs to use the bathroom. He asks her where she's going and she laughs, saying "the toilet". She might not have any marks on her tummy but her bladder is another story.

She has a quick wash before going back to bed and when she returns, Jamie is sitting up in bed. He's smiling at her as she walks in and she asks him, 'What are you looking so pleased about?'

He laughs and innocently says, 'Nothing'. Jess gets back into bed and snuggles down in the quilt facing him, so he shuffles down to her level.

She strokes his face as she tells him, 'I forgave you a long time ago, that's why I went looking for you.'

He leans in and kisses her forehead as she continues to talk, she tells him that all she wanted was to fall out of love with him, but she couldn't, that's been the hardest part of all this, still being in love with him.

He listens to her, he knows what she means as it's been the same for him. He tells her that he understands and this is the reason he came back - he needed to see if she was still here or if she'd re-married and most importantly if she still loved him, like he still loved her. She nods.

He lifts her chin up and kisses her, a long loving kiss. He's not felt this kind of love since the day he left. This is where he belongs, he knows it and he has to do everything in his power to rebuild their relationship. What happened in the past happened, nothing he can do will ever change that, but he has the chance to remedy it for the better. Jess is and always was his future - it's just taken a long time for him to find his way back.

'What time does Michael wake up?' Jamie asks.

'Ugh, Monday to Friday he doesn't, I have to wake him, but Saturday and Sunday he has no problem waking me up by seven.'

Jamie laughs and looks at the clock 2230hrs, 'You best set the alarm clock then, for 0500hrs.'

At first Jess doesn't get it, but soon realises *Oh God, he's serious*. She turns over and sets the alarm for five in the morning, and then lying back down he tells her to "lift up" as he puts his arm under her neck, pulls her in towards him with his leg over her legs. He kisses the back of her head and says good night.

She kisses his hand and says, 'Jamie, I don't know how long you're back for or what's going to happen between us, but I have tell you, no matter what, if I think Michael is going to get hurt I will cut you out of our lives once and for all.'

He opens his eyes, and pulls her closer, 'Baby, I'm not going anywhere, I know we have a lot to sort out, but I mean it, I'm never leaving you again. I love you Jess, always have and always will, I belong here with you and Michael.'

She smiles, her heart bursting with joy, for the first time in six years she can finally see a future as a family for her and Michael - with Jamie.

Chapter 33

Ready Brek

Jamie wakes up cuddling Jess, he hasn't slept that way for years, falling asleep by 2300hrs and not waking until 0440hrs. He feels energized and he smirks as he feels Jess sleeping peacefully, his "sleeping beauty" he used to call her and she's still that now.

He moves his arm gently out from under her as he needs the toilet. Walking back into the bedroom he turns the alarm off, he hasn't got the heart to wake her and he climbs back into bed and cuddles back into her, holding her close to him - he loves the touch of her naked body next to his.

He thinks about how much he's changed, he realises how selfish he was, he never thought twice about waking Jess up for sex. He could barely go a full day without it and they had sex every night, and most mornings, but perhaps that was just being young, put it down to his libido, or was it just the excitement that Jess brought out in him? He knows one thing, it won't be like that this time round, he'll be happy with a couple of times a week.

His mind starts to wonder, he can't help but think about what he needs to do next weekend, he needs to speak to Tara, it's time he was honest with her, she deserves better, he's not been the best fiancé this past year and he knows it.

He's going to see if Jess wants to spend this weekend together, he wants to get to know Michael, then he's going to see if he can stay a couple of nights in the week (Tuesday and Wednesday) along with the weekend (Friday to Monday morning). He realises its very early days and that they have a lot to discuss, but he wants to spend as much time with them as he can.

He's got no training exercises booked in until mid-January, so he'll be here for Michael's fifth birthday. He's going to tell his mum next week when he goes home, she needs to know as well as everyone else but not before he's finished with Tara.

He's worried about Rosie as she's married to Jed, Tara's brother. What effect will this have on them? After all 'blood's thicker than water' and it's bound to cause conflict with any future family gatherings, but he doesn't care, if it means him not going then he won't. It's his life and he deserves to be happy and to be with the person he loves.

The sound of Michael getting out of bed and running across the landing snaps him out of his thoughts, 'Shit,' he whispers audibly, worrying *what will he think of me in bed with his mummy?* Michael pushes the door open as he walks in, rubbing his eyes with his little hands. Jamie's heart melts, he's the most amazing little boy he's ever seen. He looks at Michael and puts his forefinger to his lips giving the hush sign, he motions to Michael to come round to his side of the bed.

Michael runs around, to Jamie's side, all excited already. *How can that be?* Jamie thinks and he smiles, *he's a morning person like me, poor Jess* he thinks.

Jamie whispers to him, 'Mummy's asleep, do you want me to get up with you?' Michael nods in agreement, so Jamie says, 'Ok, go and get your slippers and dressing gown on.' He watches as Michael runs out of the bedroom.

He can't help but wonder if he actually does walk anywhere, or always as a run. Laughing to himself, he gets up, pulls his Regimental shorts and T-shirt on, leaving Jess to sleep a little longer as it's only 0635hrs. He'll come and wake her around 0800hrs.

They go downstairs while Michael chats to him about his breakfast. He wants Ready Brek, 'Mummy makes it with warm milk. 'Do you like Ready Brek? Mummy doesn't like it,' he tells Jamie.

Jamie can't remember the last time he had Ready Brek, but he's willing to give it a go this morning, even if it's a mouthful as it's a good start, a way to start bonding with his son, even if it's just over a bowl of Ready Brek.

Chapter 34

Rise And Shine

Jamie leaves Michael to watch television and goes to wake Jess, taking her a cup of tea up. As he walks upstairs he thinks about how hard life must have been for Jess on her own with Michael - he's definitely a live wire.

He sits on the edge of the bed and strokes her face, 'Baby, it's time to wake up.' He leans forward and kisses her. She comes around, and asks him, 'What's the time?' He tells her it's 0800hrs and she opens her eyes in shock.

Jamie tells her that it's fine, he got up with Michael, he's had his breakfast and he's sat watching TV. She smiles and thanks him, taking her cup in her hands, then she looks at him and asks, 'What happened to the five o'clock alarm?' He laughs and tells her she was fast asleep, so he turned it off as he didn't want to disturb her.

He climbs over her and lies next to her, while talking about Michael being a live wire, especially in the morning. 'Sorry babe, he's a morning person just like me.'

She tuts and rolls her eyes as she says, 'Yes, I've noticed.'

'So babe, what's yer plans for today?' Jamie asks.

'We have soft play 12 - 2pm, and I need to book his birthday party whilst I'm there.'

'Ok, can I run something by yer?' He starts to tell her his idea about staying over Friday to Monday morning then coming to stay Tuesday and Wednesday night, he wants to spend as much time with them as possible. He tells her that he knows its early days but he wants her back, he'll show her he's changed, he's matured and he can see now how immature he was even though at the time he thought he was mature.

Jess agrees with him, it's a good idea, but they need to take it slow, not rush it - after all it's not just her she has to think about these days. She asks him if there's any one else, as she gets the feeling there is.

He takes a deep breath, and tells her there is but it's over between them, he's been wanting to finish it for a while but didn't have the heart. He tells her that they were due to get married next year, that she was a rebound from Jess and he thought that he'd get over her quicker - but he didn't, it just made it worse, he missed her more and more as time went on.

He continues to tell her that he's got to go home next weekend and will be telling his mum about Jess and Michael and finishing it with her. He asks her if she believes him and Jess nods and asks who this other girl is.

He knows he needs to be honest, otherwise how are they meant to start over if he's dishonest again? 'It's Tara, Jed's little sister,' he says quietly. Jess met her New Year's eve, he knows she will remember her, that's for sure.

Jess sits forward and says, 'That's who was asking for me.'

'What? Who was asking for yer?'

'When I was away, someone walked into the shop and asked if I still lived here, that she was looking for me and that I used to be her baby sitter. I've never baby sat anyone in my life. They told her I was on holiday with Michael and she asked who Michael was, so they told her he's my son.'

'When? Did they say what day she was looking for yer?'

'Wednesday, yes definitely it was the Wednesday,' Jess says, working it out in her mind.

Jamie realises now why Tara's attitude had suddenly changed. It all made sense to him, she must have thought Michael was someone else's son,

'I'm sorry babe, that won't happen again, I promise you.'

He sits up and kisses her and asks if she wants a bath or shower and does Michael have one in the morning or in the evening? She tells him she'll have a shower, and Michael only has a bath every evening at six.

'Right, off yer go and get in the shower, I'll go down and sit with Michael and once yer've finished I'll have one. Do yer fancy going out for breakfast?' Jamie asks.

She nods, as he gets up and walks out. She feels nervous, almost frightened. *Is she doing the right thing?* For Michael, yes absolutely as he needs his daddy, but should she be letting him back in her life? She needs to be cautious here, she has the feeling that things aren't all they seem.

Chapter 35

Family Time

As Jamie straps Michael into his car seat, he leans forward and kisses him on the forehead, telling him he's a good boy - he can feel how much he loves him already. As he shuts his door he opens Jess' for her and leans in and gives her a kiss also, saying, 'Wouldn't want yer feeling left out now, would we,' he winks at her and she laughs at him as he closes her door.

Heading out of the village, she tells him there's a nice restaurant that serves breakfast from ten am. on the way to the soft play area, it is part of a chain but the food is nice.

He starts to chat to her about money, asking if she ever closed the joint account. She tells him she couldn't, that she needed his signature. He was stunned, 'So it's still open?' he asks.

'Yes,' says Jess.

He then asks if there's any money in it, telling her that he couldn't check it after he'd changed his bank account with HR for his wages to be paid into as he deleted the app and that he actually doesn't remember much about the first three or four months after he left - it's all a blur.

She tells him there is still some money in the savings account and that she thought he would have transferred it out. She took the money out for her credit card the following month and never bothered with it after that, but she still has the app on her phone.

Jamie goes quiet while he's considering what he needs to do, he needs to start paying for Michael - it's his duty as his father. He asks Jess if she thinks Michael will ever call him 'Daddy' and that he doesn't want to rush it of course, but he can't help blurting out the impulsive thoughts.

She thinks about what he's said and answers, 'I'm sure he will, in his own time, don't force it Jamie. This is all a shock for both of us, you turning up like this.'

They arrive at the restaurant just as it's opened. Jamie immediately walks around to the driver's side to get Michael out and Jess can see what sort of father he would have been and is going to be like with Michael - he's very attentive, but then he always was with her, it's his caring nature.

As they walk into the restaurant, Jamie grabs Jess' hand and she looks at him shocked as she wasn't expecting it, but then smiles and remembers what he was like for his public displays of affection previously. With her other hand Jess holds Michael by his hand as she doesn't want him running off.

Jamie asks for a table for three and the young employee smiles at them both, but her eyes linger on Jamie. Jess watches very closely, she's been in here so many times in the past and perhaps the young girl is just shocked to see Jess with a man but she knows it's not that, it's because he's beautiful and hench, a real head turner.

After they've ordered their breakfast and drinks, Jamie puts his hands out on the table, reaching for Jess' hands. She feels a bit shy but nevertheless she places her hands in his. Michael is colouring and chatting away to them and they both look at him and laugh with pleasure at his obvious contentment.

'I'm going to start transferring some money into our joint account each month towards Michael and the food, it's not fair on yer, I don't like to think yer've struggled,' Jamie says, with his head bowed low from the feelings of shame and disappointment in this situation that he knew nothing about until just a couple of days ago.

'I haven't struggled Jamie, not financially. Emotionally? Yes absolutely,' Jess responds truthfully.

He looks up as he squeezes her hands and Jess is shocked with the concern in his eyes. He's way more emotional these days than he was when he left, but she likes this side of him.

She tells him, 'It's ok, we need to put the past behind us, if we're going to move forward.' Jess knows she wants him, more than ever. She felt nervous this morning but she is also determined she's going to give him a chance - she loves him, the butterflies in her belly are proving it to her even as she speaks.

Leaning close to him she quietly whispers, 'I wish you'd woke me at five, I was looking forward to it,' and winks at him.

Jamie smiles and also leans into her as he whispers back, 'Don't worry, I'll make up for it tonight.' He winks and smiles, then right in her ear he says, 'Babe, I've got a hard on,' and they both laugh out loud. Somethings never change.

Chapter 36

Soft Play

Jamie's never been to a soft play area before so he has no idea what to expect but he is looking forward to seeing Michael playing and enjoying himself.

'Bloody hell babe, it's loud in here!' he shouts over the din. They've literally just walked through the doors and immediately, the noise is deafening. There are probably more than one hundred kids all screaming and shouting and generally being noisy.

Jamie can see that Michael is excited and tells the cashier it's "one child please" as he pays for him, also asking if parents are allowed to join in. With the negative response of "not unless under two years of age, or special circumstances" Jamie looks around and laughs - it's no wonder Michael loves it here, this place is every boys dream. He bends down and picks Michael up and speaks into his ear, telling him how lucky he is to get to play on all those climbing frames. Michael puts an arm around his neck as Jamie carries him to the table that Jess has found for them to sit at.

Jess' face is beaming as she watches them come towards her - they really are like 'two peas in a pod'. Michael's arm is wrapped around Jamie's neck as he is carried, with his little bum resting on Jamie's muscular, tattooed arm. This man really takes her breath away, she is sure he looks even sexier today with his muscles and tattoos so visible.

Jess gets up to take Michael's trainers off but he tells her, 'No,' and looks to Jamie to take them off instead so Jess sits back on her chair and laughs as

Jamie sits him on his lap to do it. Then he tells Michael to go and have lots of fun.

Grabbing Jess' hand he asks her if she can get a babysitter for Wednesday or Thursday this week as he wants to take her out on a date. She's tells him she'll try but can't promise.

He leans forward and kisses her, telling her, 'Not to worry. If yer can't we'll have a date night at home once Michael's gone to bed,' and gives her his cheeky grin.

She tells him, 'I'll make sure I'm dressed for the occasion,' and looks knowingly at him and winks.

They're engrossed in conversation when Michael comes running back to them. He's all hot and sweaty and has a 'friend' in tow. He's excitedly telling his friend, 'This is my mum,' so Jess says a polite, 'Hello' and then Michael turns to his friend again and says, 'This is my dad, he's been away working 'cause he's a soldier,' and Jamie's face lights up as he says, 'Hello,' back and the two boys run off leaving Jamie with a lump in his throat - he didn't expect that, not in the slightest.

Jess leans in close again to speak to Jamie over the noise and says, 'I wouldn't worry about when he's going to call you "dad" he's doing a good job of it already,' and he nods in agreement.

'It really took me by surprise, I wasn't expecting it,' Jamie answers and then clears his throat, he needs to ask something important, there's no beating around the bush this time. 'I don't want to keep dragging up the past, but when are yer going to tell your parents?'

Jess looks at him and then says very firmly, 'Monday. I'll go and see them Monday after I've dropped Michael off at school, I'll tell them then.'

He nods, he knows it's the right thing to do, and he also has to break the news to his mum that she has a grandson, soon to be five years old.

Jess tells him she's now going to see if she can book his party for January, she just needs to put a deposit down today and then confirm the numbers the week before. As she gets up he pulls her towards him and smiles as he says, 'I love yer Jess, I hope you know that.'

She strokes his face with her hand, 'I know you do Jamie and I love you too, I'm glad you're back, I don't want to lose you again.'

He shakes his head and says, 'I'm back for good babe, you ain't gonna get rid of me now.'

She bends over and kisses him - for once she doesn't care who sees her.

Chapter 37

Adult Time

Once soft play was over it was time to go food shopping. Jamie lifted Michael into the trolley seat and strapped him in and then pushed the trolley around chatting to Michael, asking him what he likes to eat and, 'What's your favourite dinner?'

'Dinosaurs,' Michael shouts back excitedly. Jamie has no idea what kind of food that is and turns to Jess with a confused look on his face.

Jess tells him he'll see soon and then asks him what they should get for dinner tonight. Michael shouts again with excitement, 'Dinosaurs!' and Jamie laughs. He fancies either Indian or Chinese, so tells Jess he'll order them a take away once Michael's in bed.

Shopping done, including Michael's dinosaurs, Jamie is now wiser for knowing what 'Dinosaurs' are and they head home.

Pulling onto the driveway, Jamie tells Jess to take Michael in and he'll unpack the car. He leans over and gives her a kiss, then looks over to Michael and says, 'Want some Dinosaurs for dinner Michael?'

Laughing as he says it, Michael yells loudly, 'Yesss, Dinosaurs!' and Jess can't do anything but tut, roll her eyes and laugh at him as she tells Jamie, 'You're such a wind up.'

'Yep, yer better get used to it babe.'

Jess laughs at him as she gets out the car and takes Michael into the house. She puts the kettle on to make a drink while Jamie goes back and forth a couple of times with the shopping bags.

'Babe, I need to pop back to my room and get some stuff as I want to go running tomorrow.'

'That's fine, do you want a drink before you go?'

'No, I'll nip up now, get my running gear and uniform for Monday, I'll be about forty minutes.'

He wraps his arms around her and kisses her neck whispering that he's had a semi on all afternoon. He hears her giggle and tells her that once they've eaten, she's going to be his pudding.

Jess let's out a little moan at the thought of it, she feels instantly turned on and she parts her legs, she wants to feel his fingers deep inside her wet pussy now.

Jamie looks in the living room and he can see that Michael is on the sofa watching television, so he moves Jess around the doorway a bit and then unfastens her jeans, sliding his hand inside them. He kisses her hard as his fingers play with her clitoris and she pushes her jeans and thong down a bit more so he can move his hand around more freely.

Now he kisses her neck as he pushes two fingers in, her pussy is wet, he can feel her juices on his fingers, his cock is hard, it's throbbing, he wants to bend her over the kitchen sink and insert himself into her wet pussy but he can't, he has to be discreet.

He pushes his fingers in deep, Jess is trying desperately not to make any sound but is struggling, he likes this, the excitement, the anticipation of not knowing what will happen next - they're surrounded by shopping bags, the television is on and their son is in the next room.

He pulls her into him as his fingers go deeper holding the back of her head as he kisses her, his tongue looking for hers, he can feel she's going to cum any minute, he pushes his fingers deep as he kisses her harder and he feels her body giving way as she cums all over his fingers.

Jess holds onto him for a moment or two as he pulls her jeans back up and fastens them, she's smiling and he smiles back at her as he says, 'What time does he go to bed?' They both laugh and he lets her go, to continue putting the shopping away while he leaves to go and get some clean clothes, kissing Michael on his head as he walks past him on his way out.

For the first time since he can remember he feels content again. This is what he was missing. Jess, their home and the excitement she brings him - even a quick finger on a Saturday afternoon surrounded by food shopping, those brief moments of thrill and excitement.

Chapter 38

Coast Is Clear

Jess decides to give Jodie a quick call as it will take too long to text it all. She needs to tell her what's going on because the last thing she heard from Jess is "he's here" nearly twenty-four hours ago.

'Where the hell have you been? I've been worried sick,' Jodie scolds, genuinely.

'I know I'm so sorry, he's been with us the whole time. This is my first opportunity to call you.'

'I gathered, I drove past earlier, saw his car parked outside and I knew you was at soft play from twelve. Well, what's going on?'

'Christ, where do I start? He's gorgeous Jode, I can't believe how much he's changed.'

'But what about Michael and you?'

'He's going to stay the weekends and Tuesday and Wednesday nights to begin with, then by Christmas or New Year move in full time.'

'Oh, is that what you want as well mate?' Jodie is worried, she doesn't want to tell Jess to be careful not to jump in feet first, that she'll get hurt again, but she knows how much Jess loved him and still does - she let it slip one night after a few too many wines. She just wants her best mate to be happy and if it's Jamie that makes her happy then so be it.

'Yes, I really do. I just want my own little family unit Jode. It's not too much to ask for is it?'

'No mate, it isn't. So how's my little dude doing? Are they bonding?'

'Oh my God mate, it's like he's always been a part of his life, they're like two peas in a pod and he's so caring, but then again he always was.'

'Where's he gone now?'

'He's popped back to his room to get some running gear for tomorrow and his uniform for Monday.'

'Aww, have you thought about how you'll tell your parents?'

'Nope, no idea, but I'm going over on Monday after dropping Michael to school, I'm telling them everything and if they don't like it then that's their problem. I don't care anymore mate.'

'I don't blame you, just be careful babe, I love you and Michael, I don't want to see you hurt again.'

'I know, we won't, not this time, things are going to be different. I've got to go, I'll pop round Monday after picking Michael up from school.'

'Great, stay for dinner, I'll cook your favourite – Lasagna.'

'Deal,' Jess says and as soon as she has hung up she hears knocking at the front door and looks at the time. *Jesus* she thinks *we were on the phone for nearly an hour*.

Heading to the door, she picks up the spare key from the hall cabinet, 'He may as well have this back,' she says to herself out loud.

Chapter 39

Bergan

Jamie walks into his room and sees his Bergan sitting on the floor by his bed. He sits on his bed and pulls it towards him, opening the flap he fumbles around inside one of the pockets where his fingers finally touch the soft velvet box.

He lifts it out, the velvet is generally worn but fairly bold in places and it's still a lovely red colour. He's carried this box with him since he bought it on 8 May, 2020. Nobby was with him and he can only imagine what people thought seeing two squaddies in uniform looking at engagement rings - he smiles as he thinks back to that time of his life.

He opens the box, seeing the diamond as sparkly today as it was the day he bought it and still as beautiful, a classic half carat, princess cut, diamond solitaire on a Tiffany band. He can hear Nobby now telling him to "get rid of it J, it cost you over a grand, it's a lot of money mate, sell it, don't hold onto it, it'll just make you sad every time you look at it".

The truth is that it didn't make him sad, it was quite the opposite. It was his only hope, his 'ring of hope' in fact, and he held onto it because he knew there would come a day he'd present it to Jess. She will wear this ring, not as an engagement ring now, but she'll wear it on her ring finger next to a simple wedding band.

He closes the box and puts it back. He laughs to himself because that Bergan has been on so many exercises, a six month tour and three bases, actually four including this one, and the ring has been hidden inside the whole time.

He gathers his stuff - running gear and trainers, his boots and uniform, clean boxers and socks and clean shorts and T-shirt for tomorrow. Jess' house is so warm he won't need anything else on. He packs it all in his rucksack.

He takes his work watch off and puts that in the rucksack then picks up his Tag Heuer and puts it on, his twentieth birthday present from Jess - he loves this watch, it's a real head turner, whenever he wore it out with Tara she would always tell him how much she loved his watch and that buying himself a Tag Heuer was a good investment.

When he thinks about his relationship with Tara, he can see that he was never truly honest with her and that was wrong on his part. She was a rebound from Jess, though he wanted to love her and he really tried but the truth is he couldn't, she didn't excite him the way Jess does, like today for instance, he couldn't do that with Tara, she's frigid, he's always thought so but now he accepts it, they were never compatible sexually.

He can feel his libido increasing already, less than twenty-four hours back with Jess and he's had a hard on for most of it, he's excited again, his cock is hard as he smells his fingers with Jess' juices on them, he should have washed them but he likes the smell of her on him, he'll wash them once he's had a wank, he needs to sort this boner out before heading back.

He shuts his room door and walks down the corridor, he knows that by Christmas he'll be moving out and into Jess' house again, only this time it will be forever and he will be getting married next year, only he'll be marrying Jess, he's going to propose in six weeks' time on New Year's eve.

Chapter 40

Smiley Faces And Dinosaurs

Jess opens the door with a big smile on her face holding his key in between her thumb and forefinger, she waves it about slightly and says, 'You may as well have this back.'

Jamie walks in and gives her a long lingering kiss as he holds her hand with the key in it, his other hand caressing her boobs. He doesn't care that the front door is open and anyone could be walking by, he wants to strip her off here and now and fuck her up against the stairs.

Jess pulls him in and shuts the front door, not letting his kiss drop, her hand grabbing his peachy bum and pulling him towards her, she can feel her juices running already, she breaks off from his kiss and lets out a little groan and tells him, 'You've got me wet again,' and he laughs as he feels his crotch and tells her he's hard again and they both laugh. She has no idea he's just knocked one off less than ten minutes ago.

He takes his rucksack straight upstairs and Jess walks back into the living room, she tells Michael, 'Daddy's home,' and walks towards the kitchen to put the kettle on and start Michael's dinner as he's getting hungry.

Jamie comes downstairs to where Michael is sitting on the edge of the sofa, his little legs dangling over the edge and when Jamie walks in Michael jumps down and starts running around the living room with his arms outstretched making the noises of an aeroplane.

Jamie laughs at him as he walks into the kitchen, he's known his son for less than twenty-four hours and he can see already what his future will be. Jess has her back to him and he puts his arms around her waist, laughing as he says, 'We have future fighter jet pilot,' on our hands, and she nods in agreement as she nestles back into his cuddle.

Jamie asks when will she be making Michael's dinner and she tells him after she's made a cup of tea for them both - he is excited to see what these dinosaurs and smiley faces will be like, he's only seen the packets and is completely intrigued by them.

Jess lifts out the baking tray and places four smiley faces on it and two dinosaurs, Jamie is watching her and leans in to investigate them further, 'Shit babe, them smiley faces are happy little fuckers,' and he laughs out loud, it's no wonder Michael likes this kind of food, it's fun.

'Michael, up to the table darling, dinner is ready.'

She tells Jamie that they'll both sit with him while he eats his dinner and that it's important they have dinnertime together, even if they're not eating until later.

Jamie carries Michael's dinner in, smiley faces, dinosaurs and baked beans - this dinner is what dreams are made of for little boys - but he does hope that he has vegetables sometimes as well, they're important, he's not going to say anything today, he'll wait and see what they have tomorrow.

Chapter 41

Bath Time

Jamie sits on the sofa cuddling Michael, telling him about what he does as a soldier and how proud he is to serve in the British Army - that is evident in everything Jamie does, Jess can't deny that.

Jess goes upstairs to runs Michael's bath and asks Jamie if he wants to help bathe him. He looks at Michael and asks him does he want Mummy or Daddy to bathe him? Michael looks at Jess then Jamie and points from one to the other - he wants both of them to bathe him.

Jamie laughs and gets up from the sofa, bending over, picking Michael up and chucking him over his shoulder, holding his legs and pretending to smack his bum. Michael is chuckling away and Jess is thinking that this is what Michael missed - a bit of rough and tumble, he plays with Martin like this too, he's definitely a 'boy's boy'.

Jamie goes up in front of Jess and she watches his peachy bum as he walks up the stairs, she can't help thinking how much she wants to grab his bare bum with her hands tonight and as she thinks about his naked body against hers later, she wonders if he fancies skipping dinner.

Michael's bath is ready, so he gets undressed and climbs in, it's not very deep but it has lots of bubbles. Jamie kneels on the floor and starts to play with the bubbles, putting a pile on top of Michael's head and shaping them into a cone-like hat then he makes a beard around his face. Michael and Jamie are laughing heartily as Jess walks in from the bedroom with Michael's PJ's.

She laughs at how funny Michael looks and tells Jamie to smile as she takes a photo of them, the first of many she says, it's an awesome photo of the two of them with their cheesy grins, Michael in the bath with a bubble cone-hat and beard and Jamie kneeling on the floor. Jamie has the biggest smile, he looks so happy. Jess clicks on the photo and saves it as her screen saver saying, 'My two favourite boys.'

Jess shows Jamie and he asks her to send it him, it's only then that they realise neither of them have each other's number and Jess has just realised Jamie doesn't have a mobile phone with him.

Jess needs to know where his mobile is so she asks him and he tells her its turned off and in the glove compartment of his car - he's told everyone he's away training this weekend as he didn't want to be disturbed, he didn't know how this weekend was going to go.

Jess knows exactly what he means by that. He's not being honest towards Tara, he seems to have a track record of 'infidelity' and her heart sinks. Has he really changed or is this just a game? She walks away into her room and sits on her bed to think for a moment, perhaps Jodie was right, she should be careful. She feels the tears in the back of her eyes as Jamie walks in.

He kneels down in front of her and says, 'Hey, come here,' and wraps his arms around her neck and places his forehead against hers as he tells her, 'It's not what yer think. I'm being completely honest with yer, I needed no distractions this weekend, I didn't want to be sneaking off to take the odd call or sneakily answer text messages, it was easier to say I'm away,' and he kisses her.

'Baby, I've told yer I need to deal with all that next weekend, I fucked up five and a half years ago, I'm not about to fuck up again. I love yer Jess, I know it's going to take time for yer to trust me but I promise I'm never going to hurt yer again.

He pulls her towards him, her legs either side of his body as he kisses her, lovingly and passionately, she responds in the same way, looking for his tongue, her arms wrapped tight around his neck as she tells him, 'I do believe you, I'm just frightened.'

He nods, he knows how that feels, 'I'm sorry baby, for what I did I'm truly sorry.'

Jess looks at him and says, 'So, Corporal O'Halloran, you gonna give me your number or what?' and totally changes the subject and lightens the mood. She winks at him and they both laugh. She doesn't want to ruin what has so far been a perfect day.

Chapter 42

Transparency

Jamie gives Michael a kiss goodnight and tells him to be a good boy for Mummy when he goes to bed, that he's just going out to get their dinner, and he'll be back when Michael is asleep. He decided it was easier to go and collect the Indian food rather than asking Jess to use her phone, it had caused an upset once already, he didn't want to cause another.

He gives Jess a hug and a kiss telling her won't be long, he whispers in her ear, 'Feel free to get changed into your dressing gown, but leave your thong on, I'll peel it off with my teeth later.'

Jess smiles and replies, 'I will.' She's already decided to put Michael to bed five minutes early - he won't know - then she'll have time for a quick shower before he gets back. She's excited and feels like a teenager all over again. She's a woman in love that's for sure, even if he's only been back for twenty-four hours, all the feelings she had for him more than five years ago have come flooding back.

Jamie thinks about what he's got to face next weekend. He's not looking forward to it but it has to be done, he knows he'll need to sort through his photos as well - he doesn't want any of Tara on his phone, he knows that may seem mean, especially as he kept so many of Jess, but he's not hiding anything from Jess. He wants complete 'transparency'- something he heard in the past but never really understood its meaning like he does now.

She hears the key in the front door. Just as he asked, she's in her dressing gown in a clean pair of sheer lace thongs. Her nipples are erect already and he hasn't even walked through the door. She stays on the sofa when he walks in, with her legs on show as she asks him, 'Is this what you wanted?'

Jamie smiles as he walks over to her and opens her dressing gown, bends down and kisses her as his fingers play with her nipples. His cock is throbbing as he walks over to the table and puts the food down and walks back to Jess while unfastening his jeans - they can eat later.

He takes off his T-shirt and Jess' eyes light up at the sight of his body, his muscles and tattoos, suddenly so attractive like tattoos had never been before.

He kicks his trainers off as he bends down to kiss her and grabs her legs and pulls her to the edge of the sofa. Opening her legs he can see her thong disappearing inside her smooth lips, 'Mmm,' he moans as he pulls on it and Jess lets out a moan too as it rubs her clitoris.

He bends down and licks her smooth lips, pulling on her thong. He can taste her juices seeping through it and he looks up at her and asks her, 'Baby, tell me what yer want.'

She tells him, 'Your fingers,' and he smiles and asks how many. She tells him, 'As many as you want.'

'Hmmm,' he says provocatively and bending back down he carries on licking her lips, his tongue breaking through to her clit. He can feel her thong with his tongue and he sucks on her thong together with her clitoris, she's moaning with the pleasure, she can feel she's going to cum quick, she's so turned on.

He slides two fingers in her warm wet pussy as she moans some more. He wants to hear her moan louder, he loves it when she's loud, it excites him, the louder she is the more excited he is. Sliding another finger in he can feel how tight she is, he feels her thong rub on his fingers. He likes how it feels when it is rubbing against his hard cock.

She plays with her nipples, they're erect as she is so turned on, his tongue is sucking on her clit, he's pulling her thong up, it's tight, it could almost be painful but its erotic, she can feel his fingers deep inside her pussy, her juices running all over them, she's not sure how many, three maybe four, must be four it's so tight, they're deep, she's moaning louder, she's going to cum any minute, she tells him.

'Cum baby, cum all over my fingers, let me hear yer cumming, louder, I want to hear yer.'

She can't speak, she just nods as she's cumming, now making deep throated moans, it's so erotic, the pressure from her thong, his fingers deep inside, it feels euphoric.

He slowly takes his fingers out and standing up he takes his boxers and jeans off, his cock is hard, he feels like he's going to cum soon. He tells her this is going to be fast, he's not giving her any chance to get her breath, he's on his knees, he pulls her towards him and places his cock inside her pussy, its warm and very wet, he can hear her juices squelching as he pushes in.

'Mmmm,' he says, 'Baby, look at me,' and as Jess opens her eyes, he smiles at her, 'I'm gonna cum soon,' he laughs, 'Yer got me too excited,' and they both laugh as she tells him to stop talking and get fucking.

He holds her outer thighs pulling her closer to the edge, his hard cock in deep, he thrusts it in deeper, she moans loudly, he thrusts fast and hard, she's trying her best not to scream, but she can't help herself, his cock thrusting hard and fast, he's so deep, she's cumming again.

He's grunting with every thrust, it's deep, her loud moans are exciting him more, his thrusts are faster, deeper and deeper, he feels her cumming all over his hard cock, he doesn't tell her he's going to cum as he figures she probably wouldn't hear him, and then he squeezes her outer thighs as he releases his spunk deep inside her pussy, his juices mixing with hers, then he lets out a final grunt as he shudders - he's climaxed.

Chapter 43

Sunday Mornings

Jamie is out for a run at 0545hrs after waking at 0520hrs - he loves to go for his early morning runs, it gives him time out, space to think. He knows it's a cliché but thinks *there's no rules, just me and the road.*

When he gets back at 0715hrs, Michael is awake and in bed with Jess so he walks into the bedroom to see Jess cuddling into him, dozing in and out of sleep as Michael is chatting away. His heart melts seeing them cuddling and listening to Michael chatting about his school friends. Jamie asks what he was chatting about and Michael tells him he's going to tell his school friends that his daddy is back from work.

Jess opens her eyes and looks at Jamie, 'I guess there's going to be lots of gossip and questions over the next few weeks,' she laughs, 'I must text Hazel and Fred later and let them know, I don't want her finding out from someone else.'

Jamie strips off and goes for a shower, while Jess gets up and tells Michael to go and get his dressing gown and slippers on and that they'll go down for breakfast. As he's running into his bedroom he shouts to Jess, 'Dad's having Ready Brek with me a'well mum,' so excited he can hardly get his words out. Jess wishes she had his energy in the morning.

Michael hasn't actually called Jamie dad yet, but he is referring to him as his dad, she loves that he's taken to him so quickly and that they're bonding so well. It literally feels like he's been with them forever, he may have been gone physically but he was always here emotionally.

Jess pops her head in the bathroom to ask Jamie if he wants a cup of tea with his Ready Brek. She laughs as he says to her, 'Babe, a big bowl, lots of warm milk and sugar,' she nods and laughs as she goes down stairs thinking to herself *Oh my God, he actually likes Ready Brek...*

Michael is sitting at the table waiting for his breakfast, he has the television remote and is flicking through the kids programmes. He finds the Power Rangers and tells Jess that "his dad is stronger than them, he could beat them as he's the best soldier". Jess agrees with him of course and tells him he will also be the best soldier in the world because he eats his Ready Brek like Daddy does.

Jamie walks in to the living room and stands in front of the television. He used to love the Power Rangers and tells Michael that he's the Green Ranger in real life. Michael starts to laugh at him and tells him he's not, and Jamie says, 'I am, honest.'

Michael thinks about for a minute then says, 'You're telling fibs Dad, you're a soldier.'

Jamie walks towards the table and tells him, 'You're too smart for me Son,' and he bends down and kisses the top of his head with tears in his eyes that Michael just called him 'Dad' for the first time.

Chapter 44

That Dreaded Phone Call

Jamie sits on the sofa with Michael watching more Power Rangers and when she walks past him he tells Jess he could get used to this. She rolls her eyes and tells him not to get too comfy as he's got the dinner to prep while she irons Michael's uniform and her work clothes.

Her mobile rings, it's her mum - her heart sinks. Does she blank it and then text saying she's out but that she's coming to see them tomorrow? What if they're on their way here? 'Shit!' she says.

Jamie looks startled, he wonders who could be calling Jess and her not picking up. Has she been completely honest with him? What if she does have someone on the side? His heart races as he watches her expression, it's definitely a look of concern. But then he hears her and feels instant relief, he can't believe he thought that way. *I can really be a twat sometimes* he admonishes himself.

'Hi Mum,' she walks into the kitchen with her phone at her ear and a still concerned look on her face.

Jamie watches her, trying to make out what they're saying but with the television on and Michael's excitable chit chat continuing he is struggling to hear, not that he would normally eavesdrop but this is different, he wants to hear Jess saying that she's going to see them tomorrow.

Jess walks back into the living room and tells Michael that Nanny and Grandad are on the phone. As she hands him the phone to say "hello'" her heart is racing at a thousand beats a minute, her palms are sweaty and in her head she's praying *please don't say anything Michael, please don't say anything.*

She stands by the side of him listening to her mum asking him what he's doing. He tells her he's watching Power Rangers then he says, 'Nanna, Daddy's come back from work, wanna talk to him?' He then looks at Jamie and says, 'Dad wanna talk to my nanna?' and Jamie shakes his head as a massive smirk crosses his face.

Jess grapples for the phone, almost shouting, 'Michael, Michael give me the phone now!' she can hear her mum telling Michael to pass the phone back to Mummy, so he hands her the phone and she walks off into the kitchen.

Jamie picks him up onto his lap and cuddles him saying, 'Thanks Son,' he can't help laughing as he thinks *yer got no choice now babe*.

Chapter 45

Gossip

Jess and Jamie drop Michael off to school, where she introduces Jamie to Michael's teachers as there are going to be times that he will be collecting him. The mums in the playground, some of whom have only known Jess for a short time (either since Michael was born, started school or recently posted here with their husbands) have never seen her with a man. Only the women who were local to the village when Jamie was here the first time around know him.

It comes as no surprise to some of them as they say to Jess 'I wondered when it was going to come out that he's Michael's dad.' It also doesn't escape Jess or Jamie that these are the women who also knew Angela and the reason they split up.

'The gossip mongers are going to be in overdrive,' she says to Jamie, concern all over her face.

'Yeah, yer get them everywhere babe, ignore them.'

If there's one thing Jamie hates, it is gossip. Especially when it's relating to him. He heard too much when he left here in June 2020, most of which was true, for example that Jess kicked him to the curb because he fucked Angela. It didn't help the situation that she bragged about it, literally telling everyone she came into contact with.

He tries to keep his life very private now, he deactivated his Facebook account when he left, he didn't want to know what was going on back here in the village or want anyone to know what he was up to. More than anything he didn't want to change his relationship status as that would have meant explaining to people what he'd done and that would have been too much, he thinks that would have pushed him over the edge.

He knows that there's going to be a lot of gossip over the coming months, within his own family and in his Regiment once he's back there and this place, but he doesn't care, he's back where he belongs with Jess and Michael.

He's going to put a message on the Whatsapp group later, in fact he'll just put a photo up of Jess and Michael, telling the lads that they are back together and introduce his son to them, they'll all get to meet him next year when he's back with his Regiment.

He drops Jess back home after the school run, gives her a kiss and tells her how much he loves her and he'll text her later but to call him if there are any problems at her parents - he doesn't want her driving home upset, that's dangerous, he can see she's worrying about it.

As he pulls up outside work he can see some of the lads waiting, he's actually late so when getting out of the car he apologises. Ben comes walking around the corner, winks at Jamie and says, 'Saw your car in the village, I didn't know you knew Jess.'

Jamie tells him that there's a lot he doesn't know, and that he'll fill him in later. He knows he needs to tell Ben as his wife Becky will hear it from the gossip mongers. He knows she and Jess are newly acquainted friends and he doesn't want Jess to be the bad guy in this, he has to tell his side of the story, the truth of his infidelity.

Chapter 46

Time To Face The Music

Jess is feeling very nervous, she didn't sleep very well last night, she was awake when Jamie woke at five-thirty to go for his run - much to his surprise. No, she's definitely not looking forward to seeing her parents today.

She sent Hazel a text yesterday afternoon and told her Jamie was back and that they've spent the weekend together. Both Hazel and Fred are pleased for them, Fred always said it wasn't right that Jamie didn't know and Michael deserved to know who his father was - then if Jamie decided to walk away then that would have been his choice.

Hazel has invited them all to dinner on Wednesday, Jess and Michael often go Wednesday as Hazel cooks a mid-week roast. Fred likes to think it's for his benefit as it's his favourite food, regardless of which meat, Fred loves his roast dinner, but who is he kidding? It's for Jess and Michael, out of Hazel's motherly love toward them both.

She arrives at her parents' house just after 9.30am and although she heard her phone receiving text messages whilst she was driving, she leaves it in her bag when she's in the car. It's hooked up to the Bluetooth anyway for calls, and messages she'll deal with after her parents.

As Jess pulls up to the house her mother is standing at the front door with her arms folded and she's scowling before Jess has even got out of her car. This is not how Jess wanted to tell them, but like Jamie said yesterday "you have no choice now" and she knows in her heart she should have told them years ago, stood up for herself, but hindsight is a wonderful thing.

Her dad walks out to her and gives her a hug, whispering in her ear, 'Don't mind your mother, she's just going to vent, I'll have your back,' he winks, he knows who Michael's father is as he met Jamie years ago, only once and it was brief but he saw the glint in his daughter's eyes when Jamie kissed her on the cheek. He's also noticed that his beloved grandson is the spitting image of Jamie.

They walk together towards Barbara, Tony has his arm around his daughter's shoulder and he gives Barbara a stern look, as if to say 'hold your tongue'. Once inside the house, Tony takes her into the living room, he thinks this will be the best place, all sitting comfortably.

'Jessica,' her mother says frostily, 'You'd better explain what the hell is going on.'

'I will. I'm going to,' Jess replies, trying hard to hold it together and stay strong.

She starts by telling them that Michael was not conceived as a result of a fling with someone from work, he was in fact planned, that she and Jamie had been trying for a baby, but something happened and they split up, she never told him about Michael because he was posted somewhere else in the UK and that she never thought he'd come back but he did at the end of October.

'So he's a soldier?' Barbara asks with disdain in her voice.

Tony nods in unison with Jess and both Jess and Barbara turn to look at him. Jess is shocked because she realises her dad knows who Jamie is and that he met him when he took her food shopping that time, and Barbara looks surprised as she's wondering how her husband of forty-three years knows about him, yet never told her.

'Tony, is there something you're not telling me here? How do you know who he is and why didn't you tell me?'

Tony stands up slowly and turns to face them. Both women know that when he does this he is telling Barbara that he is the alpha male, that he is serious and she will listen to him. It's not very often that Tony stands up to Barbara as he likes to live by the rule that *a happy wife is a happy life.*

'I met him Barb, I took Jess food shopping that night I dropped all those cooked dinners off. He too was shopping, he gave Jess a kiss on the cheek and he had her lunch bag in his trolley, if you ask me he was a thoroughly decent young lad.'

He looks at his daughter and smiles - she's sitting there open mouthed, she can't believe it, he saw everything, yet he acted like he didn't notice, her eyes start to well up, if only she'd told her dad before, then this past five and a half years could have been so different for the three of them.

Barbara is stunned, she asks Tony why he never said anything and why has he kept it a secret all these years.

'Because love, it's none of our business what Jess does in her private life, we are her parents, it's our duty to support her not to judge.'

For once Barbara is quiet, she's shocked, she looks at Jess and asks her if this was the man she tried to tell her about that Christmas Eve and Jess nods. Barbara is speechless, she feels guilty - because of her actions her grandson has lost out on seeing his father for the last five years.

'Jessica I'm sorry, I only wanted the best for you, I thought that a soldier would just hurt you, that he's not stable, his job is dangerous.'

'Jess is a grown woman and you have no right to try and tell her what to do, look at the consequences now, sometimes Barbara I wish you would just keep your mouth shut.'

Tony is very angry with his wife, she knows it and so does Jess as he only calls her Barbara when he's angry.

'So when are we going to meet him, Michael's daddy, what's his name again?'

'Jamie, his name is Jamie.'

Both her parents look at each other, Michael's middle name is James, they never understood where that came from that there's no one in the family with that name, but now they know.

Barbara tells Jess to bring him over in a couple of weeks, they are going away with friends on Friday for a week, so the following weekend, the Saturday will be a good time to meet him, she asks Jess if they are back together as a couple, Jess nods, for the first time today Barbara smiles in the comfort that her beloved grandson wasn't the result of a fling he was in fact conceived through love. Love that his mummy and daddy apparently still have for each other.

Chapter 47

Home Time

Jess kisses and hugs her parents before she leaves. She has to head back now as Michael finishes school in an hour, she also wants to call Jamie and tell him how it went but she'll wait until she's out of sight.

'Hi, can you talk?'

'Hey, I can, let me just shut my door.'

She hears him get up and go to close his door, someone comes to talk to him and he tells them he has an important call to take, that he'll come and find them in ten minutes.

'Hi, sorry about that, are you ok?'

'Yes, yes I'm good.'

'Well, how did it go?'

'Really well, my dad knew who you were, he remembers you from when we bumped into you food shopping, he even saw my lunch box in your trolley. I can't believe he never ever said anything, to me or my mum.'

Jamie listens as Jess tells him how the conversation went, it seems he's misjudged her dad all these years, he thinks he's a pretty decent guy now, but his opinion on her mum has never changed and he doesn't think it will in the future either.

'So I'm going to meet them a week Saturday then? That'll be fun,' he says with a laugh. 'Babe, I gotta go, I'll call you later when you're home, so I can say goodnight to Michael.'

'Ok, we'll be home for 6, Love you.'

He tells her that he loves her too and to drive carefully. When he calls her later he's going to ask her where she was after school, she never mentioned that they were going out this evening but he shrugs it off as he knows he can trust her. He's only feeling like this because of his own insecurities. He needs to work on this, he'll put himself through a good hard training session in the gym later.

Jess parks by the school gates, she has at least twenty minutes until the bell goes so she decides to check her messages from this morning. Getting out of the car she sees a couple of the mums who are always early walking up the road. She's never really mixed with them but she can imagine their conversation, especially judging by the look on their faces now.

SMS from Becky: [I bet your ears are burning! You're the topic of conversation this morning. Well at least you chose a fitty, now I see it, that's why Michael is so handsome. Call me when you get the chance, don't worry I got your back xxx]

Jess replies: [Thanks mate, I'm glad someone has. I'll tell you all when I see you xxx]

Becky: [No need, Jamie told Ben this morning, about his cheating, Ben told me when he came home for lunch, as long as you and Michael are happy? Don't worry about the gossipers. Xx]

Jess: [Ok, we'll go for lunch on Friday if you're free? Got to go, bell is going xx]

Becky: [Defo, look forward to it xx]

Jess smiles, at least someone has her back around here - Becky's a good friend. She's dreading that walk into the playground, she is just going to grab Michael and go and head for Jodie's, she's been looking forward to seeing her all day and she can't wait to tell her how it went with her parents.

Chapter 48

The Longest Week

Jamie's packed his dirty clothes for his mum to wash and he's finishing early today, he has to get this over with. He's not been looking forward to this weekend, in fact he's blanked Tara most of the week, just the odd text message here and there.

He knows Jess is going out for lunch today with Becky, he and Jess have had a lovely week, Hazel cooked them an amazing roast dinner on Wednesday, in fact he even said to Hazel ''same time next week then H?''. It was lovely to see her and see how she is with Michael, both her and Fred are like his extra nan and grandad, plus they've looked after Jess, which he is grateful for.

Leaving Jess this morning was heart wrenching, he wasn't meant to stay over last night but he didn't want to go home to his mum's today having not seen Jess and Michael since Thursday morning. He feels guilty leaving her, so he's decided he's coming back tomorrow.

Jamie: [I'm just about to get on the road, enjoy your lunch date with Becky xx I love you baby xx]

Jess: [I love you too, missing you already xx]

Jamie: [♥]

Right then, let's get this over with. He drives out of the main gates, with a long two hour journey ahead of him. He's looking forward to seeing his mum and he's going to tell her about Michael before he goes to Tara's - he's no idea what will happen after that.

He's really dreading the task ahead, but he knows it has to be done. He's not a coward, he couldn't break up with her over text messages as he needs to tell her face to face, she deserves that much at least, although thinking about how she'll react, text messaging probably seems a better option at the moment.

His mum is looking out of the kitchen window, thinking how much she's missed having him home the last couple of weekends, but more than anything she's worried about him. She's worried about what's been happening as she knows in her heart of hearts that he's been seeing Jess, she can hear it in his voice - he sounds happy again - but she can't help feeling sorry for Tara, this will break her heart and she wouldn't wish that on anyone.

Anne stands at the door as Jamie gets his kit bag out and walks toward her with a beaming smile. He throws his arms around her as he says, 'Hi Mum, I've missed yer,' and she tells him she's missed him too.

He empties his bag onto the kitchen floor while Anne makes him a cuppa, she's curious to ask but won't as she wants Jamie to tell her himself and she knows he will, once they sit down with their tea - they've shared many a conversation around this table over a cup of tea, and many a tear too.

'Where do you want me to start?' he asks directly, there's no point in dilly dallying around.

'At the beginning Jamie, I know you've seen her, I can tell by the smile on your face,' Anne says truthfully, Jess is the one woman that lights up his face, she saw it six years ago and sees it today.

'I have a son, called Michael. He's turning five in January.'

Anne can't hide the shock, in fact she's upset that she's missed out on her grandson's life for five years. She asks him why Jess never told him, and what was she thinking, it's not fair on them or her grandson.

Jamie tells her how Jess went looking for him, that they'd moved two weeks earlier and about the letter she dropped off at the gate house that he never received. This still makes him angry as personal letters are to be given to the personnel, it's not up to the gate house staff to play judge and jury.

Anne is truly taken aback and asks if he has any photos, so he shows her the ones Jess has sent him over the past week. She looks at the one of the three of them together, taken on Wednesday night by Fred and her eyes fill with tears, mostly of joy but of sadness as well.

'You look so happy Jamie, he's your double. When am I going to meet him?'

All said and done Anne likes Jess and she knows she's the one for Jamie, so she tells him not to mess up this time, that he's getting a second chance in life and he shakes his head as he tells her he has absolutely no intention of it.

'What time are you heading over to Tara's?'

He puts his head in his hands as he tells her 1730hrs and that he's not looking forward to it, he never wanted to hurt her and he should have done it long ago. He tells her he's worried about Rosie, after all she's married to Jed, Tara's big brother and asks her what effect that it could have on them, his nephew and the one on the way.

Anne tells him, 'Stop worrying about other people, your sister is capable of dealing with Jed, she tells him that Rosie knows, and that Jean has been spouting off to Jed the past three weeks about what's gone on and going on, because of the way you've been with Tara.'

'Rosie has told Jed "what goes on behind closed doors is between two people, how would yer feel if it were us two?' She's told him they have to stay out if it, stay neutral or it will just cause problems in their marriage. Apparently Jed agreed, so that's what they're doing, staying out of yours and Tara's business.'

'I'm not looking forward to this Mum, I know what Tara's like, she's going to flip.'

'I know Son, but the sooner yer get it over with the easier it will be. Tomorrow's a new day, the start of your future with Jess and Michael.'

Anne is secretly happy, but doesn't want to let on yet as the timing is all wrong, besides she has some good news of her own but that can definitely wait until tomorrow, today is about Jamie.

Chapter 49

Lunch Date

Jess goes and collects Becky and Isabella, they're going out for lunch, it's going to be an extended one she's sure, as Jess needs to fill Becky in on Jamie and how he's Michael's daddy.

As they pull up to the restaurant, Becky is feeling excited. She's heard what happened from Ben but she still needs to speak to Jess, she wants to see how she feels - is she still in love with him like Jamie is with her?

The waiter shows them to their table and takes their drinks order, saying he'll come back for the food order shortly.

'Well, come on Mrs, spill the beans,' Becky giggles with excitement.

Jess has Isabella on her lap - she likes that little girls definitely make her broody - she smiles and tells her the story, about how they met, him going away training for a few weeks, getting together at Halloween and that it was instant, they fell in love over the course of a few hours.

Becky is nodding, she tells Jess that's exactly what happened with her and Ben, it must be something to do with being a military man, they know when they meet someone they can trust.

Jess has heard this before from Hazel, when she and Jamie first got together all those years ago, so she continues, telling her about her parents and how difficult her mum is, that's she very judgmental, therefore she couldn't tell them at first, after all he was only nineteen and Jess was thirty-six.

Becky shakes her head, 'Mate, age is just a number, look at you, you've got the prettiest face and a body all women would die for, there's no way you look forty-two and from what I hear from Jodie, you two were good together.'

Jess nods, 'We were, there's no lying about that,' then she tells her about the wedding they went to after Christmas, and meeting his family and spending New Year with them.

Becky is listening, chipping in with the odd, "aww" and tells her it's like a real life love story.

Jess then tells her about her being diagnosed as a teenager with amenorrhea, that if she wanted to have kids she was told she'd need IVF, and about moving here and registering with the doctor, that he didn't think she would, so she started on the contraceptive pill for three months and when that trial finished in January, she and Jamie decided they'd try for a baby.

Becky's smiling, she's feels her heart bursting with love as she says, 'So Michael wasn't from a fling, like you said?'

Jess looks into her glass and shakes her head, 'No Bex, he wasn't, he was planned, only Jamie did something stupid because he was immature and I was pathetic 'cause I didn't have the guts to stand up to my mum, and it destroyed us, he left, posted out, that was that.'

'And now he's back,' Becky says with a huge smile on her face.

Jess is brimming over with happiness, 'I know, but like I said to Jodie on Monday, I'm scared which is only natural, but I love him Bex, with all my heart, always have and always will.'

'He loves you Jess, he told Ben, that's the reason he's back - he needed you back in his life.'

Jess is nodding, she's thinking of the conversation she had with Jodie about requesting the secondment, and the reason he said he was coming back which was originally for closure.

'So when's he meeting your parents?'

Jess laughs and tells her about the telephone conversation with Michael on Sunday, that he asked his nanny did she want to talk to his daddy, 'Honestly, Bex, I shit myself, I was yelling at Michael to pass me the phone, Jamie's sat there laughing, and that's why I had to go over on Monday.'

Becky chokes on her drink, she can just imagine that little cutie pie doing that, she hasn't met Jamie but can imagine what he looks like, especially if Michael is his double, she's really happy for her friend and she thinks to herself *if someone deserves happiness, it's Jess.*

Chapter 50

The Break Up

Jamie heads to Tara's for 1730hrs and when all is said and done he's sad, sad for Tara and sad that it's gone on this long, he knows he's not loved her for a long time, he was just going through the motions.

He parks a little down the road and walks back up to the house, for the first time since he can remember Tara has not come out to meet him. He didn't know how he'd react if she did, so that's one less thing for him to worry about.

He knocks on the door and Jean answers, she looks at him with utter disgust as she tells him that Tara is upstairs and moves to one side to let him in. As he walks up the stairs he hears her say, 'I hope you're happy with yourself Jamie you seem to have a history of cheating, you know a leopard never changes its spots, remember that.'

He stops for a brief second, Jed has told her why he and Jess broke up the first time, he shakes his head, and carries on up the rest of the stairs.

He reaches Tara's bedroom door, his heart is pounding, he doesn't know what to expect from her, but one things for sure he doesn't like to see her upset and he knows this is going to be harder than he realised.

He knocks quietly as he says, 'It's me Tar,' and walks in and sees her lying on the bed. Her eyes are red and puffy and her face is swollen from crying, he wants to wrap his arms around her and tell her he's so sorry, that he never wanted to hurt her and that he knows what she's going through - but he can't, not this time.

He sits on the edge of the bed facing her, he can see the tears rolling down her face, she hasn't spoken a word and he looks past her and sees her engagement ring on the bedside cabinet.

'Tara, yer have to believe me when I say this, but I never wanted to hurt yer.'

She ignores him, as she wipes her eyes.

'Tar, I know yer drove down to the village looking for her, why? Not that it matters now.'

'I wanted to warn her to stay away, but even if I had, what difference does it make?'

'I'm sorry, I really am.'

'Yer know she has a son?' Tara says, and he nods, trying to decide whether to tell her it's his little boy or whether he should leave it.

'You're prepared to take someone else's kid on? Yet when I said about having babies you told me no...'

He cuts in, he has no choice now but to tell her. 'He's mine Tara, she was pregnant when we split up but I didn't know.'

'What the fuck are yer doing here Jamie? Have yer come to gloat' she says, then raising her voice to screaming pitch, 'Are yer fucking happy now? Are yer?'

He can see her temper starting to flare as she shouts at him, he's not going to tell her to be quiet, not this time. He needs to take whatever she has to say, this will be the last time she ever screams and shouts at him, he knows that.

'Tara, yer know I'm not happy about hurting yer, for what it's worth, I did love yer. I know yer probably don't believe me right now but I did.'

'Whatever J, just go. Go back to yer fucking family and I hope yer live a happy fucking life, 'cause the two of yers have ruined mine,' she screams.

Jamie gets up and walks out and as he shuts the door he hears her scream as she throws her ring at the door. He walks down the stairs to see Jean stood at the bottom holding the door open. He doesn't say anything, he just puts his head down and walks out as she slams the door after him.

As he drives away he looks back in his mirror, he knows he'll never have a reason to come here again, he puts his head back on the head rest, takes a deep breath and lets out a big deep sigh, for the first time in a long time he feels a sense of relief.

Chapter 51

A Mother's Love

It's just gone 0700hrs, he didn't bother going for a run this morning, he'll go for one tomorrow when he's back home with Jess.

Walking into the kitchen he pops the kettle on, his mum is still asleep, he'll make her one when she wakes up. He hasn't told her he's going back today, but his clothes are washed and dried so he has a feeling she knew he wasn't staying the weekend.

He sends Jess a text, knowing that Michael will have her up already as it's the weekend: [Good morning my Sleeping Beauty xx]

Jess: [Morning my gorgeous man xx (said in a very groggy voice lol)]

Jamie: [Babe, I need to tell you how much I love you and I'm never ever going to leave you again (other than for work) you simply are my past, present and future, you and Michael, I'll be home later, I miss you xx]

Jess: [Are you ok? Xx]

Jamie: [Never felt better xx]

Jess: [Ok xx this little man wants his ready break, text me when you're heading home, we miss you xx]

He smiles as he thinks how much he's missing his Ready Brek as well. His thoughts are interrupted by his mum saying, 'You're up early Son,' as she comes down to the kitchen.

'I didn't hear yer come down Mum, why didn't you shout? I'd have brought yer a cuppa up.'

'Oh I wanted to get up, I take it you're going back today,' and she lovingly strokes his arm as he nods his head.

'Jamie, your life is over here, you have to make a new life for you, Jess and Michael, I'll always be around and so will your siblings, this is where you was born, where you grew up but your life is somewhere else, don't feel guilty.

'I do mum, I hate to think of yer on yer own in this house.'

'Jamie, Pete has asked me to move in with him and I've accepted.'

'Really? Wow, I mean, Mum that's great, I'm seriously happy for yer, will we meet him now?'

They both laugh and she tells him the others have finally met him, 'It's just you and Sean who haven't.'

'When yer thinking mum?'

She shrugs, 'I was thinking January, start of the New Year.'

'I'm gonna sell this place then Mum, it's the right time.'

They both nod in agreement and he tells her he'll bring Jess and Michael up in a fortnight, and that they'll be up after Christmas to celebrate New Year, he'll empty the house of his stuff ready for it to go on the market and that he'll text Joe in the week to tell him of his plans. They'll split the profit fifty-fifty as that was the agreement when he bought it - Joe put down ten percent deposit and Jamie paid the mortgage.

He gives his mum a hug and kisses her on the cheek before he heads south, he can't help feeling how different his life is now, within twenty-four hours of leaving the village, he feels content. He knows where he belongs and it's not here – it's with Jess and Michael.

Chapter 52

Time For Change

Jess is getting ready to take Michael to soft play and they're going earlier than usual as she wants to be back for when Jamie gets home - he said he'll be home by lunch time.

She doesn't need to ask him if he finished with Tara as she knows by the text message. As much as she hates the thought of him being with someone else in the past, she knows Tara was in love with him and she does feel sorry for her. A broken heart is not something Jess would wish on her worst enemy.

'Michael, come on it's nine-thirty, we have to go now.'

Michael comes running in the living room asking for his dad and Jess tells him he'll be back after soft play, 'So hurry up let's get your trainers on.' He surprises her by telling her he doesn't want to go.

'But Michael, you love soft play.'

He shakes his head, she knows what this is, he wants his dad to go, so she tells him that they'll go later when daddy is home. Michael shouts, 'Yesss!' and runs around the room like an aeroplane. She can't help laughing at him as she thinks to herself *I didn't want to go on my own either*.

They snuggle on the sofa watching TV and she texts Jamie to tell him they're not going until he gets back, that Michael wants to wait.

Jamie texts back: [I'm just leaving now, will be back by noon, we'll all go then xxx]

'Michael? Daddy says he's on his way back, we'll all go then.'

She kisses him on the forehead and tells him she loves him very much, and then she finds herself thinking about Isabella and how holding her makes her feel so broody. She casually asks Michael if he would like a little sister one day and he tells her, 'Yuk, girls are mean.'

She laughs at him and says, 'Not all girls,' thinking to herself perhaps this is a conversation she should be having with Jamie instead.

Jess decides to text him there and then: [I know its early days, like really early, but how do you feel about trying for another baby? Xx]

She gets up off the sofa leaving Michael to watch TV as she goes up stairs and reaches for her box that she's not opened in five and a half years. Picking the ovulating test kit out, she has a look to see if there's an expiry date on them. It reads; Expires: June 2025. *Damn, they've expired.*

She puts them back in there and puts it away deciding that she'll order some online later once she's spoken to Jamie, after all it does need to be a joint decision. She walks back in the living room and sees Michael on her phone and asks him, 'Who are you talking to?'

'Daddy,' Michael says with a smile.

'Oh, can I speak to him?' asks Jess and Michael hands her the phone.

'Yes, definitely, yer know I like the practice anyway,' Jamie laughs on the other end of the phone.

'Yeah, that's true, that's the fun part for me as well. I'll see when you get here, drive carefully, I love you.'

She hangs up the phone and sits back down with Michael, she thinks to herself *this time next year Michael you will have a baby brother or sister, only this time Daddy will know and he'll be right beside me during labour, this time I won't need to lie or make up a cover story. We'll do it right this time.*

Chapter 53

Time To Think

Jamie gets up early and goes for his run, he's not going too far today, he wants to be back for 0730hrs - that gives him ninety minutes. He left both Jess and Michael sleeping peacefully, he so wishes he could sleep like Jess sometimes but then he thinks about when he's on exercise or away on tour, he'd never cope with the lack of sleep. No, four to five hours a night is enough for him, he'll have plenty of time to catch up later in life.

He's got his pods in his pocket instead of his ears as he's thinking about meeting her parents today. He's not going to lie, he is nervous. He knows her dad will be fine but her mum he's not so sure about. From what Martin told Jamie the other day "she's too snobby for her own good" but he liked her dad so will concentrate on bonding with him.

Well, whatever her mum thinks of Jamie he couldn't give a rats arse, he's past caring, besides he has other things to worry about. He's meeting his mum's new fella next week, the one she's moving in with but from what Joe said during the week, "he's a good man and he'll look after Mum".

They discussed selling the house and they've agreed that it will be for the best. Joe has told Jamie he only wants the deposit back, after all Jamie's paid the mortgage for the past five years and he feels that it's only fair. Jamie isn't one to argue, so he's going to give him back the ten grand deposit, and he'll bung in a bit extra for a drink.

He's arranged for a couple of estate agents to go round this week to give a valuation, he knows they've increased in value so anything over £110,000 he'll be happy for.

He's really looking forward to them all meeting Michael, they're going to love him, but he feels sad that Jed has decided not to attend any family functions on Rosie's side - that's just going to cause trouble in the future, he can see it. So much for Jed staying neutral, that'll be due to his mother and her interference. He shakes his head when he thinks of Jean, he never really liked her, he liked Brian their dad but Jean is snobby, 'Hmm' he says to himself out loud, 'just like Jess' mum.'

He puts his pods in his ears, he's thought enough for one morning's run, the rest can wait for another time and he turns his music on for the last half hour.

Chapter 54

Meeting The Parents

Jamie drives as he thinks it'll help calm his nerves by concentrating on the journey and Jess is happy to sit in the passenger seat as she likes being chauffeured.

She tells him not to worry as her dad already likes him, besides their attention will be focused on Michael most of the time as even though they live closer than before they don't see him any more than they would if they still lived an hour away. Since her dad retired he's just as busy with his hobbies, holidays and golfing as he was when he worked.

He starts to talk about his house, 'The valuations have come in and they're a lot higher than I thought babe, I bought it for one hundred thousand, Joe put ten grand deposit so I've a mortgage of ninety. The two estate agents have each valued it at £129,995 and £126,500, so by the time I've paid Joe back and the mortgage and fees I'm gonna walk away with about twenty-five grand, I'm thinking we should buy another house in the village and rent it out. What's your thoughts babe?'

'Could do. I've still not done anything with mine, just left it in an ISA, perhaps that's something we could look into in the New Year, buying a couple for rental purposes,' Jess replies

'Michael, we're here, can you see Nanny and Grandad standing in the window?' she asks their excited son.

Michael begins shouting for his nanny and grandad and Jamie laughs as he puts a finger up to his ear, he's defended him, Jess laughs at him, she knows it's a good excuse for his nerves, she leans over and kisses him telling him he looks gorgeous.

'Gorgeous enough to impress your mum?' he asks.

'Hmmm, that's a tricky one,' she says and gives him a wink.

He gets out of the car, opens Michael's door, lifts him out and puts him down on the ground, at which point Michael runs to his nan and grandad, Jess walks around to meet Jamie and grabs his hand - escorting him to meet her parents.

'Dad, this is Jamie,' she says, and the two men shake hands.

Jamie says, 'It's nice to see yer again Tony.'

'Likewise Jamie,' Tony says with genuine warmth.

'Jamie, this is my mum Barbara,' Jess says and gives her mum a stern look to say *be nice.*

'Hi Barbara, nice to finally meet you,' Jamie politely replies.

'Yes Jamie, Jess has told us all about you, it's just a shame she couldn't tell us five and a half years ago.'

'Barbara,' Tony says sternly, shooting her a look which Jess took to mean he was backing her up in her admonishment and warning to *be nice.*

Finally they all walk in the house out of the cold, it's the last Saturday in November and it's been frosty this week. Barbara has made sandwiches for them all and they each take one, Michael sitting with his on a small plate and chatting to everyone in turn. Barbara brings up the subject of Christmas and asks Jess if they all want to come and stay with them, but Jess says, 'No, not this year mum, why don't you and dad come to us on Christmas day?'

Tony says, 'Yes,' immediately, not giving Barbara the chance to say anything else, then takes over the conversation and asks Jamie what he's been up to and what rank he is now.

Jamie tells him everything there is to tell, about buying a house after leaving the base in 2020, and why he will be selling it in the New Year. He tells him of his posting to Cyprus for two years, coming back in the UK fourteen months ago, that he's on his second promotion, he's now a Corporal and this is the reason he's back on this base - he's on a twelve month secondment. He finishes up by saying that once this is up, he, Jess and Michael will rejoin his Regiment in November next year on their new posting, though he doesn't know where that is yet but is due to find out around Easter time next year.

Jess smiles, she knows exactly what that means.

Chapter 55

Catching Up

'That wasn't so bad, I think yer dad likes me,' Jamie says as Jess smiles and waves goodbye to her parents, telling Michael to wave to nanny and grandad.

'My dad likes you, he was impressed by your promotions already, and the fact you see a future with Michael and I.'

Jamie looks at her and winks, knowing that Jess actually has no idea what plans he has, other than they're all going to be joining his Regiment next year.

'It will be nice to see the old faces, I miss them. I feel bad for cutting them out of my life the way I did, especially Clementine. I did miss her,' Jess muses, with a genuine feeling of sorrow.

'I know, she didn't speak to me for over two years,' says Jamie.

'You're kidding?' Jess says and her jaw drops in astonishment at such a harsh punishment.

He shakes his head and says, 'She finally started talking to me in Cyprus when she got drunk one night. We were all out at the local bar and she told me how much she missed yer and that I was a prick, but Tommo had told her she was to forgive me, as I'd punished myself enough and he wanted me at their wedding.'

'Are they married?' Jess asks, almost unable to voice the words with the lump in her throat.

'Yeah, they got married last year, 26 October, about a month or so after we posted back from Cyprus. It was a huge wedding babe, so bloody posh, we didn't get changed out of number one's, and definitely no shots, just lager, it was a good day though.'

Jess is really upset, and for some reason she feels the need to know if he took Tara as his guest.

'Did Clementine go to university?' Jess enquires.

'No, she's a midwife, works in a hospital near to base.'

'I have to ask..,' Jess begins and Jamie cuts in.

'No I didn't. I know what you're going to ask, and the truth is I kept her away from everyone that knew yer, figured it was easier.'

'Can we go up and see them? I've missed Clem and Shelley, it was wrong of me to do what I did.'

'Baby it's fine, they understood. Yeah, they all want to meet Michael –and also see yer of course,' Jamie adds the last bit as an afterthought almost and they both laugh.

'How are Shelley and Nobby? And Oh! God, what did they have?' Jess says remembering that she hasn't even had news of the sex of their baby.

'They had a boy, Joshua, he's five now and Theo was two in September, he was born in Cyprus.'

'Oh my God, I've missed them all. What about Gavin, did he ever settle?'

Jamie laughs and says, 'No, "me brother from another mother"? He was my saviour Jess, stayed with me all the time, made sure I didn't do anything silly.'

Jess is shocked, she puts her hand to her mouth and says, 'Jamie you wouldn't have would you?'

He shrugs his shoulders, 'We went out on tour for six months the following year, May to November and I did think to myself that if we'd have been at war, I probably would have gotten myself shot.'

Jess's eyes fill up, 'I'm sorry babe, I'm so glad you didn't,' she says and a tear rolls down her face.

'Me too now,' he agrees and he looks at her, 'Aww baby, don't, we're here now, let's move forward, the past is the past.'

She nods, but she can't help thinking how much pain he must have been into want to end his life or get himself killed. No one should feel like that. She promises herself, no matter what happens in the future, that they will never hurt each other like that again.

Chapter 56

Bedtime Story

Michael is bathed and drinking his hot milk, the shopping has been delivered and put away and they're all sitting at the table having a warm drink before Michael goes to bed.

Jamie tells Michael that he's going up to meet his Nanny Anne on Friday, though Michael has no idea who she is, so Jamie tells him, 'Nanny Anne is my mummy, and you're going to meet your aunties and uncles,' and goes on to tell Michael he has two brothers and two sisters but he leaves the kids out as poor Michael is confused enough.

Jamie is also meeting his mum's boyfriend for the first time, even though they've been together for well over two years now as his mum wanted to wait until Jamie was married and moved out before she considered moving in with Pete. Jamie knows that out of all her children, he and his mum have a special bond, he worries about her and she worries about him.

'Right mate, it's bed time, I'll race you,' says Jamie and Michael jumps down off his chair and is at the door before either of them have even got out of theirs. Jamie looks at Jess and says, 'Yer know for a little guy he's seriously got some speed,' and they both laugh.

Jamie pretends to run after him and chases him up the stairs. The sound of his chuckling is infectious and Jamie immediately begins laughing with him and Jess laughs at them both.

Michael gets into bed and Jamie tells him a quick bedtime story, gives him a kiss good night, tells him he loves him and if he wakes up before he gets back from his run in the morning to get into bed with Mummy. Michael nods in agreement as he says goodnight.

Jess walks over to give him a kiss, as she's been standing by the doorway watching them both with her heart melting - this is more than she could have ever wished for.

She goes downstairs and into the kitchen, considering opening a bottle of wine tonight. They could have a couple of glasses now and use the rest later. As Jamie walks in he sees she has a big grin on her face, then he looks at the wine and looking back at her grin he says, 'Hmm, cum flavoured wine, I'll have some of that,' and he laughs as he bends in and kisses her neck.

He tells her he's going to get changed into something comfortable and asks if she wants him to bring her dressing gown down after. She nods as she walks in to the living room carrying a couple glasses and the bottle of wine, with a big grin on her face - she knows what's coming later.

Chapter 57

Sofa Sex

Jamie pops a pair of sports shorts and a T-shirt on, then brings Jess' dressing gown down for her to change into to relax - it's been an eventful day. Her dad is a decent guy, so down to earth even though he's made a lot of money in his working life, but her mum, well, she's a different story. He understands now why Jess always said "she's difficult" she wasn't wrong, however, where Michael's concerned she dotes on him and that's good enough for Jamie.

He watches Jess getting undressed. She takes off her jeans then her top, she's standing there in her black lace balconette bra and matching black lace thong, making his cock twitch just looking at her, he moves forward to the edge of the sofa and tells her to 'come here' so she walks over to him.

He opens his legs and she stands in between them, his hands rub over her bum cheeks and he gently slaps them as he kisses her belly while telling her how beautiful she is. He can smell her, she's warmed up already, her juices must be flowing, he smiles as he looks up at her and she smiles back, she knows he can smell her.

His cock is erect as he kisses along the top of her thong and spreads her legs. He moves her thong to one side and runs a finger along her smooth lips, making her juices seep out a little. He licks his finger to taste her juice and then runs his finger along her smooth lips again, only this time opening them slightly to ensure his finger tip gets covered in juices again, then he sucks his fingertips.

She bends down and kisses him, her tongue looking for his. Undoing her bra he caresses her boobs and plays with her nipples, then he stops kissing her and tells her to stand back as he gets up. He pulls his T-shirt and shorts off in what seems like one swift move and proceeds to take off her thong.

Sitting back down on the edge of the sofa he tells her to straddle him, so she sits on his lap facing him and as his hands pull her head toward him, while he's kissing her slowly but passionately, she sits down on his hard cock, feels it go deep and instantly groans out loud.

She moves up and down on his hard cock, feeling its full length deep inside, her juices leaking out all over his cock and balls, her tits bouncing as she rides up and down, moaning louder and louder as his cock goes deeper.

His arms wrap around her and feel all over her naked body, he pulls her closer still as he crosses his arms over her back, making her moans become louder.

'Louder baby,' he says as his cock goes in deeper, 'Tell me when you're going to cum.'

She nods, her moans and groans are loud, this is a new position for them and she is loving it, the feel of his cock so deep in her wet pussy, his arms holding her, she loves to feel his strength, his dominant side, even if she's on top, it's still there, in the way he talks.

His cock is throbbing now as her juices soak him, he can hear she's close to cumming and he tightens his grip on her. He loves the feel of her naked body against his as she bounces up and down on his hard throbbing cock, telling him she's ready to cum.

Her deep throated groan is loud as she cums, her head lowers onto his shoulder and his arms hold her tight as he thrusts his cock deep inside her. He thrusts in deeper and deeper, faster and faster, making her moan louder and louder. He's so excited by her moaning, he can't hold it any more as his cock explodes deep inside her, releasing his spunk deep inside her wet pussy and he holds her tight as he shudders with his climax.

Chapter 58

Snuggling Up

Jess comes downstairs after her shower to find Jamie lying down on the sofa, after his. He stops flicking through the TV channels and asks her, 'Is that better babe?' She nods, as she walks over to the table to pick her glass of wine up and asks Jamie if he would like some wine now also.

'Yeah, go on then, please babe,' he replies.

'I'm going to have this tonight and then that's it, I'm not drinking anymore in case I fall pregnant,' Jess says.

'Have yer bought any ovulation test sticks then?'

'No, I'll order some tomorrow online.'

'We'll need to get a pregnancy test once a month again,' Jamie says.

'I wouldn't bother with them, I'll know if it's anything like last time,' she says, remembering how bad it was the last time. She hopes it won't be anything like that the second time around.

She lies down on the sofa next to Jamie and he wraps his legs around her as they relax and watch the TV together.

'Yeah,' he agrees, 'although this time we'll both understand why, won't we?' Then he whispers to her, 'I'm sorry baby,' and squeezes her hand due to his feelings of guilt over the situation last time. She kisses his hand to reassure him that it's fine.

Jess is far away with her thoughts instead of following the scenes on the television. She thinks about the events of today, about him meeting her parents and what he said about all of them moving to his new base next year - she's not sure if she should sell this house or rent it out.

'You know you said about us all moving with you next year?' Jess begins with a thoughtful tone.

'Yeah,' Jamie replies, wondering where this is going.

'Well I think I might sell this house.'

'Why babe?' he says, a little surprised and still unsure where her decision is coming from.

'Well it's only got two bedrooms and as we're going to have another baby, it's going to be too small. Plus, I can't see us ever coming back here once we leave.'

Jamie lovingly squeezes her and kisses the back of her head. The thought of a baby excites him, one that he'll be around for this time, a baby brother or sister for Michael – it will be perfect.

'It's an option babe but we should try and keep a foot on the ladder or sell this like yer said and buy a three or four bedroom to rent out - that way we have something to come back to in the future,' Jamie suggests.

Jess nods in agreement and snuggles into him, lifting up his hand to kiss it, telling him she loves him. She's looking forward to the future now, something she hadn't thought much about before and if she did it was a lonely one that she envisaged - but not now, it's a future full of love and happiness with Jamie and their children.

Chapter 59

Road Trip

Jamie finished work early and Jess doesn't work Fridays, so they're leaving as soon as Michael finishes school. Jamie called his mum to say they'll be there around 1730 - 1800hrs at the latest. Jamie is very excited for his mum and family to meet Michael and to see Jess again, he remembers how well they got on the first time around.

He packs the car up while Jess makes Michael a sandwich and a drink to have when he finishes school as he'll be hungry. She doesn't know where he puts all the food he eats, she often tells Jamie "he's definitely got hollow legs" and they both laugh then Jamie will tell her "that's boys babe, yer think he's bad now, yer wait until he's a teenager - he'll eat yer out of house and home". She dreads the shopping bill by then, it's bad enough now and he's not even yet five years old.

'Why are you bringing your kit bag?' Jess asks.

'Me washing - me mam loves to do me washing when I go home,' he says, very matter of fact like she should already know.

Jess laughs and rolls her eyes and calls him a "mummy's boy". Jamie laughs and agrees with her, he really is a mummy's boy and he's not denying it. He wraps his arms around her, saying, 'Yer'll be the same with Michael, it's what mums do,' and she smiles as she nods her head.

'Right, that's the car done, yer do realise we're coming home on Sunday don't you?'

Jess looks at him a little confused at first then realises he's talking about the luggage. 'I know, but I don't travel light anyway and Michael needs some spare clothes,' Jess replies, lost in thought as if having not considered how much they seemed to be taking until Jamie brought it up.

Jamie just tuts and thinks *it's less than forty-eight hours, how many sets of outfits do they both need?* His thoughts move to what it's going to be like when they have another, *we'll need a mini bus just for the luggage*. He laughs to himself as they walk out of the house and Jess looks at him weirdly, wondering what he's laughing at, maybe he'll tell her in the car.

They pull up at the school gates and see the usual mums who are always there at least twenty minutes before the final bell goes. One of them says something and they all, very obviously, turn around to look at Jess and Jamie sitting in their car. This makes Jess feel very uncomfortable as she's not one for 'cliquey groups' at the best of times, least of all now.

'Look at them, they're like a gaggle of geese, we should give them something to talk about,' Jamie laughs.

'Don't you dare, I know exactly what you're thinking,' and despite herself, she laughs with him.

He tells her to wait in the car and he'll run in and get Michael. Besides, it's just starting to rain and he can pick Michael up and run with him if the downpour gets too heavy.

Jess watches him as he walks past the "gaggle of geese", seeing them turn and follow him with their eyes - she knows what's going on. One of them turns back and looks at Jess and then she's not sure whether to smile, give them a dirty look or stick her middle finger up. As she's not one for swearing very much she decides to smile - she's not going to play their game. *It's pathetic* she decides, and watches for her two favourite 'men' coming back to the car.

It's the first weekend in December – Friday 7, so Jamie only has a week and a bit left until shut down. He's been invited to the "lads' Christmas party" next weekend but he hasn't told Jess yet as he knows she'll be fine about it, he also thinks now about her presents and what to buy her.

'We need to sort Christmas out next weekend, it's only two and a bit weeks away,' he says to her after getting Michael sorted in his car seat and settling himself into his seat for the journey.

'I know, it's coming around really quick,' she says with genuine disbelief at how time seems to fly by these days.

'Will yer write me a list, I need some ideas for you. Do yer still have that bracelet I bought yer?' he asks.

'Yes, but I haven't worn it since... I put it away in the box with everything else.'

'Oh, ok. So give me some ideas for me and Michael to get yer.'

She nods, she has lots of ideas, probably some that are not for Michael's eyes, but she'll write them down anyway. She asks him for a list in return, she has a few ideas but it's nice to know what he also wants.

Jamie chats to Michael and asks him if he's excited to be going on a 'road trip'. Michael shouts out a loud "Yesss" and Jess looks at them both, tutting and rolling her eyes, thinking to herself *please, not in the car* she knows what's going on here, the two of them are getting excited, winding each other up, but she smiles because it's such a beautiful thing - a sight she thought she'd never see.

Chapter 60

A Warm Welcome

Anne is waiting excitedly on the doorstep as they pull up and Jess has a big grin on her face as she waves. She's feeling very nervous but also happy at the same time.

Anne walks towards the car and around to the passenger side as Jess gets out. The two women embrace each other tightly and Anne tells her how much she's missed her over the years. Jamie is sporting a beaming smile at his two favourite women - he couldn't be happier - as he gets Michael out of his seat and carries him around to meet his mum.

'Michael this is Nanny Anne, my mummy,' he says, crouched down next to his son.

Anne bends down and cups Michael's face in her hands, tears are streaming down her face as she exclaims, 'Oh Jamie, he's your double.'

'Hello Michael, how are you?' Anne asks him and Michael smiles and looks at his mummy and then his daddy for reassurance. Jamie picks him up and as he gives his mum a cuddle, Anne throws her arms around him hugging him tight, she's so happy.

Jamie carries Michael into the kitchen and Anne sets about making a cup of tea for everyone as Jamie goes out to unload the car. He calls to Jess telling her he'll show her around the house and she gets up from the table as Michael jumps down off his seat saying, 'I'll come,' and Anne follows Jess as they all head upstairs.

Anne takes Jess into her room to show her and then she shows her the box room and says to Michael, 'I hope you like dinosaurs Michael.' Anne has been out and bought a dinosaur quilt cover for Michael and a few dinosaur toys to help him feel at home.

Michael is beaming from ear to ear and Jess is smiling - she can't believe Anne has done this and she looks at Anne and mouths "thank you" as Michael walks straight into the room and picks up the dinosaurs to play.

Anne sits on the bed and Michael begins chatting to her about his dinosaurs. He asks her if she knows what noise they make and she tells him, 'No I don't, do you?' He nods and she says, 'Really Michael? You must be a clever boy to know that, will you tell me?' He goes quiet for a moment and looks at his mum and dad so they both smile at him to reassure him that it's ok.

Michael tells Anne about his friends back home in school, that they run around the playground together pretending that they're being chased by dinosaurs and they make a big loud noise like this. 'Roaaar,' he shouts loudly in his best dinosaur voice and Anne pretends to be scared. She can see Michael likes this and then he tells her, 'It's not real, it's just pretend.'

So Anne says, 'Oh good, because I was scared Michael, I bet your friends get really scared, do they?'

He nods and says, 'Sometimes,' with a satisfied smile on his face.

Anne listens to him and smiles, he reminds her of Jamie as he was a chatty one too but only if he felt comfortable in your company.

Jamie take Jess into his room, 'Look, a double bed,' he says as he dives on it and she laughs at him. She knows that he and Tara would have slept in it, but she reminds herself that that's all in the past now, it's time to move forward.

She walks around to the side and leans over to him, 'I was looking forward to the single bed,' she says and winks at him.

He winks back and laughs as he says, 'Well yer could always bunk up with Michael.'

'Cheeky,' she replies and flashes him a knowing smile.

They walk back to Anne and Michael and Jamie asks, 'Who's hungry?' He himself is starving and wants some dinner, so they all head downstairs with Michael carrying his dinosaurs tightly and holding Anne's hand. Anne's heart melts - she loves this little boy dearly already, more than he could possibly be aware of.

Chapter 61

Early Morning Sex

Jamie wakes early and goes for a run, wanting to be back in time for Michael waking. He's left Jess to get a bit more sleep before their son wakes up. They didn't have any sex last night as Anne went to bed at the same time as they did and it didn't feel right to do anything. He was definitely horny however and he woke up with a hard on, so he woke Jess up by playing with her clitoris, telling her, 'Shush, we have to be quiet,' which is something you rarely ever hear from Jamie.

She was a little groggy to begin with but playing with her clitoris always gets her juices flowing. Her legs open wide, she told him to put some fingers inside her. He started to kiss her neck, working his way up to her mouth then kissed her hard as he put three fingers in and she wanted to scream out but couldn't, so she grabbed hold of the sheet and scrunched it up.

Pushing his fingers in, feeling the juices all over them, she whispered, 'Harder,' as he pushed them in deeper, the discomfort of his knuckles stretching her was turning her on, painful but pleasurable, it was rough and she wanted to shout out that she was going to cum. Instead she just mouthed the words and grabbed the back of his head, cumming all over his hand.

He left his fingers in for a moment, feeling her pulsate around them, letting her get her breath. Taking them out they were dripping in cum and he began to lick his fingers, and share them with Jess, leaning in and kissing her at the same time, tasting her juices together.

He climbed on top of her with his erect cock throbbing, placing it inside her soaking pussy. He wasn't going to be gentle, he was in the mood for rough and fast, he told her. As he thrust his cock in hard, she bit her lip to silence herself and with another deep thrust she was cumming instantly.

Her pussy was warm and wet and he loved how this felt on his hard cock, he could hear her juices squelching as his cock thrust deeper, harder and faster. He wanted to tell her to moan but he couldn't, he was so turned on, his cock throbbing, and he told her, 'I'm going to cum baby,' as he thrust in hard, his cock exploded, his spunk mixing with her juices as they both climaxed together.

His pods are in his ears but he realises he isn't listening to any of the music at all, only thinking of their early morning sex. This is turning him on so he decides he must stop thinking and start listening, *it's impossible to run with a hard on*, he laughs and turns his music up as he feels his cock soften back down - until tonight anyway.

Chapter 62

Family Gathering

Anne has arranged for everyone to be here by noon. They're all super excited to meet Michael and see Jess again, the girls really liked Tara as they've known her since she was fourteen but they know their brother and they know he never really fell out of love with Jess and that he would one day go back and look for her.

When Jamie proposed to Tara, Rosie told their mum that she couldn't see Jamie marrying her as Tara is very spoilt and Jamie has never liked that trait in a person. Even Tara's own brother Jed would moan about her and how spoilt she is so Rosie was secretly happy when they broke up - she always thought her brother was too good for Tara.

Anne and Jess are in the kitchen preparing the sandwiches for everyone's arrival, chatting away like the old friends they are. Pete is also coming over for the occasion, due to arrive around 1.00pm, giving everyone a chance to meet Michael on the same day. She's feeling a little nervous but on the whole very excited for Jamie and Jess to meet Pete, after all she is moving in with him next month.

Breda and Steve are the first to arrive and upon entering the room, Breda throws her arms around Jess telling her how happy she is to finally see her brother smiling again. She's bought a present for Michael so Jamie picks him up to introduce him to her, though Breda wants to give him a big hug, she holds back, as she doesn't want to frighten him - she has plenty of time in the future to give her nephew a hug.

Michael excitedly opens his present, he thinks it's Christmas come early, and when he comments that it's just like Christmas, they all laugh.

'It is for us Michael,' says Anne. Breda has bought him a Nerf Gun.

Jamie laughs, 'Michael we're gonna have great fun with that later,' and they all agree.

Joe, Jacqui, Sophia and Annabel arrive the same time as Rosie and Archie. It's obvious to everyone that Rosie is visibly upset but she brushes it off blaming the "pregnancy hormones". Anne decides she will talk to her later and make sure she's ok, rather than making it any worse by bringing it up now. Jess can't believe how much the girls have grown, Annabel was just a baby the last time she saw her and is now six years old and Sofia is nine, although they don't remember Jess.

Jacqui gives Jess a hug and welcomes her back, tells her that she's missed her and asks her how she has been. Jess tells her that she's been good, but missed Jamie and everyone. She tells Jacqui that she's sorry that they never got to see Michael as a baby and Jacqui just hugs her and tells her not to be sorry, things happen, but she's back now so it's all good.

Jamie walks into the kitchen when Rosie goes to get Archie a drink, and he tells her that Jed text him late last night, telling him he'd not only ruined his sister's life but he'd ruined his life as well, as him and Rosie have separated. It said [Thanks Mate, I hope you're happy because I sure as hell ain't, you've fucked everyone's life up just so as you're happy]. Jamie didn't reply straight away, he waited until after his run, as he always thinks clearer when he's been on a run.

He puts his arm around Rosie as he tells her he knows that's the reason for her being upset today. He tells her that he didn't want to tell their mum, as he doesn't want to upset her, not today.

He asks Rosie if she wants him to speak to Jed, but when she shakes her head, he's livid, 'Why would he leave yer because of me?' he asks, so Rosie tells him that she told him to leave. She read a text from his mother calling Jamie and her family "low life tramps".

Rosie says that Jed should have stuck up for his wife, but he didn't, 'So if that's how he feels he can fuck off and live back there.' Jamie hugs her and tells her it'll be alright and not to worry, Jed will come to his senses.

Jamie decides that he does need to speak to Jed, as this isn't right. He's thinks to go out later to meet him, as he knows this is his doing - well Jean's doing, she's a nasty one, is that woman. He's very glad to be away from her but Rosie doesn't deserve this, he needs to sort this mess out. Once and for all.

Once Pete arrives, Anne introduces him to Jamie and Jess. Jamie is so pleased for his mum, she looks really happy *it's time she found someone to look after her* he thinks to himself.

Pete joins Joe and Jamie in conversation, talking about selling the house. Pete tells Jamie that he has a big enough house so when he and Jess come back to visit they are more than welcome to come and stay with them and Jamie shakes his hand and thanks him.

After a while, they all get stuck into the food, Michael plays with Archie showing him his dinosaurs and how they roar. Everyone is relaxed and laughing and Anne looks at all her children together, the only one missing is Sean, but he'll meet up with Jamie, Jess and Michael at Christmas.

Chapter 63

Man To Man

Jamie tells Jess he needs to nip out, it's nearly 1800hrs and everyone had gone by 1600hrs. He says he's arranged to meet someone for a quick chat, Jess looks at him suspiciously but he tells her it's nothing to worry about, that he needs to speak to Jed, that he's left Rosie and he needs to sort it out, what happened in their life shouldn't be anything to do with Rosie and Jed.

Jess is shocked as after all is said and done, Rosie is six months pregnant. Jess knows only too well about raising a baby on your own and she doesn't want to see Rosie in the same position, so she kisses Jamie and tells him she loves him and to be careful.

Pete is staying until later as Anne has cooked chilli con carne for the four of them and chicken nuggets with fries for Michael. She doesn't know Jamie has gone out, he didn't tell her as he doesn't want to worry her. Jess tells her he's nipped out to see someone and Anne looks suspicious but Jess tells her it's nothing to worry about.

Jamie pulls into the pub car park and sees Tara's car. *What the fuck?* he thinks to himself. One thing he's learned in his army role is how to look for someone without actually being seen.

Jed doesn't know what Jess' car looks like, so Jamie parks around the back of the pub, walks in and sees Jed on his own. So he goes to the toilet, and coming back he takes the long way round to make sure Tara isn't in the pub - to his relief she is not.

He orders a pint, and walks over to sit with Jed, who already has a pint. Jamie sits down and both men acknowledge each other without speaking.

'Jed, what's going on? Why has my relationship split with Tara caused yer marriage break up?' Jamie asks directly, no beating around the bush, as they say.

'You shit all over Tara, why would you do that? She loved you mate,' Jed replies.

'I know she did Jed, but the truth is I didn't love her, not in the way I should have.'

'So why did you ask her to marry you?' Jed asks him and Jamie shrugs his shoulders - the truth is he doesn't know himself. 'I've been getting it from all angles, me mum, Tara and Finlay, I'm married to your sister, what do you think would have happened?' Jed says, really feeling the pressure of everyone else's opinions.

'I'm sorry Jed, my life shouldn't impact on yer marriage, yer wife is six months pregnant and you've left her, why would yer do that?'

'Me mum text me, so I called her, but Rosie only saw the text, and it just caused mayhem.'

'I know, Rosie told me. Look, at the end of the day, regardless of what's gone on I'd already made my mind up I wasn't marrying her, I couldn't cope with her behavior.'

Jed nods, he knows his sister is a spoilt bitch and if she can't get her own way she has a tantrum.

'Mate, yer look awful, yer obviously not happy. Do yer still love Rosie?' Jamie asks, needing to know for his own peace of mind.

Jed nods, affirmative, as he takes a drink.

'Look mate, at the end of the day do you want to lose yer wife and kids because of me and Tara?' Jamie says and watches Jed shake his head, he does truly love Rosie, Jamie knows it. 'I'm truly sorry for what happened with me and Tara, I never wanted to hurt her but I never fell out of love with Jess, no matter how much I tried I just couldn't. It wasn't fair on Tara, she deserves to be with someone who really loves her.'

Jed nods in agreement. He understands of course, as he loves Rosie and couldn't imagine his life without her or Archie and their unborn child.

'Yer need to go home now Jed, yer should be with your pregnant wife and son, Tara will be ok, it takes time but she will.'

The two men get up and walk out of the pub together. Jamie doesn't tell him he parked around the back in case Tara was here, he just walks him to Tara's car and then waits until he leaves. Walking back to his car he realises that Jed used Tara's car as it was safer than leaving his van full of tools in the car park. He smiles to himself as he gets out his phone and texts Rosie to tell her that Jed will be home later and not to be angry with him as it wasn't all his fault.

Rosie sends a text back almost immediately: [Thank you, I love you my favourite brother (don't tell Joe or Sean, I'll just deny it) xxx]

He laughs and gets in the car, heading back to his family, the most important people in his life, Jess and Michael.

Chapter 64

Sunday Brunch

Jamie arrives back from his run by 0715hrs to find Jess and Michael lying in bed together as Michael had woken up and did as daddy had previously told him to, that if he woke before he was back from his morning run he was to get into bed with mummy.

He gives them both a kiss and as he's going for his shower, he asks Jess if she fancies going out for brunch around 1100hrs, then heading home around 1400hrs, rather than having dinner and leaving around 1700hrs.

Jess agrees it might be better, then they'll order a take away tonight and she'll go food shopping tomorrow as she's not working. She wonders why he doesn't want to stay till until 5pm, but figures it's to do with getting Michael ready for bed as well as his ironing, he normally likes to have it done by now.

Jess and Michael get up and she goes and makes everyone a cup of tea as she can hear Anne pottering around in her bedroom. When making Michael some breakfast, his favourite Ready Brek, she has to make Jamie a small bowl too, under Michael's orders.

Anne comes walking down the stairs and into the kitchen and kisses Michael on his head and tells him what a big boy he is eating all that Ready Brek. Michael shows her the muscles in his arms and both women laugh, just as Jamie walks down the stairs and into the kitchen, saying, 'Ooh is that mine babe?' and he takes a seat in front of the bowl of Ready Brek.

Jess and Anne look at each other and smirk and the term, "like father like son" crosses both their minds at the same time. Jamie tells his mum that he wants to head back around 1400hrs, so if she's ok with it they'll go out for brunch around 1100hrs instead of her cooking dinner for everyone. Anne is happy to do that as she's arranged for Pete to come and stay tonight. The change will mean he can come over earlier than 6.00pm, but she'll keep that plan to herself - her son and future daughter-in-law don't need to know about her private life.

Jess heads back upstairs to pack all their things away. The clothes that are clean she puts into the weekend case and puts the dirty clothes in a black bag, and while doing so she thinks to herself *perhaps Jamie was right, I may have brought a bit too much*. She laughs to herself, maybe one day she'll get used to this weekend away malarkey.

They all head out to a local restaurant where Breda and Steve have arranged to meet them after Breda text her mum asking what time everyone was heading home as she wanted to pop over and see them before they left. Anne told her the plans and asked her to join them and Breda is never one to turn down an invitation - especially one that involves food.

Chapter 65

Christmas Decorations

Jamie's decided not to go out tonight for the lads' Christmas drinks. It's not that he doesn't want to, he'd love to, but decides it's too early in the relationship for that, he'll wait until New Year's eve for a blow out - that way Jess will be with him and she won't be worrying about what he's up to.

They've been Christmas shopping for the family today. Jess has been doing Michael's Christmas shopping on most Fridays, but next week she needs to do Jamie's though she still has no idea what to buy him, only thinking about sportswear and everyday clothes, with some aftershave and a little surprise from her.

Once Michael is in bed, Jamie sets about getting the Christmas decorations downstairs - they'll put it all up tonight as a surprise for Michael in the morning, then tomorrow he'll hang the lights up outside. The house is going to be really Christmassy, Jamie's first family Christmas with his own family and he is so excited, Jess can see it.

'Babe, who helped you do all this before?' Jamie asks, feeling a twinge of sadness, thinking of her on her own at Christmas.

'I did, then Fred, Martin or my dad would put the lights up outside.'

He's happy she put her decorations up even if it was just for Michael's benefit, the first Christmas he met her she didn't put any up, said it was pointless as they were both away from Christmas Eve until New Year's day.

He opens a bottle of beer and offers Jess one but she puts her hand up and says, 'I'm good thanks,' intending to get herself a glass of squash or cup of tea in a bit. Leaning into her Jamie kisses her and tells her what an amazing selfless woman she is.

Half a dozen bottles of beer later, the tree, living room and hallway are decorated. Jamie stands back to admire the tree and says to Jess, 'That's a lovely tree babe, it looks almost real.'

She nods, saying, 'Yes I got it in the January sale when I was pregnant. I was chuffed with it myself,' then she wraps her arms around him and asks if they're exchanging a gift on Christmas Eve.

'Yeah, just me and you babe, once Michael is in bed.'

Jamie will break up from work next Friday and they're finishing at 1200hrs. His plan is to go straight into town and buy Jess' presents and he's got some ideas but wants to have a think this week about any last minute ideas. It's going to be an extra special Christmas and one they are sure to remember forever.

'Babe, yer still got yer butt plug?' he ventures.

'Yes, but I haven't used it since the last time we were together.'

'Do yer fancy wearing it Christmas food shopping next weekend?'

Jess laughs out loud and answers, 'What? Why?'

'It'll make it interesting, especially me walking around with a hard on.'

Jess laughs and nods at the same time, knowing she'll be turned on by it and the thought of what will happen when they get home. The chances of the shopping being put away straight away is "slim to none".

'I'm going to see if my mum and dad will have Michael next weekend, to give us the chance to get the last of his presents and the food sorted.'

He snuggles into her and responds that this is a great idea, 'Just think of all the sex we can have, morning noon and night,' he says and winks at her. She laughs at him as he kisses her, knowing this is their last Christmas as girlfriend and boyfriend.

Chapter 66

Something Special

Jess has dropped Michael off at school for his last day until 6 January. She's also finished work until the New Year as the way Christmas and New Year fell this season meant she has only had to book four days off. She was pleased that she managed to get the holiday time otherwise their plans for travelling to up to Anne's would have been ruined.

She previously arranged with Jodie to go Christmas shopping together as Jodie wants to get Martin's as well, so the two women head in to town straight after the morning school run with Jess telling Jodie that "parking should be easier this time of the morning".

They've also arranged a get-together on Sunday, with Jamie, Jess and Michael going to Jodie and Martin's house to have a few drinks, some food and exchange presents - they won't get the chance to see each other over the Christmas period as both families will be off visiting their own families in different parts of the country.

The car park is pretty empty, just as Jess thought. She likes coming to town this time of the day, it's less busy which means you get to have a good browse around the stores.

They head for a coffee shop, and a hot drink and a toasted tea cake for breakfast turns out to be too inviting, but they justify it agreeing that will hold them until they stop for a nice lunch later on the way out of town.

Jess looks at her list, it's a mixture of sportswear and designer wear. Jamie's tastes have changed a little - not that he had bad taste, quite the opposite - he used to like the high street brands but now he likes his designer clothes. It must be something to do with affordability, as his salary increased with his promotions, his shopping habits changed also.

They head for the sports shop and Jess gets him some running bottoms, a couple of T-shirts and a sweat jacket. She can't see any trainers that she likes, but decides he probably has enough already anyway.

Next she finds a little designer shop on one of the side streets and upon walking into the shop she breathes in the smell of leather and exclaims, 'Ooh Jodie can you smell that?'

Jodie has already noticed and thought the same and says, 'Mmm, fresh leather,' then both women laugh out loud at themselves.

'Fresh leather,' Jess repeats and they fall about laughing, trying to pull themselves together. 'I hope you don't say that when you next buy a piece of beef "ooh fresh beef",' she says and Jodie replies with, 'Every time mate,' and they continue to giggle uncontrollably between themselves as they browse a little more.

A salesman approaches the two ladies, greets them with a smile and asks them what they're looking for. Jess gets out her list and reads it aloud, 'Jeans, top, jumper (not too thick), belt and a shirt,' and then she asks, 'and where is the smell of leather coming from?'

The salesman goes off for a couple minutes and comes back with the new season jacket, telling her it's called "the Racer Jacket" and it's the softest leather you've ever seen with a hefty price tag, more than she budgeted for, but she loves it and can definitely imagine Jamie wearing it.

Jodie is having none of it. Martin earns good money, he's a Sergeant, but she's not spending that sort of money on him, she's happy to buy from a high street chain, though she does agree that it'll look nice on Jamie.

Jess leaves the shop with her best friend, a smiling salesman waving at the door and a very dented credit card, but she's pleased with her purchases and knows Jamie will love his clothes and "the racer jacket", now all she needs is wrapping paper, and a couple of gift boxes along with his cards.

Both women are done by 12.30pm, the town is getting busier and the car park is full, so they head back to the car with all their bags.

'Time for some lunch, I'm starving now,' Jodie tells Jess, who nods in agreement saying she is hungry herself.

'A nice freshly cooked chicken pasta with cream sauce, that's what I'm going to order,' she tells Jodie. They haven't even left the car park yet and all Jess can think about is food. Jodie laughs at her and tuts.

Chapter 67

A Special Present

Jamie's finished for this year and he wishes all the lads a 'Happy Christmas' and tells them all to stay safe, when they go home. Ben and Becky are coming round to his on Monday, as they're heading south on Tuesday to spend Christmas with Becky's mum, but are having a few drinks and dinner with Jamie and Jess before they go.

Jamie gets into town just before 1300hrs and as the queues to the car parks are ridiculous, he decides to park out of town and walk in. It's a ten minute walk for sure but as he got changed into civvy clothes already, he doesn't mind the short stroll.

His first port of call is the jewellery shop, the last time he used this shop was 8 May 2020, some five and half years ago. He's pleased to see it's still open given the state of the high street and the effects online shopping has had on most retailers in town centres.

A young sales woman approaches him and asks him if he needs any help. He tells her, 'I'm looking for a ring, something special, it's to go with this,' and he shows her the one he bought Jess when he planned on proposing to her.

'Ooh, that's beautiful, where did you buy that?' she asks.

'From here,' he replies, 'Five and a half years ago.'

The sales assistant asks him if he's looking for something simple but elegant like the ring or a bit of sparkle, nothing over the top just enough to enhance it.

He tells her simple and elegant, he doesn't want to upstage this ring.

As the ring is on a Tiffany band, she shows him a tray of platinum bands, they try them for style next to the engagement ring, and in the end he decides on a 2mm platinum court shape band. It's simple but elegant and not as expensive as he thought it would be but still it sets him back £365.00. The assistant offers to replace the ring box for the engagement ring but he says, 'No, it's fine, thank you.'

He leaves the shop feeling pleased with himself, 'Now to get her some chrissy presents,' he says to himself. The queues are awful and by the time he's bought her perfume, underwear, new earrings, some clothes and a new Pandora bracelet with a couple of charms - a mum one from Michael and a nice heart shaped one from him - his credit card has taken a battering.

He's going to have to clear it in January so he's not worried. It's not often he uses his credit card anymore and when he does he likes to clear it within a month or two, but Jamie doesn't worry about money anyway, not these days, he earns a good wage and is sensible, he's always saved right from his first pay packet.

He heads back home, wondering how he is going to wrap all this up before Jess gets back. She's dropping Michael off to her parents until Sunday so that they can have time tomorrow to finish his present shopping and go food shopping without him. Jess will however be wearing her butt plug as they agreed and his cock twitches at the thought of it, but for now he needs to get home and put the ring back in its place - the same place it's been since 8 May 2020, though it won't be long until he finally gets to give it to her.

Chapter 68

Butt Plug

Town was hell and Jess felt terrible the whole time they were shopping, she just couldn't shake the headache she woke up with. It probably didn't help that they had a late night last night and an early morning, all she wants to do now is get home, get in the bath and relax for the evening, but there's a long time to go till that time is here.

Jamie didn't go for a run this morning - he was going to but early morning sex won. He's not sure why but he's really horny just lately, all the time in fact. When he thinks about it, he must have suppressed his libido for all those years, now it's like he's nineteen again, not that he's complaining, he loves sex with Jess, it's always been the best and very exciting.

When Jess got home last night after dropping Michael to her parents, Jamie was lounging on the sofa all nice and relaxed and she'd barely walked in and his cock was twitching just at the sight of her, then she kissed him and he was hard before she'd even finished.

He wouldn't mind but he'd already knocked one off before she got home, he didn't tell her that, certainly not when she'd offered to give him a blow job. He wasn't going to refuse, when his spunk could be squirting all over her face - this just adds to the excitement.

They manage to get all the toys Michael wants and some new dinosaur pyjamas, some clothes and an electronic pad that will help with his English and Maths for school. They drop it all off at home but don't bother to hide it in the attic as it all needs wrapping with the rest of his presents. Jess tells Jamie they'll need to start wrapping that tomorrow morning before he comes home at lunch time and hide it away until Christmas Eve night.

Jess has her presents for Jamie stored at Jodie's so she'll have to go and get them Christmas Eve or before - she just had nowhere to hide it yesterday. Jamie's right about one thing, this house has no storage.

She found her butt plug last night ready for today. Jamie's been excited about her wearing it all day. She remembers how insatiable he was at nineteen and now, five and a half years later, he's no different, yet he told her he could go a week with no sex. She has no idea when that week was because he can't go twelve hours without with her, not that she's complaining.

She asks Jamie if he wants to put her butt plug in and he smiles a really cheesy smile and says 'Yes of course,' with a wink. She tells him they're not having any more sex until later tonight, laughing as she says it, and he tells her, 'Babe we ain't gonna make it out this bedroom, my cock is throbbing at the sight of yer.'

Jess has taken her jeans and thong off and she can feel her juices beginning to flow as she thinks about Jamie putting her butt plug in. She leans over the bed, in the doggy position, waiting for him. She knows she could have done it herself, but that would have been boring - getting Jamie to do it adds to the fun.

Her bare bum is sticking up in the air and her pussy lips on show as her legs are spread apart so he can smell her juices as he puts her plug in. With the purple jewel sitting perfect in her arse, he kneels down and starts to lick her pussy, he can taste she's wet and he smirks to himself as he thinks of the fact that she asked him if he could put it in for her.

His head is between her legs and she can feel his hair on her inner thighs. This excites her as she feels his tongue licking her pussy, tasting her juices. He pushes his tongue in deeper, she starts to moan, he sucks and licks harder, his head pressing against her thighs, the feel of his strength just from his touch makes her cum quickly and she knows he can taste it.

Jess is moaning with the pleasure as she feels Jamie drinking her juices, she tells him she wants him to fuck her, deep and hard, she needs to feel his hard throbbing cock deep in her pussy.

He stands up, his face still wet with her juices but he's not going to bother sharing it with her, not this time, he's too excited, he needs to fuck her with his throbbing cock. He quickly unfastens his jeans and pushes them with his boxers down to his knees, then he pulls off his top and throws it on the floor next to her jeans and thong.

Jamie holds her outer thighs and pulls her slightly towards him as he positions his cock into place, just inside her pussy. It throbs as he pushes it in and he can feel her warm, wet pussy, her juices soaking him. As he looks at her arse, the sight of the butt plug has him excited, a little too excited and he's knows he's going to cum quick.

He thrusts his cock in hard and she moans as he thrusts deeper, the harder he thrusts the louder she moans.

Holding on to her tightly with his cock thrusting in and out, fast and hard, he can feel her cumming again, all over his cock this time. He's going to cum also as he's so excited he can't stop it, he thrusts in deeper and moans as he releases his spunk deep inside her pussy, mixing with her juices, then gives her outer thighs a final squeeze as his body shudders with his climax.

Chapter 69

Excited

Tony and Barbara pull up to the house just after noon and Michael is super excited as he runs to his mummy and daddy, telling them, 'Santa's been to Nanna and Grandad's, I saw presents in the bedroom.' Jess looks at her mum, who frowns as she explains he was running in and out of her room and the room he has there, but then went running into one of the back rooms where she'd hidden all the presents.

'Well yer know what that means Michael?' Jamie says.

'What Dad?'

'If yer naughty he's gonna take them back,' he replies and he lifts Michael up and gives him a kiss and hug, telling him he's missed him.

They all walk into the house where Jess has made tea for everyone, and a light lunch as they're going to Jodie and Martin's later for dinner.

'So you finished now Jamie?' Tony asks.

'Yeah, till 5 January.'

'What about your secondment, does it not finish soon?' Tony is worried for his daughter and grandson, he's seen how happy they are and can't bear the thought of Jamie leaving them now, he knows it would be devastating for both of them.

'I've extended it until 23 October next year, then we'll have a couple weeks off before moving to my new base, I'll find out in January where that'll be.'

Jess and Barbara are in the kitchen talking about Christmas dinner and Jess shows her what she bought yesterday, Michael follows the women as he wants a drink and a cheesestring from the fridge.

'When you say "we" you mean you, Jess and Michael?' Tony asks Jamie with his voice lowered.

Jamie nods, he knows where this is going but doesn't want to say anything to alert Jess of his plans, and he sees Tony look towards the kitchen, checking that the women are not listening.

'I'm sorry Tony, I should have sought your permission first, I never thought,' Jamie says quietly, almost in a whisper.

'Well when the time is right and I'm sure you have it all planned, you have my permission, I couldn't be happier and will welcome you into our family with honour,' Tony says, feeling a lump in his throat as he's fond of him. Jamie's a hard-working, proud man and he knows how much he loves his daughter and grandson, he knew he loved her the night he met him shopping, he's just sorry he never said anything to his daughter - perhaps she would not have put herself through what she did, but it's all in the past now, it's time for them all to move forward with their future.

Jess and Barbara walk back into the living room as Tony asks what meat they got for dinner. Jess tells him, 'Turkey, beef and pork Dad, just as you like,' then she asks if they want to be picked up so they can both have a drink with Jamie but Barbara is adamant she's happy to drive. Jess also checks with them what time they want to arrive and Tony tells her he was thinking about ten in the morning as they're both excited to see Michael open his presents - they've bought him something really special. Jess looks at him suspiciously, and asks him, 'What have you got Dad?'

'You'll have to wait and see Jess, you're just like your mother, no bloody patience,' Tony says, rolling his eyes in mock disgust.

'You know I hate surprises,' Jess replies and Tony reminds her it's for Michael not her, and they all laugh. Jamie says it's probably a good idea to change the subject and motions towards Michael sat on the floor so they steer the conversation to what Michael's been up to at his Nanna and Granddad's.

Jess can't help noticing there's an air of excitement around her mum, she doesn't know what or why but she seems unusually happy. Whatever it is, Jess will find out in time to come, no doubt.

Chapter 70

Decisions In Life

Jamie sneaks the bag of presents out of the house and into the car while Jess is getting dressed, she's changing into a nice black catsuit and kitten-heeled black patent shoes. Michael is wearing his new jeans, shirt and jumper, with his freshly cut hair in a similar style to Jamie's - short on both sides heavy on the top with it brushed over.

Jamie shouts to Jess, 'Coast is clear,' meaning he's hidden the presents in the boot of her car, then they put all the Christmas lights on outside with the lamps on in the living room for when they get back, as it's going to be a later night than usual for Michael, with no bath at six o'clock or hot milk and bed for seven - it'll be more like eight or nine by the time they return from Jodie and Martin's.

Jess tells Jamie to get the bottle of wine from the fridge, she's bought a nice red for them all to drink with dinner, so she'll be driving back. She doesn't mind, she's not in the mood for drinking anyway.

Jamie drives the short distance to Jodie's house, pulls up outside and Jess leans over and kisses Jamie and tells him she loves him, and he says it back as his hand strokes her face.

Jamie gets Michael out of his car seat telling him to run and knock on Aunty Jodie's door, there's no point saying walk, because he knows Michael runs everywhere, his tiny legs going like the clappers. He does make him laugh, 'If he were any older I'd take him running with me, that'd wear him out,' he says to

Jess as she walks around from the passenger side and she smiles and nods in agreement.

Jess and Michael walk in and Martin goes out to give Jamie a hand, the two men shake hands as they've become close friends since Jamie's been back which is good for Jess and Jodie.

Once the men walk into the house, Martin takes the bag of presents from him and takes them upstairs, coming back down with another couple of bags which need to be put away in the boot of the car without Michael realising what's going on. Jamie takes them and walks back out, opens the boot of the car and puts the presents in.

As he's about to walk back to the house he looks in the back window at Michael's car seat and smiles to himself thinking how different his life is now. Only two months ago he knew nothing of Michael, was engaged to be married to someone else and was still very much in love with Jess.

Jamie knows coming back here was a big decision, it wasn't one he took lightly, he'd thought it over for months, but he now knows it was the right one. Most definitely the best decision he's ever made as he's back with the woman he loves and has always loved, and the most important part of any of this is that Michael has his daddy back from work.

Chapter 71

Broody

'Isabella, you make me so broody,' Jess whispers to the toddler on her lap.

Jamie's heart melts when he watches Jess with Ben's little girl, just turned one year old and the prettiest little girl he's ever seen, with a head full of dark curly hair and big green eyes. He can see she loves her Auntie Jess as she snuggles into her.

Isabella begins to struggle to get down, so Jess bends over and puts her down on the floor and watches as she crawls to her daddy. Ben picks her up and you can see she's the apple of his eye, Jamie knows this is how he would have been with Michael and will be with their next one, whenever that is, though he hopes it's not too much longer now as he's broody for a baby and he wants to see what Jess looks like pregnant.

Becky is helping Jess finish the cooking and he can hear them nattering about life in the village and Becky's driving lessons which she will start in January, although Ben has refused to put her on his car insurance as his car is his pride and joy and he says he'll buy her one of her own, once she's passed her test.

Ben asks Jamie what his plans are with the secondment coming to an end in the new year (6 February 2026) and Jamie tells him he's extended it until 23 October, when they'll all join up with his Regiment on their new base, but that he'll find out in January what base they're being posted to.

'All of you?' Ben asks and smirks. He knows what this means, he knows that Jess and Michael wouldn't be allowed to move on to base unless Jess and Jamie are married. Jamie nods his confirmation but gives Ben the hush sign, which is exactly what Ben will do, and he laughs and changes the subject.

Becky walks back into the room and asks Ben to sit Isabella in her high chair as dinner is being dished up. They are not having a starter today, but they have a roast beef dinner with all the trimmings and New York cheesecake with berry compote as dessert, though Michael and Isabella have a trifle that Michael helped Jess make earlier.

Jess asks, 'So what date in January are you away on exercise and has it been confirmed for how long?' then says she can't get the calendar out yet, as it's bad luck but she has a few dates she needs to add in herself. Jamie tells her that 15 January he'll be here for Michael's birthday party on the Sunday and his actual birthday on the Monday then they'll head out and be back Thursday 5 February or thereabouts.

Over dinner, Becky raises the subject of adding to their family with another baby and Jamie tells her he hopes so, as he feels it's important for Michael to have siblings. Jamie being one of five and growing up in a single parent household with older siblings helped, they all looked after each other, even now they're all adults they all look out for each other, 'a bit like what we do in our roles,' he says and looks to Ben who nods in agreement .

Jamie asks her if they plan on any more, and she tells him that when Isabella is about two and a half, they've agreed to try for another baby, as Ben has a six month tour coming up towards the end of next year and she doesn't want to be on her own with a baby while he's away for six months.

Jamie nods in agreement and tells them he's been asked if he wants to go on that tour but he happily declined, as he'll be back with his Regiment by end of November. Ben looks at him and says, 'You sure you don't want to stay? You know how much you love the Middle East.'

Jamie laughs and shakes his head, recalling his two tours of the place. The first he was living with Jess and it was a ten week tour, and then the second was for six months. He was still in a bad way then, even though it was a year after they split. He doesn't like to think of that time in his life.

'Remember when I came back from that ten week tour babe?' he says to Jess, shaking his head.

'I do, it took you a good week or two to settle back in.'

Jess looks at Becky and warmly touches her hand, asking her if she will go home to her mum's during that time. She hates to think of Becky on her own for six months and to make it worse she knows she won't be living here in the village anymore.

Becky nods and says, 'For the Christmas and New Year period yes, that's why I need to learn to drive, it's a good five hours to my mum's by car, if I go by coach it'll be about eight hours and train is just too expensive to even think about.'

Ben looks at his wife lovingly saying, 'You'll pass your test by then babe, I have every faith in you.'

Jess offers to give Becky some extra lessons in her car, once she's built her confidence up, even if it's just around the village, as it all helps. Becky agrees with her and asks if she's lost the plot. 'I can't drive your car, I'd be too scared of crashing it!'

'Perhaps driving lessons are safer,' Ben says and they all laugh and nod in agreement.

Jamie and Ben clear the table and Jess gets up to sort the pudding. Becky stays at the table to look after the children, blowing kisses between Michael and Isabella and she looks at Ben in the kitchen, he's leaning against the sink talking to Jamie. She can see these two men have a mutual respect for each other, not just because Jamie is Ben's superior in work, it's more than that, they have become good friends.

She can't help watching Ben, over six feet tall with dark curly hair, shaved on the sides. Ben is of mixed race, his dad's family are from Jamaica and his mum is a 'typical blonde' as Ben says whenever they talk about his mum and dad. Becky sometimes wonders if she'll have a blonde haired little boy like Michael, he definitely makes her broody for a son, with his big blue eyes and blonde hair. He is gorgeous and she loves him, Becky knows in her heart of hearts this is the only Christmas she'll celebrate with Jamie, Jess and Michael and this saddens her but she knows they'll be friends for life.

Chapter 72

Christmas Eve

Jamie has put some Christmas music on, playing the songs he grew up listening to. He tells Michael what it was like at Christmas with his aunts and uncles, that they would all clean the house and Nanny Anne would cook a big spaghetti bolognese for their dinner. She would also do lots of baking for Christmas such as mince pies, apple pies and sausage rolls. They never had a turkey but instead they'd have a big chicken for dinner on Christmas day, and trifle for pudding. He smiles as he thinks of his childhood, they never had a lot but they had a mum who loved them unconditionally - it definitely was a family full of love and still is.

Jess has nipped to Jodie's to collect Jamie's presents but she plans to leave them in the boot of the car until Michael is in bed. She is excited to give Jamie his special present tonight, she doesn't know how she's kept it a secret for so long, but feels happy that she has. Leaving Jodie's she gives her a hug, thanking her for all her help and tells her she'll call her tomorrow to wish them a happy Christmas.

She gets back in the car and calls Hazel to see if she wants her to collect the wine for tomorrow or will they bring it with them. Hazel tells her that they'll bring it tomorrow along with the Christmas cake she's made. Jess is excited at this news as she loves Hazel's baking even more than her cooking - it's homely and more-ish, meaning "the more you have the more you want".

Walking back into the house, she stands in the hallway, taking in the atmosphere, the Christmas music playing, the Christmas decorations, the lights, Michael's laughter and Jamie's voice. She can't remember ever feeling this happy in life, she knows no matter what happens in the future, where ever they go, she'll always be with Jamie. She never wants to be on her own again or live without him again, *this is what a family is*, she thinks to herself.

Jess tells Michael it's bath time and that there's a surprise on his bed, so Michael jumps down from the sofa and runs up the stairs with Jamie and Jess following after him. By the time Jess has reached his bedroom he's already getting undressed for his bath excited by the discovery of his new dinosaur pyjamas.

Jamie goes to start running his bath and Jess sits on Michael's bed cuddling him, asking him if he's been a good boy for Santa to bring his presents tonight. Michael nods and tells her he's been really good today and she laughs at him, 'Well that's ok then,' she says and continues to tell him he needs to carry on being a good boy and go to sleep when Mummy and Daddy put him to bed after his warm milk and cookie biscuit.

Jess goes down stairs to start the hot drinks while Jamie gets Michael dried and dressed into his new pyjamas, then she hears them 'bumping' down the stairs, on their bums bumping a step at a time. She's not sure which of them is the child sometimes - Michael or Jamie?

Jess decided to make some cookies earlier in the day and they turned out well, much to her surprise, so she's put some on a plate for them all to have with their hot drink, a little bedtime treat for Christmas Eve. Baking is not something she's done much of in the past but she enjoyed making these now that she has a family to appreciate them, it makes it worth doing.

It's her first Christmas at home, even though she's lived in this house for six years she has never spent Christmas here. Instead she has always been rushing around here and there, going to her parents' house every Christmas, but not anymore, she's staying home for Christmas from now on - *this is how it's meant to be,* she thinks to herself.

They've had a very busy but amazing week, what with dinner with Jodie and Martin on Sunday, Ben and Becky coming for dinner on Monday and then tomorrow her mum and dad and Fred and Hazel will be celebrating Christmas here in her home, the first of many future Christmases to come.

She hears Jamie saying to Michael, 'Right mate, let's get Santa's plate ready,' and he looks at Jess and winks as he says, 'and don't forget his bottle of beer,' which makes Jess laugh.

Michael tells him, 'He can't drink beer he'll be drunk.'

Jamie says, 'It's ok, he's only having one, he'll be fine,' and Jess and Jamie laugh as they all walk into the kitchen to get Santa's plate – and beer of course.

Michael places the plate on the little table, with a cookie that his mummy made earlier for Santa and a fresh carrot for Rudolph, along with a glass of milk and a bottle of beer just in case he fancies one.

Both Jamie and Jess take him to bed, like they do every night. Giving him a kiss good night, Jamie steps back and lets Jess read him a page of his bed time story book. Listening to her reading and Michael chatting is the best Christmas present he could ever wish for.

Chapter 73

Exchanging Presents

Once Michael is asleep, Jamie jumps up into the attic to get all the presents down, passing them all down to Jess. He's keeping one back for tonight though, hiding it in the inside pocket of his tracksuit bottoms. As he jumps down he tells her they may have gone over the top this year as he looks at the pile of presents in the bedroom. She kisses him and tells him, 'We have a big family babe,' and he nods in agreement, thinking to himself, *yes I do*.

They empty all the presents around the tree, and then Jess nips outside and gets all her presents for Jamie in from the car, making him go into the kitchen so as not to see what she has. She didn't realise how much she'd bought until it came to unload the car, which takes a couple trips back and forth. She's careful to keep his present for tonight hidden in the waist band of her jeans under her jumper.

Jamie cracks open the bottle of beer and hands Jess the milk, laughing at her as he does. She tuts and rolls her eyes as she laughs and snatches the cookie telling him his is the carrot. He scoffs at her and says, 'That can go back in the fridge, he won't notice,' and they both laugh.

Jamie asks her if she wants to exchange presents now, as he's finished the bottle of beer and it's nearly 1000hrs. He is feeling tired actually, which is unusual for him. Jess tells him, 'Yes, but you go first.'

He gets up, turns the light on and walks back to the sofa, staying up on his feet as he hands her the present, a square box, about four inches deep by four inches wide, perfectly wrapped. She laughs at him and says, 'I bet you didn't wrap this up,' to which he smiles and says, 'I might've.'

Jess opens it but it is empty, then looks at him confused as he says, 'Fuck, did I forget to put yer present in?'

'You plonker,' she says, laughing as she gets up to give him a kiss, then tells him it doesn't matter, she'll get it tomorrow instead and kisses him again.

'Oh wait, what's this?' he says, pretending to find something in his pocket.

She looks at him as he opens his hand to reveal a beautiful red velvet box. He bends down on one knee as he opens it to reveal the contents, a simple yet beautiful wedding ring. She clasps her hands over her mouth in shock and gasps.

'Jess, will yer marry me?'

She nods her head with tears streaming down her face, and tells him, 'It's beautiful.'

He stands back up and tells her that he couldn't find an engagement ring that represents her properly, but thought that this wedding ring seemed to be everything she stood for -simple yet elegant, classic yet beautiful.

She throws her arms around his neck and he hugs her tightly, kissing her, totally relieved she actually said yes.

'So, do you want yer present now?' she asks him.

He nods at her as she reaches behind her back and pulls the pen shaped box out from her waistband and hands it to him and says, 'I'm going to warn you, it's nothing like you got me,' and winks at him.

He rips the wrapper off, while looking at the box, feeling certain that there's a pen inside. He opens it, looks at it for a few seconds, then looks at Jess with a massive smile on his face, picks her up and says, 'Positive? It's positive, babe yer really pregnant?'

'Yes! About 5 weeks,' she giggles as she answers.

'Yer know babe, for someone who was told she'd need IVF, yer ain't doing too bad.'

'I know, I must have caught the first weekend you came back.'

'When did yer find out?' Jamie asks, still grinning from ear to ear.

'Last week, I felt really queasy in work on Thursday, and bought this on my way home just to rule it out.'

'When did yer do the test then?'

'When I went to Jodie's on Friday I did it there,' she says, also grinning like a Cheshire cat who'd definitely got the cream.

'Yer've kept it quiet all this time, how? I mean, wow.'

'I know, I so wanted to tell you but knew this would be the best way,' she admits while Jamie just nods, he can't believe it. He asks her docs she want to wait until after the baby is born to get married or get married sooner, like March or April.

'March, let's get married in March, I don't want to leave it any longer.'

'Yeah, yer've waited long enough,' Jamie replies and now Jess simply nods, as Jamie holds her head against his, both of them ecstatic, as this is definitely a Christmas Eve they'll never forget.

Chapter 74

Christmas Wank

Jamie didn't sleep much, it was a mixture of excitement that Jess is pregnant and that she said yes to marrying him. Jess on the other hand slept soundly, even with Jamie's body wrapped around hers, it never seems amaze him how deep she sleeps.

He lifts his head to look at the clock 0345hrs, he can't wake her now, it's too early and she'll be exhausted later, besides, it's going to be a long day anyway, so he'll wait until nearer 0600hrs. Michael won't stir until 0700hrs so they should have a good hour for some sex.

He's thinking about their sex life, he's going to have to be a bit more gentle, because even though she's told him it's fine and he can't harm her or the baby, he doesn't want to take the chance. He made love to her last night, not because of the pregnancy but it just felt right, it was the right time to make love.

His cock is hard thinking about it, he moves his body position a bit but he's still not comfortable, so he wonders whether he should go into the bathroom and knock one off the wrist. His cock is throbbing, so there's no way he's going to be able to go back to sleep until he's sorted this out.

He moves Jess slightly, pulling his arm from under her neck. He moves away and she still doesn't stir, he laughs at her, how she is going to wake up for their baby in the night, he has no idea. He can see himself doing the night feeds whenever he's home and he smiles at the thought already.

He gets out of bed, puts his shorts on and goes downstairs to a gently lit room as he left the lamp on last night so they could see when they walk in later this morning.

He lies on the sofa and puts the TV on. Flicking through the channels he chooses the porn channel, but leaves it on mute, deciding he'll watch a bit of 'early morning phone chat' - the girls are all fake tits and too much make up for his liking but they're fine for having a wank to.

He strokes his hard cock, still throbbing, it feels thick, definitely thicker than it used to. He likes how it feels especially when its deep inside Jess' wet pussy or her arse, now that's tight, thinking of her arse makes him throb more, he strokes harder and faster with his thumb and forefinger, wanking himself thinking of Jess standing in front of him, naked with her pregnant belly, then he feels his cock pulsate as he cums.

He lies there for a few minutes thinking, he only thought about Jess and her pregnant belly and he came straight away, which was quick, he's never done that before. The thoughts of her being pregnant is a new feeling, a sexy one in fact but he's going to have to sort this cumming quick out, there was a time he could go for hours and now it's only a few minutes, ten at the most. He gets too excited with Jess, but he figures that can't be a bad thing.

Chapter 75

Christmas Morning

To his surprise Jamie dropped back off to sleep though he's never done that before. He got back into bed just after 0430hrs, cuddled back into Jess and the next thing he knows is Michael running into the room asking if Santa's been.

Jamie lifts his head to see the clock showing 0722hrs *Wow!* He's never slept till this time of the morning, not since he started school. He kisses Jess on the cheek, and with Michael standing in front of her as she starts to rouse from her sleep, all she hears is, 'Has Santa been?' in Michael's sweet voice.

Followed swiftly by, 'Good morning Sleeping Beauty,' from Jamie.

Jess is feeling groggy, she just needs another few minutes to fully awaken so she tells Michael to go and get his dressing gown and slippers on. She knows she needs to get up, it is Christmas morning and she needs to check the turkey. You know it is Christmas when you wake to the smell of a turkey cooking in the oven.

She turns over and gives Jamie a kiss wishing him Happy Christmas and he kisses her back as he holds her naked body next to his, wishing he could have a few more minutes on their own. He loves the feel of her naked body and that early morning kiss, but they can't as its Christmas morning and they have to get up.

They all head downstairs, Jamie first with Jess holding Michael's hand. Jamie looks back at Michael and tells him, 'The lamp is on.'

Michael's face is a picture of sheer Joy as he looks up to his mummy and tells her, 'He's been,' and Jess smiles and nods in excitement at her first proper family Christmas.

They all enter the living room, with the presents all under the tree and Jamie turns the main lights on, otherwise he won't be able to see the names on the tags. A very excited, soon to be 5 year old little boy is on his knees next to his daddy looking for his presents - not that he can read the labels, but he's excited and that's all that matters.

Jamie starts to plough through the presents, putting them in piles. He hands Jess hers and she puts them next to her and he puts his to one side. Michael is surrounded by wrapping paper and presents so Jess goes into the kitchen to get a couple of black bags, she's going to start putting the discarded paper into them now or *he's going to end up losing something in all that mess*, she thinks to herself.

Jamie can't find any more presents for Michael and in any case he has a huge pile next to him still unwrapped as he's playing with every toy he opens before he opens another one. Jamie says to Jess, 'This is going to take forever,' and they both laugh as together they watch their son opening his Christmas presents - something neither of them ever really thought would happen.

Michael has opened all his presents now so Jamie tells Jess to open hers first and then he'll open his. Michael asks her if she needs his help, and she laughs and tells him that she just might, but Jamie calls him over to his lap and says, 'Let mummy open her presents herself,' and winks at him as he cuddles him, both of them spectating as Jess opens all the packages.

She picks up her last one which looks like a shoe box, she has no idea what it could be and unwrapping it she finds what appears to be an empty trainer box, so she looks at him and laughs wondering what could be inside. She opens it slowly, finding it full of shredded paper but soon finds another box which she recognises straight away. 'Pandora,' she exclaims and her eyes fill with tears, he's bought her a new Pandora bracelet.

Jamie hands Michael something and whispers to him, 'Give that to Mummy,' he didn't bother wrapping this one. Michael gives Jess a little Pandora box, which she opens excitedly to find her first charm, a beautiful 'Mum' script heart dangle charm, and she hugs him with all her might.

'It's beautiful,' she tells him and gives him a kiss on his cheek.

Finally Jamie hands her *his* charm and she can't contain her tears any longer. He hugs her as he kisses the top of her head, he knows what this bracelet means to her, only this time it won't be put away in a box and hidden in a cupboard, this one she'll wear forever and a day.

Jamie kneels by his pile of presents with Michael asking if he can help. Jess and Jamie both laugh at him, 'Of course you can,' Jamie tells him. Michael is excited about opening more presents even if they are not for him, he takes great pleasure in ripping the paper off each present, chucking it to his dad and picking up another one to open, not giving Jamie any chance to look at each one before being given another.

Finally they're on the last one, in a very big box which both Jamie and Michael open. As Jamie lifts off the lid he gets a distinct smell of Leather and he lifts his new jacket out, carefully so as not to damage it.

'Wow,' he says as he looks at Jess, he's no idea how much it cost but he knows it's a new season jacket, one he was looking at in the shop window on Friday when he was buying Jess' presents.

Jamie stands up and tries it on, even with his biceps and muscular chest it fits like a glove and looks amazing on him, even in his Regimental shorts and T shirt. *This jacket was made for Jamie*, Jess thinks to herself as Jamie hugs her and kisses her lovingly and passionately, with Michael covering his eyes as he says, 'Yuck,' and they both laugh mid-kiss.

'Kids eh?' says Jamie and rolls his eyes.

Chapter 76

Christmas Day

Jess quickly gets showered and dressed into her black catsuit with a nice silver bolero cardigan. She's wearing her Pandora bracelet, with the charms successfully added by Jamie while she was in the shower. She needs to sort the dinner out, there are still some vegetables to prepare, which she's going to get sorted while Jamie is having a shower and he's also sorting Michael out, although she can see him wanting to be in his PJ's all day - not that she's bothered today.

She hears Michael shouting, 'Grandad,' and thinks *Shit! Is it that time already?* She looks at her watch. It's just gone ten and she walks towards the hallway as Jamie comes down the stairs. She stands back a little and motions Jamie to open the front door.

He opens the door to Tony and Barbara, leaning in as he gives Barbara a kiss on the cheek and wishes her a merry Christmas. To Jess' surprise (and Jamie's for certain) Barbara hugs him back and wishes him a Happy Christmas. Jamie thinks to himself *Jesus, the ice woman is melting.*

Tony walks in and the two men shake hands, both wishing each other a Merry Christmas. Michael is jumping around trying to get his granddads attention, wanting to know if he's brought the presents Santa had left at their house.

Tony tells him to go in the living room with Mummy and Nanny, that Daddy is going to help bring them in from the car, so an excited little boy runs to join his mummy and nanny, a mere six feet away yet he manages a sprint to Jamie's amazement.

Tony and Jamie walk out to the car with Jess looking on, she can see they're chatting away and this melts her heart. She always dreamed of this day but never thought it would come, she looks at her mum and sees that she is watching her. Barbara grabs her daughters hand and squeezes it lovingly with a tear in her eye as she says, 'I'm sorry Jess.'

'Oh Mum, it's fine, today's not the day for regrets, let's just be happy,' Jess says, feeling elated that the day couldn't be going any better.

Barbara nods her head as she picks Michael up, giving her grandson a big sloppy kiss, as only nannas do, and he wipes it off with his sleeve saying, 'Yuck,' again and both women laugh at him.

Jamie walks in with a couple of big bags, smiling. He's seen why Tony was so excited about Michael's present and he puts the bags down and goes back out to get some more. Jess is watching her dad messing around in the boot of his car, then she sees him lifting something out and her face lights up as she looks down at Michael. 'Oh my God,' she mouths to her mum, who just smiles and puts her finger to her lips in a silent sssh action so as not to spoil it for Michael.

Jamie returns inside and puts the rest of the items down, saying to Michael, 'Do you want to see what Santa left at nanny and granddads for you?'

Michael can barely contain his excitement, jumping up and down and saying, 'Yes! Yes! Yes!'

They all go outside to see Tony at the end of the drive standing next to a kids quad bike. Michael is ecstatic, he's seen this one on power rangers he tells everyone, they all laugh but agree with him, he has his very own power rangers quad bike and they all stand around outside in the cold watching him riding up and down the street in his dressing gown and slippers - the happiest child ever on this Christmas Day.

Chapter 77

Christmas Dinner

Hazel and Fred arrived by noon. Jess was very excited to see Hazel and dying to tell her the good news that she's getting married and she's pregnant but she can't, not yet as they haven't told her parents.

Hazel tells Jess the table looks lovely, and asks her where she got the centerpiece from. It is a beautiful, big, round candle, the size of a dinner plate, with a gold glittery forest scene on the outside and little, clear, sparkling fairy lights on the inside.

Barbara turns them on to show Hazel and tells her that a woman she knows from the village made it, she's made her Christmas table decorations for the past five years, since she and Tony moved into their house.

The men predictably stand around, beer in hand, chatting away. Fred tells Tony about the Christmases he spent on tour and how much he enjoys his Christmases now. He looks at Jamie and asks if he'll be going away with the Regiment next year, to which Jamie shakes his head, tells him he was asked but he's not extending his secondment past 26 October as he wants to return to his Regiment and that he's missing his mates.

Fred doesn't ask about Jess or Michael as he doesn't want to hear that they'll be leaving with him. Fred is not stupid, he knows Jamie isn't going to leave them now and that they'll definitely be going with him which is going to break Hazel's heart - his too for that matter.

Jess tells Michael it's time for dinner, raising her voice to instruct him to, 'Walk please,' into the living room and tell daddy. Hazel laughs at her and calls her a spoil sport. Jess smirks and says, 'One of these days he's going to get hurt with all that zooming around.'

In true Christmas style, the men sit at the table whilst the women bring in the plates of dinner. Michael is sitting next to his granddad, Jamie sits at the far end of the table and Fred is happy to sit at the opposite end. With all the dishes served to the table, the women all take their seat - Barbara next to Michael and Jess opposite her, beside Hazel.

Jess knew Michael would want to sit between his nanny and granddad, although she knows it's a bit of a squeeze. They're happy to have their grandson between them, leaving her and Hazel with plenty of room to eat their dinner.

They all raise a toast to Christmas before eating, Jess and Barbara each have a glass of squash and the rest a have a sparkling wine - which hasn't gone unnoticed by Hazel that Jess isn't drinking.

'Oh, did I show you all what I got for Christmas from Jamie?' Jess says to everyone.

Barbara looks at her wrist and says, 'Your bracelet Jessica? I did notice it's beautiful.'

Jess looks at it and nods, but she wasn't referring to the bracelet. She puts her hand down below the table top as Jamie passes her something, then lifting her hands on to the table she opens the red velvet box to reveal the wedding ring.

'I got a proposal of marriage, and I said yes!' she exclaims, still as excited as she felt when he made the proposal.

Hazel hugs her tightly, she knows what this means, she's going to be losing her little family, the only family she and Fred have had for the past six years, *but that's military life* she tells herself. She tells Jess congratulations and that she's thrilled to bits for her - she really is, no lie.

Jess whispers to her, 'You'll still come and stay with us for Christmas next year won't you?'

Hazel nods and whispers back, 'Just try and stop me.'

Barbara hugs Jamie for the second time today - again he's not sure what has happened but whatever it is he isn't one to question it. She tells him that she's thrilled to bits and then moves around to her daughter and hugs her so tight, telling her that she's never felt so proud. That's definitely a first for Jess to hear.

Tony shakes Jamie's hand and winks at him saying, 'I knew you'd have it planned.' Jamie laughs, Tony understands Jamie, he knows that no matter what, he is a family man as well as a soldier and that he will look after his wife and children.

Once Fred settles back into his seat and they have all started to eat again, Jamie says, 'Oh, one other thing, I got this for Christmas,' and he opens up his pen box to reveal the positive pregnancy stick.

After another round of congratulations and questions of "when did you find out" and "do you know when you're due" Jess tells them all that she found out last week but kept it quiet as she wanted to give it to Jamie for Christmas. She explains that she is about five and a half weeks pregnant so probably will be due in the first week of August but will find out for definite in the New Year once she's been to see the doctor.

Everyone settles for a second time, when Tony pipes up, 'So before I attempt to eat my dinner for a third time, have you any more surprises?'

Everyone laughs, Jess and Jamie shake their heads and they all tuck in to an almost cold Christmas dinner.

Chapter 78

Making Plans

The women are cleaning up after an eventful Christmas day dinner, the men are having a beer and Fred is playing with Michael. Barbara asks Jess if she's thought about when and where they want to get married.

Jess says, 'March Mum. Jamie is away from 15 January to 5 February, so I'll be doing most of it on my own, unless you want to help?' She looks at her mum hopefully as she says this.

'I know you're good at organising things, perhaps you could lend a hand, Hazel, if you aren't busy?'

Hazel nods her head and says, 'I'll be delighted to help out, you know I will.'

'Have you thought about a venue?' Barbara asks.

'Yes, we talked briefly last night. There's a lovely hotel about two miles away, I pass it on my way to work each morning, we are going to see them as soon as we're back from Jamie's mum's after New Year.'

Barbara and Hazel both nod approvingly at this suggestion and Hazel tells Jess she's been to a wedding there, about eight years ago now "and it was a lovely day and it is a gorgeous hotel". Jess tells her she's thinking of holding the evening part here in the village at the sports and social club as they know everyone who goes in there and it'll be easier than everyone getting taxis from a venue further away.

Hazel tells Jess that this is a great idea and that way the owner will organise the disco and the food, so it will be cheaper than an evening event at the hotel.

Barbara can't help butting in at this point and says to Jess, 'If you and Jamie are worried about the money, your dad and I will happily pay for it'.

Jess looks at her and gives her a big hug and says, 'It's nothing to do with money, I just don't want to make a big fuss, not this time. Jamie and I are more than happy to sort this one out.'

Barbara is learning that her daughter is an independent woman and that this is her wedding and she's marrying the man she loves. This wedding isn't about Barbara and Tony showing off their wealth, unlike the first one, this one is about two people in love.

Hazel asks if Jess has thought about a dress yet, what style she's going to look for and that her bump might be showing by then and then Hazel smiles inwardly at the thought of the new baby. Jess tells her that she hasn't yet but again she's thinking of something simple, off the rail. *No need for a big, puffy, designer ball gown*, she thinks to herself and looks at her mum and Hazel, then says, 'We'll go shopping when Jamie goes away in January if you want to?' Both women smile and nod, Hazel can hardly contain her excitement but she has to in front of Barbara, she knows she'll have some alone time in the New Year with Jess, especially with Jamie going away on the 15 January.

Tony subtly takes Jamie to one side to speak to him, he knows Jamie is a proud man but he just wants to make sure the reason he didn't buy an engagement ring is purely due to not finding one at such short notice rather than financially.

'I know you've got this Jamie but if you need anything, you will let me know, won't you?' Tony says quietly so as not to be overheard by anyone else.

Jamie shakes his head, he knows where this is going. He looks at Tony and says genuinely, 'I got this Tony, trust me, its fine.'

Tony raises his glass, confident that his future son-in-law isn't a scrounger, not like the last one. He knows that no matter what, Jess and his grandchildren will never go without. Jess couldn't have picked a better man. Tony is a very proud father and will happily hand his daughter over to him on the day of their wedding.

Chapter 79

Packing The Car

Jamie helped Jess with the packing for this trip to his mum's as he didn't want 50,000 bags of clothes in the car like last time. They're only going to be away from home for five days, so he told her that three pairs of jeans, five tops, five pairs of knickers, three bras, makeup, toiletries and hairdryer will be enough. His mum has straighteners so she can use them and then to include an outfit for New Year's Eve. 'No more,' he says, and laughs as he walks out of the bedroom, 'and I'll sort Michael's out.'

Jamie woke around 0600hrs and decided to go for a run as he didn't go Christmas Day or Boxing Day so felt he definitely needed it today - he could feel his energy levels building and frustration starting to set in from the lack of running.

By the time he got back Michael was awake but playing in his room. He has enough toys now to open his own toy shop and to think that he still has Jamie's side of the family to go yet, he's one lucky boy - very loved that's for sure.

He packs all the presents in the car and shouts upstairs to Jess, 'There's not a lot of room left in the boot babe,' then Jess tells him she has two more small bags and he rolls his eyes and tuts. 'One bag I said, just one, what part of ONE did she not get?' he says out loud but in good humour. 'Two bloody bags, the best of it is she'll live in her jogging bottoms at me mum's,' he says to himself.

He nips upstairs to get Michael's bag, and takes it down, then he suddenly remembers something, 'Shit babe, fucking hell, I forgot I've got to empty my bedroom when we come back, it's going up for sale 3 January, we'll never get all that in the car as well.'

'I'm sure you don't need to empty it now, you can wait until it's sold or when you're back in February, you'll have a few days off to go up and get it then.'

'Yeah, I can, and I've still gotta empty my room in the block. I'll need to do that as soon as we're back.'

Jess can't help thinking this house is way too small for a family of three and it's going to be worse with the baby, perhaps they should consider buying that four bed around the corner in the New Year, even if it's for only six months. She'll speak to Jamie when they leave and see what he thinks.

'Michael, are yer ready? Yer got yer trainers on and yer coat?' He looks in the living room, 'Michael?' he says, 'what yer doing, where's yer socks gone?' Michael simply shrugs his shoulders, he's watching television, nothing will come between a nearly five year old boy and the TV.

'Jess, babe, bring down a pair of socks for Michael please.' He shouts up the stairs.

He hears Jess laugh at this and as he walks back out to the car and puts her two bags in, he says to himself, 'Fuck it, I give up, two fucking bags and no socks, why should I care? I have enough to deal with, with them pricks,' nodding towards the base as he continues muttering to himself, 'at least they all listen to me, Corporal O'Halloran, if I tell them to be ready they are, if I tell them one bag, it's one bag, not fucking two, it's one and I don't have to worry about a pair of fucking socks either.'

He shakes his head as he shuts the boot, walks back in the house and sits on the sofa next to Michael watching power rangers.

Chapter 80

Christmas Part Two

They pull up outside Jamie's house for what is probably the very last time that they'll stay here. His mum will move out 3 January to move in with Pete, and she will hand the keys over to the estate agent so they can organise viewings as and when they want to, they will also likely hold an open day - Jamie doesn't care, as long as it sells he's happy.

Jamie texts his mum to say they've left later than planned so will now be arriving around 1400hrs instead of the original time of 1200hrs.

Anne is standing on the doorstep waiting for them of course. She's so excited to see them all, for her first Christmas with her grandson, she's been looking forward to seeing him. She's missed him very much, just like she misses Jamie.

Sean is home although he and David have gone to stay in a hotel. Breda offered to put them up but she lives too far away and they wanted to be closer to the town centre, to go out and enjoy the festive season.

Jess is looking forward to seeing Sean, although she didn't know until recently that he was gay and now married to a hairdresser called Dave. "It makes no odds to me" she told Jamie when they discussed it before this trip "you are who you are and I'm looking forward to seeing him". Jamie had agreed with her on this one, commenting "you can't help who you fall in love with" and winking as she threw a cushion at him. He laughed and asked her "what have I said" to which she rolled her eyes at him. "Babe, I'm messing with yer" he had said before diving on her to tickle her, the one thing he knows she hates.

Jamie gets Michael out of the car and runs around to Nanny Anne. She opens her arms out wide to receive him and gives him the biggest cuddle and a big soppy 'nanna kiss' which he wipes off with his sleeve. Jess can't help but laugh at him, 'Exactly what he did to my mum,' she tells Anne.

Jess gives Anne a hug and tells her that she's been looking forward to seeing her again. Anne quietly says to her, 'Wait till you see what's inside,' and looks down at Michael.

Jamie hasn't given his mum a hug yet, he's been too busy unloading the car, but he tells her that he'll give her a kiss and hug once he's done, then, 'Go and pop the kettle on please Mum.'

'It's all ready and waiting for you Son, along with your favourite home-made mince pies,' Anne replies with a smile.

'Oooh, I haven't had home-made mince pies in years,' Jess says.

Jamie tells her that they're the best, and asks his mum if she has made any sausage rolls because he was telling Michael about them on Christmas Eve. Anne laughs and nods and says, 'That's the first thing Sean asked when he and David turned up on Christmas Eve.'

The car is finally unpacked and Jamie walks into the kitchen and gives his mum a big hug and kiss on her cheek, telling her he's missed her and asking if she's had a good Christmas. She tells him it's been great, that they all went to Joe's for Christmas Day, except for Rosie, as they'd already arranged to go to Jed's mum's for Christmas but they all came here on Boxing Day.

'When is Rosie due, Anne?' Jess asks.

'The first week in March, but they're saying the baby's big for dates, so she's being induced 27 February,' Anne replies.

'Do they know what they're having yet?'

'No, Rosie likes surprises, but I reckon it's another boy.'

'Oh God. I couldn't wait, I had to know, I hate surprises,' Jess says, shaking her head and they all laugh.

Jamie asks his mum what time is everyone is coming as he's excited to see Michael opening his presents. Anne tells him they're coming at 4.00pm but suggests they could open hers now so when everyone else turns up it'll be less to worry about.

They all agree and take Michael into the living room, it's like Santa's grotto all over again, 'Shit Mum is that all ours?' Jamie asks in disbelief and the huge pile of presents awaiting them around the tree. She nods, and says she got carried away last minute Christmas shopping, but she doesn't care, her son is home and it's her grandson's first Christmas with her, the first of many.

They watch as Michael opens all his presents, which include colouring books and pens, cars, a garage, some toy soldiers and some new pyjamas, power ranger ones this time.

Jamie and Jess open theirs together after - the obligatory smellies and some clothes and chocolates. Jess tells her she's going to be a beached whale by the time she leaves here, what with all this chocolate, home-made minced pies and sausage rolls and that she'll need the next size up trousers to go back to work in. Anne laughs and says, 'Anyone would think you were pregnant, talking like…' and then she stops mid-sentence. 'Oh my God!' she exclaims excitedly, 'you are.'

Jess and Jamie both nod in agreement, smiling from ear to ear. Anne can't contain herself and bursts out crying. All she has ever wanted was for her son to be happy, this is the best news she has heard and Jamie hugs her and asks if they are happy tears. She nods. 'Good,' he says, following this with 'and there is something else.'

She pulls away and looks up at him, them to Jess, then she looks at Jess' finger and sees no engagement ring on it. 'What?' She asks.

'Jamie proposed on Christmas Eve and I said yes,' Jess says with a beaming smile.

Anne is elated, hugging Jamie then Jess, asking her if that was why she asked when Rosie's baby is due. Jess nods, and Jamie tells his mum they're planning the wedding to be either Saturday 21 or 28 March, whichever date is free with the hotel.

Anne asks, 'What about an engagement ring?' as that is what threw her off the scent in guessing what the news was, so Jamie explains that he looked for one but couldn't find one that represents Jess, but he did find the perfect wedding ring and that they'll go shopping at some point together and get her an engagement ring.

Chapter 81

Family Gathering

Everyone arrived between four and four-thirty including Jed, although he was unsure whether to go. Rosie told him that he had to, they're a couple and regardless of what goes on they stick together. After all Rosie went to Jed's mum's for Christmas day, which wasn't a pleasant experience and one she won't be repeating in the future, they both agreed as from next year they'll stay at home, visit family in the morning or Boxing Day but Christmas Day is for their children - their own little family.

Jess was pleased to see Sean who introduced his husband David to her. He had already told David about Jess, long before she was back on the scene, and David whispers in her ear, 'You know Sean celebrated when he heard you was back,' and winked at her, so she squeezed Sean's hand and kissed him on the cheek.

The house is alive with kids running around playing and most of the men are in the living room while the women are in the kitchen. All the presents have been exchanged and opened now and Jamie has no idea how he's going to get them all back home. He whispers in Jess' ear, 'Babe, we need a bigger car.'

She laughs at him and says, 'Already thought about that.'

Anne has made a spread, which looks far too much for her to have been cooking for twelve adults and four kids, so she goes into the living room and tells the men to come into the kitchen, adding that she also has an announcement to make. Pete squeezes in and stands by Anne.

Jess goes over and stands by Jamie, knowing what Anne is about to say, but she's still nervous, especially as Jed is here, he hasn't really spoken to her, he has avoided any conversation - but that's fine, it will take time, he'll accept her one day.

'So, today I was informed I'm going to be a nanny again,' Anne looks over towards Jacqui and everyone turns and looks at Jacqui too.

'Don't look at me,' Jacqui says quickly, 'I'm definitely not pregnant.'

Anne then looks over at Jamie and Jess, beaming with happiness and they all turn to look in the same direction and realise who is pregnant because Jess and Jamie are smiling like Cheshire cats. Sean is the first to hug Jess and congratulate them both, maybe because he was standing right next to her or maybe the fact that his brother finally came to his senses and went back to Jess, back where he belongs. Either way he is ecstatic for his brother and Jess and his nephew Michael.

There were wishes of congratulations and questions of due dates from all around the room and Anne snuggled into Pete, saying, 'Welcome to the family.'

To which he whispers back, 'I can't wait.'

Once everyone had calmed down, Anne informed them all of another announcement, so they all looked around the room to see who else could be pregnant. It's not Rosie as she is already nearly seven months gone, Breda is never having kids so that only leaves Sean and David, who both put their hands up and shake their heads saying in synchronization, 'Nope not us,' and everyone laughs.

'So, it appears we have two weddings next year,' and that is all that she manages to say before the shouts and congratulations and a million and one questions asking "when?" begin coming.

Jamie tells everyone that their wedding is not booked yet but they're looking at 21 or 28 March and when they go home after New Year, they're going to book it at the hotel near to where they live, then it will all be confirmed by the end of next week or by the time they come down on the eleventh for Michael's birthday party. He looks at Sean and asks if he and David will be coming up for it, to which Sean nods and he says, 'I wouldn't miss it for the world.'

Jess gives Anne a hug, and asks her when Pete proposed. She tells her Christmas Eve, so it turns out she wasn't the only one to get a proposal and no engagement ring, they too are going shopping in the New Year for a ring.

Anne's sons congratulate Pete and welcome him into the family. Joe asks his mum if a date has been set yet and she looks at Pete and he nods. 'Yes,' Anne says and the room goes quiet, 'February fourteenth, Valentine's day,' and someone asks if they mean this February.

Anne and Pete both nod and snuggle together, it is evident to everyone that he loves her. Rosie is the first to speak, 'Jesus mother, you trying to send me into an early labour?'

They all laugh, Jamie hugs Jess, he can finally stop worrying about his mum, she has found a man who loves her and will look after her. She always said to him when he was growing up "be patient Jamie, what's meant to be yours will be, it doesn't matter when or how long it takes, it will always find away". It seems they were both patient in the end.

Chapter 82

New Year's Eve

'The table's booked for 1900hrs babe, yer got a couple of hours to get ready, are yer gonna be ok?'

Jess nods, she's started feeling nauseous and can't shake the headache that she has already had for two days. She tells Jamie, 'I thought I'd escaped it this time, but no, it led me into a false sense of hope.'

He kisses her on the forehead, 'We can cancel tonight if yer want? I know me mum will understand.'

Jess shakes her head, 'It will pass, we're not cancelling, it's New Year's Eve,'

He snuggles on the bed next to her kissing her intermittently, 'I don't mind, I quite fancy a nice early night, just me and you, I'll get Michael to bed for 1900hrs,' and winks. Jess rolls her eyes.

'You're so bad,' Jess says and he nods and laughs. He was looking forward to going out tonight for sure, he could do with a blowout but now Jess' morning sickness has started he's not so sure, he'd rather stay in.

'No, we're going. Sean and David have gone to a lot of trouble booking this table.'

'Spoil sport,' Jamie says with a grin and gets up and goes for a shower.

Anne is downstairs with Pete and Michael, having made Michael something to eat, as he won't be eating until around eight this evening. It is New Year's Eve so the restaurant will be really busy but the whole family are going out to celebrate. The last time they were all together on New Year's Eve was probably three or four years ago, this is the first New Year Sean has been home for at least three years.

As Anne walks upstairs she can hear Jamie's music in the bathroom, so she knocks on the bedroom door and Jess tells her to come in. Anne sits on the bed next to Jess and holds her hand, she remembers well the early days of pregnancy and that nauseous feeling, she always thought that was worse than actual vomiting.

'You sure you want to go out tonight?' she asks Jess.

Jess shakes her head, she hates feeling like this, she doesn't like letting Jamie down. 'I'll be ok,' she says, 'hopefully it'll pass, it's nothing like I was with Michael, so that's a relief.'

Anne smiles and says, 'If you feel ill during the evening, just come home, we all understand.' She turns her head toward the bathroom and can still hear the music. 'How long has that son of mine been in the shower? He does know there's three other people wanting to use it doesn't he? He needs to get Michael ready too.'

Jess laughs, 'About five minutes, so we better give him another twenty.' Anne rolls her eyes and tuts, she walks out of that bedroom and into hers and thinks how she needs to start packing up tomorrow, ready for the start of her new life - she will soon be Mrs. Anne Swift, but she can't decide whether to keep O'Halloran, after all that's her children's name.

Jess has told Anne that she's keeping Willetts. She'll be Mrs. Jessica Willets-O'Halloran, because Michael is a Willets it's only fair until they've gone through the legal process of changing his birth certificate to 'O'Halloran, and this could take a couple of years. The baby will also be 'Willets-O'Halloran.

Jamie walks into the bedroom with his towel around his waist and Jess looks at him and winks, thinking if she didn't feel so shit or his mum wasn't in the next bedroom she'd have that towel ripped off him by now - his hench body with his sexy tattoos really gets her juices flowing.

'Babe, are you going to get anymore tattoos?' she asks him.

'Yeah, I've thought of three.'

'Three? Really, what are they?'

'Yer name on my finger, as I won't wear a ring,' Jamie continues. 'Not 'cause I don't want to but because of what I do, it's too dangerous.' Jess nods, she understands that.

'Then I'm thinking on my side here, Michael's name and date of birth and this one's name and date of birth, after it's born obviously,' pointing to his left hand side, right next to his heart.

'Or, I'm thinking of a big heart shaped padlock on my forearm, with three keys, one for yer, one for Michael and the third for the baby. Each key has yer names in it with dates of birth but yours will be our wedding anniversary date.'

Jess nods, she likes that idea and she tells him she prefers the sound of that one, so he should go for that one instead. He nods in agreement and shouts to his mum that he's finished in the bathroom. He hears her say something like "finally" and he laughs as she goes for her shower.

Chapter 83

New Year's Eve Meal

They finally leave the house just after seven o'clock. It was touch and go whether Jess was going to make it, but she eventually managed to get up, showered and changed though she is not wearing any make-up tonight, she couldn't face it, the smell of her foundation turned her stomach.

They walk into the restaurant at seven-thirty to find everyone else waiting for them, except Jacqui as she's working until nine-thirty. She had Christmas off because she has a family but being a nurse has its downsides at Christmas and New Year, though she loves her job so she is prepared to make these small sacrifices.

Jess sits next to Sean and Jamie sits opposite with Michael. Breda asks her if she's okay, and Rosie leans across the table and asks her when the sickness started. Jess tells her it's not actual vomiting it is only nausea and a really bad headache, which started two days ago, inconveniently. 'Of all the times for it to start,' Jess says and Rosie tells her that it will get better once she hits the twelve week mark. 'I hope so Rosie, I had sickness all the way through with Michael.'

Rosie looks shocked and says, 'Oh God! No way, you poor thing.'

They order drinks and Jess tells Jamie to go ahead and have some beers as she'll drive back. He looks at her with a concerned 'are you sure' expression and she nods at him and says, 'Go on babe, you deserve it.' He doesn't need asking twice so he orders a pint.

They both order food, though Jess isn't sure she's going to be able to eat anything so orders a simple omelette and chips, along with Michael's chicken nuggets, chips and beans. Jamie opts for the steak with a peppercorn sauce. Normally Jess would order steak too but she doesn't fancy it and thinks it's better to be safe than sorry, so an omelette will be sufficient at the moment.

With the food orders taken, the drinks are flowing and the conversation turns to weddings. Anne and Pete have booked an appointment with the hotel Rosie had her reception at as they do civil ceremonies and have a space for Valentine's Day. She tells Jamie and Sean that they're to wear their Number One uniform for the ceremony and then they can get changed later if they want.

Both Jamie and Sean look at each other and laugh. Their mother never asks, she tells. Sean wonders if she forgets that they're adults now - perhaps not. Perhaps in her eyes they'll always be 'her little boys'.

Jess asks Anne, 'Who will give you away?'

Anne looks at all her children and says, 'I think I'll have my grandchildren escort me down the aisle, as I can't decide between the three boys.' She looks at all three of her sons, and they smile in agreement as they think it's a lovely gesture.

Breda asks her if she wants to go wedding dress shopping next week and that she'll pay for it.

'I know it's not the traditional way, but I'd love to buy you your wedding dress mum,' and the whole table agree it would be something special.

Anne nods her head and says, 'Ok Breda, that will be lovely, thank you.'

Jamie asks his mum to reserve a family room for him and Jess, there's no point staying at the house as it's too far away. He tells her she's lucky she said the fourteenth as he's away on exercise until the fifth, then he looks at Sean and asks if he has anything coming up. Sean shakes his head, there's nothing much this year but he might be going out to Kenya next year for twelve months.

David looks down at the mention of this, so Jess puts out her hand to his and tells him, 'It'll fly by David, you'll be so busy working that before you know it he's on his way back.' She remembers when Jamie was away for ten weeks - that was hard enough. She couldn't imagine him going away for twelve months.

Jamie nods, he knows it's not easy for any partner of a military man or woman, but even Jess would struggle with twelve months. That sort of posting would bring his military career into question for sure - he's not sure if he'd cope for twelve months himself, he struggled with six and he was single then.

Jacqui has finally joined them. Joe is pissed, Jamie and Sean are ordering shots, 'It's a squaddic thing,' Jess tells her and Jacqui laughs. She can't drink even if she wanted to as she has a twelve hour shift tomorrow with a 7.30am start, so Joe tells her he'll have one more and then they'll go.

They all finish up as it's nearly 11.00pm Sean and David are going back to their hotel as there's a party there. They ask Jamie if he wants to join them but he shakes his head. Jess tells him he should go, 'You're with your brother, you'll have a fab time.' Jamie looks at Jed, Breda and Steve and asks if any of them want to go. Breda and Steve are up for it but Jed declines, he's had enough for one night and doesn't fancy a hangover with Archie running around in the morning.

Jamie walks Jess and Michael to the car - his mum and Pete are going home with her. He's still indecisive about going, after all it is New Year's eve, but Jess is adamant, 'Go and let your hair down,' she says, 'Have some fun with your brother and older sister, we'll have plenty of New Years' to celebrate.'

He puts Michael in his car seat and leans in to give Jess a kiss, telling her how much he loves her and that he'll be home later. She smiles and tells him to enjoy himself. He closes her door and as she drives off, he hears Breda and Sean calling him. 'Come on Jamie, the taxi's here,' so he runs up to get in the taxi suddenly realising this is the first time he's ever been out with Sean and David, and they've been together for two years already.

He gets in the taxi and they head for the hotel. Breda shares with everyone how excited she is to be out all together like this. Steve is talking to David and Jamie quietly asks Sean if he's ok - like really ok. Sean smiles at Jamie, he really loves his older brother. He tells him, 'I'm ok for now J, now's not the time to talk, let's go and have some fun, like we used to.'

Jamie leans over and grabs him for a hug, whispering in his ear, 'Anytime Sean, just yell and I'll be there for yer.' Sean nods, he knows he will, someday he's going to need him, but not now. Now is about getting drunk and seeing the New Year in with his brother and sister.

Chapter 84

Heading Home

Jamie's packing the car up, delayed by a whole day as they couldn't head home yesterday - he was in no fit state. The fact that he was with Breda and Steve at Sean and David's hotel drinking until gone 0400hrs meant he spent most of New Year's Day either sleeping or just lounging on the sofa.

Anne has been busy packing up the house. Jamie's told her that he'll come back in February when he's back from exercise and pack his room up. They also need to sort the furniture out - he doesn't want any of it, so perhaps they can donate it to a charity shop, he suggests.

He tells Jess it's a good job he's not back to work until Monday and she nods in agreement. She's back on Tuesday but not sure if she'll make it, she's going to try and get in to the doctor's surgery on Monday, she needs to get booked in with the midwife sooner rather than later.

They're all packed up and it's just gone 1100hrs, Jess has spent the morning either in the bathroom or in bed, feeling like she's hung over. Jamie remember she was like this in the first few weeks with Michael. How they didn't realise that she was pregnant totally baffles him - immaturity perhaps? Well he knows now, when they get home she's going straight to bed, there's no point in fighting it, it'll just make her worse.

He gives his mum a big hug, thinking that he's really going to miss coming back here. His life has changed so much over the past three months, Jamie hardly recognises himself. He realises now that his mum's life was on hold because of him and he feels really sad about it. He thinks how she could have moved in with Pete long before now, perhaps that's why he wants to get married so soon, before anyone else comes back? *Fair play to Pete, he's been very patient for me mum*, Jamie thinks to himself.

Jess comes downstairs, looking like death. Anne gives her a hug and tells her to go straight to bed when she gets home and that all she should do at the moment is sleep, it'll pass. She nods and tells her she's sorry for being anti-social the past few days. Anne laughs at her, 'Don't be silly, you're pregnant, it's not being anti-social.'

Jess says goodbye to Pete and tells him the next time she sees him will be the wedding. He grins with excitement and a smile crosses her face too. She's truly happy for them both. She walks out and gets in the car, leaving Michael with Jamie. No point even trying to muster up the energy to fight with Michael and the car seat, she'll leave that up to Jamie.

Anne gives Michael a big sloppy 'nanna kiss' and tells him not to wipe it off, so he laughs as he does exactly that. She hugs him tightly telling him she loves him and she'll see him next week for his birthday party - she's coming down with Aunty Rosie and Auntie Breda. He shouts, 'Bye Nanna, love you too,' as he runs to the car laughing, with Jamie chasing after him and they all laugh at Michael's infectious giggles.

Jamie finally straps him in the car, looking at Jess and asking if she witnessed all that. She smiles and nods that she did. That's exactly the reason she left him to Jamie, she doesn't have that kind of energy right now. Jamie gets in the car and waves to his mum standing on the doorstep. Pete is standing behind her, and he can see his mum has tears in her eyes - he hopes they're tears of happiness.

He takes a long hard look at the house, he has felt quite disconnected with it these days. He's moved on and he knows it, his life has changed forever. He looks at his pregnant fiancé and his soon to be five year old son in the back. His life is a million miles away from where it was three months ago, and he couldn't be happier - he really wouldn't want it any other way.

Chapter 85

Time To Start Planning

Jamie opens his Whatsapp, clicking on the group message, 'Lads'. It used to be 'Lads night out' group, but as they've all matured, got married and had kids and so on, it was shortened to 'Lads'. He laughs when he thinks of some of the messages that have been posted on here over the past six years, good ones and sad ones, filthy ones - only where Gavin was concerned - and some soppy ones when one of them had got drunk and wanted to tell the group how much he loves them all. He laughs - yep, this group have shared some stories.

Well, he's about to shock them all. They all know about Jess and Michael, he told them after the first weekend they got back, but he's not told them that they're engaged to be married in ten weeks' time and he hasn't told them about the baby.

Jamie: [Happy New Year you miserable fuckers]

Jamie: [Pop this date in your calendar Saturday 28 March, 2026, Jamie & Jess wedding]

Jamie: [See you all in your No1s, no fucking excuses either]

He smiles - he can see everyone is typing. This is going to be a full night of messaging so thank God Jess is in bed. He goes and gets a beer from the fridge, pops his phone charger in and settles down to a night of messages.

He messages Gavin and Nobby on their personal ones, asking them both to be his best man, Gavin tells him to 'Fuck off' as he's carried him once before he's not doing it again. Jamie laughed and replied [That's a yes then Gav?] at which Gavin messaged back [Yeah mate, it's an honour].

Jamie and Nobby have a chat about 'the ring' - he tells Nobby that he hasn't given it to her, that he bought a wedding band instead, as it wasn't appropriate. Nobby understands and tells him [one day mate, you'll find the right time]. He's thrilled to be his best man and Shelley sends her love to Jess, she can't wait to see her again and meet Michael. [I'm pleased for you J, I really am].

As Jamie thanks him, he has a lump in his throat. He misses his Reg a lot, they aren't just lads in the Regiment they're his extended family.

Jamie: [Oh yeah, one other thing, we're having another baby, not sure when but she's about 7 weeks now]

Jamie: [Also, I'm away 15th Jan to 5th Feb. I'll send you Jess' number. Give it your Mrs, they can make all the arrangements with Jess]

Gav: [You don't waste any fucking time do ya, fuck me, you're worse than a pair of rabbits, you want a pair of house bricks, that'll sort ya out]

Tommo: [Nice one mate, Clem says she can't wait, roll on November I say, Married quarters R Us, just you now Gav]

Gav: [Fuck off Tommo, no way am I living in those shitty married quarters]

Tommo: [Oh yeah, cause the block's the Hilton]

Gav: [Nah, but it means I'm fucking single & it's staying that way]

Jamie laughs, he never changes, that man. He was like it at eighteen, now he's twenty-five and still the same - won't get tied down to anyone. Jamie thinks it's to do with his parents. They're rough. His mum reminds Jamie of the women back where he grew up, so he understands why Gavin is like that. He knows Gavin has a sensitive side, he's seen it and it's way nicer than the Gavin most people see. Anyway, he wouldn't change him, he loves him the way he is - his 'brother from another mother'.

Chapter 86

Appointments

Jess: [Babe I have a doctor's appointment for 11.00am, will let you know what he says xx]

Jamie: [Ok darling, you ok to drive? Xx]

Jess: [Jodie's taking me lol xx]

Jess: [Also, booked an appointment at the hotel for Wednesday, 6.00pm to meet with the wedding coordinator. Xx]

Jamie: [Cool, have they got 28th free? Xx]

Jess:[Yes, 👍😁😊😁😊]

Jess: [Can't believe we're actually getting married, I'm so excited, I love you xx]

Jamie: [Me neither, love you too xxx]

Jamie: [Sorry, got to go, let me know what doc says, love you xxx]

Jess has been practically bed bound since New Year - she can't stop being sick and if she's not sick then she's nauseous with a banging headache that knocks her off her feet. Jodie popped around to see her on Sunday and she was asleep in bed, so Jess went over to Jodie's to see her after the school run.

Jamie had to be in by 0800hrs this morning, his first day back of the New Year otherwise he would have taken Michael to school. He's told Ben about the wedding and the baby, told him Jess is ill with it.

'Oh mate, Becky was like that for the first few months, it's awful. I was up here and she was down there at her mum's, every time I called her she was either crying, spewing or asleep,' Ben shares with an expression of horror.

Jamie laughs, he can imagine how hard it was for them both, Becky more than five hours away with that pregnancy. There's no way he'd leave Jess and go and work on a base more than five hours away, if it meant him paying a fortune to private rent he would, as long as he has Jess and Michael with him, nothing else matters.

'This fucking exercise next week - the lads are giving me grief, telling me it's over in Europe, in some shitty snowy mountains. Didn't you say it was here?' Ben asks.

'It is, who the fuck told them that? Knobheads the lot of them,' Jamie laughs.

Jamie walks off to see the Sarge. He needs to make sure it's here for definite and also that he'll be back by 10 Feb at the latest, or his mum will kill him if he misses her wedding. He also needs to put in for some time off for his own wedding.

Jamie: [Fuck babe, might be a problem getting back in time for mum's wedding]

Jamie: [Ours is booked off, Wednesday 25th March to Wednesday April 1st xx]

Jamie: [Ha, just realised that's April fool's day 😄😄xx]

Jess: [What's going on? Your mum will freak xx]

Jess: [Doctor signed me off for 2 weeks, I have midwife tomorrow at 2pm, can you come? Xx]

Jamie: [I think I got all me dates mixed up, well someone has, we might be in Europe for 4 weeks xx]

Jamie: [Good, I'll see what I can do, probs yeah xx]

Jamie: [Oh it's ok we're back 12th Feb, thank fuck, see you at home, love you xx]

Chapter 87

Wedding Talk

Jess is chatting to Jodie about the wedding, telling her that they've booked the date – well, Jamie has at work for Saturday 28 March, now they just need to book the venue and then go shopping. Jodie is excited for her and Michael, but sad as she knows she's going to lose her best friend by the end of the year.

'Jode, I need to ask you something,' Jess says, suddenly becoming even more serious than she has been for the last half hour of her visit with the never ending nausea.

'What mate?' Jodie says, expecting some life altering news or a secret favour to be done that goes against all her morals.

'Will you be my Maid of Honour?'

'Of course,' Jodie says with a big smile of relief, 'It'll be an honour, are you sure?'

'What? Of course why wouldn't I be sure?'

'No idea, but I'm thrilled! Do you want me to come dress shopping with you?'

'Let me go with my mum and Hazel first as promised, then I'll take you and show you, is that ok?'

'Mate, it's more than ok, have you thought of a colour scheme?'

'I can't think of anything at the moment other than this sickness, Ugggh! I did think about red, it will go nice with their Number Ones.'

Jodie smiles, she had red, she tells Jess this. It would compliment their Number Ones beautifully with white bouquets, red for the bride. She asks what Michael is going to wear and Jess tells her a suit the same as her dad, possibly grey - they'll go shopping in a couple weeks.

'Have you sorted your cake, or flowers or photographer out yet?' Jodie asks Jess.

'Mate, I've only just about got up today, I know I need to, I'll start phoning round tomorrow. I've only got ten or so weeks. Fuck! It's gonna fly.'

Jodie is nodding and agrees with her that with Jamie away, she'll have to do it all, just as she had to do the same when Martin was away loads, but she'll help if she wants her to. Jess hugs her and thanks her.

'I'm gonna go home now, I haven't even tidied from breakfast. I'll text you tomorrow let you know how the midwife goes.'

Jodie hugs her and tells her to give Michael a kiss and cuddle from Aunty Jodie.

Jess drives home and upon realising the enormity of planning a wedding in only ten weeks, she starts to panic. She feels so ill all the time, how can she possibly plan a wedding when she feels like this? She has no choice, she'll have to call her mum - she's the best at planning stuff, she'll know what to do.

As much as Jess wanted to plan her wedding on her own, she knew the reality of it was she'd need her mum's help and assistance. She doesn't need her mum to pay for anything - not this time, this time it's going to be small and simple affair, no more than forty, possibly fifty in the day and the evening party is at the sports and social club in the village, so that's easy, she can do that one.

She calls into the club on her way back from Jodie's, *no time like the present* she says to herself.

The gaffer is there, she doesn't know his name but knows him enough to speak to about the wedding idea. He is thrilled that they want to hold the evening reception in the club, he tells her he'll put a package together - DJ and finger buffet for 100 people - he's penciled it in the diary, and will call her Wednesday or Thursday with a price.

Jess walks out feeling rather pleased with herself, she may be feeling like shit but at least she's sorted the evening event out, that's one less thing to worry about.

Getting home she downloads an app on her phone called, 'wedding planner' it's apparently everything a bride could want. It gives her tips, a countdown of what she needs to do and when and a finance page, where she can keep track of what they're spending and if they need to, they can cut costs.

It's perfect! She thinks to herself. Now time to clean up from breakfast, another hour and Michael will be finished school. *Where has today gone?* Before she knows it she'll be a married woman, a pregnant one but a very happily married woman nonetheless.

Chapter 88

A Busy Week

Jess has had what feels like the busiest week ever and with her morning sickness in full swing, most days she's just wanted to lie down and sleep. Fortunately by doing so, when mid-afternoon comes she is feeling almost human again. She attended her first midwife's appointment on Tuesday on her own as well, as Jamie couldn't get out of work.

She's been booked in for her twelve week scan on 6 February, which is a shame as Jamie will still be away, so she'll send him a copy on Whatsapp. The midwife gave her a due date of 8 August, this confirmed her suspicion that she caught the very first weekend he showed up.

Jamie has recently spoken about getting 'the snip' - it's not that he doesn't want any more children, he is thinking about Jess. His job takes him away from the family, whether it's for a few days, weeks or sometimes months, and he doesn't think it's fair on her, being left to raise the kids on her own. When he's home of course it's different, he helps out, does his bit. Jess has told him that "he more or less takes over" he's such a 'hands on' dad with Michael now, and is sure to be the same with this one, but Jamie feels that two is enough, and he doesn't want to see Jess suffering the way she does with morning sickness.

Jess is unsure about his decision, so she's going to look into having the contraceptive pill again. It's not that she wants any more herself, after all she'll be forty-three in September, but if they do change their minds and want another one she wants it to be before she is forty-five. She's told Jamie that having the snip is a good idea, but leave it a year just in case. She'll go on the pill and then if he still feels like he does today then he can get the snip.

She's updated the calendar with all the new dates: midwife 3 Feb @2.00pm, 12 week scan 6 Feb @10.30am, midwife 3 March @2.30pm, 20 week scan 3rd April @9.30am, baby due date 8 August (time tbc) she smirked when she wrote that in, if it's anything like Michael it will be on time and in the middle of night, they always seem to want to make an appearance during the night, something that's often talked about at the coffee mornings. She laughs to herself. *Hmm, I know someone else who also likes to cum in the middle of the night, I guess he's just getting me prepared for night feeds* she thinks, with a grin.

Jess starts to think about how horny Jamie's been since he found out that she's pregnant. He told her over the weekend "babe I'm not gonna lie, there's something really sexy about making love to a pregnant woman" though she doesn't feel very sexy, especially as most days she has her face down the toilet being sick, but even that doesn't put him off. If he's home he'll follow her and pull her hair back from her face and gently rub her back.

Jess has had that conversation with Jodie about how tactile Jamie is and that he was the same with her last pregnancy, with Michael, when the sickness started more or less straight away. How they didn't see the signs is beyond her. Jodie just said that he was "weird - what person wants to stand behind someone who's throwing up and be all lovey dovey?" Jess remembers laughing and saying "he's not being lovey dovey, he's just showing he cares" but Jodie was having none of it. "Nope, he's weird. When I was like that Mart would shout 'Make sure you clean that toilet when you've finished, I ain't going for a piss and seeing the remnants of your breakfast'" and they both laughed, as Jess thought *Yeah that's Martin all over, keeping it real*.

She flicks through the calendar, and lingers over their moving out date - 26 October. She's decided to sell the house, they've talked about it – it's pointless holding onto it, they'll never come back here again only to stay with Hazel and Fred. She definitely doesn't want the hassle of tenants, worrying endlessly over thought such as 'what if they don't pay?' or 'what happens when they trash it, who pays for the repairs' and then other ongoing issue that could arise like 'what if the boiler breaks down, how much will that cost to repair?'

No, she's taking a leaf out of Jamie's book and selling up. He's given Jess' number to the Estate Agent who's dealing with his house sale in case of any emergency, as he'll be out of the country for four weeks and unable to discuss anything with him, so told him he'll be best to talk to Jess. "Besides you're better at dealing with the likes of them" he told her, though she's not sure what 'the likes of them' are. Having thought over her own experience with estate agents she agrees that they do seem to be a breed unto themselves, a bit like car salesmen really, with the 'gift of the gab'.

Chapter 89

Last Minute Birthday Shopping

'Bloody hell babe, it's Friday already, where's this week gone?' Jamie walks into the bedroom with his towel around his waist, having been for a short run today - instead of leaving at 0600hrs he left at 0645hrs and back home exactly one hour later.

He woke up at his usual time of 0520hrs with a rock hard cock and decided he wasn't going to waste it, though he was too horny to knock one off himself.

'It's been a busy one, I think it's going to get busier with you going away next week.'

'I know, sorry, I really fucked up there. It didn't go down too well with everyone in work either,' Jamie says, with genuine regret showing on his face.

'Babe it's fine, these things happen. Has it caused any problems in work?'

'Nah, it's all sorted, I would've seen it in the end, going through the checklist, I think "passport" would have been a big give away,' he shakes his head and laughs to himself.

'Are yer feeling ok? I can drop Michael in, so yer can go back to sleep for a few hours.'

'I might, if I don't move I'm ok,' Jess laughs.

Jamie kneels by the bed and kisses her, pushing her hair off her face as he says, 'Any chance of a quick blow job, yer don't have to move, just open yer mouth,' and before he can finish his sentence she hurls a pillow at him, both laughing as he falls to the side.

'You're insatiable,' she scolds him, with a smile.

'Babe I'm telling yer, I'm knocking one off in work every day as well. You being pregnant has me fucking horny as hell.'

'What are you going to do when you go away next week?'

'I told Ben I'm bunking with him,' Jamie jokes and they both burst out laughing.

Jess has read about the effects a pregnant woman sometimes has on men, that they find them sexy, it ramps up their testosterone levels. Not that Jamie needs it, she swears if Michael wasn't around they'd be having sex four or five times day, maybe even more.

He woke her up this morning, nibbling her ear and playing with her clitoris, his hard cock pressed against her back and by the time she started feeling properly awake, she could feel her juices flowing, then heard "good morning beautiful".

She opened her eyes to look at the clock showing an ungodly time of 5.25am. 'I take it you aren't going for a run? she'd said.

'I will after,' he smirked as he kissed her ear, and she moved slightly so he could reach her clitoris easier, loving the feel of his fingers rubbing her juices between her lips.

As Jamie moved over so Jess could lie flat, he rubbed her juices into her nipples and they were erect already. 'Hmm, someone's horny,' he'd said as he smirked.

'Might be something to do with you playing with my clit before I'm even awake,' she told him.

He began to lick and suck her nipples, tasting her juices second hand, his finger dipping inside her wet pussy, then taking it out and sucking on it, 'Hmm tastes good,' then he moved down placing his head in between her legs and licking her sweet pussy, slowly running his tongue upwards towards her clit, 'Oh babe, you taste amazing.'

Loving the feeling of his tongue inside her pussy as he sucked and drank her juices, she began to moan, his hair touching the sides of her inner thighs and his face pressed against her vagina with his tongue deep inside her wet pussy, 'It really is the best feeling in the world,' she said out loud, between moans of pleasure.

'Rub my clitoris babe, I'm ready to cum.'

Jamie wet the tip of his finger with the juices from deep inside her vagina and rubbed her clit, hearing she was about to cum. His tongue was still deep inside her, tasting her juices as he felt her legs tighten around his head and he drank her juices as she came all over his face.

Moving into a kneeling position he pulled her closer to him, lifting her legs and resting them on his shoulders. He pushed his hard cock into her wet pussy and heard her moan as he thrust it in, 'I'm fucking hard this morning babe.'

His cock was throbbing and he thrust it in hard as she let out a loud moan. He could feel her juices all over his hard cock and her loud moans excited him. The louder she moaned the harder and faster he thrust, deep inside her wet pussy, he could feel he was going to cum soon, so he told her this and held her legs tight with his strong arms with his hard cock in deep. She screamed with her own release of ecstasy as he grunted, his cock exploding, releasing his spunk deep inside her pussy, mixing with her juices, he held tight on to her legs as his body shuddered and his brain released a cocktail of feel good chemicals with his climax.

Chapter 90

Birthday Weekend

Sean and David arrived Saturday afternoon. Hazel kindly offered to put them up, and they accepted. The thought of sharing Michael's single bed was probably not as appealing as a double bed at Hazel's house.

Saturday afternoon was a lively one, spent at the sports and social club. The Gaffer was so chuffed that Jess and Jamie chose to hold the evening reception there, he'd provided Jess with a very good quote, on Thursday as promised. He offered the room free of charge, with the DJ charging £350.00 and the food for £10.50 per head, based on catering for eighty people, so Jess was pleased with the quote and agreed to drop a 50% deposit off on Monday.

The atmosphere was lively with the lads from the base in the club. News of the engagement and wedding had spread and everyone was in a celebratory mood which meant that the shots were flowing and by the time they got home Saturday evening, it was a couple of hours past Michael's bed time, Jamie was pissed and Sean, David, Hazel and Fred were no better.

Everyone was hungry so Jamie decided to order a takeaway. A lesson now learned from this eventful day is don't let Jamie order take away when he's pissed, he'd ordered enough food to feed the 5,000. *Never mind*, Jess thinks to herself, *he's going to have to sort that out tomorrow*, because even with a hangover she knows he'll be in better shape than she will with her ongoing morning sickness.

She listens as he's telling Sean about the fuck up he'd made with the exercise coming up, that he'll be back only two days before the wedding and unfortunately he's missing Jess' twelve week scan. Sean tells him about a similar incident he had last year, fortunately like this one for Jamie, it was picked up before it was too late.

David asks if she wants him to come up for a few days and he'll go with her for her twelve week scan. Jess is very grateful for the offer but assures him that it's fine, her mum or Hazel will go with her, Hazel was with her at her scan appointments when she was pregnant with Michael.

Jamie didn't know this. Jess doesn't really talk about her pregnancy with Michael, he understands now why Hazel is so close to Jess and Michael. He leans in to Hazel and thanks her, telling her he might be drunk but he means it, he always knew she and Fred would look after Jess.

Hazel doesn't say anything, just nods. After all, they're her special little family and she will miss them desperately when they move, but all she's ever wanted was for Michael to see his daddy and for Jess to be happy again. She was secretly thrilled to bits when Jamie returned, she knew in her heart that he'd come back for her. The wait was a little longer than she had expected, but in her book, it's 'better late than never'.

The subject of conversation moves on to the wedding. David has offered to do Jess' hair, which she's happily accepted, so he's going to have a play around with it tomorrow for Michael's birthday party. He knows that she wants it semi-up and curly and instead of flowers, David has suggested diamante clips with a bit of gypsy rose feeding through the curls.

Sean asks Jamie if he's wearing his Number One uniform, and he nods, they all are, 'If you want to wear yours, do so but I am getting changed in the evening,' he tells him. 'We've reserved twelve rooms at the hotel for the weekend, so before we leave I'm getting changed.' Sean agrees with him, seeing only one problem, and asks him, 'How are you going to transport the cake from the daytime reception to the evening one?'

Jess butts in at this point, having overheard the tail-end of their conversation, 'I've already discussed this with the girl who's making it, we'll have photos with it before the wedding breakfast starts, then she's going to take it to the social club and set it up for the evening reception.'

Jess takes Michael up to bed, he's so excited for his party tomorrow. His Nanny Anne is coming down and nanny and granddad will be coming too. He's invited ten school friends, eight boys and two girls. Jess asks him if one of them is his girlfriend. ' Yuk,' he says as he shakes his head, and Jess laughs and kisses him good night, telling him Daddy will be up soon to see him. She laughs to herself as she says this, as knowing how drunk he is, Michael will be asleep by the time Jamie gets upstairs.

Jess heads up to bed just after ten, leaving Jamie downstairs with Sean, David, Hazel and Fred. They weren't making much sense, especially since Jamie and Sean nipped out to the local store and bought a crate of Bud – so Jess decided that at times like this, you retreat and say 'goodnight' leaving them all to enjoy their drunken conversation, after all they're the only ones who understand each other.

Chapter 91

Morning Sickness

Michael wakes up just before seven, full of the joys of spring, inevitably excited that his birthday party is today. Jamie is, very unusually, still asleep which she can only think is because he's had a late one, he never sleeps in - not that seven in the morning could be considered a lie-in for any normal human being, only for Jamie.

She moves away from his clutches, she doesn't know how she sleeps with him, he is literally wrapped around her, but she doesn't mind - it's when he goes away next week she'll struggle, she'll definitely be wearing pyjamas to bed again so as not to feel the cold.

As she gets up and tells Michael to go and get his slippers and dressing gown on, she can smell the food from last night - it's started to turn her stomach already. "Oh God," is all she manages as she legs it into the bathroom, closing the door behind her. She doesn't want Michael seeing her being sick.

She feels sorry for herself this morning and can't help crying, amid quiet utterances of, 'Why am I suffering like this?' and, 'Why me?'

The door opens and she tries to push it shut, but hears Jamie saying, 'It's me babe,' so she lets him in and he bends down and snuggles her. She feels like she just can't bear this anymore, she's had enough. It's her son's birthday party today and she doesn't want to ruin it, she wants to feel well.

Jamie cuddles her tenderly, feeling guilty for getting drunk last night, after all he knows how bad she is in the morning. He holds her tight as she sobs, 'I've so had enough of feeling like this all the time,' and he reassures her it will get better – it's early days. She shakes her head and says, 'I just want to be glowing like other pregnant women do.'

He has to work hard to suppress a laugh of disbelief at this, not to upset her, and he tells her, 'You are glowing babe, you look amazing,' but she tells him that she doesn't feel it so he kisses her and tells her how much he loves her.

He hears Michael chatting downstairs and stops for a moment then remembers that Sean and David stayed last night. Hazel and Fred left around midnight and he thinks he came up around 0400hrs. *Better get a towel around me then*, he thinks incase Sean or David come upstairs - *I wouldn't want to put my kid brother to shame* and he laughs to himself.

Jess manages to get out of the bathroom and heads straight back to bed, she feels like she's about to faint. She needs to eat, as she hasn't been able to eat anything solid for a few days but hasn't told Jamie. This is exactly how she was with Michael - it's no wonder he was only 5lb 9oz. She feels terribly guilty about this and cries with the guilt of not eating and causing Michael to be born at that weight.

Jamie listens to her crying and it tears at his heart. He remembers Ben saying that Becky would cry a lot "it's hormones mate"- he's not kidding. He hears a faint knock on the door and his brother saying, 'Jay, I've brought you a cuppa up,' so he tells him to come in.

'Cheers mate,' Jamie thanks him and Sean says that he'll make Michael some breakfast, so Jamie can stay with Jess for a bit.

'David is a bit worse for wear, he can't keep up with us squaddies,' Sean says and they both laugh.

'I'll come down in a bit,' Jamie tells him, grateful for his brother's thoughtfulness.

'Go down now babe, I'll be fine,' Jess murmurs from somewhere under the covers.

'It's ok Sean and David are downstairs, I'll have my drink with yer and go down in a bit.'

Sean leaves the room, telling him not to worry about Michael, 'He's fine. If I can look after a bunch of sixteen to twenty year olds, how hard can a five year old be?'

Jamie laughs, 'Don't get me fucking started, give me a bunch of sixteen year olds any day,' and Sean and Jess laugh too as Sean shuts the bedroom door.

'Babe, I'm worried about you being on yer own for the next four weeks, can yer mum come and stay?'

'No, I'll be fine, I'll get him to school and come home to bed if I have too. Fred will collect him if I can't.'

'But it's the mornings yer at yer worst, that's what worries me.'

'Babe, I'll be fine, it should start passing soon,' Jess says, with more conviction than she believes.

'You've got loads to deal with though, with the wedding and what not. Do you want me to see if your mum will sort it?'

Jess shakes her head, but tells him if it gets too much she'll let her take over. Jamie snuggles into her and tells her, 'It's not eight clock yet, try and get another hour, yer might feel better.'

He gets up and puts his dressing gown on, he doesn't usually wear it as it makes him feel too hot, but the house feels cold today - either that or its the effects of the alcohol. He chuckles to himself as he walks downstairs, he really enjoyed yesterday and last night. He's enjoyed spending time with his kid brother and new(ish) brother-in-law - he definitely needs to make more of an effort with Sean and David, and decides he will do that from now on.

Chapter 92

Michael's Birthday Party

Jess managed to get up just after eleven. Sean and David had left by then as their stuff was at Hazel's so they went there to get ready. Jamie cleaned all the food away from the previous night and put the empty beer bottles in the recycle bin, so the house very swiftly looked tidy again for his mum and sisters who were due to arrive at noon.

'Michael, I need to get you showered and dressed, so come upstairs with me,' Jamie holds out his hand and listens to Michael's excited chit-chat about his friends and his Nanny Anne coming to see him. Jamie smiles, happy that his son can talk for England and is full of confidence, *he definitely gets that from me* he thinks.

Jess is sitting on the sofa, looking very pale. Jamie asks her if she needs a drink or anything before he goes and showers Michael but she shakes her head and smiles at him. The truth is, if she tries to drink anything at the moment it will send her back to the bathroom she's certain, so she'll wait until later.

Michael comes downstairs after his shower, dressed in his new jeans, trainers, polo top and sweat jacket that Jess had ordered online in the week for today. She can't help thinking how grown up he looks already and so much like Jamie. Seeing the two of them together still makes her heart melt.

She hears the knock at the front door and gets up to answer it, a little unsteady on her feet from feeling so weak. She opens it to see Anne, Rosie, Breda and little

Archie greet her and begin to enter. Anne leans in and hugs her, saying, 'Oh Jess honey, you look so poorly,' and that's all Jess needs to hear, to set her off crying again. Between sobs, she shares with Anne just how fed up she is of feeling so ill all the time - she can't eat and she can't stop being sick and all she wants is to glow like Rosie does.

'It'll pass darling, it's early days.'

'I'm eight weeks Anne, how much longer will it go on for?'

Rosie tells her she was like it up to ten weeks, but it will get easier, she's just got to give it time.

Michael is excited running around with Archie following after him. Jamie shouts from upstairs that he'll be down soon, he's just got out the shower. Breda shouts up to him that she'll make a cup of tea for everyone as she's parched and then asks him, 'Where's Sean and David?'

Jess tells her that they're round at Hazel's place and they were here until around nine but as their things are there they needed to go and get ready. 'They're all coming here for mid-day,' she tells them, 'and I'm going to try and get ready now too.'

Anne tells her, 'Not to worry, just put something comfy on Jess,' to which she nods - that's exactly what she plans to do.

Breda is chatting to Michael in the kitchen as she's making all the cups of tea, telling him what a handsome nephew he is, and how grown up he looks in his new clothes. She asks him if he's looking forward to his party, and jumping around the kitchen he shouts, 'Yesss! Yesss!' and Breda can't help laughing at him.

'Mum, he gets more like Jamie every day, I remember Jamie being five, it's like talking to him all over again.'

'I know, I was watching him then, running around with Archie, that's exactly what Jamie and Sean used to do,' Anne smiles broadly, as she thinks of her two youngest sons when they were little.

Jamie comes downstairs and Anne looks at him. 'Ooh Son, you're so handsome,' she says and he laughs.

'Thanks mum.' He gives her a kiss on the cheek and asks her how the wedding plans are coming along. She tells him they're fine, she's found a dress and everything is booked and paid for. She's also booked the family room he asked for, that he's to pay for it when he checks in and he nods and says, 'That's fine.'

Sean and David arrive, greeted warmly by Jamie. Anne is so pleased to see her youngest son making the effort to reconnect with his older brother. They were so close when they were younger, she wonders what could have caused them to drift apart, or is that in her imagination? Maybe they're just so busy with their Army careers they haven't drifted at all and they're just doing their own thing. She even wonders if it has something to do with Jess and Michael - either way, she's pleased to see them getting closer again.

Sean was always fond of Jess - he never really took to Tara. He used to say she was too spoilt and that "Jamie's too good for her, he'll come to his senses one day mum". Anne smiles to herself, Sean always knew Jamie would come back to Jess. She would agree with Sean when he said "He's too mature for a younger woman". Jamie's always had an old head on young shoulders, she knew as a mother. Her instincts always knew he'd settle for an older woman, which is why it was no surprise to her when he brought Jess home six years ago - she was exactly the kind of woman she'd envisioned her son being with.

Jess comes down, having managed to shower and put some jeans and a top on. She tried to put some makeup on but didn't have the energy. Jamie kisses her on the lips and tells her she looks beautiful. She rolls her eyes in disbelief - she definitely doesn't feel beautiful. Jamie on the other hand looks exceptional and smells gorgeous and she tells him so and asks him if he's putting his new jacket on. He nods as he kisses her again and tells her they need to get going.

They arrive at the soft play area for 12.45pm. The party isn't due to start until one o'clock but some of the kids from school are already there. Michael goes into full on 'show off' mode, and his friends join in. Sean laughs and says to Jamie, 'You're right, sixteen to twenty year olds are a much safer bet.'

They both laugh and nod, as Jamie says, 'They sure are.'

Chapter 93

Going Away

Jamie is packing his Bergan for the off tomorrow, he's made Jess stay in bed all day. 'She's definitely gotten worse since the weekend,' he tells his mum on the phone. She's phoned every day to check on her since the party. Anne doesn't want to worry Jamie but she's definitely worried about her, so much so, she's booked a week off work and is coming to stay. Pete is driving her down on Saturday and will pick her up again the following weekend.

Jamie is relieved. If she's no better by the time his mum leaves the following week, then her own mum will come and stay. Barbara did offer to come now but Jamie had already asked his mum at the birthday party. He's also arranged for Jodie to come and collect Michael in the morning on Thursday and Friday to drop him to school and collect him, and if she thinks Jess is no better or getting worse she's to call the doctor for another visit.

Jamie took her to the doctors on Monday. He took an hour out of work and managed to get Jess an emergency appointment. Her doctor told him that it is common for women to suffer morning sickness in the first twelve weeks, but if Jess isn't eating or drinking she could become dehydrated, so he's to keep an eye on what she eats and drinks, even if it's only a little sip here and there, it still helps.

Her doctor knows Jess well and remembers how bad she was with morning sickness in her first pregnancy. He told Jamie this and tried to reassure him that it will pass, though it didn't really do much to reassure Jamie, he thinks it was just 'lip service'. The only thing he did manage to please Jamie with was sign her off work for another two weeks.

Jamie has given Barbara the wedding to organise, they spoke about it on Sunday at the party. He doesn't want any more pressure on Jess, so felt this was the best option. Once Jess is well and on her feet again she can sort out what's left, but until then Barbara can manage it. Jess finally agreed on Monday when they came to see Michael for his birthday.

He smiles as he thinks of how well Michael's birthday party went - his son was so happy, running around with all his friends. His dinosaur birthday cake was amazing, Jess had ordered it off the girl who is also doing their wedding cake - if his birthday cake was that good he can't wait to see the wedding cake. Jess has described it to him, but it just sounded like three different size sponges, a chocolate flavoured one, a lemon one and a traditional Victoria sponge, all with white icing and red flowers. He's sure "it will look lovely" as he told Jess.

He can't believe he's going away tomorrow, he's going to miss his little family. He also hasn't had sex since Saturday, but that's the last thing on his mind - he'll have plenty of time to make up for it when he's back in four weeks. Hopefully Jess will be well, he hates seeing her like this - this is exactly what she was like with Michael. He shakes his head, he still can't believe he didn't see the signs, how different life would have been for them all if he had.

Chapter 94

Best Friends

'What time did Jamie go?

'About 4.00am, I think, I know they have to be at Brize for nine and their flight takes off at eleven.'

Jodie is sitting on the bed talking to Jess, feeling terribly worried about her. So much so, that she has decided to stay over tonight and tomorrow night until Anne arrives. She'll cook Martin's dinner and leave it in the microwave and her two kids will come here from school and eat with Michael - he'll love that, he loves his two cousins, they aren't biological cousins but they're as close to him as any other biological ones would be.

Jodie has told them they can go home after they've eaten if they want. As they're both teenagers now, they more or less do their own thing anyway, but they do love 'their little man' as they commonly refer to Michael both in person and when discussing anything related to him.

'I've text him to tell him I'm staying here until Saturday when Anne arrives.'

'Oh mate, that's so nice of you but you don't have to,' Jess says, a little guilty but relived to have the company as much as the help.

'Oh yes I do. What sort of a bestie would I be leaving you like this?'

'You truly are, I'm so lucky to have you. I don't know why I suffer like this, surely it's not normal, is it?'

'Normal? Jess, is anything normal with you?' Jodie laughs.

Jess smiles weakly and says, 'Not really.'

Jodie gets up and walks into Michael's room to see if he's ready. 'Come on sunshine, it's nearly school time, shall we send Daddy a photo of how smart you look?' Michael nods, he knows his daddy has gone away again for work.

Jamie did his utmost to reassure him that he'll be back in four weeks. As good as Jess' intentions were in the early years of Michael's life, he can't help thinking that it will have lasting consequences with Michael every time he goes away with work, but that's something they both have to deal with.

Jamie: [Thanks Jode, I just wish I could have gotten out of this but I can't, I feel so guilty leaving her as she is]

Jodie: [It's fine, this is the life we chose, the wife of a soldier, you go and do your thing and I'll look after her, that's what we do]

Jodie: [<photo> Michael says he loves you and 'stay safe Daddy']

Jamie: [Aww, tell him Daddy loves him very much and yes, I will]

Jamie: [Jode, I've left a countdown calendar on his bedside cabinet, can you help him with it tonight and tomorrow? My mum will help him next week]

Jodie: [No problem]

Jodie smiles, she remembers doing the same with her two whenever Martin was away for more than a week, it is important the kids understand that Daddy is away because of the job he does but also that he will come home. The short ones aren't so bad, it's when they're gone for a month or months, she always struggled with these, she's just glad Mart doesn't go away that often any more.

Chapter 95

Hospital

Jamie: [How are you feeling babe? I miss you xx]

Jess: [I wasn't expecting a text tonight, I'm a lot better, actually eating and drinking, little but often xx]

Jamie: [Babe, that's fab, yeah, I know, I have some down time, I just needed to talk to you, well text. lol xx]

Jess: [I know, I miss you too, my mum's still here, she's said she's staying until you get home, I have my 12 week scan tomorrow xx]

Jamie: [Wow, 12 weeks already. Can't wait to get home next week xx]

Jess: [Me too, I've been in bed for most of it so I haven't noticed you've been gone lol sorry xx]

Jess is lying, she can't tell him she's actually been in hospital. Her morning sickness got so bad, her mum called an ambulance and she was on a drip for two days as she was severely dehydrated. The hospital doctor told her mum that Jess is suffering from 'hyperemesis gravidarum'. Her mum informed the doctor that Jess suffered the same during her first pregnancy and he nodded saying, "it's highly likely she will always suffer with this because it occurred during her first pregnancy, it repeats itself".

Barbara has told Jess about this information relayed to her by the doctor, which made Jess think about what Jamie said about having the snip. She now thinks it's a good idea as she can't go through this again, this was worse than her pregnancy with Michael and that was bad enough.

Jamie: [Babe, how's your mum getting on with the wedding plans? Xx]

Jess: [Ok, she's booked and paid everything, my dad has bought a new suit, Michael has the same one lol xx]

Jamie: [Fucking hell, your mum don't mess around, how much do we owe her? Xx]

Jamie: [Aww, I can't wait to see him in it, I bet he looks so grown up Xx]

Jess: [No idea about the cost, she said she'll sort it with you when you're back & yes he looks amazing xx]

Jess: [I've got a new dress for your mums wedding xx]

Jamie: [Oh good God that's next week, shit I forgot xx]

Jess: [Has it been busy? Xx]

Jamie: [Yeah, but it's been good xx]

Jess hasn't heard from him much, but that's nothing new when he goes away, sometimes he'll text and sometimes he can't. She remembers from last time, only this time she was glad of it, he would have come home if he'd have known she was in hospital. It was only for four days but what a difference they've made. Her mum still won't let her do anything though, so Jess is just lounging on the sofa eating and drinking small amounts, with fewer trips to the bathroom to be sick.

Becky's been in to see her every day, though she was sworn her to secrecy and not to tell Ben, as he would have most definitely told Jamie. It's not that she didn't want him to come home, she was just worried what affect this would have had on his secondment "besides he's only away for another two weeks" she told Becky. Becky nodded and promised she wouldn't say anything.

Jess: [Babe, I'm really tired, sorry, but I promise I'll send you a photo of the scan tomorrow xx]

Jamie: [Ok darling, I look forward to it, I love & miss you more than you could imagine, give Michael a big kiss and cuddle for me, tell him I miss him, has he been doing his calendar? Xx]

Jess gets up and goes upstairs to Michael's room, she takes a photo of his calendar and sends it to Jamie.

Jess: [He's been colouring it in each day and knows his Daddy will be home in 7 days. He's excited to see his Daddy coming home]

Jess: [Any idea what time your flight into Brize is? Xx]

Jamie: [Yeah, should land about 0900hrs, I'll be on base by 1300 hrs. My car is there, so I'll be home no later than 1500 hrs. If I'm finished before his school day finishes, I'll collect him, but will let you know once I'm back xx]

Jess: [Ok darling, speak to you soon, I love you & miss you xxx]

Chapter 96

Nosey People

Jess set the alarm for 6.30am as she's not very good first thing in the morning on the best of days. She decided that if she got up earlier she could get fully ready in time for her scan appointment without rushing. Her mum and Jodie are both going with her and she's so excited to see their baby for the first time. She's also worried, hoping that the result will show her everything is ok. With not eating or drinking very well she can't help worrying that something is wrong. Jodie tells her it's natural to feel like this, but all will be fine.

Barbara walks Michael to school. It's not raining today, so she told Michael the walk will do them good, a bit of fresh air. A few of the mums standing at the gate ask Barbara how Jess is doing. They know something is wrong because they saw an ambulance at Jess' house last week, and Jess hasn't dropped Michael or picked him up from school for three weeks now. They know that Jamie's away as they saw his mum the first week walking Michael to school and collecting him.

Barbara isn't the friendliest to people she doesn't know, and even less so to those she considers to be the nosey ones. But Jess lives here and for all she knows these could be friends of hers, although she very much doubts it, so she tells them, 'She's fine,' and walks off, putting an end to any unnecessary conversation and to Barbara having to try and be friendly to people she doesn't know.

By the time she gets back Jodie is at the house, waiting with a cup of tea and sitting with Jess on the sofa. Barbara has become very fond of Jodie, as she literally hasn't left Jess' side. She was at the hospital every day and has been round every day since Jess came home.

Jodie told Barbara that if she didn't get any better after three days she would be calling Jamie's superiors and having him brought home. Regardless of what Jess says, his place is here with his pregnant girlfriend. Barbara fully agreed with her, although if Barbara would have had her way, he'd have been back the first day she went in. But she respects Jodie and left it with her to decide if and when Jamie should know.

Jodie knows when he's back he will flip that Jess kept it quiet, but Jodie understands - she had to keep many a secret from Martin when he was away, unless it was serious like the time his dad had a heart attack and he was flown back the next day. Jodie asks Jess when she plans to tell him, and Jess replies, 'Straight away,' as Becky will no doubt tell Ben once he's back. Something Jess isn't looking forward to, as she knows the reaction she's going to get.

'How far away is the maternity hospital?' asks Barbara as she finishes her cup of tea.

'About a twenty-five minute drive,' Jess says, 'give or take.'

'Your appointment is at ten-thirty, so shall we leave about nine forty-five to be on the safe side?'

'Yeah, sounds good to me, do you fancy calling into that bridal shop you told me about on the way back?'

Jodie and Barbara smile, she's definitely feeling better. 'If you're feeling up to it darling. I thought you wanted to wait until after Anne's wedding?' Barbara asks.

'I need to start trying to get out and about, I've had enough of being cooped up Mum.'

Barbara smiles and tells Jess she'd love to.

Chapter 97

Messages From Home

Jamie turns his phone on and hears his text messages coming through. He has changed the notification tone for Jess' messages so that if he only has a few minutes he can answer hers first - he can hear she's sent him four messages today.

Jess: [<Photo>Here you go darling, picture of our baby, can't wait to meet him/her now, I love you xx]

Jess: [I've got my wedding dress, went shopping with my mum & Jodie after scan, can't wait for you to see me in it xx]

Jess: [I'm so excited, I'm going to be Mrs Willets-O'Halloran next month xx]

Jess: [I love you and miss you, can't wait to see you next week, I'm so horny xxx]

Jamie laughs at the last message and says to himself, 'Someone's definitely feeling better, and she's not the only one feeling horny,' also he wonders if she's got a 'baby belly' yet.

He looks at the scan photo again and touches it with his fingers as a tear drops onto his phone, he can't believe he's missed her first scan, *the things I sacrifice for queen and country, when most people wouldn't give her the steam off their piss* he thinks.

Jamie: [Babe, he/she is tiny lol xx]

Jamie: [I'm so sorry I missed the scan, I'll be there for your 20 week one, I promise xx]

Jamie: [I can't wait, I get to spend the rest of my life with the woman I love and have always loved xx]

Jamie: [I miss you baby, can't wait to see you next week, I'm not gonna lie, I've been so worried about you, for the first time in my army life, I nearly jacked, I wanted to come home, if it wasn't for Ben telling me you're fine, if anything was wrong Becky would have told him, I swear I'd have come home, even if it meant walking there xx]

Jamie: [So you're horny hey 😊 😏]

One things for sure, when his mum text him and told him how poorly Jess was, that even she was worried, it made up his mind, he's definitely getting the snip. He's not putting her through this again, it's too much, they'll have two beautiful healthy children anyway, they really don't need anymore.

Being away for these four weeks have been the hardest, these kind of exercises normally pass quickly as they're tiring and intense with long days, but with Jess being so ill when he left it's made it all the more challenging. He feels so detached from everything and everyone, like they're not telling him what's really going on.

He knows Jodie has been with Jess most days and that her mum is there, which gives him great comfort. Knowing she's being well looked after by those that love her and that Michael has his nan there, is a great help.

Well, he's not going to think too deeply about everything now, he's back in seven days, whatever is going on or has gone on, he will find out and deal with it then.

Chapter 98

Journey Home

It's been a 'long-arse day' for Jamie with another early start. He got up at 0300hrs, checked in by 0700hrs, took off at 0900hrs and landed in the UK at 0900hrs - the problem with different time zones is it will take a few days to adjust.

Jamie arrives back to base just after 1300 hrs and is trying to calculate the timings of the rest of the day, anxious to get home to Jess and Michael. By the time they unpack and get the equipment put away he should be finished and heading home by 1500hrs. He's not going to try to collect Michael from school, just to be on the safe side - he'll leave Barbara to collect him.

He can't wait to get home as his gut instinct tells him all is not right. He knows the baby is fine as he's seen the scan photo, but he can't work out why he's got this gut wrenching feeling that something isn't and hasn't been right.

Jamie tells Ben that he'll be glad of a few days break and Ben wholeheartedly agrees with him. This exercise was hard, and it was cold, exceptionally cold - not one he would like to go on again any time soon. Jamie nods in agreement, they just need to be dismissed now and he's out of there.

Pulling up outside the house, it's just coming up to 1530hrs. He can see Tony is here so he must have come to pick Barbara up, which must mean that he dropped her off - this worries him all the more, but he doesn't want to let it show, not in front of them, he'll wait until they've gone and he knows what's been going on.

He can hear Michael running out of the house, 'Daddy, Daddy you're home, I knew you was coming home today,' Jamie bends down and picks him up, giving him a hug and a kiss and squeezing him tight, telling him that he's missed him

'Did yer colour yer calendar in for me?' Jamie asks.

Michael nods his head vigorously with his arms wrapped around his Daddy's neck. Jess has come to the front door sporting a beaming smile. They walks towards each other and Jamie holds out his other arm so she wraps hers around him and he buries his head into her neck, letting the last four weeks of stress out - the three of them stand on the driveway, embracing each other in an emotional hug.

Barbara walks out and motions to Michael to get down and come in, she knows his Mummy and Daddy need a few minutes on their own. Jamie bends down and lets Michael go and he runs off to his nanny, who takes him by the hand and they head in doors and into the kitchen to put the kettle on, as 'Daddy's going to need a cup of tea,' she tells Michael.

Chapter 99

Stubborn Streak

Jess and Jamie walk to his car together and he gets his kit bag out, then puts his arm around her shoulders and they walk back into the house, dropping the bag in the hallway - he'll sort it once Tony and Barbara have gone.

As Jamie walks into the living room Tony stands up and shakes his hand welcoming him back home. Tony never knew what it was like to feel proud of someone before until Jamie came into their life and now he does - he's feels immensely proud that he'll be his son-in-law .

Barbara walks into the living room with cups of tea for everyone and sets them down at the table. Tony walks around the table to sit next to Barbara, Jess and Jamie sit opposite and Michael climbs on Jamie's lap, where Jamie hugs his son again and gives him a kiss on the top of his head.

Tony asks him how the four weeks exercise has been and Jamie tells him it was too cold - minus 5 degrees most nights, rising to minus one in the day. 'I could see the reasons behind the exercise but if it was up to me, I would have opted for it in July, 'he laughs.

Tony winces at the thought of those cold temperatures and tells Jamie that he remembers his days on-site, with scaffolding would be that so frozen that if you touched it without gloves you'd lose the skin off your fingers - he certainly doesn't miss it.

Jamie looks at Jess and she smiles back at him as she knows what's coming.

'So yer been signed off for another four weeks then?'

She nods, she's trying to figure out how to tell him.

'What aren't yer telling me Jess? I know something's not right, what yer hiding?' looking at her with concern, he knows easily when she's hiding something.

'I've found out why I'm constantly being sick, I have hyperemesis gravidarum.'

'What the fuck is that in English?' he says, laughing nervously.

Jess explains that it is severe morning sickness and that because she suffered with it with Michael she's prone to it with each pregnancy.

Jamie shakes his head, 'We ain't having any more after this. When did yer find out you have this unpronounceable severe sickness thing?

Jess takes a deep breath and says, 'When I was in hospital.'

A look of thunder comes across Jamie's face, 'Why the hell didn't yer tell me?' He looks at Barbara too, 'Why didn't you text me Barbara?'

Jess butts in and confesses that she wouldn't let them, she was only in there for four days, the first two being on a drip, as she was dehydrated and that there was no point in him coming home for the sake of four days.

'Jessica, there was every fucking point, what were yer thinking not telling me? Why didn't Jodie text me, I guess yer told her and Becky as well not to text me?'

Jess nods, she can see he's furious, Barbara and Tony are sitting quietly, listening. They both agree with Jamie, that Jess should have told him, he should have been with her. Tony told Barbara the day she was taken in that someone should get in touch with Jamie, even if he can't get back at least he knows, he has every right to know what's going on.

Tony can't help thinking that his daughter's stubborn streak has caused her more grief in the past than was ever necessary, her thinking she knows best all the time when the reality is she doesn't. Tony isn't surprised Jamie has gone off his head, it's exactly how he would have reacted if Barbara had ever kept a secret like that from him.

'Jess seriously, babe, I'm fucking fuming. I knew something was wrong, the whole time, yer should have told me, that's for me to decide if it's worth coming home or not.'

'I was worried about your secondment.'

'Fuck the secondment, for fuck sake,' he runs his hand through his hair, 'so you're on the sick still?'

She nods and says, 'Yes another four weeks.'

'Good, yer ain't going back. If he don't sign yer off for the rest of the pregnancy then yer hand yer notice in.'

Jess tries to butt in with some sort of protest, but he puts his hand up to her and shakes his head.

'Jess it's not up for discussion. That's it now, I mean it Jess, until this baby is born I'm not letting you out my sight,' and he grins a little through the anger at how that daft that sounded, even to himself.

Jess just smiles. She knew he was going to react like this, in fact he is being quite calm and that's because her mum and dad are sitting opposite them.

Jamie looks down and kisses Michael, turning his attention to him now. He needs to change the subject and calm down. He asks him how has school been so Michael tells him about playing 'running in the playground' and Jamie laughs and says, 'Oh, running? Just for a change hey Michael?' and they all laugh.

'Oh, my mum met the group that stand at the gate.' Jess says to Jamie, now that the conversation has turned to the school.

Jamie looks at Barbara and she rolls her eyes. He smirks, he can only imagine the reception they got from Barbara if they tried to speak to her. Michael jumps down and runs around to his Grandad. Jamie leans toward Jess, kisses her and says quietly between the two of them, 'Don't ever pull a stunt like that again, I mean it, never,' and she nods.

'I won't - next time you'll be the first to know.'

Chapter 100

First Night Home

Tony and Barbara left just after six, after they all sat for dinner together - Barbara had made a cottage pie, with roast potatoes and fresh vegetables.

Jamie received a text after dinner from Ben asking him if he was ok. Jamie text back telling him [I'm fucking fuming mate] and then shortly after [Yeah, I am now mate, thanks]. Ben replied saying he was angry with Becky, that she should have told him. [Well I guess it's not just us that keep secrets then hey mate?] Jamie nodded as he text back his agreement.

Jamie starts to sort his washing as Jess gets up to go and bath Michael, until Jamie tells her to sit back down, as he's home now so he'll sort it. She does exactly as she is told but can't help thinking *this may be a very long pregnancy*.

Jamie and Michael come downstairs after bath time to hot drinks - Jess decided that making hot drinks should not cause any problems, she herself can only manage to drink a small cup but it's better than nothing. Michael tells Jamie that Nanny Anne made him "hot chocolate with mallows in".

'Oh did she now?' Jamie says, he does love a hot chocolate with marshmallows in, so he tells Michael he'll make one on Sunday when they're back from the wedding.

'What's yer dress like babe?'

'It's really nice. Bottle green, calf length, with a front slit up to my knees,' she says with a wink.

Jamie laughs, he knows what that means, and asks her, 'With or without?'

She tells him with - she has bought a new set, white lace, she's going to wear them tomorrow then put them away for the wedding, it'll be her, 'something old'.

'So how many weeks are yer now? I'm sorry, I've lost all sense of time with being away.'

'It's fine babe, I'm thirteen weeks tomorrow, I've actually got a little bump coming now.' She stands up and unfastens her jeans to show him her flat belly.

'Where babe?' He laughs, 'How's the sickness, is it still bad?'

'Yes, but not as bad as before and I have to try and eat and drink regardless of still being sick.'

Jamie gets up and leans over her, wrapping his arms around her, 'I'm serious, I'm getting the snip, I can't see you go through this again.' Jess nods, for once she actually agrees with him.

'Right mate, let's get you up to bed.' Michael jumps down, grabbing Jamie's hand and Jess follows them as they walk upstairs. Jamie tucks Michael in, telling him what a good boy he was for colouring his calendar in. Jess gives Michael a kiss and tells him she loves him and that Daddy will be taking him to school tomorrow.

Michael smiles and says, 'Goody! Love you Mum, love you Dad, glad you're back.'

Jamie leans over, strokes his head and says, 'Me too mate.'

They leave Michael's bedroom together and on the landing Jamie pulls Jess towards him. He wraps his arms around her, 'You ain't out the woods yet Mrs, but I forgive yer for thinking yer was protecting me.' Jess smiles as she leans in and kisses him. He knows why she did it and knows she won't do it again, ever.

Chapter 101

School Run

Jamie woke to the 0730hrs alarm. On his first night home, he always sleeps well - it's a mixture of lack of sleep on the exercise and missing home. By the time he got to bed last night after finishing the sorting of his washing, he just wanted to snuggle with Jess, so he wrapped his body around hers and fell into a deep sleep, until waking to the sound of the alarm.

Jess is beginning to rouse now too but her head feels like she's had a night on the tiles. She knows she is in for a rough day by how she feels when she wakes up. She can feel Jamie kissing her and his hard cock digging in her back - she's missed this early morning wake up, despite the fuzzy head and rough feeling.

She snuggles back into him, not that she can get any closer as Jamie's already holding her tight. He doesn't want to get up but he knows he has to get Michael to school. He also has to get packed for the weekend, it's his mum's wedding tomorrow, but they're not leaving until Michael finishes school.

'How come he's still asleep?' Jamie says in surprise.

'I have no idea, but you can bet your bottom dollar he's awake by seven tomorrow morning.'

Jamie laughs and says, 'Shit, a family room, how are we going to have any sex?'

Jess laughs and tells him he'll have to wait until Sunday night once they're home, he's waited four weeks - what's another two days?

'Babe, if you need the toilet can you go now? I'm not feeling too good.'

He gives her a gently squeeze and says, 'Err, yeah, I'll go now.' He gets up and goes to the bathroom, really feeling sorry for her. Perhaps it's a good thing he didn't see her when she was pregnant with Michael, he'd never have agreed to another baby, that's why he's told her no more after this one.

'Michael, come on mate, yer got school, wake up,' Jamie calls to his son, and hears Jess going into the bathroom. He doesn't need to ask her if she's ok, as very swiftly after, he can hear her. He doesn't know how he's going to cope with another six months of this, let alone how Jess will for that matter. He's worried about the wedding as well, perhaps they should put it back from one o'clock to around four or five, give Jess the chance to get over the worst part of the day. He'll talk to her about it later, now's not the time.

'Michael, come on, I'll get yer dressed and then yer can have breakfast. Mummy's poorly so let's just get ready and leave her be' he says, helping Michael out of bed. Michael nods, he's chatting already even while still half asleep, telling Jamie that Nanna slept in Mummy's bed when Mummy wasn't there. Jamie limits his response to a nod. He's not in the mood to discuss the hospital situation this morning

Jamie goes and knocks on the toilet door. Jess doesn't answer but he walks in, finding her in a state, mid-vomit, something he's going to have to deal with. He pulls her hair back off her face and gently rubs her back. Once she's finished and feeling calmer he takes her back to bed, telling her she's to stay there for the rest of the day and that he'll sort their clothes out for the weekend.

Jess can't help thinking to herself that it would be easier if he went without her, just take Michael and she'll stay here, in bed, but she knows she can't and that it is only the way she is feeling making her think like this. Worst case scenario she stays in bed at the hotel and joins the wedding party once she's feeling up to it, whatever time in the day that will be.

'Michael, Ready Brek or Weetabix for breakfast?'

'Ready Brek, no, Weetabix, no, Ready Brek,' Michael deliberates with his head tilted to the side in concentration on the difficult choice.

'Michael, we ain't got time for this,' Jamie laughs, 'shall we have Weetabix?'

Michael nods. He opens the fridge door, wanting a cheesestring but Jamie is having none of it, he tells him, 'It's breakfast time and that's it.'

Jamie takes a cup of tea up to Jess, telling her to try a few sips, that he'll be back after the school run and kissing her on her head. He heads downstairs to Michael waiting patiently by the front door all ready to go.

Walking Michael to school he sees some of the lads who were on the exercise with him with their kids walking to school *it's always like this on returning from exercise or deployment* he thinks, *we just fit right back into normality again.*

The usual crowd were at the gate, but Jamie hasn't got time for their nonsense. As he approaches, one of them asks Jamie if Jess is ok. No one's seen her for over five weeks and rumours are rife. He looks at them and says, 'Yeah, she's great,' and walks into the playground with Michael, leaving them none the wiser.

Chapter 102

Road Trip

Jess gets in the car, trying her best to put a brave smile on and to not look like death warmed up. Most off all she is trying hard not to moan about how ill she feels or how much her head is hurting and also to stay awake for longer than a couple of hours.

Jamie has packed everything in the car and Jess simply threw on a pair of joggers and a sweater, to be comfortable. They're heading straight for the hotel as everyone is staying there tonight. Sean and David left theirs at noon, so should arrive just before Jess and Jamie. Jess is really looking forward to seeing them again, she is very fond of Sean and David.

Jamie parks up near the school gates and can't help smirking when all the heads turn to look at them both in the car. They're driving Jess' car, so it's a big give away that she is probably in it.

'Look at them! Their necks are going to break if they turned any faster,' Jamie laughs.

'They're probably wondering where I've been this past five weeks.'

'Won't they get a shock when you turn up in September with our baby?'

Jess laughs, she tells him she's going to start getting out and about as she can't continue to stay cooped up, she's going to have to learn how to cope with this morning sickness that lasts all day long.

Jamie looks at her and tells her he's not stopping her going anywhere, the fact is she can't, most of the time she's barely able to walk to the bathroom from being so weak. Jess nods, he's right - no one is stopping her going out, she just hasn't got the energy.

'How long did it last with Michael?'

'The whole pregnancy, but I wasn't this bad, nowhere near. Even Jodie and Hazel have said the same,' she sighs and Jamie leans over and kisses her.

'It'll be worth it babe when you're cuddling our baby, this will just be a distant memory.'

Jess can't think that far right now. In fact she can't even think about the next two hours - she's no idea how she's going to cope with the journey and then she's got to do it all over again.

'I'm worried about the wedding,' she says.

'I was thinking about that earlier, we should push it back to four or five, give you time.'

Jess wasn't thinking of their own wedding, she was talking about his mum's, tomorrow, but now he's mentioned it, she thinks it's a good idea too. She tells him they should go and speak to the coordinator and see if it can be put back till that time, but also, instead of having the reception at the sports club, have it there, as it's less travelling.

Jamie nods as he gets out the car, 'We'll see,' he says, 'I'll be right back.' As he walks towards the school gates, Jess watches him and the women. She watches how all their eyes' follow him, he really is a head turner - she's one lucky woman, she's not going to deny it.

Chapter 103

The Family Meal

They arrive at the hotel later than they expected as the traffic was really bad, plus Jamie had to stop at the service station as both Michael and Jess needed the toilet. Sean and David were also late arriving, as they got caught in the same traffic jam.

Anne was relieved to see them all safely together. Their table was booked for 7.30pm, and the whole family, including two of Pete's children are dining with them. His other two children aren't able to join them for the wedding as they have work commitments apparently.

Jess is sitting by Breda with Jamie opposite, trying to decide what to order to eat. Breda asks her how has she been, and Jamie butts in with, 'Oh I bet yer don't know do yer?'

Breda looks confused and says, 'Know what?' concern appearing instantly over her face.

He looks at Jess and says, 'She was in hospital whilst I was away.'

Shocked, Breda turns to Jess saying, 'What for? Why didn't you call us?'

'I didn't want to worry anyone, I certainly didn't want Jamie finding out and worrying.'

'But Jess, that's for us to decide,' Breda says, though much calmer than Jamie had been when he first heard of her hospital stay.

'Yes I know that now,' Jess laughs a little and looks down.

'So is everything ok? I mean the baby, are yer still?...'

'Oh God yeah, the baby is fine, it's me that's ill, this morning sickness, it just got out of hand. I was severely dehydrated, so I was on a drip for two days, they told me because I suffered with this with Michael it turns out I'm prone to it with every pregnancy, Not that there's going to be anymore.'

'Oh Jess, you poor thing.' She hugs Jess and looks at Jamie, winking as if to say "don't be too harsh, she's suffering enough". Jamie nods back, having understood his sisters look, showing her that he's not.

'Are yer going to be ok tomorrow, I don't want to be the bearer of bad news, but, you don't look too clever now.'

'Christ knows Breda, I'm here now, let's wait and see how I am when I wake up tomorrow.'

Jamie winks at Jess and gives her his cheeky smile. This is his "I love you and I'm horny as fuck, smile". She smirks at him as she rolls her eyes and leans forward and says, 'You're a wicked man,' and Jamie nods and laughs.

Michael comes running down the room to Jamie. He's been sat with his Nanny Anne, telling her his "Daddy is going to make hot chocolate and mallows on Sunday when they get home" and she hugs him asking if she can have one too. He excitedly tells her she can so she hugs and kisses him and he jumps down and runs to his Daddy.

'Nanny wants hot chocolate and mallows,' he tells Jamie excitedly.

Jamie laughs as he says, 'Go and tell Nanny, I'll make her one the next time she comes down.' He looks down at his mum as Michael tells her and she looks up at Jamie smiling and nods.

Looking at his mum sitting with Pete, surrounded by her family, she looks the happiest he's ever seen her. He's so relieved, for the first time in his life he knows his mum is happy and finally has someone to look after her. It's well deserved as she's worked hard and raised five kids on her own. It is definitely time that she found happiness *after all, she put her life on hold for us kids* Jamie thinks, *me especially* - something he feels quite guilty about.

Chapter 104

The Wedding (Part One)

Jamie woke at 5.30am having arranged with Sean to go for a run, just like old times. Jess wanted to get up at around eight when he got back, even though the wedding isn't going to be until 2.00pm. Jess knows she will need the morning to sort herself out.

Jamie really enjoyed his run with Sean, they managed to get a good thirteen miles in. Upon getting back to the hotel, Sean reminds Jamie that David is doing Jess' hair at 12.30pm and that Jamie can come and get ready with Sean whilst David does her hair. Jamie nods in agreement, 'Sounds like a plan.' Michael is getting ready with his mum, Breda said she'll sort him out.

Jamie walks into the room to find Michael in their bed and no Jess, but he doesn't need to ask where she is, he knows. Her plan to get up early was probably a good idea, but he knows she'll be straight back to bed as soon as she comes out of the bathroom, so he'll take a shower once she's finished.

Jamie tells Jess he's taking Michael down for breakfast, and asks her does she want anything bringing back? She shakes her head, food's the last thing she needs, she tells him she's sorry and he leans over and strokes her face as he kisses her, telling her to stop being silly. He can see she's emotional today.

Walking into the breakfast room he can see everyone has had the same idea as it is quite lively for 8.45am. He sits with his brother Joe and his partner Jacqui. She is concerned for Jess, he can see it, she looked dreadful last night after hearing she'd been in hospital and not told anyone. Jamie tells Jacqui that Jess is not good again this morning, so he'll see how she is later - worst case scenario she can miss the ceremony and join them for the wedding reception. He tells her that they're thinking of putting the time of their own wedding back to later in the afternoon, to give her chance to get sorted. Jess has assured him that she should be a lot better by then as she'll be nineteen weeks, but he's not convinced.

Rosie comes over to him and asks if Jess is ok. He shakes his head and tells her she's in bed, so Rosie gives her little brother a hug and tells him to give Jess her love as she's going for a lie down herself now, she's eight months pregnant and struggling with tiredness, so Jed has taken Archie for a swim to give her a rest.

Michael hears the word 'swimming' and asks his daddy if they can go too, but Jamie didn't pack any swim wear so tells him that he's sorry but daddy forgot to pack swim shorts so they can't. Michael puts his head down and pouts his lips in a sulk so Jamie laughs at him calling him a 'sissy la la' and Michael grunts at him. Jamie's having none of it this morning, so tells him to behave or he'll go back to the room.

Jacqui smirks and tells Jamie he seems to have a teenager on his hands already and Jamie rolls his eyes and tuts. 'I know,' he says and looks at Michael, ruffling his hair with his hand.

'Stop it,' Michael says, still sulking.

Breakfast is over and it's coming up for 10.00am so he takes Michael back to the room where they find Jess fast asleep. He doesn't want to disturb her so they go to Sean's room, where he and David are lounging on the bed. He asks them to watch Michael for a moment while he goes and gets his stuff.

Walking back into the room, Jess is stirring now so he tells her he's going to get ready with Sean and David and that his mum has said not to worry about making it to the wedding, just to take her time and hopefully she'll be well enough for the evening reception.

He tells Jess that she needs to make sure she eats and drinks something, regardless of if it makes her sick, he doesn't want her back in hospital. She nods, she has a bottle of water next to her and he can see she's been drinking it. He bends down and gives her a kiss and cuddle. He can see she's upset and he tells her, 'It's fine babe, it can't be helped,' and then assures her he'll come and check on her in a bit.

As he walks out of the room he can hear her crying and has a feeling this pregnancy is going to seem like a very long one, but he knows it'll be worth it in the end when they have a beautiful baby, a brother or sister, hopefully a little sister, for Michael.

The Wedding (Part Two)

Jamie took Michael to his mum's room for mid-day, calling into see Jess on his way back. She's sitting up in bed now after drinking a cup of tea and eating a slice of cold toast, courtesy of Jacqui who came to see her on her just after 11.00am.

Jacqui has been in touch with her friend, a midwife, as she was so worried about Jess. Her friend explained the condition and that she must try and eat and drink, little but often, no matter how much it makes her sick, so Jacqui went down to reception and asked for the toast, explaining that Jess is pregnant and missed breakfast.

He sits on the bed next to her and she tells him she's going to try and get ready, even if she doesn't wear any makeup as she wants to make it to the wedding. He smiles and kisses her, telling her he'll be back in five mins, as in that case, he's changing his previous plan and will get ready with her.

David arrives at their room for 1.00pm to do Jess' hair, so Jamie starts getting dressed in the bathroom. Jess is in her underwear and a towel at this stage, but doesn't care. She's asked David to do a 'messy bun' kind of do as she thinks it will go with her bottle-green, calf length, figure hugging, long sleeved dress with a front split to the knees. He looks at her dress hanging on the wardrobe door and smiles in agreement as he messes with her hair. By 1.30pm he's finished, so now all she has to do is get dressed.

Jamie, Jess, Sean and David walk into the ceremony room where Jamie and David go and stand at the front with Joe. Jess sits between Jacqui and David holding both their hands and smiles at them gratefully. She can feel they care so much for her and its really quite touching. She looks over to Jamie and her heart melts. He stands at the front in his Number One uniform, looking so proud and handsome, the colour accentuating his blonde hair and blue eyes. The next time she sees him in this uniform, she realises, it will be their own wedding, exactly six weeks from this day.

The registrar tells everyone to stand, and as she stands, David puts his arm around her waist holding her up. She smirks, wondering what Jamie has said to him. There's no point in challenging him about it, she hasn't got the energy.

Michael walks down the aisle carrying a pillow with the wedding rings on. He looks so grown up and Jess can't help the tears escaping when she sees him wearing his little cream waistcoat, white shirt , cream cravat and navy pinstripe trousers with his hair all neat and tidy. He's the double of his daddy and Jess is so in love with them both.

Anne enters on her own behind Sofia and Annabel, both looking so beautiful in their navy chiffon, full length dresses, both carrying cream flowers and beaming with happiness as their nanny walks behind them.

Anne is wearing a knee length straight dress and long line jacket with her hair in an up-do with tiny cream and navy flowers in it. Jess smiles as she walks by and says to David, 'She looks beautiful,' and he nods in agreement.

She watches Jamie's face beaming as his mum walks down the aisle. She knows this is all he's ever wanted for his mum, a man who loves her and will look after her. Jess couldn't be happier for both of them, Anne deserves this more than anyone she knows.

The Wedding (Part Three)

Jess couldn't believe how quick the civil ceremony was, over within thirty minutes. She hopes hers is not that quick, although she's asked Hazel and Tommo to each do a reading so that will likely drag it out a bit. She wants to savour her wedding day, she's waited long enough for it, six years, even though they were separated for five and a half years of it.

Jamie holds his hand out for Jess as he walks towards her. He's holding Michael's with his other hand and as Jess joins him, he kisses her, telling her how beautiful she looks. She smiles, thinking how sweet he is as she hasn't got an ounce of make up on and she feels like shit, but he always tells her that he loves her and that she looks beautiful.

They all make their way outside for some photos as Anne has asked for one of Jamie and Sean in their uniform as it is something she's very proud of, as are her two youngest sons to serve in the British Army. While they're having their photo taken Anne manages to have a quick word with Jess, asking her how she feels and telling her how gorgeous she looks and Jess smiles and thanks her, returning the compliment before Anne heads back for more photos.

The wedding party is small, no more than forty people, but that's exactly what Anne and Pete wanted - just family and a few close friends. Anne says at their age they don't need a big bash, it's about the people you love and who love you, and in this case it was evident for all to see.

Jess, Jamie and Michael are sitting with Breda, Steve, Joe, Jacqui, Sofia and Annabel along with two of Anne's closest work friends, Betty and Sarah and Breda is telling Jess how much better she looks today, and how amazing she looks in that dress.

On hearing this, Betty asks her if she's been unwell and Jess tells her that she's suffering with severe morning sickness, it's her second baby and it's worse this time around. Betty tells her it will pass once she's ten weeks and Jess laughs and tells her that she's thirteen weeks already. Betty's face is a picture as she says, 'Are you sure? You're so slim. I was the size of a house at three months.'

Jess laughs and tells her that she didn't show with Michael until she was nearly eight months pregnant, so it'll probably be the same with this one.

The food begins to arrive but Jess can't eat it as it's pate, so she asks if they have something else like soup. The waitress nods and brings her a bowl of tomato soup with a fresh roll instead. Jess smiles gratefully and eats as much as possible, keeping in mind that she also has roast chicken dinner to eat as well as a pudding - there's a distinct possibility that Jamie will be eating that for her, she doesn't want to over eat in case it makes her sick.

With the delicious food finished and thoroughly enjoyed, the speeches follow. Joe gives a lovely speech about their childhood and how their mum always worked hard. He tells everyone about taking his mum out for a meal when he got his first pay check and how proud he is to have Anne as his mum and finally how very pleased that Pete came into her life. 'He's a lucky fella and a brave one,' he says, looking to Jamie and Sean for agreement, with everyone laughing, then he asks all the guests to join him in toasting the 'Bride and Groom'.

The afternoon is drawing to a close and as Anne and Pete aren't having an evening reception, news of which is to Jamie's great surprise, he looks at Jess and tells her it was a good job she made it to the ceremony. She nods vigorously in agreement and great relief that she did.

Everyone has decided to head to the bar to celebrate the wedding and enjoy the rest of the evening, relaxing and chatting amongst themselves. Anne and Pete leave in a taxi at 8.00pm to begin the journey to their ten day honeymoon in Lanzarote.

Jess tells Jamie that she's really tired now so she'll take Michael up to bed, but for him to stay and have a good night with his family. She's had a lovely day and managed to last much longer than she thought she would, but now it's time to call it a day, she's got the morning to face yet, although she's only got to get from the hotel to Jamie's house, a mere four mile journey.

Chapter 105

Baby Brain

It's half term for Michael so as they're in the area they're staying over another day or two to make life easier for Jamie - plus Jamie didn't want to leave Jess home alone for a couple of days as it wouldn't be fair on her or Michael.

Jamie asks Sean if he wants anything out of the house before he leaves, his mum has taken what she wants and his other brother and sisters have had a couple of bits and pieces. Sean confirms that he doesn't want anything, telling Jamie he cleared all his stuff out over a year ago, and if there is anything else in there to just get rid of it.

Jamie needs to call the estate agent later today to tell them he's staying there until Wednesday and not to book any viewings in. That will give him the chance to sort the house out and arrange for a local charity to collect the furniture on Wednesday morning, before they head home.

Rosie has told Jamie that Jed won't be attending his wedding as he's going to stay home with Archie and the new baby. She's not particularly happy about it but Jed feels that under the circumstances it is probably best and Jamie agrees with her - he hasn't spoken to either him or Jess over the whole weekend.

Everyone is up for breakfast, some slightly worse for wear. Jamie reckons he went to bed around midnight as he didn't want to stay out too late because he knew he needed to get up with Michael. Dealing with a five year old and a hangover at the same time is not a good combination, plus he didn't get changed so he was conscious of still being in his uniform.

All checked out, it's just coming up to 11.00am and Jess is in the car, although she didn't make it down for breakfast, she managed to get up at just gone nine. Before she got in the car she said her goodbyes to Sean and David and is looking forward to seeing them next month for her own wedding.

They arrive at the house and find that the 'For Sale' sign has a 'Sold' now stuck over it which is a shock to both of them. The estate agent hasn't been in touch with either of them, not that they could have reached Jamie but he did give Jess' number to them. He'll definitely be calling them tomorrow to find out the details and to learn why they haven't been in touch. Although he's pleased, he has no idea how much was offered for it.

'Bloody estate agents,' he says as he gets out the car and hears Jess mumbling something about her mum answering her phone when she was in hospital. She tells him she'll call her mum, having vaguely remembered something now.

Jess walks in the house with Michael following and Jamie unpacks their stuff for the next couple of days. He smiles as he walks in the house, knowing that this is definitely the last time he'll ever be here in this house, the door will soon be closed on that part of his life, which is something he's looking forward to.

'Babe, my mum took the call when I was in hospital, the estate agent had received an offer for the asking price, £129,995 and I accepted it on your behalf, I'm sorry babe, I was a bit delirious.'

'It's fine babe, I'm really pleased it is sold, that was quick.'

They both nod, pleased with the situation. Jess has told Jamie of her plans to sell her house and that she doesn't want to buy anything in the village, she wants leave there with happy memories and not feel tied to it, so they've agreed they'll put all the money into long term ISAs.

Jamie has just nipped to the local store as they need some food for the next three days, when he gets a text from Jess. Parking up at the store, he checks it before he goes in, in case she needs anything.

Jess: [Babe, I've completely forgot, I have a midwife appointment on Tuesday, we'll have to head home tomorrow evening, I'm really sorry, it's my baby brain. I'd forget my head if it wasn't on my shoulders. Xxx]

'For fuck sake Jess,' he says aloud, that's his plans for sorting the house out over the next three days gone up in smoke.

Jamie: [Ok babe, xxx]

There's no point in a list, some milk, cereal and lunch stuff for tomorrow, they'll have take-away tonight now, on the plus side, they get to have some proper sex tonight. They've had a bit of a fondle over the weekend but no sex as it's not something either of them were comfortable with, not with Michael in the room.

Jamie laughs to himself as he wanders around the store thinking how true it is, kids really do nothing for your sex life, they enhance your life definitely, but not your sex life. That has to be put on the shelf from time to time, something he's learning quickly, but he wouldn't change having a family life for anything else.

Chapter 106

An Early Night

Jamie nips out later in the evening to pick up the takeaway. He actually likes the food from this Chinese, it's a shame he'll never use them again. The woman behind the counter really likes Jamie, whenever he walks in he hears, 'Aah you home, why you not call and we deliver?' he laughs, he's clearly used this take away too many times.

He orders their usual and adds chicken nuggets and chips from the English menu. She looks at him a bit strangely but he's not about to explain, only tells her that he's sold his house and is moving away for good. She makes a sad face but wishes him luck, asking him if he is still with his pretty little girlfriend.

He shakes his head, 'No we split up a while ago, before Christmas even.'

'Aah, that why she come with new man.' Jamie just laughs, he knows exactly what game Tara's playing here, she knew this is his local take away and at some point he'd call in. He can't help thinking to himself *you're pathetic Tara*.

He smiles as he says goodbye and he walks out of the shop she says, 'Stay Safe Jamie, you come back and see us in future?' He waves but thinks to himself *no, that's never gonna happen, my life is well and truly over here*.

By the time he gets home Jess has bathed Michael, all be it a little earlier than usual, and he is sitting waiting for his nuggets and chips in his dinosaur PJ's, excited to be taking them home tomorrow along with his dinosaur quilt cover that Nanny had bought him for his visits. He tells Jamie that he's going to put it on his bed straight away when he gets home. Jamie looks at Jess, 'He's going to is he? Or is that me?' She laughs and winks at him.

He didn't bother telling Jess about the conversation in the Chinese takeaway, it's pointless and irrelevant in their life, but he can't help wondering who the new boyfriend is. He might mention it to Rosie and see if she knows.

Michael went to bed a quarter of an hour earlier than normal as they'd all eaten and he'd had his bath. Jess decided she just wanted some 'alone time' with Jamie, and tells him that now she's going to have a quick shower, change into her dressing gown and just relax for the evening.

Jamie whispers to her, 'Only yer dressing gown,' and winks.

She smirks, 'That's all I've brought,' and gives him a kiss and a smile. She's feeling horny and as she's also feeling much better this evening she wants lots of sex. Although strictly no blow job as it makes her gag at the moment and she definitely can't swallow, that just sets her off being sick, but it's only for another six months or so and then they'll be back to normal, well as normal as life can be with a five year old and a new born baby.

Chapter 107

Baby Bump

Jess stands in front of the mirror, naked, seeing how much her breasts are changing, noticing how much darker her nipples are now and they definitely look fuller. She likes the shape of her boobs, she only ever imagined they'd look like this after a boob job, she laughs to herself.

She gently rubs her hands over her belly, it is definitely feeling harder and she can finally see the shape of a baby bump forming. It's not much, she has to admit, but it's there, she knows that in another couple of weeks she'll be able to feel the baby moving, a feeling that is like no other in the world.

She thinks back to when she felt Michael move for the first time, it was like little tiny butterflies in her belly, a feeling of pure love swept over her, then as the weeks progressed the movements became stronger to the point of "ouch, that kick hurt" or "your foot is in my ribs". She can't wait to start feeling this emotion again and feeling her baby move around. She knows one thing for sure - Jamie is going to be ecstatic when he can also feel their baby moving for the first time.

She puts on her dressing gown on and goes downstairs where she finds Jamie lying on the sofa. He looks tired and she realises he hasn't had any rest since arriving back on Thursday, she feels guilty that he's had to do all the driving as well as get everything ready.

Jamie sits up on the edge of the sofa as Jess walks towards him, she doesn't share with him her finding that her baby belly is starting to take shape, she wants to see if he notices it.

Jess stands between his legs and he opens her dressing gown and pins it up, pulling her towards him. He leans in to kiss her belly and then stops and looks up at her, 'Wow babe, your belly is hard, I can see a bump taking shape, it definitely wasn't like that earlier.' He smiles, feeling an emotion of pure love sweeping over him.

'No, I think it's because I'm relaxed, when I'm ill it disappears, it like sinks in really strangely.'

Jamie leans in and kisses her belly again as he starts to talk to it. 'Hey you, stop making your mummy sick, daddy needs a blow job.'

'Jamie, that's so bad, you can't say things like that, you do know it can hear you now, don't you?'

Jamie laughs. He tells her, 'She won't remember, I'll read her a bed time story when she's older about how she made you poorly and daddy had to look after you, she'll forget and forgive me,' he smiles and winks at her.

'How do you know it's a she?'

'I don't, but that's what I want and I'm sure it's going to be a girl, Michael needs a little sister.'

He stands up to kiss her, telling her how much her boobs have changed, her nipples are darker and her breasts are really full, she nods in agreement as his hands cup them, his thumb rubbing her nipples. His cock is twitching as with anticipation as he does so.

Jess moves her feet to open her legs slightly, her juices flowing, she's missed his kisses and his gentle touch. Caressing her boobs as he kisses her turns her on, she wants to feel his tongue inside her wet pussy drinking her juices as his fingers rub her clitoris making her cum.

Jess unfastens his jeans and pushes them down with his boxers, his cock is hard and she feels his smooth balls as she takes his cock in her hands.

Jamie pulls his top off and quickly takes off his jeans and boxers along with his socks. He pulls Jess into him, wrapping his arms around her. Their naked bodies entwine with each other as he kisses his pregnant fiancé, lovingly and passionately. He knows he can't be rough any more and his caring side takes over his emotions.

Jamie kisses her, loving and passionately, his tongue looking for hers, his hands caressing her boobs as his thumbs play with her nipples. He feels her hand stroking his erect cock, his kisses lingering as she wanks him slowly, he's excited, they haven't had sex for nearly six weeks.

She shuffles her feet to open her legs further, she wants to feel his fingers deep inside her, she's so horny. He smirks, he knows what she wants as his finger parts her lips, he can feel her juices seeping out of them.

He tells her to lie on the floor and he kneels down and kisses her belly all the way down to her clitoris. He pushes two fingers inside her wet pussy and hears her moan as they go in deep, he can't help worrying and tells her to tell him if he's hurting her. She nods and says she is sure that he won't, but if he does, she'll tell him.

She feels his tongue licking her clitoris with his fingers in deep, she can feel his knuckles and her pussy is tight around them. She loves this feeling of him sucking on her clitoris as he finger fucks her wet pussy, hard and deep. She can feel she's going to cum. She tells him as his fingers get faster and deeper, her moans are getting louder, gut wrenching moans as she cums all over his fingers.

Jess gets onto all fours as Jamie moves in between her legs, holding onto her outer thighs, he places his cock inside her wet pussy, hard, thick, her lips swallow it up as he pushes it in, he can feel her juices around his cock.

He slowly moves his hips back and forth, his fully erect cock sliding in and out. He's cautious not to go too deep, not wanting to hurt her. Jess can sense this and tells him it's fine he can't hurt her or the baby, no matter how deep his cock is.

She feels his cock thrust harder and faster in response. She releases a grateful moan, it definitely feels different, it feels tighter, it's exciting. She tells him, 'Go faster, go deeper,' and he thrusts harder and faster, his cock going deeper, her loud moans exciting him as he tells her, 'Louder baby, let me hear you.'

The louder Jess moans, the harder and deeper his thrusts, faster and deeper, he can feel he's going to cum, he squeezes her outer thighs as he gives one last hard deep thrust, releasing his spunk deep inside her pussy, squeezing her outer thighs as he climaxes and she feels his body shudder as she climaxes again with him.

Chapter 108

Naturally Small

Jamie wakes at his usual time, he's going for a ten mile run today. He's arranged to go with Ben, he's going to need it as yesterday was very stressful trying to sort the house out. Jess was worse than ever and Michael was bored so wanted entertaining and coupled with all this, he is trying to organise for a charity to collect the furniture from the house at a time that is convenient for his mum as they have to leave sooner than planned and she's going to have to be there for that.

The solicitor wants Jamie to go into her office within the next month to sign for the completion and he remembers taking Jess home to sort hers out. He's told her he can do a Friday afternoon and he'll book the afternoon off, drive up, sort the paperwork out and drive back home. Just that thought alone is giving him a headache but he knows once it's done it's done, finished, the door well and truly closed on his past.

He tells Ben that Jess has a midwife appointment today and he's going to take her. He's looking forward to seeing the midwife as he has some questions, mainly about the sickness and also Jess's belly - he doesn't understand why she isn't showing. He hasn't told Jess but he is worried about her size, or lack of it.

Ben tries to reassure him that from what Becky has told him some women carry naturally small babies and some are like whales, that Jess is lucky she is a small framed woman, so he can only imagine her size is something to do with that.

Ben asks him how she's been, he was shocked when Becky told him about her being in hospital. Jamie tells him she's bad, worse than he ever expected it to be, but he's just got to deal with it and look after Michael in the mealtime. Ben nods in agreement and says, 'Poor Jess.'

Jamie laughs as he says, 'Never mind poor Jess, I ain't getting a blow job as it makes her sick,' and they both laugh as Ben pulls a face, that thought is worse than Becky being sick.

By the time Jamie gets back Michael is up and eating breakfast but Jess is nowhere to be seen. He asks Michael, 'Did Mummy make yer breakfast?'

Michael nods enthusiastically and says, 'I'm going to Auntie Jodie's later.' Jamie smiles. Jess said she was going to ask if he could, so that's good, he'll be able to talk to the midwife without any distractions.

Jamie walks into the bedroom where Jess is sitting up on the bed, looking dreadful, it's breaking his heart to see her suffering like this.

'Babe, yer ok?'

'Yes.'

'What time did Michael wake yer?'

'About half six, I managed to get up and make him breakfast by half seven, he was hungry.'

'Sorry, I didn't realise he'd wake so early.'

'It's not your fault, I need to start trying to get up and moving, I can't keep lying in bed.'

'Well if you're feeling better today get up, if you aren't stay in bed, it's not a problem.'

Jamie gets undressed and tells her he's off for a shower. He looks at her and sees that she's tearful, he's not sure what's worse, the tears or the sickness, either way it's a daily occurrence.

'Hey, what's wrong?'

'I just feel guilty, you've been away and come back, you're having to do everything and I can't even get out of bed before mid-day.'

'Aww babe, it's fine, we'll get through it together.'

He leans over and kisses her, she tells him she's sorry again and he tells her to stop it, that it's just one of those things and not all women are the same in pregnancy, she's got this far and before they know it, it will be over. He tells her he's going for a shower and she is to stay there, 'If Michael needs anything tell him to wait until I'm out of the shower,' Jess nods, she can't really do anything else at the moment.

Chapter 109

Midwife Appointment

They arrive for the appointment a little early, Jess not only managed to get ready in record time when she eventually got up, but she also managed to eat some toast and have a cup of tea. She also had a very small bowl of soup before they left home, for some reason she's really enjoying tomato soup these days, since she had that bowl at the wedding. It's not something she's often eaten in the past and she laughs as she tells Jamie, 'Of all the cravings, tomato soup, it could have been chocolate or something yummy,' she rolls her eyes and he laughs at her.

They sit in the waiting room with a couple of other women, each looking very heavily pregnant to Jamie. Jess tells him she thinks the midwife must be running late, seeing that there's other women waiting. He tells her, 'It's fine, we aren't in any rush.'

The midwife eventually calls Jess in, the same midwife she had with Michael. When Jess walks in she looks at her and says, 'Oh dear, you do look poorly, has the sickness not eased off yet?'

'It's worse,' Jess says, 'I thought it would ease as I got further on in the pregnancy.'

The midwife tells her that if it hasn't eased off by now, the chances are it won't, and she strokes Jess' arm in a caring gesture, then she looks at Jamie and smiles asking him how is he coping with it. Jamie shrugs and tells her it's not easy for him but it's even worse for Jess.

She takes Jess' blood pressure, informing her that it's the best she's seen today and she wishes all her expectant mums' BP's were like this. Next Jess gets on the scales, she knows the midwife is overly nervous with Jess' weight, but to her surprise she's gained a half kilo since she was in hospital, two weeks ago. She tells Jess, 'That's good, whatever you're eating, keep eating it.'

Jess laughs and tells her, 'It's just tomato soup with a fresh bread roll,' and they both laugh.

'Well at least it's healthier than chocolate or cakes.'

Jess lies on the bed, unfastens her jeans and lifts up her top, the midwife chuckles gently as she gets her tape measure to measure Jess' baby bump saying, 'I remember when you were pregnant with Michael, you're exactly the same, but I can see a little bump forming there Jess.'

'I know, when I relax it shows, but when I'm being sick I get that sunken belly look.'

'So do you relax often?' she asks Jess.

Jess looks at Jamie and smiles. 'I don't have any choice.'

Jamie smiles at Jess and then to the midwife when she looks to him and asks, 'You're making sure she relaxes?' and he nods and tells her that he is off work this week it's half term and when he's back to work next week he'll be dropping Michael to school and has arranged with a friend to collect him. That way they won't be on their own for too long until he is home at 1700hrs. The midwife smiles and looks at Jess, who just smirks.

The midwife gets out her hand-held Doppler device and Jamie asks what it is for. The midwife tells him that it is to hear the baby's heartbeat, and his face lights up as he looks at Jess. She's smiling at him already, she knew the reaction she'd get, it was exactly how she pictured it.

Jamie sits forward on his chair listening to what sounds like white noise then all of a sudden he hears what can only be described to be like a galloping horse, 'What's that?' he asks. The midwife tells him, 'Baby's heartbeat.'

'Holy fuck! That's amazing.' He feels a gush of emotions like he's going to cry, but he holds it back, he doesn't want to come across as a twat. He's a squaddie, and squaddies don't cry.

Jess is booked in to see the midwife again in two weeks' time and she has a doctor's appointment in between to be signed off again, but the midwife tells her she's going to speak to him and see if he'll issue the certificate without seeing her.

As they leave the doctors surgery, Jamie is buzzing, he can't contain his excitement. He hugs her as he tells her he thought he was going to cry when he heard the baby's heartbeat.

'Fuck! That was amazing, did yer hear how fast it was going?'

'Yes, it is twice as fast as ours, generally.'

'Oh wow, I can't wait to see the twenty week scan.'

'Another four weeks and you'll start feeling it moving in my belly.'

'What? No way!' He's feeling emotional as they get in the car, he has no idea how he's going to cope with the scan or with feeling the baby move, these are all new emotions he's never felt before. One thing is for sure his love for Jess has just become deeper than he ever thought was possible. He never believed he could love her more, but he does. He always knew Jess was the one for him, the woman he wanted to have babies with, no one else, just Jess.

Chapter 110

Downtime

Jess has spent the week mulling around with Jamie doing just about everything for her. Since the midwife appointment and hearing their baby's heart beat he's been even more protective, he was completely blown away by it. She could see he was emotional at the time, but he kept it in.

After they got home that day, he told Jess that he is going to cook dinner from now on, he wants her to just relax and enjoy having him back home. She texted Lizzie from work asking her if she wants to pop in for a drink anytime soon, and telling her Jamie is back to work on Monday so perhaps leave it until then, but not to forget that they're bridesmaid dress hunting on Saturday.

Once Michael is bathed and in bed Jamie finally relaxes, lying next to Jess on the sofa, cuddling into her and talking about the baby, the twenty week scan and baby names. Jess says if it's a girl she'd like Elizabeth as the second name after her grandmother who died when she was pregnant with Michael.

Jamie remembers her telling him about visiting her in the home on Christmas day, she was Barbara's mum, he hugs her as he thinks of the pain she must have been in losing her Granny whilst pregnant and with no one to turn to, plus dealing with their separation. He thinks to himself *it's no wonder Jess doesn't talk about her pregnancy much.*

They've both agreed on her dad's name for a middle name if it's a boy, but Jess likes 'Toni' for a girl too, though Jamie is having none of it. He wants something 'sweet'. Jess decides she'll order a baby name book from the internet tomorrow to give them more options

They get to talking about the wedding, which is only just over five weeks away now. Jess has to go into town on Saturday with Jodie and Lizzie as they need to get their dresses for the wedding. Her mum is going to come along with the ties as Jess wants to match them up to the dresses or get as close to the same colour as possible.

They've decided to leave the wedding time as it is, Barbara has had all the invitations printed and sent out, so it's too late to change it now. Jamie tells Jess that he would like to go and see the lads before the wedding to have a kind of stag do, he's thinking of the first weekend in March. He'll go up and sign for the house, nip and see Rosie and his niece or nephew then go up to the base, stay with one of the lads, either at Nobby or Tommo's house.

Jess tells him that's a great idea, she has a feeling she'll need the break by then, she suggests taking Michael with him, dropping him off to stay with Nanny Anne and picking him up on his way back on the Sunday or she'll arrange for him to go to her mum's that weekend. He tells her they have plenty of time to think about it, but might be better if he goes to her parents.

Jess has noticed that Jamie is very gentle during sex these days. They tend to make love now rather than have sex, not that she is complaining about it, but she does love his more animalistic impulses, like when he would fuck her arse over the kitchen sink or pin her up against the stairs as he fucked her - a real turn on for both of them.

She talks to him about his gentle side, how sex really won't hurt her or the baby, but she is careful what she says as she recently read in one of her baby magazines about women who have bled after sex through being rough, so perhaps she'll leave it. She knows if she was to bleed with the way Jamie is, that would be it, sex would be off the menu until the baby is born. She is sure she couldn't cope with that.

She asks him if he wants a blow job tonight and he laughs and says, 'Fuck yeah.' That was all she needed to say and she felt his cock stand to attention almost immediately. Jess can't help laughing. Now she hopes and prays he doesn't make her gag or worse, actually sick.

She climbs off the sofa and slowly strips off in front of him, standing there completely naked as she begins to play with her nipples then moves her hand down to her clitoris - she can feel she's wet as she rubs her juices around her clit and then her nipples.

Jamie stands up and takes off his t-shirt then his shorts, revealing his erect cock, she tells him to sit back down and to stroke his cock as he watches her play with herself.

She's horny and she wants a good hard fucking, not a gentle one. She wants to feel his hard cock fucking her, she's going to take a chance.

Her finger are wet with her juices, she licks one at a time then wets them again, rubbing her clit as her juices flow more. His hard cock is throbbing, he's told her "he wants to fuck her and how fucking sexy she looks".

She steps towards him for him to suck her nipples, tasting her juices as he does so. Her fingers are wet, she can smell her own juices on them, as she caresses her nipples, with his tongue licking the juices off her fingers too.

She can hear he's turned on when he groans with pleasure as she straddles him. She places his cock inside her wet pussy and lifts her legs up and kneels on the edge of the sofa. His arms wrap around her body as she sits on his thick hard cock feeling it as it goes deeper into her wet pussy.

She moves up and down his cock, feeling it going deep, 'It's so thick,' she tells him. She can hear herself getting louder as she feels his cock going deeper. The deeper his thick hard cock goes the louder she is, she likes this feeling, sitting on his cock, feeling it going so deep in her pussy, she can feel her juices running all over his cock, she's so wet.

He holds her tight and his cock is throbbing, he tells her he's going to come soon. She can only nod as she's cumming all over his hard cock, she can feel her juices running out. Her loud moans of pleasure have Jamie so excited now.

He holds her shoulders as he thrusts his cock deeper into her, she feels him fucking her hard as she sits on his cock, she moans louder telling him, 'Fuck me, fuck me harder,' her moans and groans not yet subsided from her orgasm are loud as he thrusts hard and fast holding her tight. He grunts as his body shudders and they breathe heavily together as they climax, with Jess feeling exhilarated after the hard fucking.

She climbs off and discreetly looks to make sure there is no blood. She kisses him as she stands up and he asks, 'So what happened to my blow job?'

She winks and says, 'Tomorrow night babe.'

Chapter 111

Food Shop

It's been a good week. Jamie has been going running in the morning, taking Michael to school Holiday club and getting a couple of hours in at the gym, then by the time he gets home Jess is slightly better than when he left. She has also noticed a difference in her eating habits this week and by around lunch time she's actually starting to feel like a human being, able to get dressed and go downstairs.

Yesterday Jamie bought every brand and style of tomato soup that is available on the shelves, even the ones in the chiller, along with some fresh bread and part baked rolls - he told her it's good to have a choice and if she doesn't like some of them, he won't buy them again.

They intended to go food shopping together today, but Jess walked into the supermarket and the smell from the meat aisle was enough to set her off again, so she went and sat in the car and waited for Jamie to do the shopping alone.

While she is sitting in the car, she thinks about the sex the other night and how much she really enjoyed it. She's thinking about giving Jamie a blow job tonight, she was deadly serious about it when she said she would, she's missed feeling his thick hard cock in her mouth, her tongue licking the tip and tasting his pre cum, having him squirt his spunk all over her face.

She can't believe how horny she's feeling, her juices are flowing already just at the thought of it. She looks around to see if anyone is nearby and then moves her seat back a bit, unfastens her jeans and putting her hand down inside them, she feels for her clitoris.

With her finger wet from her juices, she rubs her clit and gets herself even hornier. She wants to feel her nipples but that will give it away if anyone walks past the car, so she lifts her hand out and licks her finger tasting her juices.

She shuffles down the seat a little and pushes her hand back down, wetting her fingers again with her juices. My God, she's horny. She starts to rub herself again, getting a little faster until she can feel she's going to cum soon. With her hips moving slightly in rhythm, she rubs her clit faster and starts to moan a little.

She discreetly feels for her nipples and caresses them through her top, she's close now, she can feel it. Still using her own wetness on her clit she rubs even faster, caressing her nipples at the same time until she feels herself cumming, her juices running out of her wet pussy soaking her thong.

She takes her fingers out, dripping wet and sticky. She can't lick them now so she looks for something in the car, finds a packet of tissues and wipes her fingers. She does her jeans back up and texts Jamie to tell him what's just happened.

Jess: [Hey, I've just made myself cum in the car waiting for you xx]

Jamie: [What? Lol xx]

Jess: [I felt really horny about giving you a BJ tonight so played with my clit, literally made myself cum xx]

Jamie: [Fucking hell, I wish I'd seen it, I'm fucking twitching thinking about it xx]

Jess: [Lol hurry up, we'll have time for a quickie at home before you get Michael xx]

Jamie: [Yeah, nearly finished I've got a semi on thinking about it already xx]

Jess watches as Jamie walks back to the car with a huge smile on his face. He opens the passenger door to kiss Jess and lifts up her hand and sucks her fingers. He is highly turned on and has a full hard on - Jess feels his swollen crotch and tells him she wants his cum all over her face .

'Fuck babe, let me get this shopping in the boot, I'm gonna fuck yer silly when we get home.'

He puts the shopping into the boot of the car, puts the trolley away and they head home with Jamie's head full of thoughts of how he's going to empty the bags in the house before he takes her and fucks her, hard and rough. His animalistic instincts are taking over.

Jess tells him she wants it hard and fast on the stairs and she wants him to fuck her arse like he has in the past. They pull up to the house where Jamie quickly unloads the car Jess goes upstairs and gets changed into her dressing gown, putting the lube in her pocket.

She walks down the stairs to where Jamie stands with his jeans and boxers pushed down to his knees and his top discarded in the living room somewhere. He wraps his arms around her as he kisses her passionately, his tongue searching for hers. She opens her dressing gown and drops it on the floor, his hands cup her breasts, caressing them as he kisses her and she wets the tip of his cock with her juices, stroking it and rubbing it with her thumb.

He turns her around and she leans over the stairs, telling him the lube is in her dressing gown pocket. He laughs as he looks for it, then rubs it all over his cock before he places his thick length just inside her arse, gently pushing it in, hearing Jess moan as he feels how tight her arse is around it.

He pushes it in deep now, it's so tight, exciting him too much. He pulls out slowly and waits a sec before slowly pushing it in again, deep. The excitement is taking over now and he starts to thrust hard and fast with Jess moaning loud. It becomes fast and deep, hard and rough and she hears Jamie telling her, 'Louder babe, I want yer screaming,' as his cock thrusts hard in her tight arse and he can feel the heat and friction on his hard thick cock.

He hears Jess' gut wrenching groans as she cums from having his cock deep inside her arse, he tells her he's going to cum too, he can't hold it back as he grips tightly on to her outer thighs as he thrusts in deep and hard, shuddering as he climaxes.

Chapter 112

Bridesmaids

Jess manages to get out for just after mid-day. Her mum arrived at 11.30am and showed Jamie the ties, telling him Tony and Michael both have a grey three-piece suit to wear on the wedding day. Jamie smiles, imagining Michael in his suit and tie - he'll look like a proper little man.

Jess has managed to get herself ready fairly easily this morning, even managing a bit of makeup - well, mascara and lip gloss. She tells her mum that they have to nip and pick Jodie up and then Lizzie is meeting them in town at the shop as she's going out after the shopping trip.

Jess gives Lizzie a big hug, having not seen her since early January. Lizzie tells her everyone is missing her at work and they all send their love and look forward to seeing her when she's back. Jess gives her some evening invites to pass out to her team and work colleagues when she sees them on Monday.

Lizzie is talking to Jodie, telling her how much she's looking forward to the wedding and that she never thought in her wildest dreams Jamie would be back, but she's so glad he is. Jodie agrees with her and tells her she always hoped he would, for both their sakes.

Jess finds a couple of possible dress styles that are high-necked chiffon material and a red colour quite close to that of the ties and passes them to the two women who nod and go off to try them on. The sales assistant then tells Jess that she can order any of the styles in red, so she tells Jodie and Lizzie, that if they don't like the dress she's picked out they can pick one of their own as long as the colour matches.

Jodie wasn't keen on the high neck, she found it irritating, so the sales assistant brought them a dress that is effectively a two-piece, with a sequined top and a chiffon bottom - they liked this idea, tried them on and decided that these were the dresses, so Jess went to order and pay for them only to find out that they take up to twelve weeks to order.

Jess is distraught, this is not what she wants to hear, so Barbara goes looking for the floor manager to see if there's any way they can be fast tracked. She comes back to the sales counter, telling the sales assistant that they can indeed be fast tracked but there will be an extra charge of sixty pounds per dress. Barbara tells the sales assistant she'll pay the fast track fee and to order the dresses, for collection in four weeks, a week before the wedding, then she looks at Jess and asks her, 'Do you think we're cutting it too fine? Should we make some kind of back-up plan?'

Jess looks at Jodie and Lizzie for their opinion. Should they look for something else or take a chance? They all agree to take a chance, worst case scenario they'll buy themselves something else if the dresses don't arrive in time, but fingers crossed they will.

Lizzie gives Jess a big hug and tells her she'll be round on Wednesday just after lunchtime, then says bye to Barbara and Jodie as they all leave town, hoping in their heart of hearts their dresses will arrive on time for their best friend's wedding to the man she's loved for as long as they've known her.

Chapter 113

Completion

Jamie's packed his car up and is only going to be in work until noon. He's pretty excited to be going back to his old base to catch up with his 'Regiment family' and celebrate his stag night tomorrow, but he is worried about leaving Jess. He tells her he's glad her mum agreed to have Michael over the weekend, so she can have as much rest as she needs. Tony is dropping him to school Monday morning and Fred will pick him up at home-time.

Jess has arranged for a few girls to pop round on Saturday evening. They're going to order a take away and have some drinks, but only pop of course for Jess. She's really looking forward to some alone time, she loves her little family so much but Jamie has been a bit stifling in all his fussing over her since his return, so a weekend away from him will be a welcome break.

Jamie called her once he was on the road, to check she was okay. Jess told him to go and enjoy himself and stop worrying about her for a weekend, she'll be fine.

He's arranged to be at the solicitor's office for 3.30pm and he's going to call in and see Rosie and his new baby nephew, who was born in the early hours of Sunday morning weighing 7lb 5oz. His mum texted him telling him they're calling him 'Harrison'. Jess ordered an outfit for him online and a card for Jamie to take up. He's sad that Jess won't get to see him, but he guesses that's just the way it is for now. He's sure it will all change once Tara gets married or at least finds someone she's happy with, Jed will start to involve himself with Jamie and Jess again

Jamie drives by the cul-de-sac to see who is there, he wants to make sure in advance that none of Jed's family have decided to visit at the same time out of spite. To his delight there are no visitors and he pulls up around the corner and walks to Rosie's.

Jed comes to the door, and politely welcomes him in, but Jamie notices Jed looking over him to see if he's alone. Jamie enters the living room to see his sister lying on the sofa snuggling her baby boy.

'Aah Rosie, he's so tiny.'

'He's cute ain't he?' Rosie says and Jamie nods and hands her the present and card, then he scans the living room looking at all her baby cards and tells her she's done well with the cards.

Jed made Jamie a cup of tea and then disappeared. Jamie asks Rosie where Archie is. She tells him he's with Tara and Jean, but he's coming home at 3.00pm, so Jamie looks at his watch and sees that it is already 1420hrs. He tells her he'll leave at 1445hrs as he has to get to the solicitors office - after all he does need to get into the town and find their office and he'd rather sit around there for half hour than risk bumping into Tara and Jean.

Jamie enjoys a little cuddle with his nephew, liking the feel of his baby warmth and that lovely new baby smell. Rosie tells him he looks much more like their side than Jed's and Jamie laughs and says, 'He just looks like a baby Rosie.'

She rolls her eyes and says, 'Typical man,' and then she asks him how Jess is and what his plans for the weekend are?

He told Rosie that Jess is pretty much the same as she was at the wedding although she's trying to get out and about more. He tells her about his weekend plans with his Regiment, having a 'Stag night' tomorrow night but it'll be nothing heavy as he has to drive home on Sunday.

Jamie's feeling nervous now, conscious of the time and Rosie notices how uncomfortable he's feeling too. She knows he doesn't want to bump into them - not because he has feelings for Tara because he hasn't, she knows he's not loved Tara for a long time, even long before they split up - he doesn't want to bump into Jean, she's the one who will give him grief, she's so bitter still.

He tells Rosie he's going to get going as he needs to be at the solicitor's office soon. He gives his sister a hug and a kiss on her cheek and tells her to give Archie one from him. The next time he sees Rosie will be at his own wedding and he's very excited about it.

Jamie arrived at the solicitors by 1510hrs and waited patiently in reception, texting Jess to make sure she's ok.

Jess: [I'm fine babe, I'm literally lying on the sofa watching telly, eating a bowl of tomato soup xx]

He laughs aloud and says, 'Bloody tomato soup.'

Jamie: [That's great babe, missing you already xx]

Jess: [Aww, I miss you too, how's Rosie & Harrison? Xx]

Jamie: [Good, he's tiny, she sends her love xx]

Jamie: [Gotta go, solicitor calling me in xx]

Twenty minutes later Jamie walks out of the solicitor's office having signed all the paperwork for the completion of his house sale. His mum arranged for a charity to collect all the unwanted furniture and anything that was left in Jamie's room she's bringing with her on the weekend of his wedding.

Jamie gets in his car and sits back in his seat, letting out a big sigh. He's finally free of the house and the life he lived back here, his life is truly on a new path, one he couldn't have envisioned as he thinks to himself *what a difference a year makes*.

Chapter 114

Stag Weekend (Part One)

Pulling up to the front gates he recognises the guards and gets out of his car to shake their hands and ask how they've been. 'Same old, same old,' they say and in turn ask him what he's doing back here. He tells them he's having a night out tomorrow night with some of the lads.

'Aah, so you need a forty-eight hour pass,' one says to him and he nods as he heads to the gate house to do just that returning ten minutes later with the job done. He waves to them both telling them he'll be on camp for a drink tomorrow if they're free to pop by and have one with him.

He pulls up outside Nobby's house, a little later than planned as he decided to have a 'drive by' of his old house, one last look. It looked empty and even though he couldn't see in the windows, he felt it. His home he shared with his mum for the past five years was now empty too. He never really thought about how he'd feel selling it, he definitely feels a little emotional about it now, but he's sure it'll pass by tomorrow *a few pints and shots should do the trick* he thinks to himself.

Nobby comes to the front door as Jamie removes his bag from the boot, walking towards him. Nobby meets him half way and they hug, they are best friends and haven't seen each other since Jamie left some six months ago.

Walking inside he hears Theo shout, 'Uncle Jamie!'

Jamie picks him up as he says to Nobby, 'Wow, he's grown.' Nobby smiles as Shelley comes down from upstairs and gives Jamie a hug and tells him she's missed him, they all have.

She asks, 'Why didn't you bring Jess and Michael to stay over?

Jamie tells Shelley about her morning sickness, how it is actually a condition she suffers with during pregnancy, and the reason he didn't bring her was she'd spend most of the weekend back and forth to the bathroom. Shelley remembers how ill Jess was when they split and tells Jamie she can't believe no one realized then what was going on. He nods his head and tells her he can't believe it either but now he knows with this one, and he grins. Shelley hugs him again telling him how happy she is that he went back to them and she can't wait to see her in three weeks but more than that, she can't wait for them to join them on the new base in November.

'Oh that's a point, Nobby have you heard where we're going?'

'Yeah, have you?'

'Yeah, Wiltshire, it's nice down there.'

Nobby and Shelley both nod but Shelley's worried it's too far from her parents. She tells Jamie it'll take around five hours to drive home to her parents or for her parents to come and visit. Jamie smiles, she knows what he's thinking as he says, 'It's the way of the Army. It's the life you chose Shelley,' and she smiles back at him - she knows.

Shelley tells Jamie she's made a lasagne for dinner tonight, that Nobby has to go and get Joshua from youth club as he goes on a Friday from five till six, then they'll all have dinner. Jamie offers to walk with Nobby as he hasn't seen Joshua since he left and he's missed his 'little mate'. Shelley tells him Joshua is excited to see his 'Uncle J' and he's looking forward to meeting Michael. Shelley has told him all about him and says, 'They'll get on well J.' Jamie nods, he knows they will.

When they get to the doors of the youth club Joshua comes running towards Jamie shouting, 'Uncle Jamie! You're back,' and Jamie bends down to greet him as he wraps his arms around him tightly. Jamie tells him he's missed him and how much he's grown.

They all walk back to the house with Joshua talking non-stop to Jamie asking him about Michael and asking "when he will be moving back to live on base with them?" Jamie tells him he will be joining up with them in November at the new base, so he'll meet Michael then.

As they walk back into the house they find that Shelley has prepared the table and started to dish the dinner up. She tells Joshua to go and wash his hands ready to eat. Jamie is starving and sits at the table, smiling and thinking to himself how many times he has done this - they really are his 'army family.'

Stag Weekend (Part Two)

Jamie and Nobby go running early Saturday morning as they both know they will be in no fit state on Sunday morning, so they decide to put a extra few miles in. Jamie tells him about the secondment and the lads, how much they remind him of them when you were all younger and not long joined up.

They both laugh at shared memories of some of the mishaps they got themselves in, the nights out and the birds they'd shagged (Jamie anyway as Nobby was already with Shelley) the lap dancing club they used to visit, 'God Nobs I think I fucked most of them,' Jamie laughs. Nobby shakes his head as he says, 'I know, you were known as the "Fuck Boy".'

Jamie looks at him with an expression that says "I have no idea what that means" so Nobby tells him, 'It's a boy who fucks all different girls and leaves them straight after, exactly what you'd do mate.' Jamie smirks, he really did, he never stayed the night, he always made sure he left straight after the sex, though he never understood why he did that.

Once they're back at the house, Jamie goes for a shower. Josh and Theo are having breakfast already and Shelley asks Jamie if he fancies anything. He tells he'll get some Weetabix when he comes down.

Nobby has arranged for everyone to meet up at The George, the pub on site, 'No later than 1900hrs for a few drinks there then we'll get a couple of taxis into town,' he tells Jamie. Jamie responds that he's happy to stay on base, then they don't have to worry about taxis and it's cheaper than the town prices, not that Jamie has to worry about money.

Shelley laughs and says, 'Well, I never thought I'd see the day Corporal Jamie O'Halloran doesn't want to go out on the lash.'

Jamie tells her that he's not been out like that in ages and he doesn't think he'd enjoy himself, then laughs with her. The truth is that Jamie isn't that person who used to love a good night out downtown, he hasn't been for a couple years now. These days he prefers the more relaxed kind of evenings than the wild ones of his past.

'He says that now Shell, wait till he's had a few shots, it'll be a different story,' says Nobby.

'Yeah true, but then again who are you trying to kid, pretending you can deal with a heavy night out?' Shelley smirks.

Jamie and Nobby laugh. They're so far removed from the "young, reckless binge-drinking squaddies" they once were. They're family men now, something neither of them would change for the world.

Jamie is full of mixed emotions. He's nervous about going out as he knows how wild and out of control it could get but then he's really looking forward to seeing his old mates. He hasn't seen "the lads" since he left in October, six months ago.

Nobby and Jamie walk into the pub at 1905hrs and it is full of all the lads from the Regiment and a few others that he knew when he lived here. Jamie is blown away to see everyone, it is rowdy already and it's only just beginning. Jamie tells Nobby that he thinks it's going to be a messy one and Nobby nods in agreement, he thinks so too.

Gavin orders a round of Jaeger Bombs and Jamie orders a round of pints to go with the shots, handing them out to everyone, he feels the old sense of 'belonging' again, he's back with his lads. He realises how much he has missed being with them, he can't wait for November when him and Jess will re-join his Regiment with Michael and their new baby.

Chapter 115

Home Alone (Part One)

Jess has been looking forward to this weekend and some alone time. Not that she would want her life any other way, she's gone from being on her own to living with Jamie and engaged to be married to him in a very short space of time after spending five and a half years on her own.

She arranged for her mum and dad to have Michael and they collected him from school today and will drop him back to school Monday morning giving Jess a complete child-free weekend, probably the last one in a very long time.

Jamie called her as soon as he left the base this morning and she could tell he was feeling guilty about leaving her but she wanted him to enjoy this weekend away with his friends in his Regiment. She knows he misses them, he's very close to a few of them and she knows he can't wait to meet back up with them in November.

They've decided not to take a holiday at the end of October as they had originally planned as the baby will be no more than three months old and they have the move straight into married quarters after his secondment to deal with at that time too.

Jess is excited about moving to Wiltshire, she's never been anywhere near that side of the country but hears that it is very beautiful and a good place for children to grow up. Though its quite possible that they won't get much chance of growing up there, as they will more than likely be on the move again in two to three years. Mind you they have discussed staying put if Jamie's post is within an hour of the new base in Wiltshire, as less disruption will help Michael and his schooling.

Jess notices now that she hasn't been as sick today, by 11.00am she was showered and dressed, not that she was intending going anywhere, she just felt well for the first time in a long time, so she made the most of it - even popping out to a little coffee shop with Jodie later in the afternoon.

When Jamie texts her late in the evening, he includes photos of Joshua and Theo and she tells him she managed to get out for a coffee this afternoon and that she thinks it's starting to ease a little, not that she wants to jinx herself but she did feel good today. She tells him she's got all her fingers crossed for a good day tomorrow.

Home Alone (Part Two)

Waking up at 8.30am on a Saturday morning is previously unheard of for Jess as Jamie is normally up and out for 6.00am to go running and Michael is always up by 7.00am, so sleeping until 8.30am and waking up on her own accord feels amazing, especially after a full twelve hours sleep. Jess can't remember the last time she slept for twelve hours, it was definitely before Michael was born, that's for sure.

She picks her phone up and straight away she can see three messages from Jamie, one from her mum and one from Jodie.

Jamie: [Morning, I'm going for a run with Nobby, you're prob still fast asleep, text me when you wake, love you xxx]

Jamie: [We're back after our 2 hour run, it's 07.35hrs, I can't believe you're still asleep, lol xxx]

Jamie: [Hey sleeping beauty, it's 08.15hrs, text me when you finally wake up, I miss you Baby xxx]

Mum: [Had a call about the bridesmaids dresses, we need to go into town on Monday, hope you're enjoying your weekend on your own. Xx]

Jodie: [Your mum has called, the dresses are in but they're the wrong ones, FFS how difficult is it to order the correct ones? Do you fancy nipping to town today and checking them out? Xx]

'Great, that's all I need now. To stress over the bloody bridesmaid's dresses,' Jess says out loud in annoyance.

Jess: [Hey, I'm awake, I slept a full 12 hours, I love & miss you too, can't wait for you to come home tomorrow 🖤 🤢]

Jess: [I'm going to try and get into town today Mum, if I don't we can try on Monday, but I really need to see what they've sent in. 😱 😢xx]

Jess: [I've just woke up Jode, haven't moved yet, so no idea how sick I'm going to be, so fed up with this now mate, I've really had enough now, but if I'm ok by lunch, yeah, I need to see what they've sent in xx]

Jamie: [Ha Babe, Glad you could join us 😄, how are you feeling, I fucking miss you, I really feel like coming home now. Xx]

Jess: [Aww, I miss you too. I haven't moved yet but I'm starting to feel queasy, stay there and enjoy yourself, I love you xx]

Jodie: [Ok, just text me once you know you're good to go, no later than 3 tho, the girls are coming at 6, it won't last forever, 🤢 xx]

Jess spends the best part of two hours to-ing and fro-ing from the bathroom, vomiting. After her third or fourth visit she is feeling very sorry for herself being home alone and is very tearful. Her memories of being alone with Michael come flooding back and with a decisive action against the discomfort of these feelings, she decides she needs to pull herself together and get out the house, no matter what it takes.

Jess: [I'm going for a shower now, can you come & get me at 1? I don't want to drive, sorry xx]

Jess finally gets in the shower just after 11.30am. She really wants to call Jamie, to hear his voice but she won't, she wants him to enjoy his time with his mates. She'll just text him later.

Jodie; [Yeah, be round at 1. Xx]

Jess: [Just out the shower mate, see you at 1 xx]

Jess: [Sorry, just out shower. Babe the bridesmaids dresses have apparently turned up already but they're wrong, so I'm going to town with Jodie to see what's going on xx]

Jess: [Hope you're having fun. Xxx]

Jamie: [Ok babe, don't stress, they're only dresses. Yeah it's good, but missing you & Michael xx]

Jess: [I know but I want it to be perfect xx]

Jamie: [It will. We will be married, that's perfect enough for me xx]

Jess nods as she reads his last message and says to herself, 'It will be babe, it certainly will be.'

Home Alone (Part Three)

Arriving in town by 1.30pm they head straight to the dress shop where Jess explains that they ordered dresses a week ago, paid a fast track fee and have received a call to say they've come in already but are not the ones they ordered.

The sales assistant looks bemused, she knows she only ordered them last week and is sure they wouldn't be in this quick. She tells Jess she'll go and find out what's going on and get to the bottom of it.

The sales assistant reappears some twenty minutes later and informs Jess that the call wasn't from them. She has also looked on the system and the order is showing with an 'in progress' status.

Jess and Jodie are confused for a moment, then Jodie remembers. 'The Bridal Shop said that your dress would be ready by the first weekend in March,' and both women's hearts miss a beat. The wrong dress is actually Jess' wedding dress. So they thank the assistant and leave, heading straight to The Bridal Shop.

Jess and Jodie sit patiently in the shop waiting nervously for the manager. The sales assistant looked very sheepish when Jess told her that the shop had called her mum. Jess looks at Jodie as the assistant walks off, both women even more nervous now.

The manager walks towards Jess with somewhat of a frown on her face, smiles as she tells Jess that she looks a lot better than when she was last here then asks how the pregnancy is progressing and is she still being sick. Jess tells her that sadly, yes, she is and she is sixteen weeks now.

'I'm sorry to hear that you are still not feeling well, but you really do look better,' says the manager, 'I'm not going to beat around the bush, your dress arrived yesterday, but it is not the one I ordered, I really don't know how it's happened.'

Jess can feel herself welling up and Jodie tells her not to get upset, to see what they've sent in first and then they'll deal with it from there. Jess tries to compose herself and nods in agreement as the manager goes off to get the dress.

'Oh God, I hope it's not a ball gown Jode, that will be my worst nightmare.'

'Mate, does it matter? You're marrying your soulmate, the man you've loved for so long. You could be in a black bag for all he cares.' Jess laughs at this image in her mind, she knows Jodie is right, Jamie wouldn't care what she wears as long as they get married.

The Manager calls them to the back of the shop where she has hung the dress up for Jess to see. To Jess' amazement it's beautiful - a figure hugging, satin and lace dress.

'It's beautiful,' Jess says, quite dazzled by it.

'It really is, Jess it will look amazing on you,' Jodie agrees.

The manager smiles with relief and informs Jess, 'This dress is called Dania - a fit and flair vintage Princess style. The straps lead into a plunging sweetheart bodice, covered in clear beads, sequins and pearl's, finished off by the satin train, which in my opinion gives it a luxurious finish.'

Jess and Jodie nod in agreement, both of them are actually speechless, sitting down just staring at this beautiful dress that has been sent in by mistake.

Jess asks the manager how much more she needs to pay for this one. The manager smiles and tells her, 'Nothing, it's our mistake, now would you like to try it on?'

Jess nods, feeling quite excited as the dress she ordered seems very plain now in comparison to this one that's arrived. She couldn't be happier when she tells Jodie, 'It's perfect.'

Chapter 116

Hangover

For the first time in a long time Jamie has woken with a full-on hangover. It's not something he normally suffers with, his tolerance to alcohol usually seems to be high which he can only put down to the fact that he's fit and maybe the amount he's consumed over the years too.

His mind wanders back to last night. It did get messy, he lost count of how many shots he had. He does remember the barman saying they'd ran out of Jaeger, but had Tequila, so the Tequila shots started. They had all given up on pints anyway by then and were just ordering shots, each round consisting of ten. He lost count how many rounds they had.

By the time they were leaving The George, Nobby was already in the toilets throwing up and Tommo was trying to tell him something about Clem but quickly gave up as he seemed to have lost the ability to talk, the rest were all pretty much the same as Jamie – legless.

He can hear Nobby spewing in the bathroom now, and Jamie doesn't feel too clever himself. Now he knows how Jess feels every day. *No wonder she needs to sleep, she's got a constant hangover* he can't imagine waking up feeling like this every day. *Poor Jess, roll on 8th August* he smiles to himself as he thinks about their baby.

Jamie needs to get up, he needs a pint of water and a shower, that should sort him out. He looks at the time 0708hrs. *Hmm, even the boys aren't awake, if I get up now I'll disturb them*. He thinks about texting Jess but he knows she'll be fast asleep, he has a hard on and fancies some sexting, but it'll have to wait till he gets home later. With Michael away they can have an afternoon of sex instead.

He gets up and quietly goes downstairs for a large drink of water and a cup of tea. He laughs to himself, thinking *it is definitely something to do with being a northerner*. He was raised on cups of tea, "Yer got a headache lad? Yer not feeling too good? Yer look sad. Have a cuppa, that'll make yer feel better". It seems to be the way of so many. "A cup of tea solves everything". He laughs to himself and thinks *it actually does*.

Shelley walks in as he's getting the milk, she looks at him, tuts and rolls her eyes. He smiles and asks, 'He's that bad?'

She nods her head and tells him he's been throwing up all night and she hasn't had much sleep as she was worried he be sick in his sleep so stayed awake to make sure he made it to the bathroom.

'I'm sorry Shell, it did get a bit messy last night.'

'I can see, but you haven't been back for a while, they've missed you J, we all have, you made up for lost time,' and she smiles as he hands her a cup of tea.

'I've missed all of you too, but I had to go back and I'm so glad I did.'

'Me too J. How did you break it off with Tara? Not that she deserved it Jamie but I never really liked her, she came across as very spoilt, you were too good for her.'

Jamie smiles, his own family said this, he can see now, now he's away from her. 'It was awful Shell, I've never felt so sorry for someone like that, I wanted to hug her and tell her it would be ok, that it gets easier but I couldn't. The truth is Shell, I didn't love her, never did really, she was just a rebound, and she didn't deserve that.'

'I know, but hopefully she'll find someone who will love her.'

He nods as he thinks about the conversation with Rosie, that she's dating a guy from work who pampers to her every need and apparently he's been in love with her for ages and when they split he made his move.

'So what time you thinking of heading back?' Shelley asks.

'I was thinking around 0930 -1000hrs, it's a three hour drive.'

Shelley nods, 'I can't see Nobs surfacing anytime today, I'll tell him what time you left, he can text or call you when he's alive, probably Wednesday.' They both laugh, Jamie tells her he's going for a shower as the boys come running down the stairs. Shelley is already getting their cereal out of the cupboard and she offers Jamie some Weetabix, he laughs and nods. He'll have them after his shower, they'll help settle his stomach, before he leaves for home.

Chapter 117

Journey Home

'Hey, you're awake,' Jamie says when Jess answers his call.

'Yes, been awake since nine-ish, still in bed though.'

'That's ok, stay there, I'll be home according to this by 12.45pm.'

'You left early then,' she looks at the clock, 9.55am.

'Yeah, I wanted to get back, spend the afternoon with you.'

'Well, we're childless, which probably isn't going to happen again for a few more years,' they both laugh.

'I know, I've really missed you this weekend.'

'I've missed you too, it felt weird sleeping on my own, more so than when you're away.'

Jamie nods, he knows what she means, he felt it himself. 'How did it go with the dresses?'

'Oh my God babe, it wasn't them, it was mine. I didn't text you and tell you, I didn't want you worrying.'

'What, have you not got a dress?'

'Yes, I have. It's beautiful, they sent the wrong one but it's way nicer than the one I chose. I'm not going to lie babe, I did think I was not going to have a wedding dress.'

'Babe, you could be in a black bag for all I care.'

'That's exactly what Jodie said,' she laughs.

'So how much more did the new one cost?'

'There's no extra cost, they said it was the manufacturer fault. Good job, 'cause I reckon it costs about two grand.'

'Shit that would be a lot for a dress you only wear once, thank God, hey babe?'

'Have your mum and dad said anything about how much we owe them for the wedding?'

'No, my dad said he'd sort it out with you, has he not talked to you about it?'

'No, I text him the other day when I was in the solicitors office and he text back saying "Barbara will let Jess know once she's added it all up".'

'They want to pay for it Jamie, we should leave it now. I know we wanted to sort it out but they're old fashioned and believe they should pay for it. You don't mind do you?'

'No babe of course not, I just don't want them to think I'm a scrounger.'

'Quite the opposite darling, my dad thinks you are the hardest working guy he's met, next to himself of course.' They both laugh and he tells her he needs to stop and get a coffee, she should stay in bed and he'll join her when he gets back. She laughs at him and tells him she loves him and to drive carefully. He tells her he loves her too.

As he walks into the service station to get his coffee, he is thinking about his wedding day. This time in three weeks he will be married. Married to the woman he's loved for over six years, the mother of his children and the only woman he ever wanted to have his babies.

When he was with Tara, he told her they were not going to have any kids, not that he didn't want any, he did, but she was a spoilt child. He couldn't imagine her having a child and losing her mum's attention, she wouldn't know how to cope and he was sure he would end up with two kids on his hands. He shakes his head as he gets back into the car, he's not sure how or why he stayed with her for so long. One things for sure, he's glad he's out of that relationship and away from her and Jean, he can finally see what everyone was thinking. He laughs it off as he starts the car to finish his journey home, resetting the satnav, with his ETA now displayed as 1255hrs.

Chapter 118

Final Fitting

Jess had her final fitting on the Saturday, just a week before the wedding. Her mum accompanied her as she hadn't yet seen the dress. Originally Jess wasn't going to have a veil but she tried on a long cathedral style one and fell in love all over again with the dress, so her mum bought it for her. Barbara couldn't help herself, her tears streamed down her face when Jess walked out of the fitting room in the new wedding dress and full length cathedral veil - she looked stunning.

'Jessica, you'd never believe you're eighteen weeks pregnant.'

'I know, but I've lost my waist and my bum has definitely got bigger, look,' Jess turns sideways and looks in the mirror at her bum, slightly accentuated by the dress.

Barbara smiles and nods, she's not sure what mirror her daughter is looking in but she certainly doesn't see Jess' bum as having grown at all. With the dress fitting over, Barbara arranges to collect the dress, veil and headdress on Friday, she'll take it straight to the hotel.

They head into town to meet Jodie and Lizzie as they also have to try their dresses on. Hopefully they don't need any alterations, otherwise Barbara will have to arrange to collect them as well on Friday - if they fit she'll take them home with her today.

Jodie and Lizzie arrived to the shop a little earlier than their three o'clock appointment, where the sales assistant asked Jodie if they found out what that call was about. Jodie told her about the wrong wedding dress being sent in at which both Lizzie and the sales assistant were totally shocked. Jodie has her suspicions that it wasn't an error, it was actually Barbara's doing but she keeps that thought to herself.

Jess and Barbara finally arrive, apologising for being a little late due to stopping for a bite to eat as Jess had been unable to eat before her fitting.

Jodie and Lizzie go into the changing rooms to put their dresses on and Jess tries to contain her excitement. She hasn't actually seen the colour of the dresses, only the sample fabric a few weeks ago –now she is nervous in case they don't look good in the red.

They emerge from the changing rooms together, their red sequined tops shimmering in the light with the bottom chiffon skirt flowing as they walk. Jess is delighted how beautiful they are, 'They're gorgeous,' she says, the colour red isn't bright at all, it's more of a rose red, exactly as she wanted.

All four women are smiling and chatting about how beautiful they are and how they'll look next to the green of the uniforms. Barbara is feeling immensely proud and tells Jess that the colour is perfect, 'The wedding is going to be amazing Jessica, definitely a day to remember.'

The dresses are a perfect fit, much to Barbara's relief, so she can take them home with her today. She'll drop them off at the hotel on Friday before she goes and gets the wedding dress. She smiles to herself, she's actually looking forward to the wedding - she's planned it well and knows it will be an amazing day.

Chapter 119

The Eve of the Wedding (Part One)

Jess is awake a little earlier than usual and she doesn't feel Jamie wrapped around her which means he's gone for a run. She looks at the clock 7.08am. She's had a good week this week in terms of her morning sickness, generally up and moving around by eleven at the latest, though it does return a bit late in the afternoon but it's not all day every day now and hasn't been for around three weeks.

The baby is moving around a lot more now. The first time Jamie felt it was a week ago, he woke up with his hand on her tummy and could feel the baby kicking - to say he was excited was an understatement. Jess received a big bunch of pink roses later that day with a note saying "The most amazing feeling in the world apart from the love I have for you was feeling our baby kick for the first time. 🖤".

She's on long term sick until her maternity leave kicks in at thirty-four weeks, then once it's over she won't be returning to work. Jess spoke with her Team Leader and HR earlier in the week and advised them of her decision – in fact they'll be living in married quarters on his new base in Wiltshire when her maternity leave finishes.

She is lying still, feeling the baby moving, her baby bump is starting to show – well, to her it is - she's only hoping it won't show in her dress tomorrow. She knows once the wedding is out of the way she won't care, she can be the size of a house for all she cares. She laughs, *if only* she thinks.

She has a million and one thoughts going through her head right now. She's looking forward to seeing his family again and she is so excited to see Clementine and Shelley as she hasn't seen them for six years or more. They've had long telephone conversations over the past couple of months though and caught up on their friendship, Jess and Shelley exchanged photos of the children and Clementine sent Jess some wedding photos.

Jess has saved one of Jamie, he was so tanned and actually looked happy, but she could see he felt uncomfortable, she remembers him telling her how they couldn't really relax, "it was very posh Jess" he says, but he loves Tommo or Tom as Clementine now calls him.

They're mature adults now, not the eighteen year old squaddie or young seventeen year old A level student as when Jess knew them six years ago. Clementine or Clem as she likes to be called is a qualified midwife and Tom is a Lance Corporal, they have matured together - she can't wait to see them both along with Shelley and Nobby.

She hears Jamie opening the front door and her belly is awash with butterflies, thinking that this time tomorrow when she wakes, it'll be her wedding day - the day she never envisioned, the day she could only dream about in the past, the day she marries the man she loves and has loved since that first encounter in The Bowl, the loudmouthed Squaddie, he truly is her soul mate.

The Eve of the Wedding (Part Two)

Jamie is feeling nervous. He is excited about his wedding day but nervous at the same time. He's packing Jess's car and his own as there is just too much to take in one car - he's very flustered and for Jamie this is something Jess has never seen before.

She calls out to him and he snaps back, 'What?' followed by, 'sorry babe.'

She smiles and says, 'I just wanted to give you a kiss and tell you I love you, but I can see you're frustrated so I'll wait.'

He comes into the house smiling as he says, 'I'm fucking nervous babe, honestly, I think me nerves have kicked in,' and he wraps his arms around her and kisses her neck telling her how much he loves her and how excited he is to finally be getting married. Then he says, 'I know we've had a few detours along the way baby, but I can't wait to finally call yer my wife, Mrs Jessica Willets-O'Halloran.'

They both smile with excitement, as she tells him, 'That car is not going to pack itself Corporal O'Halloran, don't be slacking now,' and she winks at him as he walks out calling her a "cheeky bitch" and laughing nervously.

The car is finally packed up and Michael is packing some toys in his rucksack, his car seat is in Jamie's car which Jess will drive while Jamie drive's Jess' car. They can check in any time after 1300hrs, and Jamie has put a message on the Whatsapp group during his run this morning telling them that he'll be checking in at 1300hrs, asking them all what time they'll be arriving.

Nobby: [Shelley's dropping the boys off to her parents for 1000hrs, I'm borrowing the cadets mini bus so we're all coming down together, aim to leave around noon, so should be there no later than 1500hrs.]

Gavin: [With your driving Nobbs it's more likely to be midnight, ya slow fucka.]

Nobby: [Fuck off Gav, at least we'll arrive in one piece.]

Tommo: [I think I'd have to find an alternative way if Gav was driving.]

Gavin: [Wankers]

Jamie laughs out loud as he reads the replies - they'll always be the teenage Squaddies that they were when they met, no matter what ranks they rise to and the banter will never change.

Jamie: [Just make sure you all have your no:1s and some clean fucking socks & boxers, you smelly bastards 😂😂😂]

Tommo: [Yeah Gav, no turning them inside out]

Gavin: [So my wank stains are a no go then?]

Nobby: [Gav….you're fucking walking]

Jamie is laughing, imagining the banter on the bus. Gavin will be telling them about the latest skirt he's shagging, probably going into way too much detail for the women, something that should be kept for the men's room but then Gavin doesn't have that kind of etiquette. He's still a diamond geezer or as Jess calls him "a rough diamond".

The Eve of the Wedding (Part Three)

They're finally checked in and the cars are unpacked. Jamie is sharing a room with just Gavin but all the men will be getting ready in his room tomorrow, leaving the women to get ready together - normal procedure with a wedding, which hasn't changed and probably never will with this lot.

He walks back towards Jess' room, to see if she's unpacked yet. Michael is staying in Tony and Barbara's room tonight as Jodie and Lizzie are staying with Jess, although she'd probably be better staying on her own, considering how sick she still is in the morning.

He hears chatter coming from her room, her door is ajar. Walking in he sees Tony and Barbara along with Fred and Hazel, they're all checked in and Tony is ordering some lunch for everyone, he tells Jamie, 'It's been a busy morning,' and Jamie nods - he knows full well.

On the way down to the restaurant Fred asks Jamie how he's feeling and Jamie tells him that he's ok, he was nervous this morning but he's fine now. Fred tells him how nervous he was when he got married, 'I fluffed all my lines, couldn't get Hazel's name right or anything, of course I was alright once I'd got a few drinks down me neck.' Jamie laughs, he's brought a bottle of Jaeger and some Red bull with him, he'll need a few shots before the wedding that's for sure.

Michael is sitting with his Granddad eating his own lunch and sharing his granddads too. Jamie smiles, he wouldn't change that for the world. The conversation turns to his posting with Fred asking if he knows where he's going yet.

'Yeah Fred, Wiltshire,' Jamie says.

'I was stationed there after Germany, 1997 -1999.'

'It's a gorgeous part of the country Jess, Michael will love it,' says Hazel.

'So I hear,' Jess replies.

'I've asked for a four-bedder, to give us a guest room, so yer don't be shy in visiting,' Jamie winks at Hazel.

She laughs, shaking her head as she says, 'You'll be sick of the sight of us by the time you next post.'

'What time is the meal booked for Jamie?'

'1930hrs, Tone, we'll all meet in the bar between 1830 and 1900hrs.'

'How many is it booked for?' Tony continues his questions.

'Twenty-four adults and three kids. Me sister Rosie is driving down tomorrow morning as she's not long had the baby and has Archie who is nearly three, she's then driving home after the wedding as she doesn't want to be away from them overnight.'

'I thought Rosie was married Jamie, why isn't her husband coming down?' asks Barbara.

'She is Barbara, but Jed and I had a fall out. He was invited but declined, preferred to stay and look after the kids.'

'Families hey?' says Hazel with a shrug.

Jess expertly changes the subject of conversation to the baby and that she's got her twenty week scan booked in for next Friday, and they're hoping to find out the sex of the baby.

'We need to organise your baby shower Jessica, we should have it here, it's a really nice hotel,' Barbara suggests.

'Great idea!' says Jamie, 'Barbara, do you want to organise it?'

Jess looks at Jamie, she knows he is serious, she realises he understands her mum, this will give her great pleasure, something else for her to organize and feel useful for.

'If you want me to, I'd love to,' Barbara responds with a beaming smile.

'You're the best Mum when it comes to organizing parties, book it for my thirtieth week. Should we make it a joint 'baby reveal' at the same time?'

'What? Yer not gonna tell anyone what yer having?' Jamie says, with a shocked tone.

'No, we can tell the doctor we're having a baby revealing party, that way we'll get something to open at the party.'

Barbara is smiling, she's already planning the room, the cake and the invites. 'No Jessica, I need to know what colour to decorate the room in, so I'll need to know beforehand.'

'Ok, I'll give you whatever the doctor gives us so only you'll know, then the room will be the big reveal,' agrees Jess.

They all agreed that it is a great idea and they finish lunch and walk back to the bar area. It is just coming up to 1430hrs, Jamie's family have started arriving and he's had a text from Nobby to say they had to stop off at the services so their ETA has moved to 1530hrs.

He puts his arm around Jess' shoulder, leans in and says, 'I think yer mum likes the idea, did yer see the sparkle in her eye?' Jess nods and smiles to herself, Jamie understands how her mum works now, which is a milestone she never thought he'd get.

The Eve of the Wedding (Part Four)

Jamie's ready, now he needs to get Jess. It felt weird getting ready for the evening in a different room to Jess, instead he had his 'brother from another mother' Gavin to keep him company and get ready with.

David is doing Jess' hair for the evening in a curly style, she's shown him her head dress and veil, so he decided on an up-do tomorrow to show off the low-cut back of her dress. For tonight Jess has brought a deep-purple, off the shoulder, satin knee-length dress and she's dressing it up with a thin diamante belt and diamante choker, silver low-heeled sandals and matching clutch bag.

Sean arrives at the hotel room to meet up with David and sees Jamie in the corridor. He hugs his brother, asking him how he's feeling. Jamie nods, telling him he's feeling good tonight, better than this morning and laughs. Both men walk into the girls' room and see Jodie pottering around, finishing getting ready. Martin is in the bar waiting for her and Lizzie is on her way. She was working until 4.30pm and she's coming alone, her hubby isn't coming tonight. In fact he isn't going to the wedding tomorrow either as things aren't too good between them at the moment and haven't been for a couple years. Lizzie moved into the spare room six months or so ago and she's told Jess she's looking forward to letting her hair down this weekend - she needs some fun.

'Wow baby, you look amazing.' Jamie walks over to his fiancé and kisses her on her lips, his heart missing a beat when she smiles at him. Her curly hair looks gorgeous, her make up is subtle with pink lipstick and the dark colour of her dress suits her as it shows off her olive skin tone and blonde hair with her blue eyes twinkling like her diamanté accessories.

Lizzie arrives at 6.15pm, ready for the evening in a black lace cocktail dress with black court shoes, she seems very flustered but tells Jess she is ok, she's just rushed around getting ready after finishing work. Jodie and Lizzie stay behind for a few minutes when everyone leaves, they want to take her dress out of the bag and hang it up with her veil, so it doesn't crease

Jamie holds his hand out for Jess to hold as they leave the room by 18.25pm and as they arrive downstairs and walk into the bar, they look every bit 'the happy couple'. Gavin is at the bar ordering a pint but stops and walks over and hugs Jess, telling her she looks gorgeous and how glad he is they finally got back together. She smiles as she says, 'You and me both Gav.'

By 7.00pm, everyone has arrived at the bar. Michael runs up to Jamie shouting, 'Dad, I got Granddads after shave on, smell,' as he lifts his head for Jamie to smell under his chin, laughing as he does so.

Jamie takes him over to introduce him to Nobby, Shelley, Tommo, Clementine and Gavin. Shelley hugs him and says how handsome he is like his daddy, then kisses his cheek telling him she can't wait for him to meet Joshua and Theo, that she knows they'll be best of friends, just like his daddy and Uncle Nobby.

Jess greets Clementine and Tommo. Clementine is very emotional as the two women embrace and tells Jess she looks amazing and asks her how many weeks she is so Jess tells her exactly nineteen today. Clem laughs, 'Wow Jess, it must be very well curled up inside there.' Jess nods and tells her this is exactly how she was with Michael.

Jamie mingles between his family, friends and Jess. Michael is excited, running around and showing off, but Jamie leaves him as he's excited and doesn't want to make a fuss.

They all head into the restaurant for 7.30pm where the table is set up to seat twenty-seven, twenty-four adults and three children. Jamie has paid for the celebration tonight although no one knows this yet and he's had the table decorated to celebrate the eve of the wedding. He has also arranged for six bottles of Champagne and a dozen bottles of red and white wine.

Jess had no idea he'd arranged it all, everyone is impressed and commenting on how amazing the table looks. Jess tells him, 'It's amazing. When did you arrange all this?' He smiles and tells her he did it this week, seeing as though they aren't paying for the wedding he thought he'd pay for tonight.

Barbara looks over to him and winks as she says, 'You kept that quiet Jamie.'

He smiles and says, 'I know, I thought I'd surprise you all.'

Once everyone is seated at the table, the waitresses start to take orders for drinks first then the starters and main courses. The bottles of red wine are opened to breathe ready for the food. Tony stands up and the waitresses serve a champagne glass to everyone and pop the corks on the champagne bottles, pouring everyone a glass, except Jess of course.

Tony tells the wedding party that he's very excited to welcome Jamie into his family and can't imagine what Jess and Michael's life would be like if he hadn't come back into their lives. He looks at Jamie directly and says, 'I want to thank you for everything you've done for our daughter, and continue to do, you truly are an amazing person and I'm so happy you came back.' Jamie lifts his glass to acknowledge Tony who then asks the wedding party to raise a glass and toast the happy couple, wishing Jamie and Jess congratulations.

When Tony sits down, Gavin stands up - much to Jamie's surprise.

'This isn't something I would normally do, but then anyone who knows me will know there's nothing normal about me,' Gavin says and Jamie shakes his head as he laughs along with everyone else.

Gavin begins by telling everyone about his best mate, that he is simply "his brother from another mother", how happy he is for this weekend and for him to hurry up and re-join the Regiment at the end of October, bringing his beautiful wife, Michael and the new baby with him. He finishes by asking everyone to raise their glasses for another toast to the "happy couple".

The evening goes without a hitch, with everyone enjoying the conversations, the food and the celebrations. By 10.30pm Jess starts to get tired and decides that she's had a fantastic pre-wedding dinner and doesn't want to push her luck by becoming over-tired. Once every one has finished in the restaurant and headed back to the bar, Jess calls it a day and heads up to bed, not before telling Lizzie to stay as long as she wants as Jodie is staying in the room booked with Martin for the weekend.

She works her way around the room, giving everyone a hug and a kiss as she says goodnight. Her mum has decided to take Michael to bed, as it's way past his bed time and Jacqui is taking the girls, Sofia and Annabel up to their room, warning Joe not to get too drunk so he laughs at her and promises that he won't.

Jamie walks Jess back to her room and they talk about the evening and how amazing it has been and how excited they both are for tomorrow. As they walk into the room Jess suddenly screams, 'Stop! You can't come in, I just remembered my dress is hanging up.'

Jamie quickly closes his eyes, turns around to face away from the door and laughs at her as he tells her she just scared the shit out of him. He stands in the corridor with his arms wrapped around her, kisses her goodnight and tells her that he loves her endlessly and can't wait to see her tomorrow.

Jess winks at him and gives him a final kiss, telling him to get back to the bar and enjoy his last night as a single man. Jamie does as he's told and heads back to the bar to join the rest of the wedding party who are enjoying the early celebrations of "Jamie and Jess' wedding".

Chapter 120

The Morning of the Wedding (Part One)

Jamie wakes at 0730hrs and remembers that they had all arranged to go for a run or use the hotel gym, but as last night turned into a very late one for most of them, he decides that sports are quite unlikely to happen this morning. Jamie remembers heading back to the room around 0200hrs and leaving Gav, Sean, David, Lizzie, Tony, Joe, Breda, Steve and Martin still going strong. The rest of the party, Tommo and Clem, Nobby and Shelley, Fred and Hazel and his mum and Pete had all very sensibly called it a night by 2300hrs.

Jamie looks over to see what sort of state Gav is in and sees his bed is empty and has definitely not even been slept in, 'Where the fuck has he gone?' Jamie says aloud, picking up his phone to check for messages. He sees a couple from Rosie and his heart sinks as he imagines she's texting him to tell him she's not coming.

Rosie: [Hi sorry about this, but Jed has decided to come with me, he doesn't want me driving on my own there and back, so I've managed to book a room for tonight, but can you squeeze him and Archie onto my table? Xx]

Rosie: [I'm so excited my favourite brother is marrying his soul mate, can't wait to see you all, love you xx]

Jamie smiles, as he thinks *so he should* meaning Jed should be by his wife's side. No matter what has happened, it was between him and Tara, but he's not going to worry about that any more, especially not today, today is his wedding day.

Jamie: [Will do Sis, really chuffed for you, love you too xx]

Jamie: [I know, I'm excited, can't wait to see you xx]

'Now, where is that fucker?' he says as he looks to Gavin's bed and opens the Whatsapp group for the lads.

Jamie: <Photo of Gavin's empty bed> [Anyone seen Gavin?]

Nobby: […]

Jamie: [Anyone going for breakfast?]

Tommo: [Yeah, Clem just getting dressed, be down by 0745hrs]

Nobby: [Same here]

Still no sign of Gavin so Jamie tries to think who was in the bar when he left. There wasn't really anyone he could pull unless he decided to get in touch with an old flame from when we were all based here. *Either way, he's a grown arse man, I'm not worrying about him, he'll turn up at some point.*

Jamie:[Hey, my gorgeous sleeping beauty I'm going for breakfast, just think in 6 hours' time I finally get to call you my 'Wife' I love you baby & I can't begin to tell you how much regret I have for the past, but today's not the day to talk about it, today is about our future as 'Man & Wife' 😀😑😘]

Jamie texts his mum and siblings to see who's up and going for breakfast and to tell them he's heading down for 0745hrs. He also texts Barbara to let her know Jed is coming with Archie and he'll pay the difference but can she let the wedding coordinator know to make room.

Barbara: [That's great news about your sister, I will let her know after breakfast. No need to worry about the money, it's all sorted]

Barbara: [I'm at breakfast with Michael]

He reads her message, no Tony he notices and smiles. *I bet he stayed out with Gavin all night, Shit! The twat! He'll be pissed still.*

Jamie walks into the restaurant for breakfast and can see Barbara sitting with Fred, Hazel and Michael, but no Tony. He walks over and gives Michael a kiss. He looks at Barbara, she has that stern look in her eyes and he smiles, he can't help himself, she rolls her eyes and says, 'What time did you leave the bar?' Jamie tells her he can't quite remember but probably around 2am then he asks what time Tony got in, she replies, 'Gone five.'

Jamie can see Fred and Hazel both smirking, as he thinks to himself *I wouldn't want to be in his shoes today*. He tells them he's going to get some breakfast and sit with his mum and he'll see them all later at the wedding. He gives Michael a hug and a kiss and tells him to come and see Nanny Anne before he leaves.

He sits down beside his mum in the seat she has kept for him, with Jacqui and the girls. It turns out that Joe didn't get in until gone four and that Sean, Gavin, Lizzie, Tony and Martin were still going strong when he left.

Jess: [Guess who's in the bed next to me? Xx]

Jamie: [He's a fucking twat, apparently they were out till gone 0500hrs, your dad included xx]

Jess: [I know, my mum text me & told me xx]

Jamie: [Wake him up, he needs to get the fuck out of there xx]

He smirks as he says, 'He's fucking priceless,' and everyone at the table looks at him. He shrugs his shoulders and tells them where Gavin is. He looks over to Nobby and Tommo's table and says, 'Found the twat,' they look bemused, so he tells Nobby, 'I'll text yer.'

Jamie: [Text off Jess, she's just woke up to see Gav in the bed next to her with Lizzie]

Nobby opens his message, shakes his head and passes his phone to Tommo, while relaying the contents of the message to Shelley. Tommo laughs and shakes his head as he shares it with Clem, who pulls a face as she says something to Tommo.

Nobby: [Ain't she married?]

Jamie: [Been separated 6 months]

Nobby tells the rest and they all nod and laugh. Jamie carries on eating his breakfast and tells his mum about the text from Rosie. Anne smiles and squeezes his arm, but then of course she'd already know, Rosie would have text her already anyway. In fact Anne probably booked the room for them, either way, he's just happy to have his sister and nephews at his wedding, the day he spent so long in the past hoping and praying for, is now a reality.

The Morning of the Wedding (Part Two)

Jess slept from half-ten last night until gone seven-thirty this morning. She has arranged with the wedding coordinator to send some tomato soup and a fresh roll up at eleven, as it seems to be the only thing that doesn't make her sick.

She lies there listening to the two of them snoring, real drunken snores, she can't believe they've ended up in the bed next to her - well actually this is Gavin, so there's no surprises really - but she is pissed off. It's not like it's a girls' holiday, this is her wedding day!

Jess hears knocking at the door and then Jodie's voice, so she calls out to say she's coming. Putting a dressing gown on, she opens the door and says, 'Good God, you look dreadful,' as her greeting to Jodie on her way through the door.

'I'm hanging mate, I've come to get Lizzie up.'

Jess just nods, she can feel her stomach starting to turn as she mutters a quiet, 'No' and turns to walk toward the bathroom. Jodie walks over and sits on the bed opposite Lizzie and Gavin, shaking her head. Martin told her when she woke up that she might need to check on Jess, as he thinks Gavin was going back with Lizzie.

'Lizzie, Liz, wake up. You too Gavin, it's nearly 8.30am, come on, we need to go for breakfast.'

Gavin sits up and immediately asks where Jess is, so Jodie tells him, 'In the bathroom being sick, she's not good in the morning.'

Lizzie finally starts to come around and mumbles, 'Bring me something back to the room, I daren't stand up, I'm still pissed.'

Jess emerges from the bathroom, evidently feeling awful with ashen skin and Gavin's heart sinks for her, he can see she's really bad. She gets back into bed, her head is dizzy and she feels nauseous again. Jodie tells Jess she doesn't have to get up until eleven, so try and get some more rest. David is coming to do her hair at noon and she and Liz will get ready in her room and come back here for 11.30am.

Jess nods as she gets out of bed needing the bathroom again. Gavin tells the women that he's seen enough, he's going back to his room before he ends up joining Jess. He can't help feeling sorry for her and now understands what Jamie meant when he said she's bad.

Jodie isn't impressed with Lizzie, but knows that now is not the time to discuss it. She tells Lizzie she needs to get up, bring her stuff to her room and leave Jess be for a couple of hours so she can sleep. Jodie starts to gather her bits and pieces asking Lizzie what she needs and says they'll leave the dresses here and they will get dressed at mid-day when Jess is having her hair done. David is doing their hair before that so he'll be at Jodie's room by ten.

Lizzie finally manages to get up and tells Jodie she needs a hair of the dog. Jodie's having none of it, 'You're getting strong black coffee, that'll sober you up,' she tells her. Jodie orders room service as they haven't got the time now to go for breakfast. She can't help thinking to herself *typical squaddie wedding, everyone pissed the night before and now all hanging*. She laughs, knowing it's going to be a great day - a day she'll remember for sure.

Chapter 121

Wedding Preparations (Part One)

Tommo and Nobby turn up to Jamie's room by eleven and the first thing on Nobby's mind is to check that Jamie has the ring. He nods and says, 'Safe and sound mate.'

Gavin walks out of the bathroom having finished in the shower, and Nobby shakes his head as he says, 'Yer can't help yerself can yer?'

Gavin laughs and replies, 'Nope, ya know me Nobs, if there's a bit of pussy to be had, I'll sniff it out,' and the three men shake their heads and laugh, thinking at the same time *he's one of a kind - good job I love him.*

'J, ya think Jess will make it for 1300hrs?' Gav asks.

'I hope so Gav.'

'Was she that bad Gav?' Nobby asks him.

'Well, it depends what ya call bad, in my books someone spewing every five minutes is pretty bad.'

'Ooh, is she really that bad mate?' Nobby responds and they both nod. Tommo and Jamie laugh at them, 'They really are like Tweedle-Dee and Tweedle-Dum,' Tommo says.

Jamie hears knocking at the door and goes to answer it, it's his kid brother Sean, on his way to get ready with Martin as they'd arranged last night but just stopping to say he'll be back to Jamie's room by noon, as the plan is to have a few shots to calm the nerves then meet everyone in the bar by 1230hrs.

The four of them set about getting ready, their uniform and boots shining. Even though Nobby is now a Sergeant they're as close today as they were seven years ago, there is a special bond between this lot. Tommo was thinking about leaving this year as he had an option to join his dad's company in the aerospace industry but opted to stay in, saying he isn't ready for civvy life yet, much to their delight.

Sean and Martin arrive at Jamie's room at 1155hrs and Jamie cracks open the Jaeger and pours six glasses of red bull, popping the shots of Jaeger into each glass. He hands them all one and they down it in one, then they have another before heading to the bar to meet up with everyone else.

The wedding photographer is waiting near the bar when they walk in. The six of them together are truly a sight to behold, walking in unison with each other and proud to be wearing their uniforms.

He spots Ben and Becky with Isabella, and goes over to greet them, kisses Becky on the cheek and tells her she looks beautiful, then shakes Ben's hand and Ben asks him how he's feeling. Jamie tells him he's good, the Jaeger shots have definitely worked and both men laugh, as he introduces Ben to Nobby, Tommo and Gavin.

Sean is standing with their mum and Pete and Anne can barely hold her tears back at the sight of her son in his uniform on his wedding day. She remembers the day when she really thought this was something she'd never see, especially not with Jess.

Jamie walks over to hug her, he can see she's feeling emotional and he tells her he hopes that they're happy tears and she laughs and nods. All his family is here now, including Jed. Jamie shakes Jed's hand and thanks him for being by Rosie's side, adding that he knows he wasn't quite ready but it's the right thing to do and they'll sort their differences out in the future. Jed nods, agreeing with Jamie wholeheartedly.

The photographer informs Jamie that he's going to start taking photos of them all in their relaxed mood now, then at 12.30pm he'll take them outside for some formal ones before heading to the chapel at 12.45pm. Jamie's heart skips a beat at the word "chapel" and suddenly finds himself feeling very nervous again. He shouts over to Steve and Breda who are at the bar to get him something strong as his pint is doing nothing for his nerves now.

Nobby looks over, raises his pint and smiles at Jamie. He knows that face, he knows his best mate more than Jamie knows himself, he can see his nerves have kicked in, it is exactly what happened to Nobby more than six years ago, but it'll soon pass, once the vows are said and he finally becomes a married man.

Wedding Preparations (Part Two)

Jess managed to get up just a few minutes before ten, and hasn't been sick since. She's showered and washed her hair, removing all the hair spray from last night which she realises now was actually making her feel more sick every time she turned her head and smelled it again.

She's resigned herself to taking it slow and easy, even though it's her wedding day and she feels like she should be having her makeup done by a professional and be at the hairdressers getting her hair done. This is nothing like her first wedding - for starters she's alone in her room, which is unheard of under normal circumstances but then there really isn't anything normal that involves Jess and pregnancy.

She wants to attempt her own makeup but she really doesn't have the energy just yet, so she'll wait until Jodie and Lizzie come back at 11.30am. She will have had her soup by then so hopefully will feel more up to it. Besides, Jodie did a lovely job of her make up last night, so she has no reservations in asking her to help again.

By 11.30am Jodie and Lizzie are in Jess' room telling her that David is just getting himself ready after he finished their hair, and then he will come and do Jess' hair. Her mum and dad arrive at 11.45am with her dad looking very sheepish and still very hung over.

'Where's Michael?' Jess asks.

'With Fred and Hazel, he was a bit too hyper,' Tony says and Jess laughs at her dad with a hangover. Jodie brings out a bottle of champagne and a few glasses she'd picked up from the bar, then popping the cork, she pours everyone a glass except Jess, lifting hers up as she says, 'To calm the nerves, or in your case Tone a hair of the dog,' and they all giggle like school girls except Barbara.

David arrives by 11.45am as Jodie is just finishing Jess' make up. 'Now mate, don't be getting sick, it looks lovely,' Jodie says, smiling. Jess laughs and tells her that she'll try her best not to.

'Oooh, look at that dress!' David says, 'Jess, you sexy momma!'

Jess looks in the mirror again at her dress, she can't actually believe they sent the wrong one but he's right it is a sexy but beautiful dress. 'Thanks Dave, I have to say I don't feel sexy but it is gorgeous isn't it?'

The simple yet elegant headdress is on the dressing table, with a mixture of clear crystal, pearl and diamanté adornments. David tells her, 'It will sit perfectly on the top of your head, with your hair in a simple but elegant French twist, you don't want to take the limelight from your dress or headdress.'

The bridesmaids pick their flowers up from the box, small round posies of white roses, carnations and gypsum, which look amazing next to the red dresses.

Jess is dressed by 12.30pm and her dad hands her the round bouquet of red roses to finish off the whole look. She looks stunning, her dress is simply beautiful, David can't stop himself tearing up and looks over at the bridesmaids who are also just as choked up as he is.

Barbara is smiling, feeling so proud of her daughter, 'Jess you look beautiful darling, you really do.'

They all leave the room and make their way to the wedding chapel where the photographer is waiting outside for them, he wants get a few photos of Jess and her dad before they go in.

Barbara and David walk inside, where everyone is seated. Jamie and his two best men are at the front, Barbara can't believe her eyes as she sees him standing there in his uniform, she feels a lump in her throat as she walks to her seat. She smiles and asks him if he's ok and he nods and smiles, telling her yes, he is.

Chapter 122

The Wedding Ceremony

'All Rise'

Jamie turns to face the steps, feeling his heart racing at a million miles an hour when the wedding song they chose starts to play - 'Can't help falling in love,' by Samantha Harvey, which now gives him something to concentrate on rather than his nerves.

He watches as Lizzie and Sean are the first to come down the steps. She looks stunning in her red dress and Jamie watches as Sean leads her to her seat next to Barbara on the front row and Sean takes his seat next to their mum on the second row directly behind Nobby's empty seat.

Jodie and Martin are next down the steps, both beaming with happiness as they walk to the front, Jodie smiles at Jamie and he winks back, she takes her seat next to Lizzie and leaves the last one empty for Tony while Martin takes a seat behind them.

Jamie is full of emotions, his hands are sweating and he has a lump in his throat as looks over to his son who is currently sitting on Fred's lap, his blond hair neatly combed and in his three-piece grey suit and red tie - he looks more like a little man than a five year old, and Jamie's heart melts at the sight of him.

He looks from Michael and sees her, his beautiful fiancé, standing at the top step with her dad, her slim figure accentuated by the dress hugging her curves and looking stunning. Her veil covers her face as she slowly walks down and underneath she wears a beaming smile with her hair up, showing her slim neck and shoulders.

Jamie can't help himself, his eyes fill with tears - he has waited for this moment his whole life. He destroyed everything they had for a one night stand six years ago, then disappeared out of her life but couldn't stay away - Jess was and still is his one true love.

He steps forward and Tony gives him his daughter's hand, he can see Tony is tearful, he nods to let him know he has her now and lifting her veil up and over her head, he takes her hand in his and kisses it. He turns and walks forward towards the registrar, while his two best men take their seat in the front row behind him.

Barbara looks down towards her husband, seeing that he's emotional. He looks at her with his teary eyes, this is the proudest moment of his life - giving his daughter away to the man she's loved for over six years, a man she kept secret, for whatever reason and he doesn't want to know why as he doesn't care now, he's the proudest father in the world. Barbara passes down some tissues, and Jodie keeps one for herself before passing them on as she tries with all her might to keep her emotions intact, but seeing Tony's tears is too much and it sets her off also.

Nobby looks at Tony, watching as he wipes his eyes, and feels his own emotions close to crumbling too as he watches as his best friend marrying his soul mate, a day he never thought he'd see. Nobby watched these two fall in love and also witnessed the devastating effects of that one night stand, how it destroyed both their lives.

As he looks around the room at the people who knew them when they first got together he can see this is an emotional time for them, he looks at Hazel - her tears are for a different reason, she knows she'll be losing her little family, that they'll become part of the army family that never settles anywhere for more than two or three years, but like all army families, they have a bond that's greater than no other.

Nobby continues to scan the room, first looking at Tommo, then to Shelley on his right - her face is red and blotchy from trying to suppress her tears. He smiles at her and she tries to smile back but she can't without the tears falling again. He looks at Clementine, she's inconsolable, he knows that she and Jess were close along with Shelley, the three of them helped each other cope through that ten week tour. He knows how devastated Clementine was when they separated and she refused to speak to Jamie for the best part of two years.

Nobby looks now to Jamie's family. His mum Anne is as proud and emotional as the other women, this is a joyous occasion, but an emotional filled one. The unity of these two souls, that no one ever thought would happen. Nobby looks at Gavin, he's smiling, he loves his 'brother from another mother' he was simply Jamie's rock for the first two years at least.

He turns back to watch and listen to the vows as they both say "I do" and watches as Jamie places the wedding band on her finger - finally they are 'husband and wife'.

Chapter 123

The Wedding Reception

The wedding guests take seats at their tables and the Master of Ceremonies asks everyone to stand as he introduces the bride and groom, 'Ladies and gentlemen please be upstanding for the bride and groom, Corporal Jamie and Mrs Jessica Willets-O'Halloran.'

Jamie and Jess walk in to the room to eruptions of congratulations and a round of applause from their forty guests, both of them amazed at the room - the decorations Barbara has organised are outstanding. There are four round tables each seating eight guests and a top table, on each of the round tables is a red and white flower centre piece, with a large candle in the middle, with lots of little red and white tea light holders and each chair has a big red bow on the back.

Sitting at the top table with Jess and Jamie are Anne, Pete, Nobby, Gavin, Barbara, Tony, Lizzie and Jodie, with Jamie next to his mum and Jess next to her mum. The table has a huge array of red and white flowers with three large candles among them. Jamie looks toward Barbara and tells her, 'You've done a fabulous job Barbara,' and she smiles back and thanks him.

'Babe, yer look stunning, I can't believe we're sat here.'

'Me neither, I'm glad you like my dress, it's gorgeous isn't it?'

The three course wedding breakfast consists of a choice of pate and toast, soup and a roll or a medley of melon for starters. The main course follows with pork medallions with roast potatoes, seasonal vegetables (carrots and broccoli) and gravy, followed by a pudding of either New York cheesecake with berry compote or chocolate fudge cake with ice cream and finishes with coffee and mints.

Each guest had a choice of red or white wine with their dinner and a glass of champagne for the start of the speeches and the toasts.

Once the food has been eaten it's time for the speeches. Tony stands up to give his speech, he tells everyone about the first time he met Jamie when he took Jess food shopping, This young man leans in and kisses Jess on her cheek, not only is he in a soldiers uniform but he also has a unicorn lunch bag in his trolley, which turns out to be for Jess, as she didn't have anything to take her lunches to work in. I knew then that he was the man for Jess, not only was he caring but he wasn't afraid to show his feelings for her and continues to care for her and Michael every day.'

He continues to tell them about Jess with anecdotes about the day she was born, her growing up, and how proud she's always made him. He shares with them that he never really understood why people felt proud of the armed forces until Jamie came into their lives, now he understands and feels immensely proud to have him as his son-in-law and knows no matter what or where they go as a family Jamie will love and protect them.

He finishes his speech by saying, 'So ladies and gentlemen please raise your glasses with me to toast the bride and groom.'

Now it is Jamie's turn and he stands up to do his speech, feeling nervous, he bends down and kisses Jess before he starts.

'I'd just like to start by thanking every one of you for attending our wedding, the bridesmaids, Jodie and Lizzie you both look gorgeous in yer dresses, my two best men, Nobby and Gavin, and a special shout out to my other best mate Tommo without you three I don't think I'd be here now. When Jess and I separated nearly six years ago, my world collapsed around me, but these guys picked me up, they kept me going, listened to my drunken rants, wiped my tears, kept me company in the gym or on endless miles of runs - thanks guys.' He raises a glass to his three mates and in turn they raise theirs to him.

He continues to thank his family, particularly his mum for putting up with him and pushing him to reach his goals in his role with the British Army. He tells everyone what an amazing woman she is raising five successful children as a single mum and that her strength and resilience is what has made him the person and soldier he is today. He bends down and gives her a kiss on her tear soaked cheek.

Next he thanks Fred and Hazel, firstly for introducing him to Jess back in August 2019, then for all they've done for Jess and Michael over the years. He raises a glass to Fred and Hazel and goes on to thank Tony and Barbara for everything they've done to make today so special and actually possible.

Finally he looks down at his bride as he continues, 'So now I get to thank you Jess. It goes without saying how amazing my wife looks today. Jess you truly are a stunning woman and I am so very grateful to you for taking a chance on us again. When I came back at the end of October,I had no idea if you still lived in the village or if you'd met someone else, but to my delight and surprise not only were you still here but we had a son, for which I'm truly thankful. Like his mother he amazes me every day and I find myself loving you both more and more which I didn't think possible.' He bends down and kisses her, wiping her tears from her cheeks.

He continues to talk about their life when they met the first time around and looks at Nobby as he tells them about the day two squaddies nipped into town in uniform, 'You can imagine the look on people faces and what they were thinking of us as we're looking at engagement rings, well I can tell yer, it wasn't "Aww",' and everyone laughs. 'Friday 8 May 2020, wasn't it Nobby?' Nobby nods his head as he's smiling.

'Yer see Jess I'd originally planned on proposing to yer on Saturday 26 June 2020, the day before my posting, but it never happened, so I've carried this around with me in my Bergan for the last five years and eleven months hoping one day I would give it to you.'

Jamie pulls out a red velvet ring box, now warn with age. He moves his chair back and gets down on one knee as he opens the box to reveal her engagement ring, a beautiful princess-cut half carat solitaire ring in a tiffany setting.

The tears are streaming down Jess's face as she holds her hand out for Jamie to place it on her finger next to her wedding ring.

He stands up and pulls her up to him, wraps his arms around her and lovingly kisses her - he doesn't care who is watching, he's waited a long time to give her this ring.

Chapter 124

It's Never Goodbye

Jamie hugs his mum, not sure when he'll see her next, probably in eight weeks' time - Sunday 24 May at the baby shower Barbara is organising.

He can't believe he's a married man. Yesterday was simply the best day of his life, he snuggles Jess as they say their good byes to everyone, Tony and Barbara are taking Michael back for a couple of days as Jamie and Jess have booked another night here, as they can't have a honeymoon.

All the wedding guests are either checking out now or already have. Nobby isn't in any fit state to drive back, in fact none of them are but Gavin is probably the least hungover and he hugs his buddies telling them he'll see them in eight weeks but can't wait until Jamie re-joins them at the end of his secondment.

Jess looks down at her rings and her eyes glaze with tears every time she thinks of how long Jamie's had it and how he presented it to her. It was the most amazing day, very emotional but then she couldn't have imagined it any other way.

By the time they arrived at the sports club for the evening reception, none of the women had any make up remaining from all the tears. The evening reception was pure fun, a typical night with a bunch of squaddies lots of drinking, various shots and dancing. The food was amazing, she can't thank her mum and dad enough, it was far more than she'd expected, definitely not something she could have planned.

Jamie tells her he hates this part, saying goodbye to his family and the lads. She tells him, 'It's never really goodbye darling, you'll see them all soon,' and she kisses "her husband"- a word that once upon a time she thought she'd never hear herself say or think about Jamie.

By 1.00pm everyone has left and they are alone. They walk back into their room and see just how full it is with all their wedding gifts, outfits and some of the decorations from yesterday.

'How am I meant to get all this in the car?' Jamie says and Jess shrugs her shoulders.

'We'll worry about it tomorrow. For now let's enjoy our first day as husband and wife,' she says and pulls him close to her as she tells him they've not actually consummated their marriage and winks as she kisses him, and feels her juices start flowing as she feels his tongue inside her mouth looking for hers.

His hands caress her boobs as he kisses her, and he pulls away slightly, telling her to lift her arms so he can take her top off. Undoing her bra he sucks on her nipples and says, 'Babe they're massive.'

She laughs, 'You say the most romantic things.'

Jess tells him she wants to make love, they can have sex any time but the first time being husband and wife should be about love making, he laughs and tells her that's exactly what he intended to do.

He pulls his top off and undoes his jeans, pushing them down with his boxers, his cock is hard waiting to feel Jess' juices running over it. Jess takes her bottoms off and moves towards Jamie, she wants to feel his naked muscular body wrapped around hers.

Kissing her neck and up towards her ears, he slides his tongue in and Jess gasps. His fingers are playing with her nipples and she parts her legs, her pussy is wet and waiting for his hard cock to penetrate it.

He motions her onto the bed as he follows her, climbing on top he presses against her pelvic bone, not too hard, he doesn't want to hurt her. His cock is hard and throbbing, he hasn't cum since Friday morning - he's going to enjoy this and take his time making love to Jess for the first time as his wife.

They kiss passionately, his hands caressing her boobs as he slowly moves his hips, he places his hard cock inside her wet pussy and slowly pushes it in, he can feel her juices all over it and she moans through his kisses.

His cock slides in and out slowly, while he kisses his wife lovingly and passionately, gyrating his hips. He can feel her nakedness against his, her breasts against his chest. Her naked body is warm and sexy, her wet pussy and the juices all over his hard throbbing cock turns him on.

He uses his hip movements to push his cock very slowly deeper into her wet pussy, and she moans quietly as he kisses her lovingly and passionately. He lifts his head up to look at her beautiful bare breasts, and the shift in positioning makes his cock thrust in deeper. Jess moans again, loudly this time and it spurs him on to thrust even harder.

Her loud moans excite him, he wants to hear her begging for more, he wants to hear how much he makes her cum with his thick hard cock deep inside her wet pussy, he can't help himself he needs to hear her moan louder, he thrusts hard and fast, she's cumming he can hear it in her deep throated groan, he tells her, 'Louder baby, I want to hear yer,' as he thrusts deeper.

Her hands squeeze his shoulders as she cums, his cock is in so deep, she feels him inside, thick and hard and then hears him grunt as he holds her tight and feels his body shudder from his climax.

Chapter 125

Life As We Know It

Jamie has enjoyed his time off with his new wife but he's back to work today, it is April fool's day and Michael is back to school, so he's arranged to drop Michael off at breakfast club for 0745hrs as he has an eight o'clock start, Jess can stay in bed and get up when she is ready. She's told Fred she'll go and collect Michael today as she feels she really needs to start getting back to normal again.

They've had three days alone, spending the first two at the hotel and then yesterday at home. They unwrapped all their gifts and opened their cards, sorted the gift vouchers and money - they have over £2,000 in cash and another £1,000 in holiday vouchers, which they'll use to book a holiday for next year with their two children.

They are not sure what to do with the money yet, whether to put it towards their new car, which they've not chosen yet or to keep it and buy something for the house when they move. Either way it's going into their savings account until they've decided.

Jamie kisses Jess as he leaves with Michael, asks her to text him when she gets up and if she's feeling up to it she could do an online food shop for delivery on Friday evening or Saturday morning. He gets Michael's coat and lunch box and leaves for work, thinking that this is exactly how he envisioned his life, how he knew it would feel leaving his pregnant wife in bed and dropping Michael to breakfast club.

Lying in bed this morning he had his hand pressed gently on Jess' belly, feeling his baby kicking. Even though Jess doesn't have much of a baby bump, he can feel his baby and it's a strong little thing, he's told her she's definitely a girl but can't wait for her scan on Friday, when he gets to see her properly.

Jess gets up just after 10.30am and opens her phone to text Jamie to tell him she's awake. She tells him she's going to have a quick shower, wash her hair and go round to Becky's as they've planned to go out for lunch, so she'll definitely be getting Michael from school.

Jamie: [Ok babe, but don't push yourself, if you feel tired later let Fred know, he'll get him, love you wifey 😊😊😊😊]

She laughs at the comment, but it is exciting being called wifey. She received so many photos on Whatsapp from the day and videos of the speeches so she's going into town to see if she can transfer them onto a memory stick and play it on the photo frame they got as one of the many presents.

The photographer will have the proper ones ready on a disc within a month. He's also agreed to take some at the baby shower, she can't believe how quick her mum has organised that already, she should have been a party planner or events coordinator - Jess told her yesterday "you've missed your calling in life Mum".

By the time Jess and Becky get back from lunch it's coming up to three o'clock so she asks Becky to come to the school with her - she hasn't been for nearly three months and really doesn't fancy seeing the mums at the gate on her own.

Becky laughs and tells her that she's dreading that part of Isabella going to school, all those cliquey mums. They pull up at the gates and sure enough heads spin around to look at them immediately. 'Look at them,' says Becky, 'ugh, I hate this part mate, come on let's go in then, I wonder if any of them know that you two got married on Saturday?'

They both laugh and Jess tells her, 'We'll find out in a minute.'

Walking towards the gate Jess hears one of them say, 'Congratulations Jess, I hear you and Jamie got married at the weekend,' she smiles and nods and the rest all follow suit with "congratulations". As they walk in they listen to one of them describing her dress, saying how amazing she looked in it, "it was spectacular" another one says, and she smiles to herself - her dress really was spectacular.

Chapter 126

The Big Reveal

Jess is stressing over what to wear, she's too small for maternity wear, even a size ten drowns her, she's too big for normal size ten clothes and twelves are a little too tight around her belly, so she resigns herself to wearing sports leggings and t shirts or vest tops with a hoodie. She tells Jamie she looks more like a chav than the chavs on the streets do.

'Jess, babe, you look amazing.'

'You're just being kind,' she says, rolling her eyes.

She's found a nice slim pair of treggings (a mix of trousers and leggings) with a slim fitting long line shirt, it's fitted in the back but loose around the front. Her feet have started to swell so she's wearing flip flops, but she can get away with it as it is nearly summer.

Her twenty week scan seems so long ago now and they left the appointment none the wiser at knowing what they're having. They gave the letter straight to Barbara who hasn't said a word since but has been busy organising the event.

'Yer know this is going to be like our wedding, another celebration with yer mum having the room decorated as a surprise.'

'Yes, it's what she likes to do.'

'Babe, in all seriousness, where are we going to store all this baby stuff? The pram is at Fred and Hazels, we have a cot and crib in our room already, we're running out of space and it ain't even here yet.'

Jess laughs, 'Don't forget we're buying a bigger car in September. Michael James are you ready?' She says to Jamie, 'That child is worse than a woman, he takes forever to get dressed,' and he laughs at her, normally it is him getting stressed over Michael not getting dressed, but he tells her he'll go up and help him.

Jamie's family have travelled down for the baby shower, Sean and David have been here since Friday staying at the hotel. Sean is off to Kenya in September for twelve months, so they're spending as much time as possible with the family before he goes.

Barbara and Tony arrive to collect Jess, Jamie and Michael. Barbara is outwardly excited, they've not seen her like this ever, she tells Jess she's not slept for weeks with excitement and Jess can believe it. Tony tells her, 'I've had no problems sleeping, I don't know what all the fuss is about,' and Barbara tuts and slaps him playfully.

'This car's nice Tone, when did yer get it?' Jamie asks, admiring the new 4x4.

'I've got it on a forty-eight hour trial, Barbara thinks it's too big.'

'Why don't we get one of these babe, surely we'll be able to fit a baby in it?' They all laugh at how that sounded, though they know what he means.

'What is it Dad?'

'Land Rover Discovery, Jess.'

'Seriously babe, we should trade in both cars, and get one of these.'

'Great idea, I'll give my mate a call on Tuesday that sorted this out for me, he'll do you a great deal. If you want me to that is Jamie?' Tony offers.

'Yeah Tone, that'll be a great help, thanks.'

Tony looks at Barbara and smiles, Jess sees it, she has a feeling this was a set-up, that they've discussed this already, she can tell by Jamie's reaction. She smirks as she looks out of the window, if she knows her dad and her husband there will be one of these sitting on the driveway by next weekend.

They arrive at the hotel at 1.40pm, the baby shower is due to start at two so they have plenty of time. Her mum sent out fifty invites, of which she has had forty-five acceptances and only five declines, strangely from people living locally which is bizarre, as a lot of the attendees are travelling up to three hours to attend.

They walk into the bar, packed with friends, family and work colleagues. Jess is overwhelmed by it all, it feels like her wedding day all over again. Everyone hugs her, kisses her and congratulates her, she sees Michael running around with Archie, Joshua and Theo and she looks at Jamie and says, 'Well that didn't take long.'

Jamie laughs and says, 'Nope, he's sociable just like me babe,' and she nods, he really is.

The coordinator comes into the bar and informs them that the room is ready if they'd like to follow her. She takes them into a side room, with sliding doors leading to the function room. Everyone waits patiently, Jamie is holding Jess by the hand and they hear everyone count down from ten, nine, eight, seven, six and when they get down to one, the doors don't open! For a split second it goes quiet then an array of pink balloons fall out of nowhere.

Jamie picks Jess up and swings her around saying, 'I told yer! See, I knew it was a girl.'

The partition doors open to the most amazing baby shower, a live band starts to play, the room looks beautiful, decorated in pink and white, with sweet trolleys, afternoon tea on the tables, nappy cakes, trees decorated in baby rattles, bottles, dummies, packs of vests, you name it the room is completely decorated in every item of baby girl clothing.

Barbara had the best eight weeks, shopping for her granddaughter, she doesn't know how she kept it quiet with her excitement, but she doesn't have to now, she can share it with the world that her daughter is having a little girl.

Chapter 127

The Announcement

'Jode, can I drop Michael round? Jess has gone into labour,' Jamie says when Jodie answers the phone.

'No, no Jamie, I'll come round to you, leave him in bed.'

'Ok, see you soon.'

'What time is it?' Martin asks from beneath the covers, his voice dry and slurry with sleep.

'It's two-thirty, go back to sleep, love you.'

'Breathe babe, in through yer nose and out through yer mouth,' Jamie says, remembering what he's seen on the television.

'For fuck's sake Jamie, stop rubbing my back, I know how to breathe,' Jess says, trying to deal with the current contraction ripping through her groin and lower back.

He lifts his hand up as she leans into him, he really doesn't know what to do, he'll wait for her to tell him what she wants, it's probably the safest option, even between the pains when she gets a little respite.

'Jodie's on her way round, so we can leave Michael in bed.'

Jess nods as she gets yet another contraction, her waters have gone and her contractions are getting stronger and closer together. She's breathing in through her nose and out through her mouth and trying to relax in between each contraction.

'Babe we need to get downstairs, will yer be ok?'

She nods, her suitcase and baby bag is ready in the hallway and Jamie's unlocked the door for Jodie to walk straight in.

'Have you called the hospital?' Jodie asks when she arrives.

Jamie nods, telling her that Jess' waters went all over the bedroom floor and he hasn't had time to clean it up, so be careful walking in the bedroom. Jodie nods and she helps them out to the car, Jamie is panicking, Jodie can tell he doesn't like seeing Jess in pain and she can't help thinking how he's going to cope when she's in full blown labour and delivering - she thinks Jamie should have had some one there to support him, let alone Jess and she laughs to herself.

'You ok getting in?' Jamie asks, trying to help her into the car.

'Yes, yes, why you had to swap the cars for this monstrosity thing is beyond me, you should have waited until ... owww, shit this hurts.'

'Breathe mate, deep breaths, you need to breathe through the pain. How long between each contraction J?'

'Five mins I think,' Jamie says, looking a little unsure.

'Call the maternity ward, tell them her waters have gone and her contractions are five minutes apart, they need to get her straight in.'

Jamie just nods, he's shitting himself, he can handle anything the enemy throws at him, he's trained to deal with getting shot at, dodging IEDs, you name it he can deal with it, what he's not trained to deal with is his wife in labour and crying out in pain.

He arrives at the maternity hospital twenty mins later where a porter and a nurse are waiting for them with a wheel chair to take Jess straight in, he tells them her contractions are less than five mins apart.

'Mrs..?' the midwife prompts as she begins to wheel Jess through the corridor.

'Jess, just call me Jess.'

'Okay Jess, we need to get you into the delivery suite, I need to examine you to see what's going on and then we'll see where we go from there is that okay?'

Jess nods and asks for some gas and air, she needs help with this pain but the midwife tells her once she's in and settled and they know what's going on she can set it up.

Jamie follows behind them, feeling glad that he got the snip last month as there's simply no way he could watch Jess go through this again, he told her two is enough, let's enjoy life and each other.

The midwife asks Jamie if he can help Jess onto the bed, so he puts the bags down to help her and she throws her arms around his neck and leans into him as another contraction begins. He holds her head to his chest, kissing the top of it, not saying anything. He's learned very quickly not to speak or do anything, just be there.

'You're eight centimetres Jess, keep breathing through the contractions and you'll be ready to deliver before you know it,' the midwife says. 'Was your due date today? 8 August?'

Jess nods as she tells the midwife that this one's brother was on time as well. The midwife smiles as she continues with her paperwork then Jamie asks her how much longer before the birth. The midwife tells him that if she carries on the way she's going then probably by 5.00am, he looks at his watch, 3.45am - 'Holy shit! That quick?' laughing nervously as he says it.

He gets his phone out to text every one that Jess is in labour and as soon as the baby is born he'll send them all a photo or at least let them know.

Barbara: [I'm awake, call me as soon as you can when she's born]

Jamie: [Will do.]

Jamie texts his Sergeant for when he wakes, letting him know that Jess is in labour, so he won't be in, his two weeks paternity starts now. He is so looking forward to spending time with his baby daughter.

'That's it Jess, one last push.'

'Babe! She's here, oh my God, she's born and with a mass of dark hair.' Jamie is emotional, tears are streaming down his face, this is definitely the most amazing moment of his life - seeing his daughter coming into the world. He kisses Jess and tells her she's amazing, how much he loves her and how beautiful their little girl is.

The midwife comes back with their daughter and hands her to Jamie, he asks what weight she is and the midwife tells him "5lb 2oz". She is tiny. He looks at her and feels a rush of emotions and the feeling of pure love sweep over him, this is what he missed with Michael. He buries his face into her and sobs.

Jess tells the midwife that Jamie is in the army so wasn't around for their son's birth and the midwife smiles, she sees a lot of women whose husbands are away on deployment when their babies are born. She tells Jess that he'll spoil her, they always do, and Jess nods.

They take Jess, Jamie and their daughter up to the ward and the midwife tells them both she'll be discharged by 4.00pm today as she had no complications and the baby is fine. Jess nods, she needs a sleep now, so she tells Jamie to go home and get some rest and come back at four. He looks at her like she is crazy and tells her he's slept in worse places than a hospital chair, so he's staying with her until they're both discharged. She's to get some sleep he will look after the baby if she wakes up and needs feeding.

Jess is way too tired to argue, and is reminded of the kind of man her husband is and wonders why she even suggested he go home. She asks him for a kiss before she falls asleep and he leans in, brushes her hair off her face and tells her he loves her and kisses her.

He opens his WhatsApp messages, clicking on the 'Lads' conversation.

Jamie: [<photo> Welcome to the world Charlotte Elizabeth Willets-O'Halloran, born 0455hrs weighing in at 5lb 2oz, she's perfect]

Jamie looks over at Jess sleeping in the hospital bed and his daughter sleeping in the cot - his life is complete.

Epilogue

So the day has finally arrived, Monday 26 October. The house is all packed up and the removal men will be arriving by 8.00am. Jess has given a set of keys to the estate agent who is dealing with the sale, she was surprised that it had increased in value so much, she paid £120,000 for it in May 2019 and seven years on it has been valued at £159,995.

Charlotte woke up for her 5.00am feed on the dot and Jess tells Jamie, 'She's like you with her body clock.'

He laughs and says, 'No one can sleep as much as you babe,' and he goes downstairs to make a cup of tea for them both and leaves Jess to feed and change Charlotte.

Jess is playing with Charlotte's hair, it's starting to fall out, exactly as it did with Michael before growing back blond. She can't believe the moving day is here already, she's excited but sad, really sad to be leaving her friends and family, particularly Fred and Hazel, but "that's army life" as Hazel and Jodie have told her repeatedly over the last couple of weeks.

Michael finished school on Friday for the half term break and Halloween is coming up on Saturday. It will be seven years to the day since Jamie and Jess got together, she will no longer dread 31 October, instead they will celebrate it with their children.

He'll be starting at his new school on Monday 2 November with Joshua, although he'll be a year older than him, and they'll all walk to school together. Tommo and Clementine announced their baby news in

September, their little one is due next May. Jess is ecstatic, she's told Clem they can do baby dates together, go to soft play and mums and tots. Clem agreed, she's looking forward to it already.

Jess was up and showered by 7.00am, Charlotte was dressed and in her pram and Michael was left for Jamie to deal with. 'He may be five and a half but he's as stroppy as a teenager,' Jess tells Jamie.

The removal men start loading the van and packing anything that isn't already packed. Jess is looking around her house, so many happy memories and so many sad ones, but she doesn't think of the sad times anymore, that's all in the past.

By 9.00am, they're ready to get on the road, Michael is in his booster seat, Charlotte strapped in her baby seat, her pram in the boot and Jess has made four bottles and packed some extra clothes in case of emergencies.

Jamie hands the keys to the removal man, he's to post them through the letter box once they've finished. Getting into the car, he looks at Jess and asks her if she's ok. She nods and they reverse out of the drive and make their way through the village, past the base and out the back road heading to Wiltshire, where their new base and the start of their new life back with Jamie's Regiment will begin. Back where he belongs.

Printed in Great Britain
by Amazon